AN INTRODUCTION TO LOVE

Gretchen barked again.

"Quiet," he ordered, glancing down impatiently. "Can't you see that we are—Oh, damn."

Tina followed his gaze, and was dismayed to see that the lead now encircled their legs. Gretchen had bound them together with her pacing.

Gerard sighed. "Here, give that thing to me so I can untangle us—"

Undoubtedly he would have done so if Gretchen had not spied the hare. Later, Tina would recall this moment with a shudder of mortification, but at the instant it happened she was conscious of nothing but Gerard's sudden grip as they lost their balance and toppled to the ground.

Tina lay in shock. Laverstoke was almost atop her, his face inches from her own. In fact, he was so close she could actually smell his masculine scent, so close she could almost feel the heat of his flesh through his clothes. Oddly, he did not move, but lay looking down at her with a strange expression. "I do beg your pardon, ma'am," he said, in an even odder tone, "but I believe this calls for an introduction."

As his lips found hers, all lucid thought drained from her head. Tina forgot her outrage, her sense of misuse, the resentment she had been harboring. She even forgot the cold. It all receded, washed away in a mist of pure, primitive longing. *Human contact. Elemental, necessary, impossibly exciting. . . .*

THE TIMELESS CHARM OF ZEBRA'S REGENCY ROMANCES

CHANGE OF HEART (3278, $3.95)
by Julie Caille

For six years, Diana Farington had buried herself in the country, far from the gossip surrounding her ill-fated marriage and her late husband's demise. When she reluctantly returns to London to oversee her sister's debut, she vows to hold her head high. The behavior of the dangerously handsome Lord Lucan, was too much to bear. Diana knew that she could only expect an improper proposal from the rake, and she was determined that *no* man, let alone Lord Lucan, would turn her head again.

The Earl of Lucan knew that second chances were rare, so when he saw the golden-haired Diana again after so many years, he swore he would win her heart this time around. She had lost her innocence over the years, but he swore he could make her trust — and love — again.

THE HEART'S INTRIGUE (3130, $2.95)
by Evelyn Bond

Lady Clarissa Tregallen preferred the solitude of Cornwall to the ballrooms and noisy routs of the London *ton,* but the future bride of the tediously respectable Duke of Mainwaring would soon be forced to enter Society. To this she was resigned — until her evening walk revealed a handsome, wounded stranger. Bryan Deverell was certainly a spy, but how could she turn over a wounded man to the local authorities?

Deverell planned to take advantage of the beauty's hospitality and be on his way once he recovered, yet he found himself reluctant to leave his charming hostess. He would prove to this very proper lady that she was also a very *passionate* one, and that a scoundrel such as he could win her heart.

SWEET PRETENDER (3248, $3.95)
by Violet Hamilton

As the belle of Philadelphia, spirited Sarah Ravensham had no fondness for the hateful British. But as a patriotic American, it was her duty to convey a certain document safely into the hands of Britain's prime minister — even if it meant spending weeks aboard ship in the company of the infuriating Britisher of them all, the handsome Col. Lucien Valentine.

Sarah was unduly alarmed when her cabin had been searched. But when she found herself in the embrace of the arrogant Colonel — and responding to his touch — she realized the full extent of the dangers she was facing. Not the least of which was the danger to her own impetuous heart . . .

Available wherever paperbacks are sold, or order direct from the Publisher. Send cover price plus 50¢ per copy for mailing and handling to: Zebra Books, Dept. 3642, 475 Park Avenue South, New York, NY 10016. Residents of New York and Tennessee must include sales tax. DO NOT SEND CASH. For a free Zebra/ Pinnacle Catalog with more than 1,500 books listed, please write to the above address.

A Valentine's Day Fancy

Julie Caille

ZEBRA BOOKS
KENSINGTON PUBLISHING CORP.

ACKNOWLEDGMENT

This is to express my gratitude to my mother, Priscilla Burns, who very kindly came to my rescue when I required my characters to compose poetry. She is the true author of Gerard's love sonnet, as well as Valentina's composition for Gerard. Thanks Mom. I love you.

ZEBRA BOOKS

are published by

Kensington Publishing Corp.
475 Park Avenue South
New York, NY 10016

First printing: January, 1992

Printed in the United States of America

Valentine's Day, 1814
Lynsted Manor, Kent

"If only Christian were here."

With a wistful sigh, Miss Valentina Jardine set aside her sketchbook, watching idly as her mother selected another hank of silk from her workbasket. "Oh, Mama, I miss him so much," she confided, putting voice to emotions that had been swirling inside her for weeks.

Her mother's lips pursed. "Aye, 'tis a pity," she agreed. "I must own I am surprised. After all, for your betrothed to miss your eighteenth birthday is no small thing. I see no reason why he could not make the journey. He's had since mid-October to claim his estates and whatever else he's had to do."

This buttressing of her own disquiet was not what Tina wanted to hear. Hating the weakness that made her voice shake, she swallowed and said bravely, "Perhaps he has had second thoughts about the wisdom of our marriage."

"I trust he has not," responded her mother tartly. "You need to wed him now, my love, since your father's"—she stopped and corrected herself—"some of your father's investments have gone awry. At any rate, why should his sentiments change?" she added, at last providing some measure of reassurance. "He's mad with love for you, darling. Everyone for miles knows that. And he *has* spoken to your father,

5

after all, so it's not as though it is not settled. The two of you are betrothed, and as soon as he returns, he and your father will negotiate the marriage contract. Once that is signed you will have no more worries."

Unable to sit still, Tina rose and wandered to the window. "Strange," she mused, "I always used to like that I was born on Valentine's Day, but today it seems—"

She stopped, unwilling to confide her melancholy premonition. Instead, she gazed out at the bleak Kentish landscape and said, "If only his estates were not so far away. I wish he had not inherited them at all. Or at least not 'til after we were wed."

Since her mother said nothing, Tina continued to look out upon the snow-encrusted ground, remembering the day when she had first learned that Christian was to leave.

It had been little more than four months ago, when summer's laziness was first giving way to autumn's wilder glow. As usual, she had met Christian in their place for secret trysting—a small copse midway between their two homes—and as always, she had flung herself into his arms. . . .

"Oh, Christian," she murmured as he pulled her close. "I've missed you so."

"What?" His hands spread across her back while his lips brushed her hair. "When it has only been three days since last we met?"

"It seems more like three years." His gentle chuckle emboldened her to confess, "I wish we could be married tomorrow."

His arms loosened. There was a pause. Then, "Tina, there is something I must tell you."

She raised trusting eyes to his face, drinking in the sleek male beauty that haunted her dreams. "What is it?"

"I am leaving this afternoon."

"Leaving?" Alarm shot through her system. "Why? Where are you going?"

He released her and turned away, and for a moment it was as though he were retreating from her life. All she could see was his back, his broad, magnificent shoulders,

6

his dark, curling hair.

"I have inherited an estate. And a title — a barony." When she did not speak, he started to pace. "It is something I never expected to happen. There has been a tragedy. My father's cousin, Lord Rewe, was drowned in a yachting accident three days ago, along with both his sons. And I" — a lilt entered his voice — "I am the next in line. I'm a wealthy man now."

When she only looked at him, he walked over and took her hands. "It will make no difference to us," he soothed, raising her fingers to his lips. "We can be married, exactly as we planned. But I must go to Oxfordshire for a while."

Strangely, she did not feel as relieved as she ought. "I understand, but . . . when will you come back?"

"I hope to be back by Christmas. If not" — he smiled and brushed her brow with his lips — "I will certainly be back for your birthday. My Valentine's Day girl."

Reassured by the familiar endearment, she gazed up at him. "So long," she whispered. "Weeks, perhaps months. However shall I bear it?"

"And how shall I?" All at once his eyes darkened with a hunger she had learned to recognize. "Shall I leave you with a memory to keep you warm at night?" he murmured. And then, as she had longed for him to do, he fastened his mouth on hers.

Since he'd asked for her hand, they had kissed many times, so this was not a new experience. And because he was her betrothed and beloved, Tina had allowed him liberties, pleasant liberties such as skimming his hands over the curves of her body and cupping and squeezing her breasts. She had not minded at all; indeed she'd found that she enjoyed it, a fact she'd shared with him.

However, it soon became obvious that this time was different. He wanted more. And being a girl of gentle birth, and having been raised with strict regard for the proprieties, Tina resisted when he sought to urge her to the ground. Again, Christian set about to smooth away her doubts, his

7

voice as coaxing and gentle as the breeze that ruffled the trees overhead.

"It's all right, darling, I'm not going to hurt you. But the ground is dry and soft as a mattress, and you are sweet beyond belief." With honeyed words, he persuaded her to do as he wished, to sit upon his lap while his fingers eased the fastenings to her gown.

She shivered in the cool air. It was the first time he had bared her flesh and she was a little embarrassed. Anxious, however, to please this divine man who had chosen her, she passively allowed him his will, telling herself that they would soon be man and wife and one more harmless pleasure was really of small consequence. So when he pushed her down upon the blanket of autumn leaves, she simply closed her eyes and her mind to the knowledge of where this could lead.

Instead she thought about Christian's inheritance, and that subject, once broached, would not be dismissed. As his future wife, she supposed she ought to be happier about it, but all she had ever desired was a simple life. She knew girls who yearned for houses in London and wealthy, titled husbands, but all she had ever wanted was a home of her own, a husband to love, and children. And now Christian, a mere squire's son, was to be a wealthy and titled aristocrat. When they married, she would be Lady Rewe. She was unsure how she felt about that.

While she was mulling this over, Christian suddenly lifted himself up. Startled by the shock of air, her eyes automatically flew open, then widened in dismay. When had he loosened the buttons to his breeches? Surely he did not think — ? Before she could complete the thought he was spreading her knees, one strong hand sliding beneath her skirt in an urgent, sensual probe.

Instantly, half of her dissolved into panic, while the other half railed against her own mindless stupidity. She'd thought that he'd only wanted a little more — not everything.

Not this.

She wriggled sideways to avoid the intrusive contact.

"*Christian,*" she gasped, "*what are you doing?*"

"*You know what I'm doing.*" He breathed the words against the base of her throat. "*And you love it, you know you do. Just relax and don't worry, darling. I won't get you with child. I give you my word.*"

Beguiled by his promise, Tina's misgivings faded. Of course he did not mean to dishonor her; of course he recognized that marriage must come before the final intimacy. She had merely misunderstood. But that belief soon vanished.

Thinking back to that day, Tina still felt distressed, but that was tempered by her desire to make excuses for the man she adored. Christian had many wonderful qualities, she thought. He was splendid, witty, handsome, even godlike, but like the gods of old, he was weak and prone to self-indulgence. That was no sin. Indeed, in her eyes such humanness made him all the more lovable.

Smiling sadly, she touched her fingers to the cool window glass. Of the two of them, it was only she who had possessed the strength of will to put a stop to things.

And she had.

Oh, Christian had sulked briefly, but then he had kissed and teased her and called her his dearest little prude. He had brushed the leaves from her clothes and coaxed her to smiles and refastened the ties to her gown. They had exchanged apologies and renewed their vows of love.

Yet four long months had passed and he had written only twice. Why? Had she driven him away? Had he been angrier than she'd realized?

Depressed by the notion, Tina turned and studied her mother. Above all, she longed to pour out her fears, but as she watched her mother's face she knew she would not do it. It was not the sort of confidence one made to one's mother, who had enough to plague her right now, what with her father's propensity for choosing the wrong ventures in which to invest his funds. Already they were having to practice the strictest economies, and Papa had said he was going to take another mortgage on the Manor.

Concealing a sigh, Tina retrieved her sketchbook.

She would always recall the exact moment the post arrived that day. Their maid entered precisely as the clock was striking four, Christian's letter on the silver salver in her hand.

Tina did not open it until the girl was gone, then with shaking fingers she broke open the wafer. As she skimmed the letter, her face drained of color.

"What is it?" said her mother sharply. "What's wrong?"

Slowly, Tina's head bowed. Feigning a courage she did not feel, she spoke without inflection. "Christian is betrothed to an heiress. Her name is Allegra Marchant."

"Marchant!" repeated her mother, aghast. "But the Marchants—she is your own cousin! He cannot!"

"He can and he has," Tina said, after a small pause. "The girl's guardian has given his consent. It has been in the London papers. The settlements are drawn and signed."

Mrs. Jardine simply stared helplessly. "My dear . . . what can I say? Dear heaven, how could he do this to you on your birthday? 'Tis outrageous! Why, the Marchants are connected to us through my great-aunt's marriage to"—she paused, rapidly calculating—"the second viscount's fourth daughter's third son," she ended, as if that could prevent the marriage from taking place.

With a shuddering sigh, Tina's eyes fell to the letter. "Christian is very unhappy about the marriage. He says that he was maneuvered into it, that it is a question of honor, not of choice."

"Who is the girl's guardian?"

Tina glanced down again. "Viscount Laverstoke. Her brother."

"But of all people, *he* should know better!" declared her mother in a wretched tone. "Oh, this is dreadful! What shall we do? What shall we tell your father?"

"Tell Papa the truth," Tina retorted. "As for what we shall do—what can we do?"

And, indeed, there was nothing to be done.

One

January 1819
Gloucestershire

Her posture rigid, Valentina Jardine clutched at a strap as the conveyance she occupied — a light traveling coach — fishtailed its way along the icy Cotswold road. Outside, the wind howled and heavy flakes fell from the sky, transforming what could have been a pleasant journey into one fraught with risk.

"This is madness!" she exclaimed, as the coach lurched again. "We never should have tried to travel on such a day!"

The entire day had been disagreeable from start to finish, but her young cousin, Miss Felicity Winton, looked no more than bored.

"It is your own fault, Tina. You ought to have waited for a fair day to acquaint Mama with the contents of Miss Steeple's letter. It was a bird-witted thing to do." Felicity yawned and pulled the fur rug more tightly about her person. "In any case, you worry too much," she added with the insouciance of the young and overindulged.

Tina burrowed her feet into the sheepskin mat. "It simply never crossed my mind that your mother would respond in such a fashion," she said defensively. "I only wanted to discover if she would permit me to pay Cousin Libby a visit *some time in the near future*. I never expected to be thrust into a carriage within an hour of asking the question!"

"I daresay if Miss Steeple had chosen to live anywhere but on Lord Laverstoke's estate you would not have been," put forth Felicity shrewdly. "But Mama has been boasting for years of our connection with the Marchants, and Miss Steeple's invitation is our first opportunity to get a foot inside their door. If Papa had not been so ill, I expect Mama would have come with us."

"I expect so." Tina's voice was wry. "I suppose I ought to have guessed what would happen. But I did not."

"Ah, but you lacked the vital piece of information! The *viscount* is in residence!" Felicity leaned back and closed her eyes. "Mama is amazing, is she not? She would have made a wonderful spy. Imagine how difficult it must be to ferret out the precise whereabouts of every eligible bachelor in England, as well as the size of their respective fortunes." Her lovely lips curved. "We now know what rewards she reaps from all that diligent correspondence."

After two years of living with Felicity's mother, Tina failed to find the matter amusing. "Your sense of humor leaves much to be desired," she replied.

"Come now, you know Mama amuses you, too. I've seen your lips quiver when she makes some of her sweeping, nonsensical statements. Own it!"

Tina smiled reluctantly. "In truth, I ought not. You know how much I am indebted to your parents."

"Oh, fiddlesticks, for what? For taking you in when your mother died, and then turning you into a servant? You know perfectly well Mama pays you too low a wage, and demands a great deal more of you than what is right. So do I, for that matter. Of course, Papa is too lost in thought to demand very much of anyone. I doubt he has even noticed that you live with us. Or if he has, he likely thinks you're another of his daughters. He is not very good with faces," she finished irreverently.

Tina grimaced as the coach gave another sideways slither. "If I had my way, we would never have left the protection of your father's roof. This is turning into the worst blizzard of the season. The poor coachman!"

"Poor Tina," her cousin corrected, rather mockingly. "Mama expects *such* things of you!" Sitting forward, she puffed out her bosom in an excellent imitation of her mother. *"It has long been my dearest wish,"* she mimicked, *"that my darling Felicity form an acquaintance with our esteemed cousin, Viscount Laverstoke. I expect you, Valentina, to do all you can to bring it about."* Felicity's eyes danced with roguery. "And I shall never, ever forget the look on your face when she said it!"

Tina's heart sank at the reminder. "A thousand other mothers in this country share her wish," she said sharply, "but I, for one, do not see the merit of the goal."

"Do you not? He is one of the most eligible men in England, and certainly one of the richest. And," she added complacently, "you and I have the good fortune to be related to him."

"Only distantly," Tina countered. Unsettled by the subject, she drew her rug a little closer. "You and I may share a grandmother, but our connection with Lord Laverstoke is far more remote. It is quite possible he will not acknowledge us." *After all, he had not acknowledged her existence five years ago, had he?*

Felicity, however, was full of confidence. "I scarcely think that is likely." She fluttered her eyelashes meaningfully.

Tina sighed. "As far as I am concerned, the sole purpose of our journey is to visit Libby Steeple, not," she emphasized, "to secure an introduction to Lord Laverstoke." The fine line of her jaw tightened. "And since Libby resides in the Dower House, I think it unlikely we shall meet him at all. In fact, I hope we do not."

"What?" The younger girl arched her brows. "When Mama specifically bade you to parade me in front of him?" Her head tilted consideringly. "Of course I can just as well parade myself if I've a mind to."

Tina frowned. "I know you are jesting, Felicity. The man

is too old for you, surely."

"Perhaps. But to capture such a prize would be a feather in my cap, would it not?"

"And what of Mr. St. Hillary? I thought you had a *tendre* for that young man."

The young beauty tossed her auburn curls. "On the contrary, I would not marry him for anything in the world!"

"Ah." Tina glanced toward the window, but could see nothing except that it was nearly dusk. "You had a row, did you?"

If Felicity had been standing, she would probably have stamped her pretty foot. "No one could have a row with Eugene," she said crossly. "How could one, when one never sees him?"

Despite her somber mood, Tina smiled. "Poor Felicity."

"Let us not discuss him. I wonder what Lord Laverstoke is like? I make no doubt he is as handsome as a dream."

Tina's smile faded. "I am sure he is quite dissipated and repulsive," she said repressively, "and very likely has the gout as well."

"The gout?" Felicity blinked. "Is he not too young to have the gout? Mama says he is only three-and-thirty, which of course is very old, but not as old as my uncle the baronet, who did not become goutish until he was past forty."

Being rather too tired to consider her words, Tina embroidered upon the image she had formed long ago. "He will have the gout and he will limp," she declared. "His breath will be bad and he will have missing teeth."

"He will *not* limp," protested Felicity, who loved to argue, "and his smile will be beautiful."

"Not only will he limp, he will have a nasty, calculating nature." Tina would have gone on had she not, at this point, recollected the imprudence of sharing her opinion of the man who, if not directly responsible for her current situation, had at least in some way contributed to it.

As it was, Felicity was eying her with open curiosity. "You sound as though you dislike him."

"I do." It was too late to disclaim.

"But why?" asked the other girl in bewilderment. "Have you ever met him?"

"No." Unwilling to explain her prejudice, Tina folded her lips. "Nor do I wish to." Once more she looked toward the window, half covered by flakes the wind had driven against the glass. "We must be nearly there," she said abruptly. "Perhaps we will make it through unscathed."

At the instant she spoke these words, the coachman—no doubt even more anxious to attain their destination—sought to churn the horses into a canter on a straight stretch of road. The result was disastrous. In less time than it took to count to five, the coach hit a patch of ice and sailed sideways, its wheel falling into a deep rut which the snow had made invisible. As the vehicle toppled to its side in a snowdrift, the young ladies pitched from their seats.

For a moment Tina lay quite still, conscious only of the discomfort of Felicity's weight.

"Tina, oh Tina, are you hurt?" screeched the weight, wiggling in a manner that sent a stab of pain through Tina's arm.

"Yes, I'm fine, Felicity, but your elbow is pressing into my—yes, that's better. We must try to climb out of here."

As Felicity groped for the handle, the coachman wrenched open the door, sending a shower of cold flakes raining upon their heads.

"Death an' the deuce! Are ye 'urt?" he cried, peering down at them. " 'Twas no fault o' mine, 'pon my grave. 'Ere now"—he reached out a hand—"ye'll 'ave ter git out. I disremember the last time the roads was so terrible. 'Tain't fit for man or beast out 'ere, let alone two nice young ladies like yerselves."

The coachman, whose name was Rawlings, went on making excuses while he helped them out of the coach. After assuring himself that they had sustained no injuries, he then stomped over to the groom, who was attending to the unhappy horses.

Tina shivered and looked about. It was growing dark,

but it was possible to tell that the surrounding Cotswold hills would have been beautiful beyond description in the light of day. At the moment, however, she was in no mood to admire the prospect.

"How far are we from Laverstoke Park?" she asked, walking over to the two men.

Rawlings swiped at his reddened nose and exchanged glances with the groom. "Mebbe another mile, miss, with the Dower 'Ouse a short distance beyond that. 'Twas why I thought ter press on, 'stead o' puttin' up at the inn back in Norton. The mistress told me to git ye ter Laverstoke this day, snow or no snow. She don't 'old wi' young ladies stayin' in public inns."

"An inn would have been preferable to this," snapped Tina, who had long since lost all patience with Mrs. Winton and her demands. "Well, Felicity, we shall have to walk. We have no other recourse."

"Walk!" squeaked Felicity, her teeth chattering. "Oh, T-Tina, I cannot possibly walk! I am too c-cold!"

"Fustian," said Tina. "Walking will warm you far better than standing about. Rawlings, shall you be safe if we leave you?"

"I reckon as I can manage, miss," replied the coachman with respect. "I'll just keep walkin' around and stompin' me feet 'til someone comes." He drew a flask from the pocket of his greatcoat and winked. " 'Sides, I got a drop o' somethin' in 'ere ter 'elp."

As the sharp wind whipped at her cloak, Tina nodded. She turned her gaze to the groom. "Very well, then. Harris, you had better come with us. We will send help as soon as possible."

At much the same moment, Gerard Marchant, 5th Viscount Laverstoke, was cozily ensconced before a roaring blaze in his library. Having but a short time before partaken of an unfashionably early dinner, he now held a glass of port in his hand, from which he took an occasional sip

16

as he gazed meditatively into the flames.

"Are you game for some chess?" The idle question came from his brother, who lounged opposite him with equal laziness. "I'm in a reckless enough mood to challenge you, if you like."

Gerard's gaze shifted. "You look tired. Is your leg paining you again?"

"Devil a bit," James admitted with a sigh. "It's this damned weather. The cold always makes it ache. The plight of an ex-soldier. Do you want to play or not?"

"Certainly, if you wish it." Gerard rose and went to a cabinet, from which he retrieved a box of chess pieces. "Have you made up your mind about Sussex?" he inquired.

"No." James looked vaguely irritated. "What the devil makes you want to go there? Is it that Chalfield woman?"

"Beatrice?" Gerard smiled sardonically. "I suppose she is part of the reason." Without bothering to summon a servant, he moved one of the rosewood sofa tables—the one with the chessboard set into the top—over between the two chairs and set the box upon it. "And since she already has a husband," he went on, "I am spared the customary tricks and ploys. Bridals interest her no more than they do me."

James grinned. "Poor Gerry. Fame and fortune have their drawbacks, eh? It must be devilish hard having all those females hurling themselves in your path."

"Well, it is," replied Gerard, his tone bored. "You may laugh, but if one more female loses her slipper or drops her fan or has an accident on my doorstep, I swear I will strangle her. Christmas at Allegra's was a mere sampling of what I have had to put up with these past months."

"Ah yes, our dear sister had three prospective wives lined up and ready for the great diplomat's delectation. And you chose to be displeased." James leaned back, linking his fingers behind his head. "They were all well-qualified, too. Miss Gladstone was proficient on the harp—"

"Miss Gladstone was proficient at dampening her gown," corrected Gerard acidly. "Her figure wasn't worth the trouble either. She was shaped like a bell."

James's eyes twinkled. "Miss Rudgwick was gifted with blue eyes, golden hair, a luscious figure—"

"—and not a brain to occupy the space between her ears."

"True," acknowledged James. "But then there was Miss Fenchurch, who could converse intelligently *and* sing, though not at the same time. What, pray tell, was wrong with her?"

"A great deal," answered Gerard coolly. "She wasn't my style, and her teeth were bad. And she lacked even the rudiments of a sense of humor."

"You are difficult to please."

Gerard's lips curved in a scornful line. "Hardly. I simply have an aversion to being pursued. I prefer to do my own hunting."

"Ah." James hid a smile. "And do you?"

"Do I what?"

"Hunt."

This time Gerard's face was genuinely amused. "Oh, yes. When the mood moves me."

James began to set up the chess pieces. "What of Vienna? I heard the Princess Balgration lusted after you quite openly."

Gerard snorted. "She lusted after every man she saw, and had most of them, too. Excepting Talleyrand, of course, who disliked her as much as I did. Go ahead."

James opened with his king's pawn. "Yes, but consider the political advantages," he remarked. "She could have been a useful ally. Was she not one of the tsar's favorites?"

"One of many," Gerard replied imperturbably, moving one of his own pawns. "Yet I managed to do without her. Do you wish to discuss my past amours, or shall we play chess?"

With another of his infectious grins, his brother denied all interest in his sibling's mistresses, past or present, and proceeded to concentrate on the game. Half an hour later, the two men's absorption was interrupted by the appearance of the viscount's butler.

"My lord?" The butler cleared his throat, a sure sign that he was perturbed.

Gerard glanced up. "Yes, Bissett?"

"My lord, a situation has developed."

"Don't tell me Marcel has given notice again. Where shall I find another cook in this weather?"

The butler coughed delicately. "It is not Marcel, my lord. You have, er, some visitors."

Gerard frowned. "Who?"

"Two young ladies, my lord. Their coach met with an accident. I put them in the Blue Saloon."

James guffawed. "Good God, they follow you everywhere, don't they? Though if they are pretty, perhaps it may not be such a bad thing. Shall I come with you to see?"

After a brief silence, Gerard rose to his feet. "No," he responded, quite curtly. "Allow me to deal with them myself. I shan't be gone long."

As Tina warmed her hands before the fire in the Blue Saloon, she could not help admiring the room. On either side of the chimneypiece stood walnut pedestals supporting Delft porcelain vases; these were surmounted by portraits of a man and a woman dressed in Restoration fashion. As for the rest of the room—the elaborate frieze and wainscoting, the walnut armchairs, the settee, the giltwood sidetables, the paintings and Turkey carpet—it all surpassed anything she had ever seen. However, after a brief study, Tina discovered that the elegance was having a profound effect upon her nerves. The whole day had been extremely trying, and now she was forced to seek refuge under the roof of the one man in England for whom she cherished an abiding resentment. It was the final straw!

Fuming inwardly, she concentrated on the pleasure of the fire's heat. Though she had relinquished all of her outer garments, she found herself longing to pull off her boots, for her toes were nigh to frozen. However, since she was not about to conduct an interview with Viscount Laverstoke in her stocking feet, she valiantly ignored the discomfort.

Inches away, Felicity was crouching down, her hands close to the blaze. "Oh, T-Tina, I'm still so c-cold," shuddered the kneeling girl. "I don't think I've ever been so chilled in my life. I could not have walked a step farther, I swear."

Felicity's cheeks and nose were pink from the chafing wind, a reflection of her own, Tina knew. Wishing she had been given the opportunity to tidy her appearance, she said only, "A cup of hot tea will help. I'm certain Lord Laverstoke will provide that, if nothing else."

Felicity glanced up. "If Mama were here, she would say that all our trouble had been worth the while." Her wide-eyed gaze swept the room. "Look at this place! The entrance hall alone is bigger than the whole of Mama's drawing room. Mama says the viscount is very rich, but I did not bargain for anything as grand as this. And to think he is a bachelor! Mama says it only goes to show that he must be very particular, for countless girls have set their caps for him, even if he does have the gout. But it is his duty to marry, she says, and at this time of year he is more like to be bored so—"

"For heaven's sake, Felicity," Tina cut in with impatience. "Someone might hear."

As she uttered these words she sensed a presence in the room, though there had been no discernable sound other than their own voices and the wind whirring in the chimney. She was therefore unsurprised when, upon turning, she found a tall gentleman in buckskin breeches and a mulberry coat surveying them from the doorway.

He had a distinct air of breeding, and a countenance that was far from ill-favored. His hair was a burnished gold most women would have killed for, a curious contrast to his brows and lashes, which were as dark as though he'd been born a brunette. His eyes were measuring, their color a sharp, steel gray that made her think of a pair of rapiers she'd seen in a Bristol shop window. As for the rest of him, he was as well-made a man as she had ever seen.

Including Christian.

Thrusting aside the disloyal thought, Tina rose from her crouch. "Are you Lord Laverstoke?" she asked in a tone just short of accusing.

The gentleman advanced several steps into the room, his eyes assessing her in a discomfiting manner. "No," he said, after a brief pause. "I am his brother James. The viscount is otherwise engaged at the moment."

Felicity had also risen. "Then you must be our cousin, too," she said, holding out her hand and smiling prettily. "We have come to visit. I am Felicity Winton."

The dark brows rose as he bowed over her hand. "I don't recall my brother mentioning the imminent arrival of any cousins," he murmured.

Detecting his irony, Tina stepped in before Felicity could answer. "I beg your pardon, sir," she said brusquely, "but I must ask that you send someone to assist our coachman. Our coach is stuck fast in a drift a mile back on the road, and poor Rawlings is there with the horses in this dreadful weather."

To her relief, Mr. Marchant reached instantly for the bellpull. When the butler appeared he said, in a dispassionate voice, "There is a coach stuck in a drift somewhere between here and — ?" He glanced at Tina.

"Norton," she supplied, her annoyance mounting.

"Norton," he repeated. "I wish you to dispatch several men to assist the coachman and convey the horses to our stables."

The butler bowed. "Yes, m—"

"At once, Bissett," he cut in. "My brother would not wish you to delay." The butler sent him a peculiar look and withdrew.

Well! thought Tina indignantly. The house might belong to the viscount, but James Marchant's orders were obviously obeyed as though it were his. She wondered why the knowledge annoyed her so much.

He turned back to them with a hard light in his eye. "Am I to understand that you have just walked a mile through the snow?" He sounded so skeptical that Tina's hackles rose.

"Indeed we did," she said challengingly. "And it has been a most unpleasant experience." She tried hard to imply that the unpleasantness was by no means over.

"Oh, it was dreadful!" chimed Felicity, unconscious of nuances. "I don't think I shall ever grow warm again."

Mr. Marchant subjected them to a penetrating scrutiny, then at last his mouth relaxed. "Then we must do something to remedy that. Pray be seated and I will order refreshment."

As he reached once more for the bellpull, Felicity planted herself on the nearby settee, and after a short pause, Tina joined her.

"What a lovely room," her cousin exclaimed, casting her blue eyes about in ingenuous admiration. "I cannot wait to meet Lord Laverstoke."

Mr. Marchant's mouth curled—unpleasantly, Tina thought. "Unfortunately," he said smoothly, "my brother intends to depart tomorrow to visit friends in Sussex. He will be desolated to have missed you." He turned as the door opened. "Some tea for the ladies," he commanded the hovering servant. "And something to eat."

"Oh, thank you," uttered Felicity. "I am famished, are not you, Tina?"

"No," stated Tina, whose stomach was rumbling. "Sir, contrary to what you appear to think, it is not you we have come to see—"

"I'm well aware of that," he interpolated.

"—nor are we interested in your brother," she continued, her cheeks burning. "I am sure he must be a magician if he thinks to travel tomorrow, however that is neither here nor there, and no concern of mine. Felicity and I have come in response to an invitation from our mutual cousin, Libby Steeple. It is her we have come to see."

He regarded her blandly. "Indeed? Miss Steeple said

nothing of this to me."

"Need she have?" Tina retorted, on her mettle. "Is she required to ask permission before she invites visitors?"

Ignoring her question, he said with a trace of mockery, "Well, you have come to the wrong place. Miss Steeple resides at the Dower House."

"Where Lord Laverstoke banished her," she retorted. "I am well aware which house my cousin resides in."

"Yes, I rather thought you were," he replied. He sat and crossed his legs, his expression enough to rile a saint.

Tina controlled her temper with difficulty. "Despite what you obviously believe, Mr. Marchant, we have not come to encroach upon his lordship's hospitality. If it were not for the coaching accident, we would not be here at all, but since yours was the closest house — oh, why am I explaining?" Despite her intense weariness, she forced herself to her feet. "Come, Felicity. We will go to the Dower House now."

His eyes glimmered strangely. "Are you planning to commandeer one of my carriages?" he inquired. "If so, I fear I cannot oblige you."

"I would not dream of using anything that belonged to you or your wretched brother," she snapped. "Felicity and I will walk—"

"Oh, no! No, Tina, I will not!"

"No, you will certainly not," he agreed.

At that moment, the servant returned with the tea tray. To one who had not eaten since the morn, the sight of plum cakes, tartlets, gingerbread, biscuits, and a pot of tea was a mouth-watering temptation. Tina swallowed hard.

"Do have some tea before you set out." Across the intervening space he was watching her, obviously deriving amusement from her discomfiture.

Feeling foolish, Tina bit her lip and accepted the steaming cup the servant was holding out. With inward thankfulness, she sipped the hot beverage, then said, with as much crispness as she was able: "At any rate, Mr. Marchant, neither of us has the least desire to spend the night under your roof. Surely you must see that it would not be proper."

"You have little choice," he pointed out. "You should have planned this better, should you not? Or perhaps you planned it precisely right." Again, that ironic nuance to his voice that made Tina yearn to deliver a cutting set-down.

Felicity rose to his bait. "Oh, no," she said between mouthfuls of gingerbread, "it was Mama who planned the whole scheme. She would have come herself if Papa had not been ill, but I think it better that she did not. She would have had the vapors when the coach went over and we were thrown from our seats—"

"Were you injured?" The dark brows snapped together.

"No—at least I was not. Tina's arm hurts, I think."

Again, Tina found herself subjected to a penetrating stare. "I am quite well," she said stiffly.

"You ought to take those boots off and warm your feet," he remarked. "You, too, Miss Winton. And while you do so, perhaps you will be good enough to explain how it is that we are related."

Still chewing, Felicity bent at once to do as he suggested, but Tina was determined to give this abominable man no quarter. Something of this must have shown in her expression, for she saw the corner of his mouth twitch.

"You never told me your name," he prodded. "Are you another long lost cousin?"

"I am Miss Jardine," she informed him with chilling hauteur. "And my connection with your family, sir, is quite remote."

"Jardine," he repeated, giving it the same soft French pronunciation that she had used. "I do vaguely recall the name from somewhere or other. The name Winton is also familiar."

"Oh, we're in your family tree," said Felicity, as she trotted over to set her boots before the fire. "Or at least *you* are in *ours*. You must go back to the second viscount to trace the connection." She returned to her seat and reached for a plum cake.

"Ah," he said, his lazy smile putting Tina in mind of a

cat toying with its prey. "I daresay you are right. Perhaps I ought to study the family bible more often."

"Yes, I daresay you should," Tina said shrewishly.

His look was so quizzical that she blushed. "How is the tea?" he said mildly.

"It's . . . very good." Tina made the admission grudgingly.

"You'd be warmer if you took those boots off. Shall I do it for you?"

"N-no!" she choked, her eyes flying up.

"Can you feel your toes?"

"Mr. Marchant, I do not wish to discuss my feet with you. Your concern should be for our coachman, who is far more likely than I to have taken frostbite."

"Oh, he will be attended to, never fear. My people will provide him with all that he requires."

"Your people?" Tina echoed. "Is this not your brother's house?"

"My dear Miss Jardine, I grew up here," he said, almost gently. "I speak out of habit."

"What is his lordship like?" inquired Felicity with a wistful sigh.

The broad shoulders rose in a careless shrug. "He's only a man, like other men. There is nothing especial about him."

"Mama does not think so," Felicity confided. "She will be odiously disappointed if we do not obtain an introduction. Are you certain he is occupied? She expressly wanted me to"—she caught Tina's glare—"to, ah, convey her respects."

Ignoring the question, James Marchant leaned forward and refilled both their tea cups. "It seems curious to me that Mrs. Winton was willing to allow you to go jaunting about in weather that can only be termed hazardous. Where is your maid?"

"Oh, Tina is my maid," said Felicity blithely. "Well, not precisely my maid," she amended, as he shot her a look. "I used to share a maid with Mama but now . . . Tina lives with us and . . . helps. Mama says she could not manage without her. She has such a way with a needle, and always knows exactly how one's hair should be arranged and that sort of thing. I have gotten into the habit of relying on her to help me dress, so you see I do not need a maid. That is what I meant."

"I see," was the noncommittal answer. "Well, all I can say is that the two of you will have to stay here for the night. Your transportation to the Dower House can be arranged in the morning." He rose. "If you will excuse me?" Without waiting for an answer, he walked from the room.

"Well!" said Felicity, reaching for more gingerbread. "Mama would have been better pleased if *he* had been the viscount, but perhaps we shall meet him yet. I found Cousin James quite handsome, did you? I wonder if Lord Laverstoke resembles him. Surely the weather is too bad for him to travel anywhere."

"One would think so," agreed Tina, eying the food longingly. Casting pride aside, she took a biscuit and bit into it, reflecting that Lord Laverstoke could not possibly be any more arrogant than his brother. However, it would do no good to brood over past troubles when present ones were at hand. Indeed, as tired as she was, it was all she could do to match wits with James Marchant.

They had been left alone for quite some time, then: "Your coachman has arrived safely." Tina started; again she had not heard James Marchant's steps. "Your baggage has arrived," he went on, "and been conveyed upstairs. I think it best if you allow our housekeeper to show you to your rooms now. As for dinner, Mrs. Bissett will bring you each a tray."

Struggling to hide her fatigue, Tina squared her slender shoulders and stood up. "Thank you. I hope all this is not inconvenient." Her tone was designed to put him in his place.

He gave her a curious smile. "Did I suggest it was? How rude, if I did. By the by, I have sent orders that a bath be prepared for each of you." To Tina's outrage, his

26

gaze flicked over her figure in a faintly interested manner.

"A bath will be perfectly delightful." Felicity sighed happily. "You are so kind, Cousin James. Pray tell Cousin Laverstoke that we hope to see him at breakfast before he departs."

"I will do so," he said dryly. "But I can promise nothing."

Two

When Gerard returned to the library, his brother appeared to be asleep. Reclaiming his chair, he regarded the sleeping man with affection, then looked down at the board. James, he saw, had made the expected move, the move he had planned for him to make. Conscious of vague disappointment, he slid his bishop across the lacquered surface. "Your move," he said, very softly.

As he had suspected, James was not asleep in the true sense of the word. Nearly seven years as a soldier had given his younger brother the ability to doze lightly and for short intervals, a habit he still retained. In fact, he was awake and alert in an instant, his eyes assessing the chessboard as if he had never slept at all. "Hang it," James said, quite genially, "that's not what I meant for you to do."

"I know." There was an apology in Gerard's voice. "You thought I would take your rook."

"Where the devil have you been all this time? If my leg hadn't been throbbing, I'd have come to look for you."

Gerard reached for his half-finished drink. "Actually, I'm glad you did not."

"Oh? Why?"

Ignoring the question, Gerard shifted enough to extend his long legs, and swallowed the remainder of his port. "It seems," he said finally, "that the two ladies who managed to have a coaching accident are distant cousins of ours. They aim to be here for a while." His tone was pensive.

"So?" said James. "What are they like?"

Gerard studied his empty glass. "The younger girl is unquestionably a diamond of the first water. Auburn curls, green eyes, dimples. Spoiled, but not mean-spirited. Her name is Felicity Winton. She tells me we are in her family tree, so I suppose she must be in ours."

His brother lifted a brow. "Good lord, where is this charmer? Surely you did not cast her out into the snow!"

"I would hardly behave so shabbily, Jay. She is upstairs, recovering from her ordeal."

"And the other girl?"

"She is older than Miss Winton, though not by many years." Gerard hesitated. "At first I thought her quite ordinary."

"At first?" James repeated.

"My second assessment is that she is not ordinary, but"—Gerard paused—"I cannot say I like her."

Several seconds passed. Then, "Is she pretty?"

"Not in the common way. Her hair is black but she wears it most unbecomingly. Her eyes are blue." Unwilling to admit that he had found Miss Jardine unaccountably stimulating, Gerard merely shrugged. "She is tall for a woman."

"And her figure?" His brother's tone was sly.

Gerard smiled reluctantly. "Quite passable. You may judge for yourself tomorrow. I shall be gone by then."

"Gone!" James blinked. "When we have visitors?"

"They did not come to visit us," Gerard said dryly. "They are here at Miss Steeple's invitation. But from what I overheard before I went in, Miss Winton's mama has her ambitions well in order. Miss Winton is yet another applicant for the role of viscountess."

James rubbed at his thigh and sighed. "I wish you would not go, Gerry."

"Come with me, Jay. I have no wish to leave you behind."

James snorted. "That *would* be shabby, wouldn't it? Only think what our cousins would say if we both ran out on them."

Gerard was silent for a moment. "I own you have a point, but it may be . . . awkward. I fear I have done something impulsive."

"You? Impulsive?" James shifted in his chair. "What the devil did you do?"

"I said I was you."

"What?" His brother stared. "The deuce you say!"

"I thought to fob them off," Gerard said evenly. "I said Lord Laverstoke was occupied." He laughed shortly. "That was before I learned they were connections of ours."

He turned and stared at the fire, wondering how large a part Miss Jardine's accusatory question had played. *Are you Lord Laverstoke?* God, he could have sworn she'd been ready to scratch out his eyes if he said yes. Irrational annoyance shot through him at the thought.

James was no less annoyed. "So you're simply going to ride off to Sussex and leave me to mend matters," he complained. "Devil take it, you're the diplomat, Gerry. What the devil am I going to say to them?"

Approaching the problem with his usual logic, Gerard said reasonably, "Well, you can either confess the truth or pretend to be me for a while. I recommend the latter."

James scowled. "Aye, and how long do you think it would be before the truth came out? *You* do not walk with a limp. *I* do. The mere notion of such a masquerade is tomfoolery. Even if I bribed every servant in the place, Miss Steeple knows the truth."

"Very well, then. Confess, or come with me to Sussex. Those are your choices."

James ignored his remark. "You know, you've made me devilish interested in these ladies," he commented.

"What are they doing now? The hour is not advanced. Surely they did not wish to retire so early."

"Have patience," said Gerard plaintively. "I've managed to get rid of them. Let well enough alone, I beg. I make no doubt you'll see enough of them before they're gone."

James glanced toward the window. "And if you cannot leave? Do we keep them barred in their rooms until the roads are clear?"

Gerard followed his gaze. By this time it was far too dark to see the flakes, but he knew they were there, just as he knew, deep inside, that he had no intention of leaving. He exhaled a deep sigh of resignation. "If I'd realized it would be like this I'd have left this morning."

James didn't bother to hide his grin. "Time to restrategize, old fellow. Ah well. You diplomats are good at that, eh?"

Gerard flashed him a look. "True," he said mildly. "One must always be ready to adapt to new situations."

"And one must remain open to new ideas, must one not? New ideas, new concepts, new . . . fancies?"

New fancies? Once more, Miss Jardine intruded upon Gerard's thoughts—which was very odd, since she was not at all in his usual style. Did he fancy the girl?

"Let's play chess," he said with a frown.

After a delicious dinner, Tina was savoring the luxury of a warm bath. The tub was set before the fire, while on the other side of the screen, a maid lingered to serve her needs.

It was heaven. Sheer heaven.

She had always washed in cold water in Felicity's home, while back at Lynsted Manor, bathing had always been done in a small room off the kitchen. Tina's mother had considered it a great waste of effort for the servants to lug water up and down the stairs.

"Do you need more hot water, miss?" inquired the maid.

"Not yet," answered Tina, sinking lower into the water. The seductive warmth wrapped around her, making her sleepy, coaxing her to spend as long as possible in its luxurious embrace. She stared at the fire. Deep in the dancing flames she saw James Marchant's face: harsh, thin-lipped, aristocratic, yet handsome in its way. His was not a face she could easily forget.

She hadn't cared for him at all, yet it was he who was responsible for her present comfort. He was a strange man, she decided. An enigma. She was certain he hadn't cared for her either, yet when he'd mentioned ordering their baths, his gaze had suddenly lost its detachment. His eyes had swept over her in an appraisal that had been very swift and very masculine. But why? She was not a woman to draw men's stares—that was Felicity's role in life. But he had not looked at Felicity.

Baffled, Tina looked down at her breasts, which, though well enough, could hardly be said to be curvaceous. On the other hand, she was better endowed than Felicity—oh, the devil! Why should she think about such things? She was a spinster and a virgin, and was destined to remain so forever because her true love had been stolen from her.

Stolen by Lord Laverstoke's sister.

Immediately, her lips curved. It sounded so much more melodramatic than it used to, didn't it? *Destined to remain so forever.* How impractical. How foolish. The past few years had done much to rip the melodrama from her heart. And yet, underneath, she still cherished a resentment toward the Marchants. Perhaps it was illogical, but there it was.

Five years, she brooded. Five long years since she had last seen and spoken to Christian. It seemed a lifetime ago; so much had changed. Her father had died in June of '14, leaving her mother sadly in debt. They had had to sell the Manor and move into a smaller place, and even then they'd had to struggle to make ends meet. A year

32

later, in early November, her mother had caught a chill which had soon blossomed into a full-blown inflammation of the lungs. Two weeks later, Mrs. Jardine had succumbed to her illness, leaving her daughter alone.

Tina opened her eyes and shivered. "I'm ready to get out," she said to the maid, who immediately stepped around the screen with a towel. A short while later, Tina sat, garbed in her dressing gown, while the maid carefully combed the tangles from her damp, waist-length hair.

"Your hair is right pretty, miss," the girl, Annie, complimented her. "Black as night, and with such a nice bit o' curl."

"Why, thank you," Tina murmured in surprise. "I never thought of it as pretty. I've always rather wished it were blond, like yours."

"Oh, but miss, black is ever so pretty and rich-looking. Look at the ripples in it. And look how dark your lashes are, miss. Mine are so light they fade to nothing."

This mention of dark lashes made Tina think of James Marchant. "Do Lord Laverstoke and his brother spend much time here?" she asked.

"Oh, his lordship comes and goes, miss, but Mr. James stays here most o' the time, him being the steward and all. They both been here since Twelfth Night. Christmas weren't the same without the family here, but Miss Allegra—Lady Rewe, I should say—insisted they go to Chandling this year."

"Lady Rewe?" repeated Tina, her nerves jumping.

"His lordship's sister, miss. She's a great beauty, and her husband, Lord Rewe, is nearly as handsome as his lordship. I do hope you get to meet them, miss."

Tina's jaw clenched at the horrifying thought. "Perhaps I will," she murmured.

Annie put down the comb. "Now you just sit by the fire and dry your hair," she said kindly, "and I'll fetch you up a nice cup of hot milk to help you sleep."

Tina had been alone for no more than three or four minutes when Felicity drifted into the room. "I don't feel ready to retire for the night," she complained. "I wish we could go down and meet Lord Laverstoke."

"Lord Laverstoke is occupied," Tina said dryly. "And I have the impression that James Marchant does not relish our presence overmuch. I have the distinct feeling that we have been sent to our rooms for the night."

Felicity plopped down on the edge of the bed. "You didn't like him, did you?"

Tina shrugged. "I thought him arrogant. No doubt he is jealous of his brother." *His brother, the great diplomat,* she wanted to sneer.

"Perhaps." Felicity reclined at her ease, her head propped on her hand. "I wish we could dress and go down. What excuse can I use? I know!"—she snapped her fingers—"I cannot sleep and need a book to read."

"Look in your cupboard," advised Tina. "If it's like mine, it contains a varied selection of literature, including poetry and gothic romance."

"Oh." Felicity looked disappointed. "Well, that's no good then."

"And anything you desire can be brought to you." Tina pointed. "There's the bellpull. We each have a maid assigned to us. Any excuse to return downstairs will be construed for what it is—sheer impudence. Pray remember that we are here as uninvited guests."

Felicity sighed audibly. "You are no help at all, Tina. What am I to do?"

"Read or sleep. I know I'm tired. Why should you not be?"

Felicity sat up suddenly. "I know. Let's go exploring! The house is so vast that we could—"

"No." Tina covered her ears with her hands. "No, no, and no! Honestly, I don't know where you get these ideas."

"Oh, very well," her cousin capitulated. "I suppose I

am a little tired." With catlike grace, she stretched and rose from the bed. "I shall see you in the morning, then," she said with a yawn. "Good night."

"Good night," Tina replied, a trifle absently.

If she were not so tired she would have pulled out her sketchbook, but instead she went to peruse the selection of books. At once, her interest was caught by a slender volume of Shakespeare's sonnets.

As she retook her seat by the fire, Annie returned with the milk. "Here you are, miss," she said, setting the cup by the bed. "It should help you sleep. Of course, it's early for that, but I expect you're tired."

"I'm exhausted. Thank you, Annie."

"I've put a hot brick in the bed, miss. Be you needing anything else?"

Tina shook her head. "Thank you, no. I'm going to read for a while."

She sat for nearly half an hour after Annie was gone, then, growing drowsy, she hung her dressing gown in the wardrobe and climbed into bed. Settling back on the pillows, her eyes roamed the room, taking in its elegance a shade wistfully. She was not accustomed to such lavish surroundings, but, oh, how exceedingly pleasant it was. Even the book was handsome, with its green leather cover and gold embossing. How wonderful it must be to own such beautiful things, she thought. She'd almost forgotten that there was another world out there, a world of pleasure and wit and culture that did not revolve around household chores and the endless monotony of performing one's duty so that one might be worthy of the pittance of a wage one was paid.

Ah well. She would return to that world soon enough, a world far removed from the likes of the odious Marchant brothers. She might as well enjoy this episode of self-indulgence while it lasted; it was not like to be long.

With a pragmatic sigh, she propped herself on the pillows and settled the book in her lap. Then, as she had been wont to do as a child, she opened the book at random just to see where it would fall. The words which met her eyes made her smile wryly.

*Is it thy will thy image should keep open
My heavy eyelids to the weary night?*

It was an ironic choice, she reflected, considering that she was having some difficulty keeping James Marchant from her thoughts. Still, the lines beguiled her and she read on, lured by the beauty of a language filled with imagery and sensitivity, the language of Shakespeare's world. As she read, she sipped the milk, which, as Annie had predicted, exacerbated her drowsiness. Little by little, her eyelids grew heavy until at last they drifted shut without her conscious knowledge.

How long she dozed she did not know, but it must have been a good while later that the quiet closing of a door brought her to alertness. She looked about in vague alarm, but there was nothing to be seen or heard except . . . light footsteps tapping down the hall.

Felicity.

Tina sat up, throwing off the covers. Had the foolish girl decided to go exploring after all?

Shoving her feet into slippers, she wrenched open the wardrobe and snatched up the first wrap she could find, which happened to be a Paisley shawl. She then hurried over to throw open the door and peer into the corridor.

There was no sign of anyone, which sent small prickles down her spine as she recalled every haunted house story that she had ever heard. Now stop it, she told herself sternly. Summoning her courage, she walked along the passage to the next door and rapped lightly.

"Felicity? Are you in there?"

There was no answer.

Tina opened the door and looked in. The bed was turned down and rumpled, but there was certainly no one in it. A quick search assured her that Felicity was not in the chamber at all.

Considerably vexed, Tina pondered her next action. She was, in effect, the girl's chaperon, so it was her duty to find her, and persuade her to return to her room. But where in the world should she begin her search?

Returning to her own chamber, she retrieved the candle that was still burning by her bed and walked down the corridor until she reached a staircase. She peered over the balustrade, but saw no sign of Felicity. Drat the girl! Where the devil had she gone?

Again she debated. Should she return to her room to dress? Or would the delay allow Felicity to go even farther, perhaps penetrating the area of the house which their two male cousins inhabited? Annie had told her that they were in the east wing and that the viscount and his brother occupied apartments in the south wing, two sides of a square built round a central courtyard. But then, the hour was not advanced. The two men might be anywhere in the house. Not that Felicity would be in any danger from them, but James Marchant had made it clear that their presence was, if not unwelcome, at least not a cause for celebration. Felicity's intrusion might be deemed a nuisance, which was hardly what Mrs. Winton would have desired.

If only she knew what direction Felicity had taken! After a moment's deliberation, Tina decided to slip down the stairs to the first floor. Mayhap she would find Felicity simply by using her ears.

The staircase was carpeted, its walls decorated with murals—scenes of gods and goddesses parading about in flowing garments, allegorical in nature. Halfway down, there was a niche containing a marble bust, a noble-looking gentleman with disordered locks and a decidedly austere countenance. She glanced at it as she passed, thinking it reminded her of James Marchant.

At the foot of the stairs she paused again. This was

not the grand staircase, but another set closer to the end of the house. Stretched out ahead lay a string of dark, eerie rooms; save for the wind and the usual creakings of an old house, complete and utter silence prevailed.

Tina raised her candle. Surely Felicity would not be skulking around down here in the dark! Perhaps she should go back and look for her upstairs. Yet between her candle and the light of the moon shining through the windows, there was just enough illumination to hint at the splendor.

Then she looked up, and her interest was caught. Slowly, tentatively, she walked forward, her eyes raised to the deeply coved ceiling ornamented with elaborate plasterwork. This truly was a magnificent place, she thought wonderingly. Earlier, she had been too cold and overwrought to take much notice of the dwelling that Felicity's mother had likened to places like Chatsworth and Knole, two of the greatest houses of England. To Tina, it had only been large, and the road leading up to it had been far, far too long.

Now, however, she could fully appreciate what Mrs. Winton had meant. Forgetting Felicity for a moment, she kept walking, feasting her eyes on her surroundings. How beautiful it was, and how much more intriguing it would be in the light of day. What was that over there? A pair of bronze and ormolu urns. And that? A set of birds cast out of silver. How charming. And that?

Somewhere nearby, a door opened and a set of footsteps echoed. They were slightly uneven, as if their owner limped, and were accompanied by a soft, tuneless whistle.

In a flash, Tina snuffed out her candle and pressed against the wall. How foolish she would look if she were found like this—and in her nightgown, for goodness sake. Yet at last the footsteps receded, and it was once more silent.

But now she was stranded in the dark, and it was suddenly very cold. Could she find her way back? Possibly, but she disliked the notion, and if she were not mistaken, there was a light coming from a room up ahead. If she could only relight her candle. . . .

Very cautiously, she crept forward, straining for sounds of human habitation. She heard nothing. And then she realized she had reached the end of the house, for there were no more rooms. The glow she had seen came from a corridor to the left, off of which lay a room with its door open.

Approaching quietly, Tina peeped in. It appeared as empty as the others, but much warmer—someone had occupied the room until recently. Her nerves tingling, she stepped inside and glanced around. It was a library, and a very handsome one at that. Hundreds of volumes lined the walls, their highest shelf surmounted by a frieze of bas-relief classical figures. The furnishings were lovely and comfortable-looking, and before the hearth, a chess table had been set up between two wing chairs.

Suddenly, she was flooded with memories of her father. Emotion welled in her throat; she moved forward and stared longingly at the ebony and ivory chess pieces. It had been so very, very long since she had played chess with Papa. Without thinking, she set down the candlestick, her hand reaching out to touch one of the pieces.

The library door closed with a snap.

Tina spun around. "Y-you startled me," she gasped, nearly losing her shawl in an attempt to gather it more closely.

James Marchant leaned negligently against the shut door. "So I should think," he answered. He said nothing more as he sauntered forward, his cold gray eyes sweeping over her in an insolent manner. "What are you doing prowling around my house at this hour?"

Tina's cheeks reddened. "I . . . I was looking for Felicity. She left her room and I thought . . . she might have come down here to . . . to . . ."

39

"Play chess?" he inquired, his voice very soft. "Look for a book? Come now, Miss Jardine, that's doing it a shade too brown."

She tried to form a retort, but instead she could only look at him, mesmerized by the disturbing quality of his gaze.

"Do you always walk around strange houses in your nightdress?" he asked, his tone conversational.

"No, of course not!"

"Oh, so it's only Laverstoke Park you favor. I am honored, I assure you. But I own I am also puzzled. What is it you want, Miss Jardine?" Reaching out, he lifted her chin. "Is it this?" Before she realized what he was about, he bent and kissed her, full on the mouth.

Stunned, she shoved hard at his chest, inadvertently loosing her shawl in the process. "Oh!" she breathed, twisting her face to the side. "*Oh,* how dare you! For shame! Is this the way you treat a guest?"

He laughed and captured her wrists, imprisoning them loosely. "An uninvited guest," he reminded, his flinty eyes doing a slow perusal of her figure.

Trying not to think how little lay between his gaze and her bare flesh, Tina flung back her head and said proudly, "Is Lord Laverstoke even aware he has guests? Has anyone taken the trouble to tell him?"

Her captor looked amused. "Oh, yes. He knows."

"Well, I should not think he would approve of his brother mistreating a woman who has sought the protection of his roof—through no fault of her own, I might add."

"Perhaps he would not," he agreed. "However, I am not mistreating you, and I do not apply to my brother for approval of my actions." He released her abruptly and bent to retrieve her shawl. "And I'll return this when you tell me the truth."

"The truth?" Tina repeated indignantly.

"About why you are here, and not in your room."

She had crossed her arms over her breasts, but could not so easily shield her embarrassment. "I told you already," she stated with dignity. "And I do not intend to repeat myself."

His eyes gleamed silver in the firelight. "You were looking for Felicity?"

"That is correct."

"I had the impression you were looking at the chess pieces."

"Well, I was, but . . . but only for a moment. *Will* you give me my shawl?" she added crossly. "I am cold, and you are behaving most unchivalrously."

He smiled at that, and to her surprise arranged the shawl around her shoulders with the tenderness of a lover. "Better now?"

Oddly, much of her rage evaporated with the gentle inquiry. "Yes," she admitted with a shiver that had nothing to do with the cold. "And now if you will excuse me—" Anxious to escape, she tried to step past him.

His hand caught her elbow. "Don't leave."

"You do not want me here—"

"Now I do. Stay and talk with me."

"Mr. Marchant, I am sure you realize that it is completely improper for me to be here in my nightdress—"

"Quite improper," he agreed. "But since you are already here, and I have already seen"—he paused—"what there is to see, there is nothing worse that can happen, is there?"

She controlled an urge to moisten her lips.

"I *am* a gentleman," he said softly.

Now she knew what to say. "Are you? Gracious, Mr. Marchant, for a moment you quite had me fooled."

His smile, she discovered, held a charm that was extremely potent. "If you don't sit down, Miss Jardine, I shall steal your shawl from you again."

Tina regarded him warily, her grip on the threatened garment tightening. "I should leave."

"True," he acknowledged. "But do you always do the things you *should* do? I don't." He stepped back a little. "Sit with me for a while. Do you play chess?"

Her eyes went to the table. "Yes. I was used to play with my father a great deal before . . . before he died."

"My brother did not care to finish the game. Would you like to take his place?"

Ignoring the voice in her head that told her it was unthinkable, Tina said frankly, "That depends entirely on which place is his. One of the players was in the process of being soundly trounced, Mr. Marchant. You cannot bamboozle me about that."

He bowed. "You may have your choice, Miss Jardine. Which shall it be? Ebony or ivory?"

Discretion warred with her desire to cross swords with this man. "Very well, sir," she said, after a brief hesitation. "I shall be ebony. Might I inquire whose place I am taking?"

"No, you may not," he answered. "There's no point in giving you every advantage, you know."

She smiled at him. "Very well, then. From the looks of it, the game should be over in a very few moves."

"Indeed. But perhaps it can be delayed. The first move is yours."

The shawl folded virtuously over her bosom, Tina tucked her feet under her and propped her elbows on the table. While she studied the pieces, he added a log to the fire. "Are you warm enough?" he asked, sitting down.

"Yes," she said absently.

"Would you care to play for stakes?"

She glanced up. "Stakes? What sort of stakes?"

"How about if I win, you give me . . . another kiss?" His eyes gleamed wickedly.

"That's absurd, Mr. Marchant. I thought you said you were a gentleman."

"Being a gentleman hardly excludes one from liking

kisses, my dear. But I see you fear my skill. Perhaps you feel this is a man's game."

"Hardly," she countered. "I can play chess as well as you, sir, any day of the week."

"So why won't you take the bet?"

"What if I win?" she demanded. "What will you give me?"

"A kiss?" he suggested.

Despite every resolution to the contrary, Tina's lips twitched. "There will be no wagers, Mr. Marchant," she said primly.

He leaned back in his chair and studied her. "You're a great deal prettier with your hair down," he commented.

Tina's color heightened. "If you continue to try to distract me, I shall not play."

"I beg your pardon, Miss Jardine. I will keep still."

True to his word, he did not tease her anymore, but bent himself to the task of challenging her intellect. Half an hour later, they had each made five moves, and though she was acquitting herself well, Tina knew she had somehow lost the advantage.

She was by no means an indifferent player — her father had taught her well — but her opponent was skillful beyond any player she had encountered. He seemed to know exactly what move she would make, yet it seemed impossible to predict what *he* would do.

By the time the clock tolled eleven, Tina had forgotten her surroundings. Unbeknownst to her, the shawl had slipped from her shoulders, but the cascade of black curls hid her charms just as adequately. Her bottom lip tucked between her teeth, she held her breath and moved her bishop. "Check," she said, making her voice triumphant.

He studied the move. "You can't do that," he pointed out.

"What? Why not?" Tina raised her brows innocently.

"Because your bishop is pinned. Moving him puts *your*

43

king in check." He seemed puzzled by her ignorance.

"Oh, of course. I must be tired." She put the bishop back. "Very well, then. I'll do this instead," she added, nonchalantly moving a tiny pawn one space forward.

He frowned. "That," he said, "seems an odd move. What do you think to accomplish— Oh. Ah. Clever girl."

She watched in disappointment as he shifted his queen. Somehow, he'd managed to ascertain her strategy four moves ahead of time. The placement of the pawn had been but the first step in a complicated plan she had formed, a plan that was to have culminated in his defeat.

"Devil take you," she muttered. "How did you know?"

"Experience," he assured her. "I've a great deal of it, my dear."

"Yes, I'm sure you do," she said dryly. Quite suddenly, her shoulders sagged. It had been such a long day.

"You're tired," he remarked. "Let's finish this tomorrow."

"Tomorrow I am going to the Dower House. Cousin Libby needs someone to take care of her—"

"Oh? Is she ill?" He looked surprised.

"Not that I know of. But she is old and lonely, and has no one to see to her needs."

"No one to—where did you get that idea?" he demanded.

"From her letter," she said firmly. Almost idly, her attention wandered back to the chess game. Suddenly, she saw a move she could make, a move so diabolically clever that he could never have foreseen it.

"Oh, Miss Jardine," he groaned a moment later. "My dear Miss Jardine. I really did not think you would do that."

For a moment she thought him annoyed, then it dawned on her that she had fallen into a gaping hole of a trap.

Her cheeks reddened with chagrin. "Oh, drat. You distracted me, or I would have realized."

"Shall I let you take it back?"

Her eyes flew up and connected with his. "But that would be wrong," she said slowly. "I made the move of my own free will, Mr. Marchant."

He smiled. "Very well, then." His hand went out to make the final move. "Checkmate, Miss Jardine."

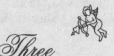

Three

The words broke the spell. Tina suddenly realized that she was staring at him like a moonstruck ninnyhammer. How ridiculous she must look with her hair down and . . . dear God, where was her shawl? How could she not have noticed its absence?

"Is something wrong?" he asked in apparent concern.

Flooded with embarrassment, she jumped to her feet; the shawl lay crumpled on her chair seat. "I must go," she mumbled, snatching it up. She did not dare to look at him.

He stood. "Yes, I suppose you must." His tone was impersonal, reminding her once again that reality had intruded.

Clutching her shawl as if it were a shield, Tina focused on the center of his cravat. "Good night, Mr. Marchant," she said stiffly. "And thank you for . . . a pleasant interlude."

He inclined his head in acknowledgment. "A pity you did not accept my wager," he murmured.

"I hope I have more sense than that."

He smiled faintly. "If you'd any sense at all, you'd not be dressed like that in my company." He relit her candle and handed it to her, then took her arm and propelled her toward the door. "We'll play again," he said. "From start to finish next time."

46

Tina's head shook. "I'm no match for you." As they paused near the shadowed threshold, it flit through her mind that his height made her feel dainty and feminine. "I doubt a rematch would be more than another trouncing," she added. "Your skill far surpasses mine."

"You belittle yourself without cause. The outcome was never a sure thing." One side of his mouth curved slowly. "But that wager would have made things interesting."

"I wish you would not speak of it," she said uncomfortably.

"Then I won't do so again." He let go of her arm, but only to smooth back a lock of hair that had fallen too close to her eye. It was an intimate gesture, completely at odds with his next formal words. "Good night, Miss Jardine. Can you find the way to your room?"

"I . . . I think so." She was too aware of him, too distracted by the way her candle cast the planes of his face into relief.

"You sound unsure. Do you want me to escort you?"

"No!" Her voice was too high-pitched; once more she must seem the veriest ninny. "I mean"—she moistened her lips—"thank you, no. I can find it again."

"If Miss Winton is still not in her room," he instructed, "pray summon a servant. I will see that a search is made."

Tina opened her mouth, then shut it again, knowing it was what she should have done in the first place. She turned from him then, tearing herself from his presence with amazing difficulty. As she stepped into the corridor, she could feel his eyes on her back.

"Sleep well." His parting words hovered in the air, and drifted with her all the way back.

Of course, Felicity was sound asleep in her bed. Too tired to do more than assure herself of this, Tina crawled into her own bed with a sigh of relief. Cold and weary,

47

she pulled the blankets up to her chin and closed her eyes.

Yet sleep proved impossible; the more she tried to relax, the wider awake she became. Images of James jangled through her head, accompanied by disjointed bits and fragments of their conversation. Perversely, her mind seemed determined to come up with the replies she *should* have made rather than the ones that had actually come out her mouth. And the new replies were far more witty and sophisticated. Hindsight, she decided, was frustrating.

Rolling to her side, she gave up trying to sleep. There was obviously no use in it, just as there was no use in denying her attraction to James. Yet how could she be so attracted when she still loved Christian?

Yes, even after five years she still loved him—poor, darling Christian who had been too sweet and good and honorable to recognize Allegra Marchant for what she was. And because she had trusted him, Tina believed with all her heart that Christian would never have jilted her if he'd had a choice. Like a fish in a net, he had been ensnared by a wicked, scheming girl who had maneuvered him into some sort of compromising position. Tina could imagine how the girl must have lured him to some private spot, picturing how Christian would have gone, all unsuspecting and agreeable. This being so, how could she, Tina, take a fancy to any member of the Marchant family?

Stabbed with guilt, she felt as though a deep-buried wound had just been reopened. Of course, she knew that James Marchant was not to blame, for her mother had discovered, quite by accident, that he'd been honorably engaged with his regiment at the time. No, Tina blamed Viscount Laverstoke for not fulfilling his duty. What kind of a guardian allowed his ward to trap another girl's fiancé into marriage? A man of his power and position should have been able to prevent such a shocking occurrence. But then, she reflected cynically, such men were often ruthless and uncaring. It was how they gained their influence in the first place.

Having rehashed all this, her thoughts returned to James. He was nothing like Christian, so why did she find him so attractive? Was it the direct way he looked at her, or his air of quiet authority? Or was it his undeniable intelligence? God, the man must have a wonderful mind to be able to play chess so well.

She wondered what he had thought of her. He had said she was prettier with her hair down, which must mean that he thought her unattractive with it scraped up into its usual, severe style. Of course he was right, but what need had she to make herself attractive? She'd worn it that way ever since . . .

Don't, she scolded herself. It was a bad habit of hers, to label everything "pre-Christian" or "post-Christian" as though her insignificant history were a milestone against which all things were measured.

Neither Felicity nor any of the other Wintons had ever been told about Christian. Tina's mother had protected her from much of the gossip, and later on, as the months passed, it had become old history. Only Libby knew. Dear, dear Libby.

Libby Steeple was an aged spinster, related to Tina through her mother's side of the family. Left virtually unprovided-for by her spendthrift father, Libby had been denied the chance to marry and have a home of her own. Lack of beauty and dowry had forced her to earn her own living, so for five-and-thirty years she had served as genteel companion to one wealthy matron or another. In between situations, she had made her home with the Jardine family, for Mrs. Jardine had always held Libby in particular affection. But though these visits had sometimes lasted for months, pride had always made Libby take on a new position.

Libby's last stint as lady's companion had been with

Viscount Laverstoke's mother, who had died a year and a half after taking Libby on. Free once again and eager to see Tina, Libby had paid a brief visit to Felicity's home in Avon, where Mrs. Winton had made clear she regarded Libby as an inferior, penniless nobody. Thus snubbed, Libby had soon returned to Laverstoke Park, for Lady Laverstoke had grown so fond of her that she had specified in her will that Libby make her home there for as long as she wished. Then Lord Laverstoke had come home and banished Libby to the Dower House—a house that had not been occupied in years!

What a heartless man he must be, Tina thought fiercely. The place was probably cold and damp, worm-eaten and draughty. She was likely all alone there, with nary a servant to see to her wants. Her letters had been cheerful—they always were—but Libby had never been one to complain. Her latest letter had contained a broad hint that she was lonely, which was why Tina had taken a chance and spoken to Mrs. Winton this very morning.

And now look where she was.

Rolling to her back, Tina stared up at the ceiling and thought once more of James Marchant. His kiss came back to her with crystal clarity: somehow her memory was able to recreate the exact, electrifying sensation of his lips pressed against hers. She shivered. She might admire his intelligence, but it was not his skill at chess that put that queer quiver into the pit of her stomach. She still felt it, in fact. Which brought her to a review of her own behavior. The man had taken shocking liberties with her person. And what had she done?

Had she slapped his face? Forced him to apologize? Screamed or fainted?

No, she had not.

She had sat down and played chess with him! Chess, for pity's sake! And to make matters worse, she had not even the wit to defeat him!

And what must be the repercussions of such conduct?

He obviously thought she was immodest or he would not have suggested that outrageous wager. Thank God she had at least retained enough modesty and sense to refuse it. Well, she must be sure to disabuse him of any notions he might have concerning the impropriety of her conduct or the immorality of her disposition. Beginning tomorrow, she would be very cool to him. That would teach him what sort of woman she was.

And with that resolution lodged fast in her mind, Tina punched her pillow once more and concentrated on ridding herself of the disconcerting suspicion that she was looking forward to teaching him that lesson.

Gerard remained in his library for some time after Tina had gone. The fire had burned so low as to be almost out, but he neither added a log, nor rang for a servant. Ignoring the chill, he stared down at the smoldering wood, his thoughts on the episode that had just taken place.

He had met women from the lowest to the highest rank, yet none had stirred his interest the way Tina Jardine had just done. And the hell of it was, he could not fathom the reason, except for the rather obvious fact that she had not been trying to attract him—which he had to admit was a refreshing change. At first he had thought otherwise; for her to wander into his private library wearing nothing but a nightgown and a shawl that kept slipping—well, frankly it reeked of premeditation.

He sighed and stretched out his legs, crossing them at the ankle. He had obviously spent too much time in those cologne-scented Viennese drawing rooms, where seduction and betrayal were as commonplace as breathing. There, every look had been an invitation, every pouting lip an enticement, as the ladies sought to manipulate the powerful men who had gathered to settle the balance of power in Europe. Politics and sex had ever had a curious attraction, he thought cynically.

But seducing him had been the furthest thing from Tina Jardine's mind — he was a good enough student of human nature to know that, even if he had kissed her just to be sure. Her agitation and distress had been as genuine as her embarrassment at being seen in her nightdress.

That kiss, then.

It was the source of the problem. What else could it be? Although her face was memorable she certainly was not beautiful, and though, contrary to what he'd told James, her hair was truly lovely, that was scarcely a reason to have invited her to stay — or to have enjoyed her company so much when she did. Such fine, soft, silky-looking hair, he mused. He'd wanted to twine his hands in it and *really* kiss her. And that had been the most arresting aspect to all of this: his body's unexpected, jolting response to the touch of her lips.

He fancied she'd been unaware of it. She'd been too busy sputtering to know what she had done to him, and likely too innocent as well. He wondered if she had the least idea how provocative that prim white nightgown had been. The knowledge that nothing lay between his eyes and her naked flesh but that one thin layer of fabric — it had acted on him strangely. Potently.

Gerard closed his eyes, pushing aside the memory of Tina's shapely body before it could cause him further discomfort. He sucked in a deep, full breath, quelling his arousal with the force of sheer will. Obviously it had been a mistake to let so much time pass since his last visit to Beatrice. Beatrice, Lady Chalfield, could loosely be termed his mistress if one stretched the term to include the kind of casual relationship they enjoyed. How many weeks had it been since he had last been to her? Five weeks? Six? Too long, he thought irritably. He was a man, not a monk.

Yet despite his desire to journey into Sussex to seek Beatrice, Gerard felt himself hesitate. His diplomatic

52

training had taught him to listen to his intuition, and now that intuition was bidding him to linger here, and to further his acquaintance with a woman who was too respectable to play the role that Beatrice did. It was a decision that cost him regret, for tonight, now, his body ached for a woman.

A few minutes later, Viscount Laverstoke went off to his bed, feeling a good deal lonelier than he had the night before.

"Good morning! Are you awake?" Felicity plopped onto the mattress with enough force to intrude upon the most interesting dream Tina had had in months.

Tina cranked open an eye and stared up at her smiling, fresh-faced cousin. "I am now, Felicity," she said, not veiling her sarcasm. "What time is it?"

Felicity, she noted, was dressed to the nines in a morning half-dress of French-figured muslin, her hair arranged *á la Sappho,* and a handsome Norwich shawl draped negligently across her elbows. Dressed to kill, Tina thought grumpily. If she wasn't murdered first.

"It's past seven," Felicity informed her reproachfully. "I made sure you would be up by now, for pity's sake. You are normally such an early riser."

"Exactly what is the hurry?"

Felicity's cheeks flushed a delicate pink. "Good gracious, Tina, don't you know? If we are to meet the viscount before he leaves for Sussex, we ought to go down at once. We may have missed him already, although there is so much snow outside I don't see how he can think to travel."

Tina tried to pull the covers over her head, but Felicity jumped up and yanked them off. Tina yelped as the cold air rushed in.

"Come on, slug-a-bed I thought you went to sleep early."

The remark reminded Tina of what she wanted to say. "And where were you last night, miss?" she said crossly.

"Last night? What do you mean?" Felicity's face was as innocent as a newborn babe.

Tina sat up, shoving her hair from her face. "Last night when you weren't in your bed," she accused. "I heard you go out, Felicity, so don't pretend otherwise."

Felicity renewed her perch on the bed. "I only went for a walk," she replied. "It was nothing to signify."

"A walk," repeated Tina, eyes narrowed. "Where?"

Her cousin shrugged. "Just about the house a bit. I explored some of the rooms on the ground floor. And if you don't stop scowling at me, I won't tell you my secret."

"What secret?"

"Promise you won't scold?" At Tina's nod, Felicity said, with sparkling eyes, "All right then. I saw the viscount! And oh Tina, he is very handsome—even more handsome than his brother! His hair is the same gold color, but his face is more . . . more pleasing somehow, and far sweeter in expression. And you were right, Tina, he does walk with a limp! But even if he does have gout, he is still very handsome."

"Did he see you?" asked Tina abruptly.

"Oh, no," Felicity assured her. "I was careful to keep in the shadows. But I saw *him* quite clearly. He was whistling as he passed. After that I followed him up another set of stairs until he disappeared, then I came back to bed."

Tina decided to say nothing of her own adventure. "Wretch! You know perfectly well you did wrong. How could you have done such a thing? What if you had been caught, for pity's sake?"

"But I was not," Felicity pointed out.

"What has that to say to anything? And what would your mama have said? Did you consider that?" Tina stalked across the room to survey her reflection in the cheval glass. Her hair was a sad mass of tangles; she obviously ought to have braided it. "She would have held *me* responsible, you know. Any untoward consequences would have been laid at *my* door, not yours."

Felicity looked contrite, but before she could answer, there was a light rap on the door, followed by the appearance of Annie. "I'm sorry, miss. I came by before, but you was still sleeping so I went away." She bobbed a cheerful curtsy. "I'm here to help you dress, miss. Which gown will you wear today?"

Half an hour later, Tina and Felicity were directed to the breakfast parlor, which they found without much difficulty in the back section of the house. A footman ushered them in, while two more stood at attention at either end of the table.

"Ah, you must be my cousins," said a sunny voice. A blond gentleman in a coat of olive green superfine limped forward to receive them with an affable smile. "I was hoping you were not late sleepers. Some ladies will sleep until noon every day, but I am not accustomed to that, having been a s—" He broke off with a cough. "Ahem. So sorry. A crumb in my throat." He turned to Felicity first. "Let me guess," he said to Felicity. "You must be Miss Winton. How do you do?"

"And *you* must be Lord Laverstoke," Felicity simpered, giving him her hand.

He inclined his head and turned to Tina. "And you must be Miss Jardine. I am charmed to make your acquaintance."

Tina regarded him with animosity, but could find nothing to dislike in the attractive, genial countenance. "How do you do, my lord," she said coolly. "I hope you do not object to our seeking the protection of your roof. I'm afraid we had no choice—"

"Yes, my brother told me. How could you do other-

55

wise? I am delighted that it *was* my roof whose shelter you sought. We are very dull here this time of year, and shall be very glad of some company."

"Then you are not leaving?" asked Felicity hopefully. "Your brother gave us to understand that you were going on a journey."

He smiled mischievously. "No, how can I? Look outside. Have you ever seen the snow piled so high? We are trapped here, all of us." He gestured toward the table. "Do come and join me for breakfast. Come, don't be shy."

Shy was the last word one would use to describe Felicity. Approaching the sideboard, she took three times more food than Tina did, heaping her plate with slices of ham and fowl, an omelette, a pastry, a slice of toast and two scones, all the while chattering nonstop of their mishap.

"—and Tina said we had to walk, but I was so cold, my lord, you can have no notion! But walk we did, and once, when I fell, Tina actually had to lift me to my feet. I am very delicate, you see," Felicity added demurely.

"Yes, I can see that you are," said their host, watching in apparent fascination as Felicity added a breakfast tart to her collection. He appeared to drag his eyes away with some effort. "Coffee, Miss Jardine?" he asked courteously.

Tina accepted a cup from the footman. "Thank you. Shall we be able to move to the Dower House today, do you think? I am sure Cousin Libby will be needing us, particularly when the weather is so adverse."

Though she made the remark in a pointed manner, nothing of guilt flashed across his face. "Oh, Miss Steeple will be all right," he responded, as they sat down. "She goes along famously most of the time. She's a tough old bird."

Tina stiffened, her expression meant to convey indignation at the remark, but he was too busy trimming the fat from his ham to notice. "Though she may ask you to walk Gretchen," he added, spearing his meat. "If she does, be careful. She's very strong."

"Is Gretchen that large?" asked Tina in amazement. "I had the impression she was quite a small animal."

Their host grinned as he lifted his fork. "That's because Miss Steeple calls her 'my dear little Gretchen.' However, dear little Gretchen must weigh—"

"—at least ten stone and consume as much as a small horse," finished a familiar voice. Looking annoyingly rested, James Marchant strolled into the room, glancing directly at Tina as he approached the table. "Miss Jardine," he said smoothly. "And Miss Winton. I trust you slept well?" He took the chair at the end opposite his brother, and accepted a cup of coffee.

Tina lifted her chin. "Yes, thank you, Mr. Marchant. Both Felicity and I slept very well indeed." Let him interpret that how he wished, she thought.

"But if we are all cousins," objected the voice at the opposite end of the table, "must we be so formal?"

Felicity fluttered her lashes at the viscount. "No, why should we? You may call me Felicity, if you like. And of course, Tina's name is Valentina."

"Valentina." It was James who spoke.

Hearing her name on his lips disconcerted Tina so much she nearly dropped her toast. "I don't think Mrs. Winton would approve," she said. After all, this abominable man must be shown that they were respectable females, not ingratiating connections with a loose regard for proper moral behavior.

Unfortunately, Felicity chose that moment to display her unamiable temper. "Tina is my watchdog," she said with a pout. "She is the starchiest creature alive, with nothing to recommend her beyond a sharp tongue and an excellent understanding of the proprieties."

An excellent understanding of the proprieties.

Instinctively Tina's eyes flew to James Marchant, whose arched brows were so eloquent of incredulity that she blushed fiery red. When he spoke, however, it was only to say, in a rather mild tone, "I beg to differ with you, Miss Winton. I should rather think Miss Jardine has a great deal to recommend her to anyone."

The reproof was gentle, but direct enough for Felicity to grasp. "I beg your pardon," she said at once. "That was an odious thing to say, but I did not mean it the way it sounded. But I truly do think Mama would not object if you called me 'Cousin Felicity.' Indeed she always refers to you as our cousins," she added reasonably, "so why would she object?"

Lord Laverstoke set down his coffee cup. "Is that acceptable, Miss Jardine?" he asked eagerly. "May we call you 'Cousin Tina'?"

Subjected to scrutiny from three directions, Tina capitulated. "I can see I am outnumbered," she said tartly. "Very well—Cousin."

"Capital!" he responded, his blue eyes twinkling.

Try as she might, Tina found the golden-haired viscount impossible to dislike. James Marchant aroused far more powerful emotions in her breast; even now she could feel him watching her from under those thick, dark brows.

Determined to prove that she was not intimidated, she turned and looked him straight in the eye. "Have you breakfasted already?"

"An hour ago," he answered gravely. "I rise early."

Doubtless he was trying to tell her that he had had no difficulty falling asleep, she thought.

"I had to drag her out of bed," Felicity told him, obviously bent on saying exactly the thing Tina least wanted her to say. "Although I don't suppose there is very much for us to do today," she added, looking hopefully toward the viscount.

His eyes crinkled with laughter. "Well, we shall cer-

tainly do our best to see to your entertainment, won't we
. . . James?"

"We are going to the Dower House," Tina reminded
them all.

The two brothers exchanged looks. "Very true," replied
James, his voice bland. His gaze shifted to Felicity, who
was eyeing the sideboard with longing. "Do have some
more, if you like," he said politely.

"Oh, thank you," Felicity said gratefully. Oblivious to
his sardonic amusement, she rose and piled high her
plate once again.

"Was Miss Steeple aware that you were to arrive yesterday?" asked James.

Tina knew he'd timed the question so it was she who
had to answer, for by now Felicity had her mouth full.
"No," she admitted, avoiding his look. "Libby had not
mentioned any particular day she wished us to arrive on,
but . . . Felicity's mother wished us to leave at once.
Libby is all alone," she added defensively. "A woman her
age needs someone to look after her."

"Indeed," said James, his brows rising. "I had thought
Miss Steeple to be doing nicely, but perhaps you are better informed than I am."

"Libby and I have been corresponding for years," she
retorted. "Before my parents died, she was used to visit
us often. I know her very well indeed."

He leaned back. "I see."

"I am very fond of Libby," she said challengingly, "and
will permit no one to take advantage of her."

"Our mother was very fond of her also," James said
softly, "which was why she made such generous provisions for her in her will."

There was a short silence, a moment of respect for the
deceased viscountess, then Tina said, "And did those
provisions include a life of solitude in the Dower House?
Surely it would have been kinder to have allowed her to
stay here, at Laverstoke Park?"

59

"Do I detect a note of rebuke in your voice?" James's tone was both cool and mocking.

"It is simply that I do not understand—"

"Then I suggest you make yourself acquainted with the facts," he interrupted. "Then, if you still harbor any doubts concerning Miss Steeple's welfare, I will be more than happy to discuss the matter."

Conscious of the set-down, Tina flushed. "I beg your pardon," she said icily. "I shall indeed do as you suggest."

To her annoyance, he looked amused. "I am gratified," he said, gesturing the nearest footman to refill his coffee cup.

As the servant obeyed, Tina eyed him with hostility. Contrary to expectation, it was Lord Laverstoke who was the more amiable of the two, and though she still harbored bitterness toward the viscount on account of Christian, he was clearly such a good-natured gentleman that it was going to be difficult to sustain.

"I don't believe you ever answered my question," she said. "Is there any possibility of our going to the Dower House today?"

Though she was clearly addressing the viscount, it was James who answered. "We can send you over in the sleigh," he said, "providing the runners haven't rusted off with disuse."

Tina longed to give him a set-down, but bit back the retort that entered her head. Once more she addressed the viscount. "I beg you will let us know if this is possible," she went on, as though James had not spoken, "for I should very much like to see Cousin Libby as soon as possible."

"To see for yourself that she has not wasted away with deprivation," mocked the voice at the other end of the table. "We perfectly understand. Don't we . . . Gerry?"

"If you say so, brother."

Gritting her teeth, Tina rose to her feet. "Come, Felicity. We have things to do before it is time to leave."

"Oh, but I am not done—"

"Yes, you are," Tina countered, finality in her voice. "Lord Laverstoke will not object if you do not finish that tart."

Both gentlemen had also risen. "Take it with you," said James politely. "Or better yet, take the lot of them."

Felicity's eyes widened with delight, but Tina said quickly, "Absolutely not. You have eaten quite enough."

James laughed, which prompted the viscount to say with sympathy, "Don't mind him, Cousin Felicity. He's an odd fellow, with an even odder sense of humor. You'd never know him for a dip—"

"We shall send word when the sleigh is ready," James cut in. "Don't feel obliged to hide in your rooms, though, for it may be an hour or more." He sent Tina a speculative look. "I'll be in the library," he added.

"I doubt I shall see you before I leave," she answered frostily, "so I will bid you good day, sir."

"Cousin," he corrected.

"Cousin," she repeated unwillingly. She gave him a stormy look, but his gaze held nothing but amusement.

Incensed, she turned on her heel and left, leaving Felicity to trail behind.

Four

An hour later, outside the massive front door, a gray mare stood hitched to a sleigh whose gleaming runners displayed a conspicuous lack of rust. It was, in fact, as well maintained as everything else at Laverstoke Park, Tina noticed, as she shaded her eyes to study it. She supposed she ought to have expected it, even if she had not expected that the two Marchant brothers would personally oversee their excursion.

"Do you prefer the front or the back?"

Behind her, James Marchant's voice was pleasant and courteous, which was no reason at all for her heart to give the odd little leap that it did. She turned, thinking rapidly. One might reasonably assume that the viscount would drive, but with these two nothing was certain. She glanced covertly at Felicity, who was flirting with Lord Laverstoke at the top of the snow-swept steps.

"Oh, the back," she said, wishing Felicity would cease her dawdling. "Felicity will wish to sit in the front."

James looked at her quizzically. "And do Felicity's wishes always come first?"

"They must," she answered ruefully. "I am being paid to see that they do." The moment she spoke she wondered why she had answered so frankly; she usually made light of the fact that she was, in essence, an employee in the Winton household.

"A pity," he said. He glanced casually at Felicity, then

his light gray eyes returned to her face. "Allow me to assist you into the sleigh, Cousin Valentina." Again politeness, but this time with a hint of challenge.

Tina hesitated again, then accepted his aid, for the step up was a considerable one and she did not want to slip. To her discomfiture, he climbed in beside her and settled the folds of his great-cape.

"Have you ever ridden in a sleigh before?"

Tina was oddly grateful to him for asking the question, for otherwise she might have been flustered into saying something harebrained. "No," she admitted. "But it looks fun."

"It is," he agreed. For a moment it seemed he would say something more, then his head turned. "Come on, you two," he called out. "It's too cold to tarry."

It *was* cold, but until he spoke of it, Tina had scarcely noticed. Now she shivered, burying her hands in her muff.

Lord Laverstoke hurried over, Felicity's hand tucked under his elbow. "You're going to enjoy this," he told Felicity. "Shall I lift you up?"

Felicity's giggle clearly signifying assent, he put his hands at her waist and swung her inside. As he did so, Tina saw him wince just a little.

Then they were off, flying over the snow as if blown by the wind. In contrast to the day before, the sky was blue and cloudless, turning the surrounding landscape to a stark, glittering paradise.

Tina sat silent, her gaze averted from James Marchant. In itself this ought to have adequately conveyed that she did not wish to converse, but he was clearly not a gentleman to take a hint. Indeed, he sat staring at her so hard it seemed certain he was trying to discompose her.

"Are you very angry with me?" he said finally, against the wind.

Tina's eyes went to the couple in front of them, who were engaged in animated conversation. "Angry?" she repeated, unsure which transgression he might be referring to. "For what, pray?"

He leaned closer, thus insuring that only she could hear his words. "For kissing you last night, and then teasing you about it. I should apologize, I expect."

"Oh, don't give it a second thought, Mr. Marchant—"

"Cousin," he corrected.

"Cousin," she repeated, through clenched teeth. "Your conduct was infamous, but I promise you I did not lose any sleep over it." Her eyes lowered to her muff, her sense of fair play forcing her to add, "I am well aware that my own conduct was not without fault. I know I must have looked"—the words were terribly difficult—"dressed as I was, I mean . . . I must have looked . . . looked . . ."

"Seductive," he said helpfully.

Her eyes flew to his. "Mr. Marchant—"

"Cousin."

"Mr. Marchant," she continued, "you are trying to put me to the blush."

He had the temerity to smile. "Am I?" he said lazily. "Yes, I suppose I am. You do it delightfully, you know."

"You, sir, are shockingly adept at blandishment!"

"You think I am flattering you?" One side of his mouth curled oddly.

"I don't know what you are doing—"

"—but whatever it is you don't like it." Draping his arm along the back of the seat, his eyes fixed on her intently. "Tell me, do you always dislike what you don't understand?"

"Indeed not," she said defensively. "If I don't understand something I try to become better acquainted with it so that—" She broke off, sensing a trap.

"Ah," he said, looking self-satisfied. "Then you will have no objection to becoming better acquainted with me."

Before she could come up with a reply, he added, "Here we are, my dear. The Dower House. A bleak little place, isn't it?"

Tina looked. The Dower house could not have been one-fifth the size of Laverstoke Park, but it had to be one of the most charming houses she had ever seen. In proportion and elegance it likely had no match, while its situation and prospect must, at a warmer time of year, have been pure heaven.

Tina avoided his eye as the sleigh drew to a halt a few feet from the front steps.

"Here we are," announced the viscount. He jumped down from the sleigh, waving to the servant who came striding up. "Hullo, Ben. We've some visitors for Miss Steeple. Is she—uh oh! Watch out!"

Having just given her hand to James, who had already stepped down, Tina looked up to see a huge animal bounding toward them.

It was a dog. It had to be a dog, she told herself, for what else could it possibly be? Tail wagging, jaws spread wide in canine delight, it uttered a bark and hurled itself at James with as much joy as a child greeting its long-lost mother.

Fortunately he was ready, but a lesser man might have been knocked flat. James, however, managed to hold his ground, although Tina, her hand mysteriously still in his, was jerked off balance. Consequently, instead of stepping from the sleigh in a dignified manner, she somehow found herself sprawled, most unceremoniously, over James's left arm. The very fact that he caught her at all was nothing short of a miracle, but Tina, hanging over his arm like a limp rag, was not in a position to appreciate this—particularly since Felicity had gone into a peal of laughter.

"Down!" ordered James, warding off the dog.

"Yes, down!" Teeth clenched, Tina struggled to free herself. "Put me down at once!"

Immediately she was set on her feet in the snow. "Better?" he inquired.

Tina thrust out her jaw and glared at him, whereupon he added, quite reasonably, "Well, at least I didn't drop you."

Before Tina could form a suitably withering retort, the beast turned and nuzzled her hand, as if seeking to apologize.

She regarded it wrathfully. "I suppose *you* are Libby's dear little Gretchen?"

The animal snorted and grinned at her foolishly, its thumping tail spraying snow up into the air.

Despite her ruffled dignity, Tina's vexation melted under those liquid brown eyes. She reached out and risked a tentative pat. "Hello, Gretchen." While Gretchen whimpered ecstatically, she glanced at James. "She was certainly glad to see you," she remarked.

"Yes, well, I occasionally take her for walks," he said calmly. "Let's go in. Ben, take Gretchen around to the stables, will you?"

They were admitted to the house by a middle-aged woman wearing a maid's cap, who ushered them into a small, delightfully appointed drawing room with a respectful curtsy. Avoiding a certain pair of sardonic gray eyes, Tina's gaze wandered over the room, her chagrin mounting as she took in its immaculate condition. She had been completely wrong about the Dower House.

A moment later, familiar footsteps sounded, and a diminutive, white-haired lady bustled into the room. "Valentina!" she cried, rushing forward to enfold Tina in a plump, violet-scented embrace. "What a charming surprise! I never expected to see you so soon—oh, and you have brought Felicity with you! How do you do, my dear?"

"Very well, ma'am," answered Felicity.

Too conscious of James, Tina struggled to keep the emotion from her voice. "Oh, Libby, it's so good to see you. I was afraid that you . . . I mean I thought . . . but you are looking so well!"

"And you look more like your mama than ever!" Libby hugged her again, then turned to greet the two men, her faded brow wrinkled with perplexity. "I can see you are all acquainted, but I do not at all understand how that can be."

Immediately, Felicity launched into a rambling explanation, which Tina was eventually forced to clarify for the sake of everyone's patience.

"Good gracious, you poor girls!" exclaimed Libby at the end. "Well, you did the sensible thing, of course, and I am glad it all came to rights." She reached up to straighten her mobcap, which had gotten slightly askew. "Goodness, where are my wits? Let us be seated, and I shall ring for refreshment. Perhaps a spot of warm tea?"

"I think not," said James, glancing at his brother. "We should leave you ladies to celebrate your reunion in privacy. Perhaps, however, you would consent to dine with us some night soon. Perhaps tomorrow evening?"

"Indeed, yes," put in Lord Laverstoke with an easy smile. "We insist that you do."

Libby looked pleased. "How kind! I am sure we would all be delighted!"

James bowed. "We'll send the sleigh for you then. About seven? Or would you prefer to dine earlier?"

While Libby assured him that seven was perfect, Tina looked him straight in the eye for the first time since they had entered the house. In response, his brows lifted in a mocking salute that, unaccountably, made her feel as though they had just crossed swords once again.

When the two men were gone, Libby sighed happily and urged them to sit down. "Lord Laverstoke is such a kind man," she declared. "And his brother, too, is everything that is most obliging! And now you must both tell me all about everything. I hope things are well at home, Felicity?"

"Yes—except Papa is ill, that is. We are not receiving callers at the moment and life is very dull. So when Tina received your letter, Mama said she might go if she brought me along. Mama was certain you would not object. Of course she knew Lord Laverstoke was in residence," she added breezily. "Mama said we would be

67

foolish to toss aside a chance to make his acquaintance."

Libby's sharp eyes examined Felicity. "That sounds like your mama," she remarked. "And having met Lord Laverstoke, what do you think of him?"

Felicity spread her hands. "Well, he is very handsome, is he not? They are both handsome, of course, but Lord Laverstoke is by far the more amiable. He was not nearly as proud as I expected."

The expression on Libby's face was difficult to decipher. "And you, Valentina? Did you find Lord Laverstoke agreeable?"

"He seems," she said carefully, "a gentleman who would be hard to dislike." Even if that were untrue, she was not about to air her grievances in front of Felicity. "I thought him a great deal more good-natured than his brother," she added, as an afterthought.

Her answer seemed to surprise Libby. "Really?" she answered with a blink. "But that is exactly what— hmmm. Dear me, let me see. Yes, yes, we'll have tea first, and something to eat. I daresay you must be hungry—"

"Starving," Felicity assured her.

"We have eaten," countered Tina, frowning at her cousin. "Felicity, you will be fat as a sausage if you don't stop eating so much. You know very well your mama does not approve."

"Oh fudge. Who cares what Mama thinks? When I am from home, I will eat as I choose. And when I am married I will eat even more." Felicity turned to Cousin Libby. "I would love some scones, if you have them."

"Felicity, you cannot be serious!"

"Now, girls," soothed Libby, reaching for her bell. "Let us have no squabbling. Felicity will eat what she likes, and if she grows too wide for her gowns she will have to pay the consequences. And now, Valentina, tell me what you have been doing since last we met."

* * *

68

Holding the gray at an even pace, the true Lord Laverstoke guided his sleigh back to Laverstoke Park with a skill that had earned him recognition as a notable whip. "I thought you were going to tell them at breakfast," he remarked.

James grimaced. "Well, I meant to, you know. But when Miss Winton smiled so prettily and said I *must* be Lord Laverstoke, I found it devilish hard to disagree."

"So?" Gerard's voice was cool. "How long do we continue this charade?"

"I doubt it will be long. Miss Steeple will let the cat out of the bag sooner or later. If she don't, we'll have to confess."

Gerard frowned. "I suppose so. Ah well, it can hardly signify. We'll call it a joke."

"I doubt they'll find it amusing."

"Probably not. However, 'twill be amusing to watch how swiftly Miss Winton's smiles transfer to me," Gerard said cynically. "The chit has the subtlety of a coal-heaver."

It was James's turn to frown. "You judge her harshly, Gerry. I find her charming enough, and no different from any other girl of our class."

Gerard's silence was eloquent.

"You're not going to Sussex?" asked James, at length.

"If I was, I would have been gone by now."

"Why?"

Gerard chose to misunderstand. "Why, the storm, of course. It's too treacherous to travel."

James's eyes narrowed. "Is that all of it?"

"All of what?"

"This change of plans wouldn't have anything to do with Cousin Valentina, would it?"

"Come now, Jay. You know me better than that." The viscount spoke with the unruffled calm of one who keeps his own council.

"Do I? I thought her figure quite excellent, by the way."

Gerard smiled.

"She isn't precisely pretty," mused James, "and yet she has a great deal of style. I'd call her a striking young woman with a great deal to recommend her. Wouldn't you?" he added craftily.

"I'd call her an intelligent young woman caught in an intolerable situation, but that doesn't mean what you're implying. I've no thought of courtship."

The sleigh entered the drive to Laverstoke Park, following the ruts made by their earlier excursion. Ahead, the house loomed up before them, its mullioned windows winking like diamonds in the sun.

James absorbed the remark for a few moments. Then, "You told me you hunt, when the mood moves you."

"Ah, but that is different," Gerard said suavely. "When one hunts, there's an end in view."

"The kill, you mean."

"Precisely. And I'm not such a blackguard as that. Miss Jardine is quite safe from me."

"Ah, but surely a little light flirtation would not come amiss?"

Gerard's lips twisted. "Something tells me that Miss Jardine is uninterested in flirtation."

"I'll wager you could persuade her to change her mind. There's obviously something about you that women like." James nudged him in the ribs and grinned. "All those females must be swooning over *something* other than your blunt."

By this time they had arrived at the stables, where they turned the sleigh over to the head groom with the instructions that the ladies' baggage was to be conveyed to the Dower House and would be sent down forthwith. The two brothers then headed for the house.

"Shall we finish that chess game now?" James said suddenly.

Gerard gave him a sidelong look. "We'll have to start anew. The other game was . . . finished."

James looked offended. "I may be no great dab at

70

chess, but the game was not over, not by any stretch of the imagination!"

"I'm sorry to contradict you, but it is most definitely over. I—we—finished it without you."

"We? Who the devil did you cozen into playing?"

"Valentina." The words were spoken with a nonchalance that was not quite convincing.

James stopped dead and stared, then hurried to catch up. "Oh, come on," he objected. "What gammon are you trying to pitch?"

"None at all. She came to the library last night after you went to bed. We finished the game."

"Good God, why the devil should she do that?"

Gerard's lips twitched at the memory. "She was looking for Felicity. Don't ask me where Felicity was, for I've no notion and I don't care. However, since I was certain the chit was merely playing tricks, I invited Valentina to play chess. And she accepted. She took my place, and I took yours."

"Somehow there seems to be a great deal missing in that explanation," complained James, who was nonetheless diverted. "I cannot imagine the virtuous Miss Jardine invading your sanctuary so boldly." No answer was forthcoming. "Did she win?" he asked with interest.

"No." Gerard smiled.

James looked disappointed. "Damn. I thought perhaps you'd met your match. *That* might account for your odd behavior."

"Would it?" Gerard reflected. "Perhaps. She plays well."

"Yet she did not win."

"She could have. Her state of dishabille disturbed my concentration enough."

"Her state of—" James stared. *"Dare* I ask?"

"Her shawl slipped," Gerard explained, just as they reached one of the side doors to the house.

"Her shawl—! Gerry, what the devil happened?"

"Nothing," answered Gerard, on a note of faint regret.

"I'm a gentleman, am I not?"

"You said she was safe from you," persisted James.

Gerard sighed, and opened the door. "She is. Damn it, she is."

Scones and tea having been summarily produced, Felicity sat munching while Tina and Libby embarked on their first face-to-face conversation in almost two years.

"What have I been doing?" echoed Tina evasively. "Gracious, you know that from my letters, don't you?"

Libby made a clucking sound with her tongue. "Oh, I don't mean all those tasks you do for Felicity's mother. I mean, what have you been *doing?* Do you still sketch? Do you still read literature and poetry? Have you any suitors?"

The last question brought a flush to Tina's cheeks. "Of course not, Libby. And, yes, I still sketch occasionally, but I've little time for it, or poetry either." When Libby's brow creased, she added, "What I long to hear is what *you* have been doing. You said you had come to live here"—her eyes wandered around the snug little room—"but I never fully understood why, when Lady Laverstoke had specified that you stay at the main house. I assumed it was because Lord Laverstoke was too proud and heartless to allow a poor relation to live in his home, but—"

"Oh, my dear, no!" Libby looked quite distressed. "No, no, it is nothing like that at all. I was *ecstatic* to be given the opportunity to live here. It is quite like having my own home, something I have lacked for nigh on thirty years. I am sure dear Lady Laverstoke would have approved if she had thought of it."

Bewildered, Tina said, "But in your letter you said you were lonely, so I assumed—" She broke off as Libby touched her hand.

"I did not mean I was unhappy, dear. I am quite, quite content. Oh, dear me, yes. Lord Laverstoke takes such good care of me. I have my own cook, you see, as well as four other servants to pamper me." The sweet, wrinkled face beamed with delight. "In fact, I have never been so mollycoddled in my life. Of course I still mourn dear Lady Laverstoke, but otherwise I am very well indeed." Then her voice took on a guilty note. "I confess, however, that I was so anxious for you to come that I . . . I may have misled you, just a trifle."

"Well, I am relieved to hear it," said Tina truthfully. "I honestly feared you were being mistreated." She paused, then added with constraint, "Obviously his lordship is not the ogre I imagined." She did not add that James Marchant better fit her perception of a ruthless, arrogant manipulator of other people's lives.

"Indeed no," said Libby eagerly. "I am pleased to hear you say that, Valentina, because I had quite hoped—But there! I do not want to be boring you with my fancies. How are the scones, Felicity?"

"Delicious." Felicity proved this by reaching for her fourth.

"Do you always eat like this, my dear?" asked Libby curiously.

"I always *want* to," Felicity admitted. "But Mama raises a dust if I do. I don't know why either, for I don't run to fat."

"Mr. St. Hillary does not seem to mind." Tina spoke suddenly, remembering Felicity's infatuation with their neighbor's son. "He brought you macaroons once, did he not?"

"Once," conceded Felicity with a scowl. "But he was merely trying to bribe me into forgiving him for being the most stuffy, priggish man alive."

"Oh dear," ventured Libby. "He sounds most disagreeable."

"He is," said Felicity darkly.

"Actually, he is a very pleasant, well-behaved young man," Tina said crisply. "Moreover, he is in the process of embarking upon a promising career in the government."

73

Felicity wrinkled her nose. "If you ask me, he has a very high opinion of himself because of it. He thinks himself quite a fount of information—all of it confidential, of course. We mortals cannot begin to comprehend the Great Matters which occupy his time." She pouted. "He cannot even find time to come home and visit his mama, much less me. And everyone knows he only holds some mundane position in the Home Office!"

"But he has the potential to advance," Tina pointed out. "He is intelligent, industrious, honest, and, I think, kind. You could do worse, Felicity."

"Are you suggesting I should throw myself away on a mere mister? Mama says that with a little effort I could snare myself a lord! She says I am pretty enough, and my uncle the baronet is to settle a goodly sum on me, besides what Papa can do."

"Pretty is as pretty does," murmured Libby, sipping her tea.

Felicity's green eyes flashed. "I shall not throw myself away on Eugene," she declared. "In fact, I have half a mind to marry Lord Laverstoke."

Libby choked on her tea, and went off into a coughing fit.

Concerned, Tina patted the elderly lady on the back until she recovered, then fixed Felicity with a piercing stare. "I think you are being a trifle premature," she pointed out. "You and the gentleman have only just met."

Felicity raised her chin. "True, but I like him very well, and I think he likes me, too."

As Tina sighed, Libby said tactfully, "But my dear Felicity, surely you wish to have a Season? Think of all the young men you will meet."

Felicity's hands clasped together. "Oh, I know, Miss Steeple. But if Papa dies—"

"Good gracious, is he that ill?"

"Well . . . I don't know precisely. But Mama says if anything were to happen . . . if he were to, well, *you* know, then of course there would be no question of my going to London." For the first time, her voice trembled, and a teardrop glistened at the corner of her eye. "He is not at all well, I'm afraid."

"That may be true," Tina said bracingly, "but he is not as ill as your mama makes him out to be either. Your mother is prone to exaggerate."

Felicity brightened. "Yes, she is, isn't she? At any rate, yes, I *do* want a Season, but if Lord Laverstoke were to make me an offer, couldn't I still have one?"

"I suppose so," Tina admitted. "But this notion of yours is ridiculous."

"Why?" Felicity looked affronted. "Why is it ridiculous?"

"Because marriage should be based on affection! And because you scarcely know the man! What do you know of him? Can you name one thing?"

"Certainly I can. I know from his smile that he is kind. I know that he is loyal and good-natured because it doesn't trouble him when his brother gives orders in his house. I know that he is brave because he bears the pain in his leg so nobly. I know that he is—"

"Wait a moment," said Libby in perplexity. "What did you say?"

Both girls looked at her questioningly.

"You said something about his lordship's leg. I don't understand."

A cold feeling crept over Tina. "What do you mean? Lord Laverstoke walks with a limp, surely?"

Libby's head shook. "No, dear," she said gently. "James walks with a limp. He was a soldier, and was shot in the hip some years back. Those naughty boys have been playing tricks on you."

"Tricks," Tina repeated, as everything shifted into perspective. She stared past Libby, her anger slowly escalating as scenes from the previous night flashed through her head. "Tricks!" she said again, her voice climbing. "Good God, now I understand why he kept referring to the house as his! It *is* his! Oh, I could . . . I could *shoot* him!"

"But my dear, why are you so angry?" inquired Libby. "It was very wrong of them, I grant, but it is no great matter after all."

"No great matter?" Tina pressed her fist to her mouth to control the sweeping tide of her emotion. "He made a fool of me—of both of us! I consider that a very great matter!"

Libby looked dubious. "I am sure they will apologize. When we see them tomorrow night, I will—"

"I shall not go! I shall not give him the satisfaction of . . . of . . ." Tina's voice dwindled when she could not think of a satisfying way to finish the sentence.

"Of course you'll go, dear. I have already accepted for us all. I never thought you could be so foolish, Valentina."

Tina's hand fell to her lap. "Indeed, I think I am a fool," she said despairingly. "The greatest fool alive."

Libby's face softened. "No," she said. "My dear Valentina, you have never been a fool. But where men are concerned, we women are sometimes very foolish. Now I want you to sit down and have a scone and stop worrying. And while you do, Felicity is going to tell me more about this Eugene . . ."

Five

The following morning, Tina rose at her customary hour and breakfasted with Libby. Felicity was still abed, which might have provided them with an opportunity to discuss private issues, however by tacit agreement the conversation was kept to such innocuous topics as the best way to roast a partridge and how often the floors should be sanded. Neither Marchant brother was mentioned.

In fact, Libby had never said very much about them in her letters, so Tina had always presumed there was nothing to say. However, during the time between Napoleon's abdication and his infamous escape from Elba, Laverstoke had figured so prominently among the diplomatic corps that one could scarce pick up a newspaper without reading his name. Tina had been sick of hearing about him then, and (she told herself firmly) she had no wish to discuss him now.

At Libby's urging, Tina returned upstairs to fetch her sketchbook, and was in the process of retrieving it when her ankle struck the edge of a stool. With a sharp yelp, she sat down and rubbed the offended area. Staring at her foot brought back the memory of *him* (she was not yet ready to call him Laverstoke) making that incorrigible offer to remove her boots. Would he really have done so if she'd agreed? Of course not. He'd merely been trying to humiliate her. And with this conviction came the echo of Libby's warning. *Where men are concerned, we women are sometimes very foolish.*

How true. And Libby did not know the half of it.

How could she, after all? Libby had never been wed, and (to Tina's knowledge) had never even had a beau, so she could know nothing of what went on between a man and a woman. Well, Tina amended, Libby might know in theory, but she certainly could not appreciate the indefinable spark that could exist between a man and a woman.

With a rush of bitterness, she thought of Christian. He had been so sweet, so warm and likable, so perfect for her. Of course, there had been those occasions when he had sulked like a child, but everyone was entitled to a few flaws. Most of the time, he had been mild and uncritical and loving, and until that last tryst, he had never tried to push her to do aught her conscience would not allow. She sighed heavily. If they had married, she would have given herself to him happily. She would have borne his children, as she had so longed to do.

But Allegra Marchant had intervened.

Tina shuddered as she recalled her actions of the previous evening. Dear God, if she had known it was Laverstoke, she would never, ever have played chess with him! He had lied to them both, and (she had no doubt) then inveigled his brother into joining the deception. He clearly had few scruples, which was just what one would expect from someone who allowed his sister to trick a man into marriage.

She despised him.

And yet, ironically, she still found him attractive. Of course, she had imagined him quite differently and had not yet had time to adjust to the reality of his appearance. Perhaps because of her prejudice, she had always envisioned him to look something like Felicity's uncle, the baronet, who was an unpleasant, dissipated man with a fixed sneer. Lord Laverstoke, on the other hand, was as far from that portrait as cream from sour milk.

Rising up from the stool, Tina walked to the mirror, but her eyes were too unfocused to see her reflection. Instead, she saw a man—a tall, black-browed, elegant man whose mere glance possessed the disturbing ability to send shivers racing over her flesh.

With a frustrated oath, Tina made a horrid face at herself. "Impressionable pea-goose," she scolded. "I daresay that monster Bonaparte had a charming smile, too!"

Determined to waste no more time with thoughts of Lord Laverstoke, she tucked her sketchbook under her arm and headed for the door. She was *not* going to let any of this spoil her day, she reflected. At long last, she had a respite from Mrs. Winton, and she was going to enjoy it!

Marching down the corridor, she descended the stairs and headed for Libby's sitting room. At the threshold, however, she froze, for the sight of a huge, four-legged monster plunging across the carpet in her direction had a distressing effect upon her nerves. Resigned to her fate, Tina closed her eyes and waited for the impact, but Gretchen, displaying the natural suspicion inherent in the species, decided merely to sniff about her feet. At last, apparently satisfied that Tina bore no resemblance to anything edible, Gretchen thrust her wet muzzle forcefully under Tina's hand.

"Ah, good. She likes you," said Libby sedately.

Tina reopened her eyes and beheld the panting dog with misgiving. "I'd hate to see what would happen if she didn't," she retorted. "She, er, looks as though she wants something."

Libby touched a hand to her cheek. "Dear me," she mused, "she probably has to go out. Cook's son usually takes her about this time, but he is fast up with a cold. Oh dear, and Ben has gone into Norton on an errand. I wonder if—" She hesitated. "My dear Valentina, I hate to ask it of you, but—"

"You expect *me* to take this beast for a walk?" said Tina incredulously.

Gretchen's ears perked.

"She will be good," Libby pleaded. "Won't you, Gretchen?"

Gretchen lifted her head and whined.

79

"She nearly knocked Lord Laverstoke to the ground yesterday." Tina carefully omitted any mention of her own ignominious experience.

"Oh, but that's because he is a man," said Libby in an excusing tone. "Dear little Gretchen is perfectly aware of the difference. Aren't you, Gretchen?"

Gretchen leered as cockily as any tavern wench.

"But I don't know anything about dogs. You know Mama always had cats. Cats take care of themselves."

Libby's face fell. "Well, I suppose *I* could take her—" she began.

"Oh, no," Tina said bravely. "Of course I shall do it. Actually, a walk sounds lovely. If someone could just be sure she is wearing a good, stout lead . . ."

Twenty minutes later Tina stepped out into the snow, her spirits higher than they had been for days. In truth, it had always been her preference to take an early morning walk, but she had gotten out of the habit since Mrs. Winton frowned upon it. An invigorating walk would be just the thing, she told herself firmly.

If only the dog would behave.

So far, Gretchen displayed no disposition to do anything but conduct herself with absolute propriety. She was walking daintily at Tina's side, her head thrust slightly forward, her nose quivering in the cool, crisp air. Since the lead had seemed rather long, Tina had looped it several times around her hand, but perhaps that had been unnecessary. The lead was slack, Libby was right, and the dog really did have manners.

At the outset, Tina had intended to head east, but made no objection when Gretchen indicated her preference for a westerly course. It mattered naught what direction they took, as long as the animal was happy.

And judging from the eager little noises in her throat, Gretchen did seem happy.

"Good girl," said Tina tentatively, and was rewarded by

a look that seemed positively affectionate.

Gretchen, she decided, was a nice dog.

However, she was not a particularly attractive dog. She was part mastiff and part something else—what, even Libby was unsure. Cousin Libby had told them the story of Gretchen last night at dinner.

Gretchen had come to her four years before as a pup, the offspring of a mastiff owned by the blacksmith in Norton. Libby had gone into Norton one day on a shopping expedition, and had twisted her ankle a short distance from the smithy's yard. "He carried me inside," Libby had said, "and his wife tended me like I was her own dear mother. So sweet, they both were, married only a few months, and her already in a delicate situation. And there in the corner of their parlor was the mastiff and her litter, and the runt of them all was my dear little Gretchen." Libby had smiled fondly at the reminisce. "I always loved dogs. My ankle was fine, but by the time Lady Laverstoke sent the carriage to fetch me home, Gretchen was mine."

Tina glanced down. Yes, Gretchen *was* a nice dog. Not little, but nice. She reached down to ruffle the fur on Gretchen's head. "Nice Gretchen," she remarked. "I don't blame you in the least for wishing to knock Lord Laverstoke into the snow. Indeed, I wish you had done so."

Gretchen ignored the remark, having picked up a scent which piqued her interest. Her pace increased accordingly; the lead was no longer slack.

"I am not normally a vindictive person," Tina went on, her stride lengthening to match Gretchen's. "I wouldn't have wished you to knock down his brother, you understand. James is pleasant and unpretentious. But Lord Laverstoke undoubtedly deserves to be taken down a peg or two—"

Gretchen was not attending, but Tina continued talking, finding it oddly soothing to voice her grievances to a disinterested party who could not repeat her confidences.

"—and if I had only been paying attention I would have seen that his knight was there. But I did not, and so— You are going too fast," she complained. "You must have misunderstood. I am supposed to take *you* for a walk, not the other way around. Is there something you wish to see? If so, I wish you would try to be a little more—oh!"

Gretchen chose this moment to forget it was a lady she was walking.

"Gretchen!" Tina gasped, her arm nearly wrenched from its socket. "Do slow down. Stop! Heel! Oh, dear lord—"

As Gretchen's gait blossomed to a full gallop, Tina lost her purchase and fell. Yet Gretchen plowed on, etiquette forgotten, relentlessly dragging Tina facedown like a sleigh without runners.

Unfortunately, there was no question of letting go of the lead—it was wound too tightly around her hand. Cursing inwardly, Tina closed her eyes and mouth and concentrated on breathing. Even so, the snow was worming its way inside her pelisse and down the front of her dress. . . .

"Gretchen!" said a male voice. "Heel!"

Incredibly, Gretchen heeled.

Tina lay still, panting and gritting her teeth because she knew very well who it was.

"Cousin Valentina," said the voice with distinct amusement. "What do you think you are doing?"

She raised her head at the same time Lord Laverstoke squatted down. "I'm taking Gretchen for a walk," she said acidly. "Isn't it obvious?"

The viscount flicked snow from her face, his eyes alight with laughter. "Oh, yes, perfectly. I do beg your pardon. It was a silly question."

Before she realized what he was about, he lifted her to her feet and commenced brushing the snow from her clothing. "Why the devil are you doing it?" he began. "I thought Ben or young Joe—"

"I beg your pardon, my *lord*," she said in arctic tones, "but I don't think I gave you permission to touch me."

Laverstoke's hand froze, and he straightened. "So you know." His smile was gone; only a question remained. "I suppose that means I'm in your black books."

"As a matter of fact, it does. And I take leave to inform you that I find your deception wholly disgraceful. Why you chose to play us such a trick, I have no notion at all. I can only suppose that your sense of humor is . . . is . . ." She groped for an adequate word.

"Warped?" he supplied.

"At the very least! Perhaps all that time abroad has addled your wits," she ended waspishly.

The dark brows rose, but he did not look as angry as she expected. "You have a sharp tongue," he said mildly. "What a fishwife you'll make the man who weds you. Down, Gretchen!" he added, as the dog jumped on his arm.

Tina made a furious sound. "You are impertinent! I suppose you think you are entitled to special observances simply because of your title—"

"Oh, certainly," he agreed. "I demand obséquiousness from everyone I meet."

"From the first moment I laid eyes on you, you have behaved without any respect for propriety—"

Without warning, he reached out and clasped her chin. "And you have?" he inquired in a smooth, gentle drawl. "You know if you keep abusing me, sooner or later I'll be forced to defend myself."

Tina drew back from his grasp. "So you defend your odious deception," she shot back. "No doubt it amused you to make mock of us. Did it amuse your brother as well?"

Gretchen was growing bored. She paced around Gerard, making small, irritated sounds, then brushed past Tina's skirts, moaning softly.

"No, I can't say that it did," he retorted. "But Jay is a good fellow. Always game for a lark."

"A lark!" she said scornfully. "Is that what you call it? Surely you're too old for that. You must be at least—"

Gretchen paced by Laverstoke.

"—three-and-thirty," he told her cordially. "And you,

my dear? You look old enough to know better than to run around half naked in front of—"

Tina slapped his face.

Gretchen barked.

"That hurt," he admitted. "But not nearly as much as if you had hit me with your fist. Has anyone ever shown you how?"

Gretchen barked again.

"Quiet," he ordered, glancing down impatiently. "Can't you see that we are— Oh, damn."

Tina followed his gaze, and was dismayed to see that the lead now encircled their legs. Gretchen had bound them together with her pacing.

Gerard sighed. "Here, give that thing to me so I can untangle us—"

Undoubtedly he would have done so if Gretchen had not spied the hare. Later, Tina would recall this moment with a shudder of mortification, but at the instant it happened she was conscious of nothing but Gerard's sudden grip as they lost their balance and toppled to the ground.

Oblivious to the two humans she had displaced, Gretchen strained at the lead and barked madly at her retreating prey. She made no headway, however, for the addition of Laverstoke's weight made pursuit impossible.

Tina lay in shock. Laverstoke was almost atop her, his face inches from her own. In fact, he was so close she could actually smell his masculine scent, so close she could almost feel the heat of his flesh through his clothes. Oddly, he did not move, but lay looking down at her with a strange expression. "I do beg your pardon, ma'am," he said, in an even odder tone, "but I believe this calls for an introduction."

As his lips found hers, all lucid thought drained from her head. Tina forgot her outrage, her sense of misuse, the resentment she had been harboring. She even forgot the cold. It all receded, washed away in a mist of pure, primitive longing. *Human contact. Elemental, necessary, impossibly exciting.* This kiss was not a simple brush of lips.

This kiss was real—as real as Christian's—and yet it was different enough to be a completely new experience.

A throbbing shudder ran through her as his tongue probed her mouth. This kiss was hungry and insistent, lingering and savage. His breath grazed her cheek, warm and soft, an echo of her own spreading heat. Weakness pervaded her limbs; he tasted so male and virile that she wanted to whimper with the sheer wonder of it.

But Laverstoke was not Christian, and so there could be no reason at all for her to respond with such helpless enthusiasm. There could be no reason at all for her to grip his powerful shoulders through the layers of his greatcoat as though she yearned to pull him closer still.

When at last he raised his head, she lay staring up at him, gasping and dazed. And then came the flood of shame—and the outrage, in full measure.

"Dear heaven, get off me! What on earth do you think you're doing!" Pretending it was what she had meant to do all along, her shaking hands rammed at his shoulders.

Though his sardonic look told her he wasn't fooled, he rolled off her and sat up. "I have a fairly good notion what I was doing, but do I really have to explain?"

Tina pushed herself up, her cheeks stained crimson. "You must be mad," she said in a suffocated voice.

"I daresay," he said dryly. Reaching for the lead, he reeled Gretchen in like a fish. "Sit," he ordered.

Gretchen sat, looking as though she had no idea what the fuss was about.

He then reached for Tina's left hand and proceeded to unwind the lead. In itself the action was not objectionable, however when he proceeded to pull off her glove, she tried to pull away.

"Does it hurt?" he inquired, chafing her numbed fingers.

"I can hardly tell," she snapped, "since there is no feeling left anywhere else in my body to compare it with." In truth, she was not as chilled as she feigned; the sun shone warmly down upon them, and the wind was presently at a lull. And the effects of that wretched kiss had by no means worn off.

He extricated their legs from the lead and stood up. "Poor Valentina," he murmured, looking down at her. "You've had a devilish week, haven't you?" Reaching down, he pulled her to her feet and held out the glove.

Tina accepted it silently, her lips tight with suppressed emotion. Then, without a word, she turned and walked back the way she had come, following the path of footsteps in the snow.

Both Laverstoke and Gretchen caught up with her at once. "I suppose I've passed beyond the point where one might reasonably hope for forgiveness."

Tina stared straight ahead. "Why did you do it?"

"Which? Deceive you or kiss you?" He spoke lightly, as though trying to soften her mood.

"Deceive me," she said curtly.

He hesitated, as if trying to make up his mind. "Well," he said finally, "when you said 'are you Lord Laverstoke?' in such an unflattering tone, it seemed expedient to say no. 'Twas a craven impulse, I admit."

"And childish," she said flatly.

"Indeed. I am aware of that."

They walked in silence as taut as a whip.

At length, he said, "I've the feeling you disliked me before we met. Am I right?" His tone was curious, yet it also held a note of . . . what? Dissatisfaction? Pique?

Tina was loathe to discuss the subject. To attempt to put yesterday's pain into words would be beyond her capabilities right now. It would come out all wrong, and he would brush it off as something small, a past event unworthy of serious discussion.

"I don't want to talk about it," she said sharply. "Here, I'll take Gretchen now." Not waiting for a response, she reached out and snatched the lead from his hand. "You don't need to come back with me. I don't want you to."

It was a graceless thing to say, but she had not expected his face to harden as it did.

"Very well," he said, his cold pride matching hers. "I'll see you this evening then, if you're still inclined to come." With a short nod, he strode off in the direction of Laverstoke Park.

And as Tina turned her back on him, her heart felt as though it had just been ground into the snow.

Gerard was furious, both with Tina and himself. In diplomatic circles he was known for his ability to remain detached, yet each time Tina Jardine crossed his path that ability diminished, involuntarily and without warning.

Why the devil had he kissed her, for God's sake?

He stomped through the snow, filled with impotent frustration at his inability to unravel the mystery. The woman did something to him, that was all. He'd spent years encasing himself in a layer of cool indifference, training himself not to react too quickly, mastering the art of staying aloof. He'd spent years learning to observe, to look for the advantages and hidden meanings, to make sure what came out his mouth was exactly what he meant and nothing more. And then, fiend seize it, Tina Jardine came along and he forgot everything—or as near to it as made no difference. And he did not have the least idea why or how.

Beatrice had never had this effect on him, he thought irritably. He always knew exactly where he stood with Beatrice. He knew what she wanted, and why and when and how. He knew what he could expect from her; he understood what made her tick.

And Beatrice understood him, too. She knew exactly how to arouse him and had never failed to do so. Yet he had never kissed her anywhere but in the privacy of a bedchamber—nor wanted to, for that matter. And he had never lost his temper with Beatrice, as he had so nearly done with Valentina.

Still wondering if physical deprivation was the source of the problem, Gerard summoned an image of Beatrice lying naked on her bed. Rather to his surprise, the vision did not affect him, a fact he found vaguely disturbing. Curse it, it *ought* to affect him; Beatrice was a voluptuous, desirable woman, a pink-and-gold beauty whose passion had always awakened his most basic male instincts.

Ah well, perhaps it was because he was cold. After all, how could one think of sex when there was snow in one's boots?

When Tina arrived back at the Dower House she was still very shaken. Cook's son met her in the drive to collect Gretchen, so that Tina was able to enter the house through the front door. As she mounted the steps, it crossed her mind that the boy showed no outward sign of illness. In fact, he had looked remarkably robust.

As she turned over her outer garments, she realized that it was not yet nine o'clock. She had been gone little more than forty-five minutes, but it seemed more like hours, or even days.

"Oh, there you are, Valentina." As Tina walked into the sitting room, Libby welcomed her with a smile. "Did you have a pleasant walk?"

"Pleasant?" Not wishing to distress her relative, Tina weighed her answer carefully. "Well, it was cold, at any rate." She crossed over to kiss Libby's cheek, then held her hands to the fire. "Gretchen seemed to enjoy it tremendously."

"Did you . . . meet anyone?" To anyone who did not know Libby, the question would have sounded perfectly guileless.

Tina looked up sharply. "Was I meant to?" Catching Libby's expression, she went on, "Libby, for heaven's sake! Did you know he would be there?"

The picture of innocence, Libby raised her brows. "Who, my dear?"

"Lord Laverstoke!" Tina's fingers curled into knots; she tried to keep the accusation from her voice. "Did you plan that we should meet?"

Libby sighed. "You were always so clever, Valentina. It is a trait I have always admired." As Tina's eyes flashed, she confessed, "Well, he does often walk at that hour, though of course with the snow I could not be certain."

"And Cook's son?" Tina went on. "You bamboozled me about him, didn't you?"

Libby hung her head. "Well, he did sneeze twice yesterday. I made certain he did, because I heard him myself."

"Libby, are you . . . are you *matchmaking?*" asked Tina thunderously.

"Oh, no, dear," insisted her relative. "Gracious, no. I simply wanted to give you an opportunity to patch things up with his lordship. It distresses me to see you angry with him. He is a good man, my love."

"His conduct has been unforgivable," she said in a curt voice.

Libby regarded her anxiously. "Do you truly feel you cannot like him?"

Tina stared down at her fingers. They were long and shapely, and she had always been rather proud of them.

"Oh, Libby," she said finally, "you don't understand. You know as well as I do that it is he who was responsible for—" The words stuck in her throat.

Libby's soft eyes were genuinely puzzled. "Responsible? My dear Valentina, I fear I do not follow. Responsible for . . . what?"

"Christian." The word was clipped.

"What about Christian?" Slowly, comprehension dawned in Libby's face. "Dear me, surely you do not blame Laverstoke for what happened?"

"Of course I blame Laverstoke—at least to an extent! If he had been doing his duty as a guardian, it all might not have happened. And if he had ceased his raking around long enough to make the least inquiry about Christian, he would have learned that he was already—" She drew a breath. "I know we were not formally betrothed, but our attachment was no secret. Everyone knew. Perhaps he thought a country nobody like me did not count, but—"

"But surely," interrupted Libby in deep distress, "surely, my dear, you must see that the fault lies with Christian."

"No, I do not!" Tina flashed. "You did not know Christian as I did. He was tricked into marriage! He told me as much. His letter said that he still loved me and wanted me, but honor was forcing him to marry Allegra."

Libby's head bowed. "I'm sure he did love you, or thought he did. But what's done is done. I thought by now you must have faced that."

Tina's hand raised and fell in a helpless little gesture. "But I have faced it, Libby." In a tired voice, she went on, "I suppose she must have been in love with him to do what she did. Christian always had such a way about him, besides being so very handsome."

So handsome, she thought, her throat aching. *Dark hair and dark eyes, a slow, dreamy smile* . . . "Any young girl would be impressed," she added. " 'Twas her guardian's duty to . . . to know."

Libby's brow furrowed. "Dear me," she uttered, looking vague. "Things have reached a much worse pass than I feared. If I'd had the least notion—! But there, I do not want to go on about my fancies, do I? We shall see. Time will tell. And in the meanwhile, my dear, you must try to enjoy yourself. Shall you show me your sketchbook? You know, I really would like it if you could draw little Gretchen."

Six

The men were out with their shovels when Gerard arrived home. He saw them pause in their work, felt them watch his approach, but he ignored them and concentrated on the crunch of his own footsteps in the snow. No doubt he was a curious sight, walking alone and on foot, but they should be used to his habits by now.

He was twenty yards from the house when James rounded the corner astride a huge bay. He rode over to Gerard, his brows arched in surprise. "Good God, did your horse throw you?"

Since parting from Tina, Gerard's mood had inexplicably worsened. "I didn't take a mount," he said shortly. At his brother's inquiring look, he added, enunciating slowly, "I felt like walking. I do that sometimes."

James looked down at him quixotically. "I know. But dear heaven, Gerry, in this weather? There'll be bellows to mend when Henries sees those boots."

"My valet receives a wage. Let him earn it."

"My, my, something's put you into a dudgeon. Let me guess. Was it one of our fair cousins?"

Gerard ignored him and resumed walking. James's voice followed. "I was looking for you earlier. Did you pay them a call?"

"No." Laverstoke tossed the surly word over his shoulder. He gained the shallow stone steps leading up to the door, and turned. "Where are you going?"

"I thought I'd pay a call on Millie." James spoke uncomfortably, as though caught committing a *faux pas*.

The hardness in Gerard's face faded to compassion. "You'll be allowed to see her?"

James shrugged, affecting a nonchalance Gerard knew to be false. "Probably not. You know what Lady Buckden wants for the girl."

"Me." The monosyllable was succinct and without arrogance, a statement of flat fact.

"Either you or some other fellow with a title and the fortune to go with it. But I promised Millie I'd keep trying." The words were spoken sadly, but with grim determination.

"Invite them to dine with us tonight, if you will. To meet our cousins. It's as good an excuse as any."

James looked visibly cheered. "I say, that's a good notion. You don't think Felicity or Tina will object, do you?"

At the moment, Gerard didn't care if they did. "I'm sure they'll be delighted," he said silkily. "And it should help smooth things over, since the ladies have discovered the truth about us."

"Have they, now." James looked thoughtful. "How do you know?"

Gerard tapped his hand on his thigh. "I came across Valentina while I was out walking. We, er, exchanged words."

"In a bad skin, was she?" James grinned. "Did she give you your comeuppance?"

"She tried." Gerard scowled, and changed the subject. "About Millie. Are you able to talk to her at all?"

"We talk with our eyes. And once in a while, at a dinner or such, we are actually able to use words. But never for long." His mouth curved bitterly. "Her mother always intervenes."

Gerard sighed. "I'd like to throttle that woman. If the Park were yours, she'd change her tune fast enough."

James heard the guilt in his voice. "Dash it, don't start on *that*. Second sons may lack the advantages, but we lack the obligations, too. It suited me to join the army, don't forget. I was always army-mad."

However, they both knew that James's career in the army was at an end. Finally and for all time, Boney had been defeated, and even if that were not the case, James's leg was too weak to permit further action. A ball in the joint had taken care of that—and nearly robbed him of his limb.

"You *are* my heir," Gerard reminded him with a frown.

"True enough, but if you think not to wed only so I may inherit, then think again. It won't fadge, Gerry, and I won't allow it. Believe it or not, I'm happy as a grig just working here as your steward."

"I've no wish to wed," Gerard pointed out.

"That's because you haven't met the right woman yet. Or at least—" James broke off from whatever he'd meant to say. "When you do," he said instead, "you won't give a fig about me inheriting. You'll want her, and sons of your own."

"Shall I?" As Gerard considered this, an image of Tina entered his head—tall, black-haired, elegant, and proud, her eyes sparking blue fire, her lips soft and yielding. It was from such a woman that he wanted children, not from some fawnlike society creature with sensibilities so finely edged that he must treat her like a china doll. Perhaps that was why the thought of marriage had never tempted him. He wanted spirit and passion in a woman, but he also wanted a wife who was gently bred and refined, physically attractive and intelligent. And none of the girls thrust at him over the years had ever struck him as possessing this rare blend of qualities.

"Perhaps you are right," he said curtly. "But your wishes count a good deal more than Father's in this matter. His desire that I wed Lady Millicent was based purely on whim and the fact that Lord Buckden was his crony.

If he'd lived long enough to know it was you she favored, I know he'd have given his blessing."

"Unfortunately, Lady Buckden is not so accommodating," said James dryly.

"Lady Buckden is an ambitious shrew. Do you really desire her for a mama-in-law?"

"If it means I can have Millie," James said simply, "then yes. I would put up with it."

Mentally tossing up his hands, Gerard turned to mount the steps. "Invite them to dinner," he advised over his shoulder. "They have a sleigh. They can manage."

By the time Felicity sailed into the sitting room, Tina had recovered her temper sufficiently to greet her cousin with composure. Oddly, Gretchen had played a large part in soothing her agitation, for the dog had apparently conceived an adoration for her sometime during the course of their walk. In fact, Gretchen had devoted a number of minutes demonstrating this by rubbing against her leg, uttering such piteously apologetic moans that Tina had had to laugh. She had then given Gretchen a thorough petting, which must have sealed the bond between them for the dog had promptly draped herself over Tina's feet and fallen asleep.

"Good morning everyone!" said Felicity cheerfully. "Oh, look at Gretchen, how charming." Stepping over the dog, she plopped down next to Tina on the sofa. "You do not mind if I breakfast in here, do you, Miss Steeple? It is tedious eating in one's room. I told the maid to serve me in here."

"Of course you may," responded Libby politely. "Did you sleep well, dear?"

"Yes, thank you." Felicity turned to Tina. "What are you drawing?"

Tina turned her sketchbook around, holding it so both women could see her portrait of the dog.

"But that is wonderful!" Felicity clapped her hands in awe. "I had no notion you could draw so well! Why did you never tell me?"

"One's talents are not something one boasts about, Felicity. And anyway, it is not very good."

"Not very good!" repeated Felicity and Libby in a single voice.

Tina returned the sketch to her lap and studied it. "No. It lacks something," she said finally. "The proportion is right, but something is missing. The dog in this picture looks too placid. I see nothing of mischief in its face."

At the word "dog," Gretchen's head lifted.

"What do you think?" Tina asked, lowering it so the dog could see.

Gretchen whimpered.

"You are quite right," Tina said gravely. "It looks like you, but it is not you. I do much better with people, particularly when I am acquainted with them."

At this point, Felicity's breakfast tray arrived, so that Gretchen was forced to sit up at full alert.

"No, Gretchen," Felicity scolded. As she reached for her toast, her eyes returned to Tina's drawing. "Do you think you could draw me?"

"Oh, I have. Many times, in fact." Tina flipped back a page in her sketchbook. "Here is one," she said, rotating it around.

Tina knew the likeness was remarkable, for not only was it technically accurate, it captured much of Felicity's temperament as well. The girl in the picture was clearly her mama's pampered darling, a girl whose intrinsic good nature warred constantly with the vain, selfish streak her mother did everything to nourish. The latter showed in the petulant curve of the soft, pretty mouth; the former in the dancing, roguish eyes.

Felicity must have seen something of this, for she looked a trifle taken aback. "That is how I look to you?"

The toast hung slack in her fingers.

Tina closed the sketchbook, conscious of having exposed more of her sentiments than she normally cared to do. "That is how you sometimes appear," she temporized, her voice quiet.

"Oh." Felicity's hand completed its arc to her mouth; she bit into the toast and chewed pensively.

"Well, I think the sketch of Gretchen is equally fine," said Libby tactfully. "You are a very talented young woman, Valentina."

Embarrassed by the praise, Tina shrugged. "It is something I enjoy doing," she said, "just as you enjoy tatting."

Libby glanced down at her lacework, then held it up for Felicity to see. "Yes, I do like to keep busy," she agreed. "And you, Felicity? What do you enjoy?"

"Other than food, you mean?" Felicity jested. "Well, I play the pianoforte and take dance lessons, of course. And sing. At Seminary they tried to teach me to draw and paint and speak French, but I hated all that. However, Mama says I must be accomplished if I want to capture a lord." She paused. "I like to read, but if Mama catches me at it, it gives her nervous palpitations." Suddenly her eyes turned mischievous. "What I really like to do is ride," she went on. "And I very much enjoy looking at the gentlemen—"

"Felicity!" Tina reproved automatically.

"Well, but I do, Tina. Gentlemen are the most fascinating creatures! At Miss Bletchley's Select Seminary, that is all the other girls talked about. I used to think they were silly, but that was before I met—" She broke off, swallowed, and continued, "Lord Laverstoke and his brother, for instance. You cannot deny that *they* are fascinating."

"I refuse to discuss it," Tina said repressively. "And as far as reading goes, I fear I must disagree with your mama. During this visit, you will have opportunity aplenty to indulge yourself. I strongly suggest that you do it."

Felicity's mouth fell into a mulish line. "When you talk like that, Tina, you sound a great deal like the elder Miss Bletchley. She was a hopeless spinster, you know. Everyone called her the queen of the ape-leaders behind her back." She tittered nastily. "I do hope that doesn't happen to you, for if you don't get a husband, what on earth will you do with the rest of your life?" The jeering words hung in the air, backwash from her mother's attitudes that Felicity had unconsciously absorbed.

Unable to think of a retort, Tina sat stock-still, her face a little pale. There was nothing she could say, for had she not asked herself that same question, time and again?

What was she to do with the rest of her life?

Most of the time she shut it from her mind, but when she did ponder the matter, the future looked bleak. She was practically three-and-twenty, with neither prospects nor suitors on the horizon. She was presently employed, but for the sake of her sanity she knew she must eventually leave the Winton household. And though she would be happiest with Libby, *that* was not a viable solution, for it would mean accepting charity from Lord Laverstoke. Perhaps, she thought heavily, it was time to seek employment in some other capacity, perhaps as a schoolteacher or governess. . . .

Even as these thoughts flashed through her head, Felicity was apologizing. "*Do* forgive me, Tina. That was a horrid thing to say. I don't know why I said it. Sometimes I think there are devils inside me." She hesitated. "It is what Eugene most dislikes about me," she added, her voice low and melancholy.

"And what does he say?" asked Libby gently.

Felicity sighed. "He wants me to be more like his sister, who is a pattern card of tact and propriety. Indeed, I don't think Melissa has ever said a cross word to anyone.

97

And she speaks French *and* Italian with a perfect accent."

"She sounds perfectly odious," said Libby comfortingly. "But even when a lady lacks accomplishments, my dear, she must always consider the feelings of others. Otherwise she does not deserve to be called a lady."

"I know." Felicity toyed dejectedly with her eggs; astonishingly, she appeared to have lost her appetite. "I have been so blue-deviled and bored lately. Perhaps that is why I have been so cross with you, Tina. I can think of no other reason." She heaved a long, wistful sigh.

"Well, we shall have to find something to capture your interest," Tina said dryly.

Later in the afternoon, during a period when she was alone, Tina was seized with an uncontrollable urge to draw the viscount's face. Though she had made an honest effort to put the morning's encounter from her head, the moment she gained the privacy of her bedchamber she was compelled to give in to the pull of her artistic instincts.

At first, it was easier than she expected. In order to sketch from memory, she typically had to know the person well, but in this case it proved otherwise. Her charcoal pencil skimmed effortlessly across the page as the image in her brain flowed directly to her fingers. In a manner of minutes he was there, staring up at her with very much the same expression he had worn this morning, just before he had kissed her.

However, it was not the expression she had wanted to capture. She had wanted to show his insufferable arrogance, his harshness, his disregard for the feelings of others, but instead she had somehow caught his sensuality and strength.

Disturbed, she studied the drawing, her brow creased with thought. She ought to destroy it. She ought to rip the page from the book and cast it into the fire, yet, oddly, that seemed a horrific act. She could not do it. The sketch was too real. Just looking at it made her heart skip a beat.

Lust. That was all he felt for her. The purpose of the first kiss had been to insult her, but the second — it had been based on pure animal lust. There was no other possibility.

Yet the knowledge that she had attracted a man in a physical sense played oddly with her emotions. She was not the sort of woman to do that, she had learned. Oh, she had used to consider herself attractive, in a quiet sort of a way. Christian had seemed to find her so, at any rate. But since Christian there had been no one — no one to talk to, no one to laugh with, no one to touch. And until this moment, she had not realized how lonely she had been.

Staring down at her drawing of Lord Laverstoke, she considered his kiss with bewilderment. Whatever else he felt for her, his passion had been real.

And so had hers.

That was yet another cause for puzzlement. For as much as she had adored Christian, she could not remember his kisses ever producing such wooziness in the stomach. For pity's sake, she and Laverstoke had been lying in the snow! Under such circumstances, how could she possibly have enjoyed his kiss as much as she had?

He had known, too. That was the worst of it, the most humiliating aspect of the whole situation. She had vowed to be cool to him, to show him that she was a good and decent woman — and instead she had done just the opposite. After all, he could not have failed to feel her response. She had done more than allow the kiss — she had been an active, enthusiastic participant.

And now, no doubt, he thought her a brazen hussy, and perhaps he was right. Perhaps, she thought uneasily, deep down in her soul she *was* an immoral woman—a trollop trapped in the body of a confirmed and hopeless spinster.

Slowly, Tina closed the sketchbook, her face a little pale. No more. If she had a weakness for Laverstoke, then she would have to fight it.

She had never fought her weakness for Christian. Eager to please the man she adored, she'd allowed him to kiss and caress her in a way a respectable woman ought never to have allowed. Perhaps it had been this willingness that had made him think she would consent to his lovemaking. The disquieting notion had never occurred to her before. Perhaps Christian had recognized the wantonness inside her, just as Lord Laverstoke did now. But where Christian had genuinely loved her, Laverstoke did not.

In a few hours, she was to dine with him. How would he behave toward her? How *did* a gentleman behave toward a lady he wished to seduce? In public, she supposed he would feign indifference. But then, too, the indifference might be real. After all, her rudeness to him might well have cured him of his lustful intentions. She ought to hope this was so. Yet deep down, in the heart of her heart, she found the notion of his indifference more disturbing than anything else.

It was when she was dressing for dinner that she found the book. Tucked inside the wardrobe, along with the rest of her personal belongings, lay the copy of *Shakespeare's Sonnets* she had read at Laverstoke Park. The maid, Annie, must have packed it mistakenly, and Cousin Libby's maid had put it away before Tina had known it was there.

Tina picked it up, thinking once more how lovely it was. She would have to return it, of course. Laverstoke might think she was stealing from him. Yet, as if drawn to it by some mysterious force, she once more opened it to a random page.

> *Since I left you, mine eye is in my mind,*
> *And that which governs me to go about*
> *Doth part his function and is partly blind,*
> *Seems seeing, but effectually is out;*

She closed the book with a snap. Shakespeare certainly had a way with words, she thought testily. Every emotion she was experiencing had been felt before, every human fear and affliction had already been endured. And the world went on, didn't it? So what right had she to complain?

Setting the book aside, she went over to the mirror, studying her reflection with a critical frown. As usual, her dress was outmoded, while her hair was parted in the middle and drawn severely back in a style that had become a symbol of her inability to look or feel attractive. The dress she could do nothing about, but the hair . . . Suddenly, Tina knew she would not wear it thus tonight. No matter how she felt about Laverstoke, the thought that he might be indifferent to her was unendurable. Loathe her he might do, but indifference she could not and would not tolerate.

"May," she called.

Libby's maidservant scuttled into the room, having just completed aiding Felicity with her *toilette*. "Yes, miss?"

Tina smiled self-consciously. "I'm sorry. I hate to trouble you, but my hair . . . it doesn't flatter me much, does it?"

"No, miss." May clapped a guilty hand to her mouth. "That is to say, miss, it could be a mite more becoming. If you'll sit down, I'll fetch the curling tongs and we'll see what can be done."

Thanks to her hair's natural tendency to curl, the transformation was completed in very short order. Tina's hair was still drawn back, but in a much softer, more feminine fashion. Delicate ringlets now framed her face, displaying her features to far greater advantage than before.

"Do you like it, miss?" asked May earnestly.

"I think so," Tina said cautiously. "It makes me look . . . different."

"Much prettier, miss, if you don't mind me saying so."

"The wind will probably ruin it."

"Not if you wear your hood, miss. Would you like to try some rouge?"

"Rouge? Do you have any?"

"It's Miss Felicity's, miss. Didn't you know?"

"No," said Tina in a dry voice, "I didn't." She wondered how Felicity had managed that one, but decided she didn't want to know that either. "Do you think . . . I should?" she asked hesitantly.

Of course she was insane. She had never used rouge in her life, not even for Christian.

"Oh, just a mite won't hurt, miss. A bit o' color in the cheeks makes 'em look like roses."

Moments later, May set a rouge-box onto the dressing table. "You just need the smallest mite," she stated as she applied the hare's foot to Tina's cheeks. "There!" She stepped back, admiring her handiwork. "That's perfect, miss. 'Tis lucky you are to have such fine skin. There's nary a spot or a freckle anywhere."

Tina was too amazed by her reflection to answer at once. "Thank you, May," she finally managed to mumble. "Pray tell Miss Steeple that I am ready."

As Laverstoke had promised, the sleigh arrived for them promptly at seven, driven, on this occasion, by the viscount's groom. As before, the ride was accomplished very quickly; within minutes they were sweeping up to the front steps of Laverstoke Park.

Inside, Tina pulled the book of sonnets from the

pocket of her cloak before relinquishing it to the digni-fied Bissett, at the same time glancing at her reflection in a large gilt mirror. As May had prophesied, her ringlets had survived the journey.

They followed Bissett up the stairs to the drawing room, where she was surprised to find that they were not the only guests. She hid the book behind her as Laver-stoke stepped forward to introduce them to two very fashionable ladies.

The elder woman, Lady Buckden, nodded politely, but examined them with brittle eyes as they exchanged "how-do-you-dos." Her dark hair was swept up as severely as Tina's had been earlier, and her face possessed a hard, domineering quality that Tina found repelling.

The younger woman was her daughter. Lady Millicent Quigley was a soft, pretty creature with dark hair and large, scared eyes which darted about like a bird's. Tina's impression was that she was terrified of everyone—of her mother, of the three newcomers, and most particularly, of Laverstoke.

As for Laverstoke, he gave no sign that he noticed the change in Tina's appearance, yet he managed to observe that she was holding something behind her back.

"What do you have there, Miss Jardine?" The question was phrased every bit as courteously as the introductions, but Tina sensed a chill in his tone.

Good, she thought ferociously. *He is still angry.*

She raised her chin and held out the book. "I found it among my things," she said defiantly. "The maid who did the packing must have thought it was mine."

"Ah, yes. My volume of Shakespeare's sonnets," he said casually. "You may keep it a while longer, if you like."

Despite the offer, he took it from her hand, an action which caused Tina to say, with equal coolness, "There is no need, my lord. I am finished with it."

As Laverstoke set it on a nearby table, Lady Buckden,

obviously scenting scandal, said sweetly, "Oh? Did you spend a night at Laverstoke Park, Miss Jardine?"

For a moment, Tina thought that Laverstoke would answer, but a swift glance at his face showed his gaze to be quite noncommittal. Cursing him inwardly, she forced herself to smile at Lady Buckden.

"Our carriage overturned," she said calmly, "and we were forced to seek shelter under our cousin's"—she emphasized the word ever so slightly—"roof. It was either that or freeze to death."

"How shocking," said Lady Buckden, after a moment's pause. Then she pursed her lips and looked at Felicity. "Well! I would never permit Millicent to travel alone. I am surprised at your mother, Miss Winton."

Felicity deliberately misinterpreted the remark. "Oh, Mama reposes great confidence in our cousins' ability to keep us out of trouble," she said with a toss of her head. Her flirtatious smile encompassed both men. "So far, they have been very obliging," she added, batting her lashes at Laverstoke.

Tina ground her teeth. Clearly, the evening was going to be extremely trying. Felicity was in a dangerous mood, Laverstoke was out of temper, Lady Buckden was far worse than Mrs. Winton, and Libby had lapsed into a dreamlike silence. Only James seemed his usual, cheerful self.

As the evening progressed, however, she revised her opinion of James. He was, she decided, distinctly unhappy about something. As for Lady Millicent, she might be afraid of everyone else in the room, but she was not afraid of James. In fact, they exchanged glances so often during the course of the first hour that Tina began to suspect a romance. However, if James cherished a *tendre* for the mouselike Millie, he received no encouragement from her mother. Lady Buckden's hopes clearly centered on the viscount.

As for Laverstoke, his air was detached. He had spoken little, but his penetrating gaze rested on Tina just often enough to make her fidget. Each time their eyes met—which was often—she had the oddest feeling she was being challenged, but in what way she did not know. For the most part she attempted to ignore him, but once or twice, when no one else was looking, she gave him back stare for icy stare.

From the vein of her remarks, Tina soon realized that Lady Buckden viewed Felicity as her daughter's rival. "It is too bad you have not a harp in the room," she complained at one point. "Millicent has been practicing a piece she would love to perform for you, my lord."

At once Lady Millicent shrank back into her chair.

"There is a harp in the music room, of course," the viscount responded. "Unfortunately, it has a broken string."

Lady Buckden frowned. "How vexatious," she said. "I wonder you do not have it repaired. Millicent is excessively musical, as I'm sure you are aware. She is equally proficient on the pianoforte. She practices for hours every day."

"Do you really?" inquired Felicity with awe. "I have always hated to practice my playing."

Lady Buckden looked pitying. "So many girls lack the necessary resolution to practice as they should. Millicent's French is excellent, and her Italian is superb. It should be an asset, should her husband be required to travel in foreign lands." It was a pointed reference to Laverstoke's diplomatic career, but the viscount said nothing.

"Perhaps," said James tautly, "Millicent's husband will not care to travel."

Lady Buckden cast him a look of dislike. "Millicent's accomplishments," she stated, "must make her a suitable wife for any gentleman of rank. She does everything well."

"Can she draw?" asked Felicity.

Surprisingly, it was Millicent who answered. "Not very well," she admitted with an apologetic air. Then her eyes widened, as though she were shocked at her own daring.

"Tina can draw," announced Felicity. "She can draw anything and make it look quite real."

"I'm sure we all have talents if we could but find them," Tina said quickly.

"Well said, Miss Jardine." It was Laverstoke who spoke. "Would anyone care for some more wine?"

Lady Buckden ignored the hint. "Millicent is blessed with a natural modesty that precludes her from speaking of her achievements." She waved a waggish finger. "That is left for her mama to do. It is a mother's prerogative."

Felicity surveyed Millicent with mild interest. "Are you to have a Season?"

"Of course Millicent will have a Season," Lady Buckden informed her. "She will be eighteen in February. *All* the Quigleys"—she made it sound as though there were hundreds of them—"make their bow to Society at that age."

"I'll be eighteen in February, also. Which day is your birthday?"

Millie gave her mother a hesitant look. "The fifteenth," she responded, after a little pause. "Which is yours?"

"Mine is the fifteenth also!" Felicity gurgled in delight. "And Tina's is the fourteenth! She was a Valentine's Day baby, you see. That is where she gets her name."

James glanced at his brother. "Perhaps we should have a party," he suggested. "Surely three birthdays rate some sort of celebration."

Felicity almost squealed with excitement. "But which day shall it be on?"

"Valentine's Day," put in Laverstoke unexpectedly. "Most assuredly it should be on Valentine's Day."

Seven

For a long time after his guests departed, Gerard sat alone in his library, cradling a snifter of brandy. He was well aware that inviting Lady Buckden had been a tactical mistake. He'd suggested it to make James happy, but that had clearly been a blunder on his part. He should have realized that when a person craved a sweet, to dangle it before him was more cruel than kind. Normally, he was not so thick-skulled, but his encounter with Valentina had left him too unsettled to think in his usual, logical manner.

Leaning back in his chair, he stared upward at the frieze. It was past midnight, but he felt no inclination to seek his bed. Oddly, what he really wanted to do was to challenge Valentina to another game of chess, but of course this was impossible. She was back at the Dower House now, safe in her chaste little bed.

And it was probably just as well.

She had looked different tonight. More alluring. She had done her hair in a softer style, but it was more than that. What had it been? Her eyes, perhaps. He had been acutely aware of her, conscious of the soft curves beneath her out-moded dress, conscious even of the rise and fall of her breasts as she breathed.

What amazed him was that Lady Buckden actually thought it was Felicity who interested him. The woman obviously had no conception of what pleased a man — or perhaps it was only that his taste was not the same as other men's. Certainly he was very different from James, who had hankered after the mouselike Lady Millie since she was fifteen.

However, Gerard reflected, Felicity Winton did nothing for him. She was too youthful, too ingenuous, and too superficial. No, he corrected fairly, superficial was too strong a word. She merely stood too close to childhood to have developed the depth of personality necessary to attach a sophisticated man like himself. Without effort, he could call to mind dozens of her kind—lovely English apple blossoms prepared to burst upon Society in all their pink-faced glory. He'd seen too many of them to bother looking twice.

He sensed something deeper in Valentina. She was like a secret, and secrets had always intrigued him. Perhaps that was what he had most liked about his career, the need for prying out secrets, the deciphering of what lay behind the simplest of words. He smiled reminiscently, recalling the machinations he and Castlereagh had gone through in the past. Manipulating foreign powers into doing what England wanted was not child's play, but he had loved the challenge of dealing with such intricate men as Talleyrand and Metternich and Alexander of Russia.

Hidden meanings. Secrets.

And though he hoped he was done with all that now, it seemed to be as much a part of him as ever. The curiosity, the heady delight of a challenge was ever-present, enmeshed into his personality like threads in a carpet.

That must be the answer, then. Valentina presented a challenge.

From the first, he had felt her hostility. He had not a clue to its cause, but his first instinctive response had been a natural one—to try to charm her out of it. He supposed that was why he had kissed her yesterday, to see if he could penetrate the prickly hostility wrapped round her like a layer of nettles.

But it had not worked. Oh, he had gotten through briefly. He knew she had enjoyed his kiss, but that was unsurprising. After all, he was no novice at kissing a woman—or at any other facet of lovemaking for that matter. Not only had she enjoyed it, but she'd responded with unrestrained passion, something he doubted the Felicity Wintons of the world would have done, at least under similar circumstances.

For a moment, Gerard cast his eyes about the room, recalling the evening's dinner party with a small sigh. He supposed it could have been worse. Felicity's mother could have been present as well, and he might have had two ambitious matchmaking mamas pitting their forces—with him squeezed in the middle. Praise God Valentina did not have a mother, he thought wryly. That was one less Mama to plague him.

And now, he thought resignedly, they must have a Valentine's Day party.

Or a ball.

As one might have predicted, Felicity Winton desired a ball. So did Lady Buckden. Millie had not offered an opinion, and as for Tina—what she thought was a mystery.

Recollecting the brandy in his hand, Gerard lifted it to his lips and drained it. As the fiery liquid seared his throat, he recalled his sister's come-out ball in the spring of '13, which in turn reminded him of his need for a hostess. For a moment he frowned, then relaxed as he remembered Allegra. Not only was she the only woman suitable to fill the position, he felt sure she would delight in arranging the thing. However, knowing Allegra, she would want to make it into a full-blown house party with a ball to culminate the event.

And that was when the idea occurred to him.

If they were to have a house party, and if Valentina and Felicity were to be guests of honor, didn't it make sense that they—and Miss Steeple, of course—should move into the main house in order to mingle properly? Yes, absolutely. They would invite Millie and her mother, too—everything circumspect and aboveboard so no one could point a finger. Mulling the idea, Gerard straightened his posture and stared down at the papers on his desk.

109

Yes, it was an excellent plan.

And without even realizing it, he smiled the smile of a man who is hunting in earnest.

By the following afternoon, Tina had made up her mind to tell Lord Laverstoke that she would not be coming to his ball. Moreover, she would make it a point to suggest that he hold it on the fifteenth of the month, the day that Felicity and Lady Millicent turned eighteen. Why make it a Valentine's Day ball anyway? It was nothing but an obscure lovers' holiday, which made it a silly idea. Laverstoke had only said it to discompose her.

Yet as soon as she made the decision, she was gripped with a strange restlessness. For a while, she twitched around the house, flipping through books, peering out windows, until at last she came to the conclusion that fresh air was what she required.

"No," she told Gretchen, when the dog tried to follow her outside. "You've already had your walk today. I know you have, so don't look at me like that. I won't play the willing victim twice."

Gretchen wagged her tail hopefully, but Tina was adamant. Telling herself that she simply could not cope with Gretchen at the moment, she suppressed her guilt and left the house.

During the night the wind had piled the snow into drifts, and the morning's sun had hardened it to a smooth, brilliant sheen. Blanketed by gleaming white, the gentle Cotswold hills were profoundly, unutterably beautiful, and as Tina walked along, she was conscious of a sense of peace. There was something deeply satisfying in the stark silhouettes of leafless beech trees, etched as they were against a flawless blue sky. In some indefinable way, the sight of those skeletal branches touched her soul, as though they were, in some mysterious way, offering something precious to their Maker. She'd had no time to observe such things during her walk with Gretchen.

A reluctant smile tugged at her mouth as she pondered yesterday's outing. If she'd been anything but a participant in that ghastly scene, she supposed it would have been funny. After all, who would have thought the abhorrent animal would wind the lead around their legs and upset them like that? And the two of them going splat in the snow while Gretchen barked and strained after a hare that was long gone—it really was rather amusing. If it had been anyone other than Laverstoke, she might have been able to laugh about it at the time it occurred, but since it *had* been he, she'd merely been mortified. Of course, no one but Laverstoke would have behaved in so shocking a fashion.

Tina's lip curled cynically. She hadn't known it until a year ago, but Lord Laverstoke possessed quite a rakish reputation. She narrowed her eyes against the wind and brightness, trying to recall exactly what she had heard about him.

It had been something to do with an opera dancer, that much she knew. Mrs. Winton always tended to talk loudly to her husband, perhaps in the belief that a boost in volume might cause him to pay her more heed. She remembered standing stock-still outside the door to the Winton drawing room, hearing an account of how Laverstoke had been involved in some shocking scandal.

No doubt he was very successful with women, she thought bitterly. After such exotic places as Paris and Brussels and Vienna, he likely found the quiet of the Cotswolds dull. It would certainly explain why he had chosen to dally with *her*, wouldn't it? Without knowing why, the knowledge enraged her beyond all logical reason.

Tina pulled up short as, without warning, the tenants' cottages came into view. Even from this distance she could see their honey-brown masonry, bleached limestone turned tawny by time and exposure to the sun. Each small, gabled cottage glowed with a quiet dignity all its own, each pristine chimney trailing its thin, gray line of smoke. It was so beautiful, so simple, it made her throat ache.

She sighed and turned away. She did not have to look in

the windows to know that Laverstoke took proper care of his tenants. She did not need to knock on those doors to know that each and every family adored their lord and master. She would find no fuel for enmity here.

Enmity. Hatred.

They were strong words. And out of place, too, for although she did not like Laverstoke, she certainly did not hate him. How could she? Instead of the dissipated, gout-ridden roué of her imagination, she had found him to be a lean, graceful, well-formed man of remarkable intelligence. And it unsettled her.

Tina stomped her feet to warm them as she wended her way back, but her steps faltered at the crest of the hill which brought her within view of the Dower House. To her dismay, a sleigh was pulled up to the front door, and a tall, familiar figure stood beside it, still as a sentinel.

Tina kept walking, trying to behave as though she did not know he was watching her approach. As the distance between them shrank, she took silent stock of him. He wore a greatcoat but no hat, and appeared to be as much at ease as she was discomposed. The wind tousled his hair as it did hers, and the peculiar fancy crossed her mind that he was feeling exactly what she felt, at the exact same moment in time. Until now their lives had taken different paths, but right now those paths had intersected. They were like two straight lines crossing each other, meeting briefly only to separate again, inevitably, and for all time.

At last she was close enough that she could no longer ignore him. "Lord Laverstoke," she said, acknowledging him curtly. When she would have hurried past him, he stepped forward, his hand extended.

"Cousin," he said quickly. "A moment, if you please."

Tina looked at him, her brows arched haughtily.

"Would you"—he paused, as though unsure how to phrase what he had to say—"would you care to go for a sleigh ride?"

Several seconds slipped by before Tina answered, suspiciously, "For what purpose?"

"For the purpose of pleasure," he replied. There was a hint of mockery in his tone, yet beneath that lurked something other than nonchalance. "Afterward, I thought we might return to Laverstoke Park. I thought to offer you the chance to take your revenge."

For the length of a heartbeat, she thought he was referring to Christian. "My revenge?" she said faintly.

His gray eyes missed nothing; ever so slightly, his brows pulled together. "At chess, my dear," he said. "That was the purpose of my call. I have already been inside and paid my respects to the other two ladies. Miss Steeple does not object to my borrowing you for a while."

"I . . . see." What she saw was that Cousin Libby had not given up her attempt at matchmaking. That was nonsensical, of course, but, discarding that, there was a real allure to the offer.

She knew she ought to refuse, but having long cherished an aversion to cutting off her nose to spite her face, she hesitated. To be wholly honest, there was nothing she would enjoy more than to pit her skills against Laverstoke once more, but that battled her decision to avoid the man.

"Well." Tina moistened her lips. "I hope you did not tell them of . . . that other game. I fear poor Libby would be shocked."

"No." Again, that undercurrent of mockery. "I am rather more discreet than that, my dear."

Wondering if he considered a liaison with an opera dancer "discreet," Tina tried to match his mockery. "And Cousin Libby voiced no qualms?"

"Let us say," he said smoothly, "that she trusts me implicitly with your welfare."

She widened her eyes in challenge of his statement. "And you can promise that my being alone with you will in no way compromise my reputation?"

"If it did, I would be forced to offer for you, wouldn't I?" This time the mockery was more pronounced. "Rest assured that I would not so easily be snared. It has been tried," he added.

"I see." Very much provoked, she tried to brush past him, but his arm shot out to bar her way.

"Don't be angry, Valentina. I merely stated fact."

"Indeed? And if the fact implies an insult, must it still be stated? I thought you were a diplomat."

"Diplomacy is an art I reserve for those occasions I require it. I speak to you as a man, Valentina, not as a diplomat." His gloved hand went out to settle on her shoulder. "Come, it is too cold to stand about. Will you accept my invitation or not?" His tone intimated that he would not ask again.

As she glared up at him, she could feel her objections evaporating. Anticipation churned in her stomach, the urge to put herself in opposition to this man so strong that it cast aside every other consideration.

For the moment, she knew she would yield—or at least she'd allow him to think so.

Their sleigh ride was surprisingly harmonious, largely because Laverstoke skillfully steered the conversation to light, unexceptionable topics. More than once, Tina found herself laughing at his dry remarks; despite the wind, she was warmer than she'd any right to be.

When they arrived back at Laverstoke Park, Tina's cheeks were pink, and her hair, a mass of tangles. Annie, the maid who had served her before, assisted in the resurrection of her hair, so that when she descended to the library she was able to pass the handsome gilt mirror at the foot of the staircase without actually cringing.

Laverstoke stood with his back to the fire, looking unperturbed and elegant. Tina felt herself blush as his eyes went over her with approval.

"Allow me to commend you," he remarked. "It's a rare female who can make herself presentable in ten minutes. Would you care for some sherry?"

Tina took a breath, then tossed discretion to the four winds. "Yes, thank you." She sat down in one of the chairs facing the chess table, watching as he poured.

"Tell me," she said suddenly. "Is there really a broken string?"

He glanced up, his face blank. "A broken string?"

"On the harp in the music room."

His mouth slowly lifted in a smile that transformed his face. "You've caught me, I confess. How did you know?" He walked over and handed her the goblet, then took the opposite chair.

Ignoring the queer butterfly flutter in her stomach, Tina shrugged and set it down. "Everything in this place seems so well maintained. I thought you must have been shamming it."

"And you don't approve?" Laverstoke's look turned quizzical.

"I don't approve of lying, if that's what you mean."

"I prefer to call it prevarication." His fingers tapped the table in a light rhythm. "Why? Did you wish to hear Lady Millicent perform?"

"You are missing the point," she said impatiently. "If I could see through your sham, then very likely Lady Millicent could also. You might have injured her feelings."

"I doubt Lady Millie's feelings are so tender," he retorted. "You much mistake the matter if you think that poor girl wished to be put on exhibition. She's as shy as bedamned, in case you hadn't noticed."

"Of course I noticed. And making her think you don't wish to hear her play is scarcely the way to set her at ease."

Lord Laverstoke allowed several seconds to slide by before he answered, very gently, "Once again, my dear, you are operating under false assumptions. Acquaint yourself with the facts, then if you still wish to berate me you may do so with my goodwill."

Reminded of her sharp condemnation of his ousting of Libby, Tina's color deepened to a rich hue. "I should apologize," she began stiffly.

"Don't." His eyes were glittering and indecipherable as water. "Apologies bore me."

Struggling with her rising temper, Tina wondered whether he was purposely goading her to lose it. "Very well, then," she snapped. "I certainly don't wish to bore you."

"Oh, I don't think there's any danger of that. I would not have invited you otherwise."

"No doubt I would be flattered if I thought you did not say that to every female who crossed your path." Thinking herself clever, she waited triumphantly for him to show some sign of discomfiture, but instead he leaned forward, his response blunt and deliberate.

"In fact, you are the first recipient of that particular tribute, but that is neither here nor there. What is more to the point is this: you are determined to dislike me, and it's not because I pretended to be James. Nor do I believe it's because I kissed you, though in that I may be wrong. So I beg you will enlighten me. What is it about me that puts you so out of humor?"

Tina stopped breathing. It was the moment she had been waiting for, the instant she could hurl his past negligence in his teeth. And she found she could not do it. It was as though a blockade were set up between her mind and tongue; she could not form the words, nor gather any of those much-rehearsed phrases that would accurately convey the heartache she had experienced.

Instead, she forced a smile. "You are imagining things, my lord."

"Am I? How odd. I am not a fanciful man."

"I thought we were going to play chess," she said uncomfortably.

He gave her a long, hard look. "Yes, we are. But I wish you'd come clean with me first."

"There is nothing to say," she said desperately.

"Is it something you read in the newspapers?"

She searched for an answer that would put him off. "The papers did nothing but sing your praises, my lord. You are one of our national heroes."

He dismissed her comment with an impatient gesture.

116

"My part was minor. The true heroes are the men who fought and died—or lived, according to the will of God." Reaching for his glass, he lifted his sherry to his lips.

As he drank, Tina studied his face. Its individual features were hardly perfect, yet the sum total—the chiseled nose, the firm chin, the startling, golden hair, the deepset gray eyes surmounted by the dark, heavy brows—added together it was a potent, very masculine combination. And underneath it all, like a powerful current, ran a streak of confidence, perhaps unconscious but nevertheless there, manifest in the set of his broad shoulders, in his body movements, in his bearing and speech. It ought to have set up her back, but, curiously, it had the opposite effect.

He was exciting. In his presence, she felt more alive than she had in years, more attuned to every sight and sound and smell within her sphere. She was absurdly aware of the light clink of his goblet as he set it down, of the fire in the hearth and the wind in the chimney, of beeswax and lemon oil on gleaming mahogany, of the shimmering sherry within her glass and the kid leather of a host of books with titles stamped in gold and silver. She was aware, too, of the man, of the dark blue of his coat and of the hard muscles underneath. All this and more flowed into her consciousness, like rain replenishing a well gone dry.

Fearing he'd guess the reason for her silence, she said quickly, "I'm sure you must have done something worthwhile. You could not possibly have spent all your time—" She broke off with an involuntary gasp at what she'd nearly said.

He cocked an eyebrow. "Wenching?" he inquired. Watching her face, he said mockingly, "My dear Valentina, is *that* why you've been looking so stern? Can it be that you've heard of my association with a notorious young opera dancer calling herself . . . Delilah?"

Flustered, she began, "Well, I never actually heard her name—" before realizing that once again she had betrayed herself.

"Ah." His mouth twisted ruefully. "That was during the

117

spring of 'Fourteen, my dear, just prior to the Allied Sovereigns' visit to London."

Tina said nothing.

He stared past her into the shadows. "Politically speaking, I chose a dashed awkward time to make her acquaintance," he admitted. "Castlereagh raked me over the coals for it, too, when it mushroomed into the latest and juiciest *on-dit*. Ordinarily something like that doesn't get into the papers, but the Whig Opposition set an obnoxious young newspaperman on my tail. His stories were highly inventive, but close enough to the truth to do damage."

Some devil prompted her to ask, casually, "Wasn't that the year of your sister's marriage?"

"Aye, and the scandal didn't do Allegra any good either." There was deep regret in his voice, along with a thread of weariness. "Let's play chess, Valentina. I should not be discussing such things with you. It is wrong."

Gerard watched her as she studied the board, so intent upon the game she seemed oblivious to his regard. Tiny tendrils of hair curled round her face; one, at her brow, kept falling over her eye. Her eyebrows were pulled together with the intensity of her concentration, twin black wings topping beautiful eyes hidden by long, sooty lashes. He realized that with each exposure to those smoky blue eyes he was becoming more and more attracted to her—as well as more intrigued.

Was his short-lived, well-publicized liaison with the infamous Delilah the true reason for her hostility? He frowned slightly, his eyes riveted on her full lower lip. Any woman who kissed like she did ought not to be so prudish in her opinions. After all, he had behaved so well afterward that Castlereagh had permitted him to attend the Congress of Vienna. Then the newspapers had been only too glad to sing his praises.

In the subsequent years he had served England well, and having more or less retired from the diplomatic corps, was now entitled to enjoy the life of a wealthy, titled gentleman who conducted his *amours* with discretion. The only trouble was, he was not really happy with his life.

No, he thought suddenly. His instincts told him there was something else, something more complicated troubling Tina than mere puritanical condemnation of his love affair with Delilah. And he'd relied on his instincts enough times to know that they were seldom wrong.

What could it be, then? As he sat, cudgeling his brain, he saw her hand drift out to touch her queen.

"Check." She looked up at him exultantly, her blue eyes glowing.

He had to admit that she played very well. She had the capacity and the guile to beat him at this game, and he discovered that the knowledge delighted him.

"Very good," he praised. "I must ponder this carefully."

He did not ponder it long, however, for there were only two moves he could make. The strategy he chose was to interpose his rook in the path of her queen, cutting off the threat, while at the same time exposing to danger a lowly pawn he knew she was saving for something special.

"Oh, Laverstoke," she said in frustration, "why could you not move your king? Nine out of ten people would have done so!"

"Because I did not wish to," he replied imperturbably. "Do you desire to win on your own, or is it your preference that I play badly apurpose?"

"Of course I do not want you to *let* me win," she said indignantly. "What would be the pleasure in that?"

"That's what I thought," he replied. "Pray note, then, that I have enough respect for you as an opponent to do my damnedest to outwit you."

"Oh," she said, blinking at him. Then, gruffly, "Well, thank you for that, at least."

"I suspect you've lacked recent practice," he went on. "When was the last time you played?"

"Not since . . . since before Father died, in August of 'Fourteen."

"Nearly five years," he said gently. "Enough time for anyone to grow a trifle rusty." He cleared his throat, and added, encouragingly, "A few more games and you'll be quite up to snuff."

"A few more—!" she sputtered, her eyes so full of wrath that he could not repress a smile. "I've practically beaten you now, in case you've not noticed."

"Are you so sure?" he teased.

He watched her survey the board anxiously, thinking that he wished she would win, for it would please her so much. And it came to him then that, above all, he wanted to please her more than any woman he had ever known. And that was why he would do her the courtesy of playing to win.

The game resumed with increased vigor. Valentina was determined to lock horns with him, and he fought back with all his skill.

Another hour passed before it was over. She had fought valiantly, but her last attack was just a trifle too bold. She knew it, and he knew it, too.

"I'm sorry," he said sincerely, hoping she was not too disappointed.

"Don't apologize," she replied. Then she smiled, and surprised him by saying, "Apologies bore me."

"Do they, now." He smiled. "I'd have thought you'd love to see me on my knees."

As her smile widened, he noticed her dimples for the first time. "Defeating you would satisfy me far more," she said demurely.

His emotions swirling, Gerard gazed deep into her eyes. "I'll be happy to give you the opportunity, Valentina. My Valentine's Day girl," he added, for no reason at all.

He was stunned to see her smile vanish, replaced with an expression that was almost antagonistic. It was as though, he thought in confusion, the past few hours had never been, and their relationship had reverted to exactly what it had been at their moment of meeting—whatever that had been.

120

"That reminds me, Lord Laverstoke," she said coolly. "I quite forgot to mention it, but I have no intention of attending your ball. I think it would be much more appropriate if you held it on the fifteenth of the month."

"Why?"

"Because"—she faltered, as though she had not anticipated the question—"because it implies something neither of us wishes to imply. People will talk."

"Let them," he retorted. "I think Valentine's Day is a perfect day for a ball. It's . . . romantic."

If he had made her an improper proposal she could not have looked more disdainful. "Well, do what you will, then. But I shall not be attending. I'm not looking for romance, Lord Laverstoke. Especially from you."

Eight

Lord Laverstoke's expression altered. It was almost imperceptible and yet it was there, this change, chilling Tina as effectively as if he had flung her face-first into the snow.

Especially from you.

The cutting words hovered in the air like an echo, sounding more and more intolerable with every passing moment.

"Shall I take you back now?" His low, toneless voice was like a door slamming shut in her face. Without waiting for an answer, he rose to his feet and stood looking down at her, tall and still and utterly controlled, his gray eyes unwavering and cool.

Tina looked up at him unhappily. "Laverstoke," she began, "I . . . know that sounded beastly . . ." She bit her lip.

Good gracious, why should she care how it sounded? The last thing she should do is apologize to this man, of all people. Particularly since apologies bored him.

"Yes, I'm sure you did," he responded with a slight, ironic bow. "At the risk of boring you, Miss Jardine, pray allow me to apologize for whatever I have done to so offend you. Perhaps someday you will be inclined to tell me what it was."

She looked down, unable to bear his stark, wintry look. Surely she should be pleased to get back a bit of her own at this man. But where defeating him at chess would have ranked as a victory, wounding him with words only made her feel cheap and small, like something nasty that had crawled out from under the carpet.

She stood. "Yes, I suppose I should go." Her voice was constrained. "Libby will be wondering why I have been so long."

Yet when she turned toward the door, he spoke once more, still distantly, without any noticeable inflection. "There is something else. I almost forgot."

When she looked back, he was holding a small book in his hand. "I meant to ask if you would like to borrow this again." His patrician features were set with disinterest. "I may be wrong, but I had the impression that you returned it before you were through."

Tearing her gaze from his, she saw that it was the book of Shakespeare's sonnets. How could she reject what was so obviously a peace offering?

She moistened her lips. "You . . . do not mind?"

"Not in the least." He shrugged and held it out. "I've another copy if I've a mind to read poetry. Actually, this one was my mother's."

After a moment's hesitation, she accepted it. "Well, I suppose . . . if you are really quite certain."

"I do not object, nor would my mother have done so." He added, obscurely, "She had talents, too."

"Talents?" Tina repeated uncertainly.

"Miss Winton said you could draw."

"All young ladies can draw, my lord. It is one of the essential polite accomplishments."

"Essential for what?" he returned, walking past her toward the door. He opened it and stood waiting, a sardonic look on his face. "Snaring a husband?"

Involuntarily, Tina's eyes squeezed shut, his words like a needle pricking a wound that had never quite healed. When she opened them an instant later, she saw that he was frowning.

"Yes, if that is what one desires," she said unsteadily.

Suddenly there was moisture in her eyes; she almost stumbled in her haste to move past him and out the door. Vaguely, she knew that his hand reached out, but she evaded it, leaving him to follow behind her as he willed.

The ride back was replete with silence; the moment the sleigh drew to a halt, Tina propelled herself out as though to sit for an instant longer would cause her physical pain. She walked several paces toward the door before she dared to turn around. "I . . . I suppose I should thank you," she began.

She flinched from the aloofness in his gaze. "Don't mention it," he said tonelessly. To her surprise, he added, "When you're ready for a rematch, I'll oblige you."

Tina shoved a curl from her face. "I . . . I'm not sure we ought to . . . oh . . . goodbye!" And, spinning round, she fled like the coward she knew herself to be.

Once inside, she leaned against the door, breathing deeply, knowing she could not possibly let anyone see her in this state. Surely her agitation must be writ on her face. Yet Libby's housekeeper made no remark as she relieved her of her outer garments, and Tina merely told the woman she was going to her room.

Once there, she threw herself on the bed, her face buried in her hands. "Oh God," she said aloud. "What am I to do?"

In seeming answer, a loud, canine yawn emanated from the far side of the bed; Tina peered over to find a pair of liquid brown eyes gazing into hers. "Oh, Gretchen," she sighed. She rolled off the bed and sat on the floor, wrapping her arms about the dog's neck. "If only my life were as simple as yours."

Gretchen's long, pink tongue crept out to wash Tina's fingers.

124

"He's the one, you know," she whispered. "I've tried so hard to blame him and his wretched sister for what happened, but now that I've met him"—she gave a long, shuddering sigh—"I just don't know what to do." Her fingers stroked through the shaggy fur. "You don't understand, do you? You probably think I'm behaving like a twit."

Gretchen offered no opinion; her tongue shifted to Tina's face.

"And now I feel guilty for behaving as I did, which is simply not fair. Is it?" she asked, rubbing the area behind Gretchen's ears. "What a nice dog you are. I forgive you, you know, for upending us in the snow."

Gretchen panted softly, her malodorous breath fanning Tina's cheek.

Tina turned her head away. "And he gave me the book of poems back, which makes it even harder to dislike him. But what difference does it make when we are worlds apart? Honorable intentions are the furthest thing from his mind, even a twit like me can tell that. He diverts himself with me, that is all."

Obviously bored by confidences, Gretchen lay down and commenced washing unmentionable parts of her body.

Tina frowned. "A fine friend you are," she scolded. "The least you could do is listen to my problems."

Gretchen went on washing.

"Of course, it's not right to burden you with my troubles, when you clearly have more important matters to attend to," she said reproachfully.

The bathing continued, but the tail thumped, and Tina sighed again. "Is it wrong of me not to go to the ball? Perhaps that would only make things worse than they already are. And what difference does it make if he wants to call it a Valentine's Day ball? It's nothing to do with me, really. To make a fuss about it shows a want of good sense . . . I suppose."

With a last, satisfied lick, Gretchen raised her head and regarded Tina soulfully.

"You think I am right?" Tina said doubtfully. She gazed past Gretchen toward the window, but instead of clouds or sky she saw Gerard Marchant's face as it had been a short while before: cold and remote, an austere reflection of her own inner turmoil.

And what else could she expect?

Once more wrapping her arms around Gretchen, Tina buried her face in the dog's fur. It felt good to have another living thing to touch. It seemed so long, so very, very long since she had felt loved. Sometimes she did not know if she could live her life without it, or face the bleak emptiness that loomed ahead. As many times as she had pushed her needs aside, there were just as many occasions that she ached for something more, something that would make her life complete in a way that it had never been, nor was ever likely to be.

She was alone.

Perhaps it was the gentle rise and fall of Gretchen's ribs that brought this home with painful clarity. Her own family was gone, and the Wintons hardly treated her like one of their own. While addressing her as "cousin," they saw her more as an upper servant, even paid her a wage as a sop to her pride and their consciences. Not that she had ever minded that, she thought moodily. God only knew she needed the money. But what she yearned for more than anything was a family of her own. She wanted a husband, someone she could love and hug and touch, a kind, constant, caring man who would love and cherish her and give her children. Yet, other than Christian, she had never met a man she could envision in that role.

Until now.

Dear God, what was she thinking? Laverstoke felt nothing but lust for her, and after the way she had spoken to him this afternoon, very likely even that was obliterated. At any rate, setting aside the fact that he was

126

who he was, he hardly fit the description of the man she sought. Oh, she was willing to concede that he was not the effete libertine she had imagined, but he was sophisticated in a way that Christian had never been. Why, he'd probably seen and done things she could never even imagine; certainly he had met people far more interesting than herself. He had dealt with rogues and royals, princes and princelings and heads of state—even the Tsar of Russia. And he had known women, many women, all of them more witty and worldly than herself.

And yet, knowing this, the memory of his kiss still flooded her with trembling. That worried her. Of course, it *might* only be the artist in her craving sensory stimulation, but that was difficult to believe, particularly when her knees and heart and mind turned to jelly every time he smiled. Lackwitted girl. She had been going to fight this weakness, and she had not so much as drawn her sword.

Thoroughly exasperated with herself, Tina sat up and swiped at her tears. "Well, just look at me, Gretchen. Here I am crying over a man. I never cry, for pity's sake."

Gretchen, however, had been callous enough to go to sleep.

Tina stretched out on the bed and stared up at the ceiling with a heavy heart. At least, she consoled herself, she need not see him again for several days. Perhaps longer. But what was meant to be a solace felt more like a penance.

The penance was to prove short-lived, however, for an hour later Tina discovered that Libby had invited the viscount and his brother to dinner.

"I wouldn't normally do it," insisted the elderly woman rather self-consciously, "for he is such a busy man. Yes, indeed. But he seemed to have nothing better to do, and

I knew that Cook was planning one of her little specialties, so I just sort of *hinted* that they would be welcome and he accepted at once." She beamed happily. "I must say I'm surprised he did not mention it to you, Valentina."

Tina struggled to conceal the maelstrom of emotion in her breast. "I daresay he must have forgotten," was all she could manage, though that seemed unlikely. Laverstoke was not a man who forgot anything.

"Who won the chess game?" inquired Felicity, eying a plate of macaroons on the table beside her with relish.

Tina laced her fingers together in her lap to keep them from twitching. "He did," she answered. "He is an excellent player. He could probably have beaten Papa."

Libby was watching her intently. "Are you feeling well, my dear? You look a trifle pale."

"I am fine, Libby. A little tired, perhaps. I did not sleep well last night."

"Perhaps you should rest a while. There's at least an hour to fill before we must dress for dinner."

Libby sounded so worried that Tina forced a smile. "Oh, I'm not that weary. I'd rather stay here and be with you and Felicity. After all, I was gone for most of the afternoon." She searched her mind for some harmless topic. "Tell me more about Lady Millicent."

"Well, I scarcely know her, Valentina. Do not forget that until a year and a half ago I was only Lady Laverstoke's companion. Lady Buckden is not a woman who cares to mix with those below her station—"

"What do you mean? Your birth is every bit as good as hers!"

Libby smiled gently, with only a trace of bitterness. "Yes, but you see, the moment I became a companion, I stepped outside the charmed circle. To Lady Buckden, I daresay I have less worth than a piece of furniture."

"She was polite to you last night."

"Ah, but that was because Lord Laverstoke was

present." Libby's smile became affectionate. *"He* is unfailingly courteous to me, and she takes her lead from him. She dares not do otherwise, you see."

"No." Tina frowned slightly. "I don't see."

"Dear me. Lady Buckden wishes her daughter to become the Viscountess Laverstoke, and is willing to do almost anything to achieve it."

Tina's frown deepened. "So I gathered from her remarks last night. I thought her shockingly obvious."

Libby nodded. "But she is not the only one, you see. Laverstoke has always been a target for the matchmaking mamas, but since he has won such political acclaim, he has been more ruthlessly pursued than ever."

Suddenly, a number of things slid together in Tina's mind. "Good lord, do you think that he thought that *we—*" The idea was so insulting she could not go on.

Libby answered hesitantly. "Yes, unfortunately I think he did. I think that was the explanation for that naughty charade he and James played."

Tina stared down at her hands. The knowledge that he had sat there, judging them . . . it stung her to the quick. Doubtless he had heaped them in the same pile as the Lady Buckdens and Mrs. Wintons of the world, she thought wrathfully.

Aloud, she said, in clipped tones, "No doubt you are right. He is certainly arrogant enough to have made such unpleasant assumptions. I can hardly blame Lady Millicent for disliking him."

"Oh, I don't think Lady Millicent dislikes Lord Laverstoke," corrected Libby mildly. "He is kind to her, you know. The business of the broken string on the harp—I thought it quite resourceful of him." When Tina said nothing, the elderly lady went on with a sigh, "Anyone can see the poor lamb hates being put on display. When her mother takes her to London, I fear it will be that much worse."

"She seems to like James."

Libby's head shook gloomily. "Aye, she does that, but she'll never be allowed to have him. Second sons are not the matrimonial prizes their older brothers are. James Marchant's expectations are nothing remarkable—and remote. His mother's sister, Lady Sarah Fitzmartin, has pledged to leave him a goodly sum, but it qualifies as no more than an independence. And by all accounts, Lady Sarah is in excellent health. It may be years before James inherits anything."

Felicity had been nibbling macaroons and gazing abstractedly into the fire, but at this her head turned. "What a pity," she said. "He's such jolly good fun. And he must be very brave. All soldiers are, you know."

"Are they indeed?" said Tina tartly. "And how would you know that?"

"Well, it stands to reason." Felicity's pretty face grew animated. "In fact, I think he's quite the most amiable man I've ever met. I've half a mind to marry him instead of Lord Laverstoke." She picked up another macaroon and eyed it lovingly. "Mama would hate it if I married a soldier."

"And *ex*-soldier," Libby corrected. "James is now his brother's steward. I suspect that's another of Lady Buckden's objections."

"What a dreadful woman," remarked Tina with vehemence. "I would think she would find it admirable. I certainly do. There are so many less worthwhile things he could be doing."

"Such as?" asked Felicity innocently.

Tina and Libby exchanged a look. "Never mind," said Tina. "And do stop eating, Felicity. You will grow too fat for your gowns."

The first to enter the drawing room that evening, Tina paced around nervously, the skirt of her rose-colored gown swishing as she moved. It was the same gown she

130

had worn the previous evening, but the deficiency in her wardrobe was not something she could easily correct. And anyway, she thought with a toss of her head, she was certainly not going to pretend to be something she was not, as Lord Laverstoke had done.

While dressing for dinner, she'd had plenty of time to ponder her latest discovery regarding the motives for his deception. And while it rankled that he'd made assumptions about them, she could scarcely blame him too severely when in truth Felicity *had* been sent for the express purpose of catching his masculine eye. So in a way he had been perfectly correct, and that being so, she should not mind what he had thought.

But, illogically, it bothered her that for *any* length of time he had believed that she, Valentina Elizabeth Jardine, was party to such a low-bred scheme. And she *had* been a participant, albeit an unwilling one; even now she could hear Mrs. Winton's imperious voice dictating lofty instructions: *"I expect you, Valentina, to do all you can to aid my daughter in attracting Lord Laverstoke's notice. Try to create situations where she may meet him, then be as unobtrusive as possible. If he seems disposed to admire her, a little time alone will not come amiss."*

Tina's teeth clenched. She did not care what Mrs. Winton wished; she would rather die than do anything so obvious, so calculated, so vulgarly common. As far as she was concerned, If Laverstoke wished to make Felicity the object of his gallantry (which she strongly doubted) he could jolly well do the work for himself.

She was still mulling this over when the guests were announced. Unfortunately, she was also still alone, but thanks to James, any awkwardness attached to the circumstance was instantly overcome.

"Good evening, Cousin Tina," he said, smiling roguishly. "You are looking very fetching this evening. I like what you've done to your hair." As he bowed over her hand, he glanced over at the sofa-table with a twinkle. "Only two macaroons? I can see what Miss Felicity has been doing."

Tina was uncomfortably aware of Laverstoke's eyes traveling over her with far more thoroughness than was necessary. "Feel free to have one, if you like. Libby and Felicity should be down at any moment." Then she blushed, realizing she was getting things backward. "Please sit down," she added quickly.

Choosing a chair, James popped a macaroon into his mouth. "I hear you took Gerry on at his best game. I was hoping you'd win, you know. I've never beaten him myself."

"What, never?" Tina was unable to conceal her astonishment.

James smiled. "Oh, I'm not a very good player. I've no patience, y'see. Gerry's the one with all the guile. I just trip through life by whim and fancy, never looking ahead to see where I'm going—"

"—and so you frequently trip and fall," finished Laverstoke, speaking for the first time. "That is a disadvantage, you must admit."

"On the contrary," countered his brother. "My way is a great deal more diverting than yours. I never look ahead, so life is continually a surprise."

Tina smiled at him. "I think that's a fine way to be," she said. Some devil prompted her to add, "And despite what you say, Lord Laverstoke, I think you are sometimes a little more rash than you admit."

"Indeed?" Though the viscount's voice was tranquil, Tina sensed he was disconcerted. "What makes you say that?"

At this juncture, Felicity and Libby entered the room, thus relieving her of the necessity of answering. For once, she was actually grateful to Felicity for her babbling, though within five minutes her sentiments on that theme would alter.

It soon became plain that her young cousin, having

132

been unable to decide which brother she wished to set her cap for, had (by way of a compromise) settled upon them both. Indeed, Felicity divided herself between the two men with the dexterity of an accomplished flirt, leading Tina to speculate upon just where and how she had acquired such skills. Perhaps, Tina reflected, such talents simply came naturally to those who were born with genuine beauty.

If so, they apparently grew stronger with practice. At one point during dinner James began teasing Felicity about the rigors of making one's bow to Society, whereupon Felicity fluttered her lashes and responded, "La, but sir, it is my *duty* to go. Mama is depending upon me to make a splendid match, for I must find husbands for my three sisters. But I am fortunate. My uncle is to pay the expense of my Season, though"—she sighed faintly— "a court dress is naturally out of the question. But I don't care for that, really, for I find the idea of wearing hoops with a high-waisted gown quite absurd. And all those plumes! I should look such a quiz . . ."

For some time Tina had sensed that Lord Laverstoke was growing bored, and as she studied his lean, hard face she grew convinced of it. Boredom. It was there in the set of his mouth and the expression of his eyes as they rested on Felicity.

Tina watched his face as Felicity chirped, ". . . and I would much rather be presented at Almack's anyway. Mama cherishes high hopes of procuring vouchers for me. She says our connection to you, my lord"—her melting gaze settled on the viscount—"must weigh heavily in my favor."

"I am happy to be of service," said Laverstoke with an irony that made Tina wince.

"And once I am seen in Almack's, Mama says my future is quite assured . . ." While Felicity chattered on, Tina squirmed with embarrassment, acutely conscious of every subtle change in Lord Laverstoke's expression.

At last she could no longer keep silent. "Felicity, for heaven's sake!" she broke in.

Everyone looked at her, and Laverstoke arched a brow. For the first time since he'd arrived a hint of amusement entered his eye.

Mercifully, the meal was at an end so that Libby was able to lead the way into the drawing room without it seeming too abrupt. The gentleman, refusing an offer of port, chose to follow them at once, making it impossible for Tina to issue a warning to Felicity. For a few moments there was awkwardness, as though no one knew what topic of conversation to introduce. It was left to Libby to break the silence. "Are you to stay at Laverstoke Park for long, my lord?"

"That is something I have yet to decide, Miss Steeple. It . . . depends." On what it depended no one ventured to ask.

In the short pause that followed, Felicity said, "Well, it must certainly be for at least a few weeks, must it not? After all, there is the ball to plan." She looked to James for support. " 'Twill be ever so exciting! How many people shall you invite?"

James winked at her. "Oh, hundreds!" he teased. "Perhaps thousands!"

"And the ballroom will be decorated in red and white," Felicity went on dreamily. "And I shall wear pink and receive ever so many valentines."

"Actually," said a cool voice, "I've been reconsidering the idea. Upon reflection, I find the notion of a Valentine's Day ball rather . . . outlandish."

If the viscount had hurled his drink across the room no one could have been more astonished.

"Outlandish!" repeated James, staring at his brother. "I should rather say it was a bang-up idea. What the dev — I mean, what's amiss with it?"

When Laverstoke said nothing, Felicity's eyes filled with tears. "Yes, my lord, why? Is it because of Tina?"

134

Libby looked hesitantly from one girl to the other. "Why, what can you mean, my dear? What can Valentina have to do with his lordship's decision?"

The tear drifted down Felicity's cheek. "Tina says she will not go."

"Not go!" echoed James. "Cousin Tina, why?"

Once more all eyes went to Tina, but only Laverstoke's were hard and mocking.

"I . . . I thought it should be for the younger girls," Tina said feebly. When Laverstoke's gaze challenged her, she raised her chin and added, "I hope you will not abandon your plans because of me, Lord Laverstoke."

"I don't have to," he said gently, "and I won't . . . if you will agree to come."

It was blackmail, pure and simple.

Lips compressed, Tina searched her mind for some way to put him in his place, while at the same time couching the set-down in such veiled terms that its true meaning would be camouflaged from the others. Regretfully, she came to the conclusion that this was not possible.

"Well, if that's the way you feel about it," she mumbled. Her clenched hands were the only outward evidence of her wrath.

"Splendid," he said with a gleam. "We shall look forward to your presence then."

Felicity dabbed at her eyes and sniffed. "You mean we can have the ball, after all?"

"Yes," Laverstoke told her in such a kind voice that Tina ground her teeth. "A Valentine's Day ball, just as we planned."

"Oh, *thank* you!" For a moment Felicity was all smiles, then once more her face grew anxious. "Oh, but I have just had a thought, Cousin Laverstoke. You have no hostess, do you?"

His elbows on the arms of his chair, Laverstoke steepled his fingers and smiled. "On the contrary, my sister will be delighted to undertake that role. Allegra thrives on just such exertion."

Though she heard the words, it took Tina several seconds to assimilate their meaning. *Allegra would come,* she thought numbly. *Allegra, Lady Rewe. And Allegra, Lady Rewe, would bring Christian, Lord Rewe. Christian would come.*

Sick dread clutched at her heart. She would have to face Christian.

Nine

For the rest of the evening Tina yearned for the privacy to unburden her soul of its strickened emotions, yet when at last she was alone, the tears would not come. Confused, she sat up and stared over at the carved oak wardrobe, focusing on memories of Christian.

She could still remember his face, couldn't she?

Of course she could! How many times had she pictured him, smiling at her, laughing at something she'd said? She could never, ever forget Christian! It was impossible.

So why was his face such a blur in her mind?

Alarmed, Tina leaped up, impatient to reach her sketchbook where every detail of Christian's face was recorded with loving accuracy. Carrying it over to the bed, she flipped it open and immediately found views of every angle of his beloved countenance. Relief and memory surged together as one.

"Oh, Christian," she murmured. "How could I forget, even for an instant?"

Turning a page, she touched a finger to her favorite sketch, a detailed portrait for which Christian had sat and posed. The boyish, handsome face on the page smiled up at her, quickening the ache in her chest.

How clearly she could recall the day she had made this.

Unable to bear the memory, she began turning pages. Amid other drawings of Christian, her parents and various friends and neighbors had been painstakingly reproduced.

137

She lingered briefly over her parents, but that caused such a wrench of pain that she was forced to go on, turning quickly past her drawings of the Winton family on the way to the page where her sketch of Lord Laverstoke awaited.

Naturally, she had not forgotten *his* face; she doubted it would ever be possible to erase such striking features from her memory. As she studied the drawing, she puzzled over his behavior this evening. His method of forcing her hand coincided with her vision of him as an unscrupulous manipulator, and yet somehow she could not be insulted. In fact, she was rather gratified that he should care whether or not she attended his ball. For a moment, Tina allowed herself to toy with the fancy that he was not, after all, indifferent to her; that he wished her to go because he enjoyed her company.

Then her mouth hardened. What a simpleton she was. Laverstoke was no callow youth to be impressed by her unspectacular beauty or unremarkable wit. Without a doubt he had some hidden purpose in mind, just as he did when he played chess. But life was not a game of chess, she thought angrily. And she was certainly no pawn.

Still, as she considered exactly what his ulterior goal might be, a tremor fluttered in the pit of her stomach. Was it all an elaborate prelude to an intended seduction? She believed him capable of it, but was perplexed as to the reason. Why should a man like that trouble himself so? Didn't he have some opera dancers tucked away somewhere?

Then at last she did what she had intended to do all along—she flipped back to the picture of Christian and held the intervening pages aloft so that she could view both men at once. As the impact of the two faces hit her, she swallowed hard. Amazing how different they were, and more amazing still how what she knew of their characters showed in their expressions. Christian looked so sweet and pliable, Laverstoke, so strong and sensual and ruthless. Such a contrast. How curious, too, that Christian, with his dark hair, should be a creature of impulse and light, while Laverstoke, with his locks of burnished gold, should offer darkness and mystery. There was nothing to link them together, no basis for commonality. Nothing except . . . herself. Abruptly, Tina slammed shut her book of memories.

Damn them both.

Was this what hopeless spinsters did? Sit and stare and dream of the men who touched their lives, destined never to know or feel what it was like to actually *have* those men? Agony pierced her breast. Right now, she hated herself, she hated Christian, and most of all, she hated Lord Laverstoke.

Well, she would go to his precious ball, and she would meet Christian, if that was what Fate decreed. But she would never allow them to guess how much it cost her.

Never.

"Faith, Gerry, I don't know what's come over you. One moment you're ready to cancel the ball because Tina"— James shot his brother a sideways look—"refuses to attend, and the next, you behave as though she has the black plague. It's been three days now, and you haven't called on them once."

Nudging his stallion to a trot, Gerard pondered his brother's words. "I'm not avoiding her," he lied. "I simply have other things to do." He allowed his gaze to wander over the surrounding landscape, wishing he could capture some of its tranquility for himself. Unfortunately, the emotion eluded him, as it had done since the day he had met Tina Jardine.

James's frosty breath whooshed out. "I think you're afraid to face her. What other reason could the blackmailer have for avoiding his victim?"

"I wasn't blackmailing her."

"Weren't you?" Gerard heard the grin in his brother's voice. "It sounded like it to me. You're intrigued by her, aren't you?"

Gerard shrugged. "I suppose that's as good a word as any."

"So why avoid her, you great fool? Go over there and charm her! You're well able to do it, by all accounts."

"You very much mistake the matter if you think she would welcome my attentions. Tina dislikes me, Jay. And I'm damned if I know why."

"She looks at you often enough."

"Oh, she's attracted to me," Gerard answered coolly. "But lust is transient, you know, and arbitrary in its choice. I don't think it means anything."

"But why should she dislike you?" demanded James. "Do you think its because of that ridiculous deception?"

"I've no idea." Gerard drew in the sharp, cold air in an effort to dispel his nagging headache. "At any rate, she cannot become my mistress and I've no fancy to take a wife. So that is an end to the matter."

Gerard was by no means as sure as he sounded, but he was not about to confide that the memory of Valentina's lips haunted his dreams. And he was certainly not going to confess that erotic fantasies of the lady surged through his head day and night, or that his present surliness was a direct result of this self-inflicted torture. Nor was he going to explain that this was why he had decided not to see her again—until he had himself on a tighter rein.

But because James was grinning at him in such an imbecilic fashion, he felt obligated to offer a part of the truth. "It's merely that I'd like to solve the mystery of her dislike," he said shortly.

James thought this over. "Mayhap it's only disapproval," he suggested. "What if she's heard about Delilah?"

Gerard's head shook. "No, I mentioned that to her, and her reaction wasn't what I expected. It may be a part of it, but it's not the whole explanation." He wasn't completely certain of that either, but again he didn't admit it. Force of habit made him play every hand close to his chest.

" 'Pon my honor, Gerry, what will you tell me next!"

"I've written to Allegra."

The laughter faded from his brother's eyes. "And?"

"And I await her response. I doubt I shall be refused,

but with our sister, one can never tell. She's surprised me in the past."

"Yes." The syllable was abrupt. "That husband of hers—" James stopped. "Well, I suppose it's worked out. When all is said and done, Rewe's an amiable enough fellow."

"When all is said and done," repeated Gerard. "An apt phrase, that."

"The child is the image of him."

"Fortunately." Gerard's voice was ironic.

"He's faithful to her, isn't he?"

Gerard shrugged. "More or less. A little less than more, perhaps. I thought his attentions to the three young ladies last December a trifle too assiduous, particularly the brainless Miss Rudgwick. However, Allegra made her bed."

"Yes," agreed James, a little sadly.

Gerard's lips compressed. He didn't want to think about his sister's marriage, or about that worthless fribble she called a husband.

James reached over and cuffed him on the arm. "Don't worry, Gerry. Allegra will hostess our ball and Rewe will behave himself. If he flirts with anyone at all, it will be Felicity Winton." He shifted in his saddle. "Damn leg," he muttered.

"Do you want to go back?"

"No. What I want is to have a few words with Millie."

"I think we could arrange that." Gerard paused, thinking rapidly. "Tell me, do you think you could do something for me in return?"

James shot him a keen look. "Of course. You need only ask."

"I need you to lay a little ground work that will serve both our ends." There, *that* sounded like he knew what he was doing, he thought sardonically. It was another habit he'd picked up during his service under Castlereagh—always pretend you know more than others do.

"Ah." James's eyes gleamed. "A mission."

"It occurs to me that if the ball is to be held in honor of

three ladies, they all ought to be residing under our roof for the duration of the house party."

"We're having a house party, too?" James looked startled.

"Allegra will wish to," Gerard explained calmly. "And I believe Lady Buckden will be agreeable if I make the suggestion." He paused meaningfully. "The other ladies may be more difficult to persuade."

"You mean Tina."

"Precisely. Do you think you can do it?"

James's grin was a little twisted. "I think so. I've learned something of your techniques these past years."

"Indeed?" Gerard's brows rose.

"Of course. I don't pretend it's easy, but if necessary, I am as capable of manipulating people as you are."

"Manipulating?" Distaste flickered across Gerard's face. "An ugly word. I prefer to call it influencing. Or guiding, if you will. Don't mistake, Jay. I have no interest in coercion. I simply desire an opportunity to . . . to learn more about Tina." He made the admission with a faint flush that he hoped the sharpness of the wind concealed.

James's smile returned. "Good God, don't think I am judging you! Don't forget I know your virtues better than anyone."

"I'm afraid my virtues are fewer in number than you would have them."

"And more numerous than you would have them," retorted his brother. "At any rate, I like your idea. With Millie installed at Laverstoke Park, perhaps . . . oh, hell, I don't suppose it will make any difference. Her mother will guard her every bloody instant."

"Oh," said Gerard grimly, "I imagine we can deal with that."

Gerard's failure to call at the Dower House would not have occasioned much remark had not his brother visited so frequently. However, only Felicity made any comment;

Libby was too tactful to mention it and Tina pretended not to notice or care.

Instead, Tina made every effort to content herself with activities she normally would have delighted in pursuing. Yet, somehow, they did not seem to be enough. Nothing was enough to stifle her growing restlessness.

To make matters more difficult, Felicity was becoming bored, which meant that she was more trying than usual. Now that the novelty of being away from home had worn off, her pretty young cousin was beginning to miss her sisters and the various beaux who had constantly found an excuse to call at the Winton manor, rain or shine. And so, while Libby dozed in her chair, Felicity sat and poured her woes into Tina's long-suffering ear.

"Of course, I adore Cousin James," she moaned, "but when he visits he stays for no more than an hour, and beyond that, what is one to do with the rest of the day? I read a book, as you suggested, but too much reading makes my head ache. And I hate embroidery, and there is no pianoforte, and I am no good at cards and—"

"Let's go for a walk." Tina reached down and scratched the furry head that rose hopefully. "You've done nothing but sit in that chair all day. The exercise will do you good," she added firmly.

Felicity shivered. "But it is so cold! And you know what Mama says about the wind and one's complexion."

"Haven't you noticed that the sun is shining? I think winter is beginning to lose its grip. Surely that dripping we hear is the sound of melting snow."

Felicity tilted her head, listening intently. "Why I think you are right." Rising, she hurried to the window, her pretty features animated. "I hope it stays like this for the ball. How dreadful it would be if it snowed like it did the day we left home." For several seconds she stared out, then heaved a great, melancholy sigh. "I wonder what Eugene is doing."

"You do care about him, don't you?"

Felicity turned around. "No!" Then, "Yes—no—oh,

what am I saying? I used to care for him a great deal until he took that silly position in the Home Office."

"Perhaps if you wrote to him, he might be able to attend Lord Laverstoke's ball. I am sure we could procure an invitation if you wished it."

Felicity arched delicate brows. "Don't you think James would view Eugene as a rival?" She sounded rather pleased by such a notion. Then her expression went glum. "But I am not permitted to write to him. Mama says it is not proper."

Tina hesitated, knowing it was her duty to enforce Mrs. Winton's strictures. Finally she said, "I suppose I could write to him in your stead, if you liked."

Felicity's eyes grew large. "Would you? Would you truly do that for me? Oh, Tina, you are so very good! I am sorry for every mean thing I ever said to you! You are not at all stuffy after all!"

"Why, thank you," Tina said dryly.

Felicity looked at her curiously. "I always think of you as being old, but you are not, are you? You are only five years older than me. And how romantic to be born on Valentine's Day! I wish I had been born a day sooner. Then we might have shared a birthday."

"Instead you share one with Lady Millicent."

Felicity sniffed. "The poor girl is dreadfully insipid. How her mother expects her to attract Lord Laverstoke is beyond my comprehension."

Tina ignored the latter statement. "Lady Millicent is merely shy, Felicity. Not insipid."

"Lord Laverstoke thinks she is," argued Felicity. "I'm surprised Lady Buckden does not see it." She reached down to scratch Gretchen's ear. "I wonder why he has remained unwed for so long? He seems quite old to me."

"Many men do not marry until they are older," Tina pointed out. "And three-and-thirty is not old."

"Eugene is four-and-twenty." Felicity counted on her fingers. "And when he is three-and-thirty, I shall be . . . oh, dear heaven, I will be six-and-twenty!" Tears of self-pity

144

welled her eyes. "I will be older than you!" she added mournfully.

"A terrible fate indeed," responded Tina with irony. "Come on, Felicity. Let's go for a walk."

"Oh, very well," agreed her cousin with a sigh.

They had scarcely set foot outside the door, however, when James rode up on a large bay gelding. At once, he gallantly swept off his hat.

"I see I'm too late. I had hoped to call earlier, but some estate business prevented me. Miss Steeple may have told you that I am my brother's steward."

Tina could only marvel that he stated it so cheerfully. Here was a man who was not corrupted by bitterness, a man who took what life offered without railing against fate. Laverstoke had everything and James had nothing, and yet he smiled. It ought to be a lesson to her, Tina reflected.

"We're going for a walk," Felicity informed him happily. "Won't you join us?"

James agreed, and they waited while Cook's husband was summoned to take the gelding round to the stables. That accomplished, their handsome cousin offered his arm to each girl. "I am fortunate," he remarked, "to have you both to myself, but I hope you are wearing stout boots. The snow is turning to slush."

Felicity laughed with delight. "Soon it will be spring," she cried. "How I love the flowers and sunshine."

For a while James and Felicity talked some nonsense, while Tina strolled along, listening with only half an ear. Then her attention was caught by the words: "—so the best thing is for all three of you to remove to Laverstoke Park."

"Oh, we shall," promised Felicity in rapturous accents.

"There will be planned activities," he explained. "I don't know exactly what yet, but I am persuaded you will not wish to miss them—"

Tina's head turned. "I beg your pardon?"

James met her eyes. "You were not attending? I was saying that there is to be a house party. And since you and Felicity are to be guests of honor—"

"Yes, I heard that. But I don't see any reason why we must stay anywhere but at the Dower House."

"Oh, but Tina, Lady Millicent will be there," cried Felicity, "and it will look most singular if we are not."

"But—"

"Now, Cousin"—James spoke with such smoothness that Tina was reminded of Gerard—"I beg you will consider. There will be no impropriety involved, and Felicity is right. Your absence would make things very awkward for Lady Millie. And the point is for you to mingle with the other guests," he went on.

Tina did not answer immediately. While she understood what he was saying, she could not imagine voluntarily putting herself under the same roof as Laverstoke and Christian and Allegra. It was a horrifying notion. But already she could see Felicity's pout, which reminded her how much moaning she would have to listen to if she refused.

"I . . . see your point," she said at last. "But I shall have to think about it, and . . . consult Libby's wishes. There are reasons why I am not entirely enthusiastic." Dear God, that was an understatement. "It is nothing to do with you, of course," she added quickly.

James rescued her far more chivalrously than his brother would have done. "Think it over as long as you wish. Naturally you must do as you think best."

Tina hesitated, then asked the question utmost in her mind. "Does Lord Laverstoke know of this scheme?"

James's brows rose. "My brother has put the arrangements of the event in my hands. Allegra, when she arrives, will assist with the invitations and such, but the initial preparations are under my authority."

"I see." It did not precisely answer her question, but she was oddly reassured.

"The real problem is what we shall wear," inserted Felicity. "I shall send for clothes from home, but you, Tina, what will you do?"

"I shall have to wear what I have," Tina said wryly. "I own no ball gowns—which is another reason why my attendance seems foolish."

James's smile flashed. "You know, an easy solution presents itself to me. You and Allegra are very much of a size. I think I can prevail upon her to lend you a gown. Her coloring is different from yours, but I daresay something can be found."

It was all Tina could do to prevent herself from exclaiming that nothing would prevail upon her to wear anything that belonged to Christian's wife. Instead, she only said, "Perhaps she would not like that," in rather a low voice.

"Oh, Allegra won't care. Rewe buys her more clothes than she knows what to do with. She'll bring most of 'em with her, too," he predicted. "You should see the cavalcade when she travels."

The casual reference to Christian was like a pin jabbing her flesh. "She sounds . . . most generous," Tina mumbled.

He gave her an odd look. "Oh, she can be—when the mood moves her—but she's an unpredictable creature. When we were children she used to drive me insane. Sometimes she still does," he added reflectively. "I don't know how her husband puts up with her."

"I daresay he loves her very much." Tina knew the question was foolish, but a part of her longed to know the truth no matter how much it hurt.

To her surprise, James merely shrugged. "Oh, I suppose so. He dotes on the child."

"The child?" All at once, Tina was conscious that it was winter, that her nose and feet and heart were cold, and that thick, gray clouds had gathered to obscure the sun.

"Yes," he went on, unconscious of her pallor. "Dickon's a capital little boy, the very image of his father except for the color of his hair."

The image of Christian.

There was a funny, tight, curling sensation in her stomach. "How very fortunate for them both," she muttered, through lips gone strangely numb.

James glanced at her sharply. "Yes, it is. Cousin Tina, are you feeling quite well?"

"Yes, I'm . . . only a little cold."

"Let's go back," he urged. "The wind is picking up."

"I'm cold, too," offered Felicity, peering up at him through her lashes. "You will join us for tea, won't you, Cousin James? You had best agree, for I won't take 'no' for an answer . . ."

Tina ignored them as they went on talking. All she could think of was the staggering news that Christian was a father. Why it should tear at her heart like this was unclear. She only knew that any beautiful, laughing little boy who looked like Christian ought to have been hers.

The pain of it was almost physical. Why, why, *why?* Why did it have to hurt so much? Would it hurt even more when she faced Christian? *Could* it possibly get any worse?

Considering this, she began to wonder. Perhaps it could not. Perhaps she had already reached the apex of suffering, and there was nowhere to go but down. The possibility furrowed her brow, but in an odd way it made sense. And, indeed, it was beginning to look as though she had no choice.

Little by little the idea caught hold, lifting her spirits at the prospect of making a conscious choice rather than simply falling flat into a situation for which she was not prepared. Until now she had taken no steps to deal with her past — yet here was an opportunity to look it squarely in the face and if possible, outbrave it.

Yes, by heaven, she would do it. She would go to Laverstoke Park; she would meet Christian, greet his wife, and pat his little boy on the head. She would be stronger than she had ever been before.

She only hoped Laverstoke would not think it was his victory.

Ten

Ten days later, the three female inhabitants of the Dower House — along with one four-legged inhabitant — were, with competence and care, removed to Laverstoke Park. Exactly why this was necessary so far in advance of the house party was, in Tina's view, never adequately explained. James tossed around words like "convenience" and "practicality," but Tina privately thought Machiavellianism was a more fitting term. For, without a doubt, it was Laverstoke pulling the strings — and she resented it.

Her opinion notwithstanding, she was once again installed in the room she had formerly occupied, her things unpacked, her clothes pressed and hung — and her emotions acutely unsettled by the entire business. Three days after that, she was no less at ease.

Frequent encounters with Lord Laverstoke had left her somewhat tetchy, for their verbal exchanges were replete with undercurrents so strong she could only wonder that no one else noticed. However, she congratulated herself that she was handling him well — her defenses were mounted, her wall had no chinks. And if, beneath his grave formality, he secretly found her amusing, well, she was not going to let him see that it annoyed her!

Beyond this, the knowledge that Christian and Allegra were due to arrive very soon frazzled her nerves. Escape, however, was not to be considered; even if she were not so determined to deal with her Achilles' heel, she was duty-bound to watch over Felicity. And so she waited, hiding her agitation beneath a mask of rigid composure.

Of course, Libby guessed. Midway through the morning of their fourth day at Laverstoke Park, Libby found her in the Long Gallery, staring broodingly up at the face of a Marchant ancestor who bore a striking resemblance to the present viscount.

"Ah, there you are, Valentina," exclaimed the elderly lady, hurrying over. "I have been looking all over for you." Her gaze troubled, she glanced around, seeking a place where they could sit.

Knowing she could not fob Libby off, Tina allowed herself to be shepherded to a nearby bench. "Now"—Libby patted her arm—"I want you to take a deep breath and tell me what the trouble is."

"Trouble?" Tina had slept poorly the night before, and was not at all certain she had the energy for this.

"You don't have to pretend with me, dear. I know you are unhappy." Libby peered around, making sure there was no one within hearing range. "I know you're dreading Christian's arrival," she added, "and I hate to see you suffer so."

"Of course I am. Would you wish to meet the man who jilted you? Would you wish to see his child, knowing that it might have been yours?" Tina looked down at her hands. "I know you cannot understand."

At first Libby did not answer, then she said the last thing in the world Tina expected. "I understand better than you think. You see, something very similar happened to me once, a very long time ago."

Tina looked up, surprised to full attention.

"His name was Percy, and I thought I was very much in love with him. I thought him prodigious handsome and charming, and I wanted to marry him very much."

"What . . . happened?"

Libby stared off into space. "I discovered that he was in love with someone else. A dear friend of mine, in fact.

150

Only he didn't want to marry her because she wasn't wealthy."

Tina frowned. "But you weren't wealthy either."

"Oh, I had a sizable dowry. But when I jilted Percy, because I could not bear that he should not love me, my father was furious. He ranted and raved, and said I'd get no second chance, that he'd give my dowry to my sister instead. There was only enough for one of us, you see." She sighed, but her voice was quite normal. "In the end, Percy married a third girl—a wealthy girl. He gave her nine children before he died." Her eyes met Tina's squarely. "And not a day goes by when I do not thank God that I was spared having him for a husband."

"Libby!" Tina's mouth fell open. "Why?"

"For a great many reasons. Oh, I was like you—I dreaded the meeting, but it came, eventually, while I was employed by Lady Stanley. And to my horror I discovered that Percy was not the knight in shining armor I had believed. He had pouches under his eyes, his temper was bad, and he was nearly as fat as our Regent. He also had a wandering eye. Even when his poor wife was present, he had the vulgarity to ogle any woman with the remotest claim to beauty. He also flaunted his mistresses in public, quarreled with everyone he knew, and ran himself into debt with his gambling excesses. Within his household, he was reputed to be a tyrant. Need I go on?"

"I . . . don't think so," said Tina, feeling incredibly depressed.

Libby pressed her hand. "What I am trying to say, Valentina, is that one's first love is not necessarily one's last. Or one's best and truest."

Tina eyed her doubtfully. "And you never met anyone else?"

"Yes, I did," replied the elderly woman, this time with real sadness. "And I was fortunate enough to have my affection returned. Unfortunately, he died before we could wed."

"Oh God, I'm so sorry." Tina reached out to clasp Libby's blue-veined hand between her own. "So very sorry."

Libby's face gentled. "At least I had the gift of his love for a short while, my dear. And that is what counts."

Before Tina could answer, the sound of approaching footsteps warned her that someone was coming. A moment later, her heart jerked as Lord Laverstoke strolled into the Gallery, Gretchen at his side. He was dressed in a well-cut black coat, plain white waistcoat, buff-colored trousers, and half Wellingtons, and looked every bit the aristocrat—and very handsome.

"Hello," he said, smiling at them. "I've been wondering where you two ladies were hiding. Are you gossiping? Or merely admiring my illustrious ancestors?"

Patting Gretchen absently, Tina said, "You appear to have a great many of them."

She realized how foolish it sounded when she saw the twitch of his mouth. "So must we all," he replied, with a gravity she knew to be false. "In fact, I daresay they are as much your ancestors as mine."

"I would hardly call them that," she retorted. "The connection between us is—"

"Slight," he finished, his face mocking. "You have informed me of that several times, my dear cousin. Slight but indisputable, according to record. Shall I escort you somewhere warmer? There is always such a draught through here during the winter months."

Libby rose, and Tina could do naught but follow. "I thought you would have gone out," she remarked, referring to the fact that he and James (and Gretchen) had gone out shooting hares the past two mornings.

"No," he replied, frowning faintly. "My brother's leg is paining him today."

"I am sorry to hear it." She hesitated. "Is there aught that can be done for it?"

His head shook. "Rest helps. The battlefield doctor suggested opiates, but our physician advised against it. Prolonged use of such substances is very bad. Jay takes laudanum occasionally, but that is all." He added, in a voice that made Tina shiver, "He is lucky to be alive. His regiment saw a good deal of action at Waterloo."

He took them to the library, where they found James stretched out upon the sofa, a glass of sherry in his hand and a plate of muffins at his elbow. His leg, minus its boot, was propped upon a pile of pillows.

The moment they entered, James shifted his posture. "You should have warned me!" The words were directed at Laverstoke, though his eyes twinkled at Tina. "Our cousins will think I am a poor creature to be lolling about like an invalid."

"No such thing," Tina told him kindly. "Pray do not allow us to disturb you, sir. It will not do."

After a small hesitation, James returned his limb to the pillows. "It's dashed annoying to be laid up like this," he confessed, "but at least I'm alive. Many of my friends aren't." A shadow crossed his face.

"I'm so sorry," Tina murmured. As she spoke, she realized how often she seemed to be saying those words. What right had she to mope? Her troubles were surely of a mild nature compared with the sum total of human anguish caused by the recent war with France. So many had died. At least she had the whole of her life ahead of her, even if she did have to spend it alone.

Sighing slightly, she sat down and glanced toward the viscount. He was studying her again, this time with an air of puzzlement.

"I'll pour you some sherry," he told them. "Down, Gretchen."

Tina watched him reach for the decanter, noting his economy of movement, and the pleasing shape of his hands. The amazing thought flit through her head that she was glad it was not he who had been hurt.

As he handed her the glass, his fingers brushed hers, sending a tingling shock throughout her entire system. Weakness flooded her body as she recognized how aware she was of him physically. Dear God, why was it so? Once again, she was struck with the disquieting fear that there was some unnatural, wanton streak in her nature.

As he selected a chair near her own, Laverstoke's impassive countenance told her the awareness was not reciprocated. He had clearly lost all interest in her as a woman, yet here she sat, quivering like a blancmanger simply because he had touched her. Staring down at her lap, she grappled with this flaw in her character.

She wondered what he would do if he knew it. The mere thought that he might choose to take advantage of her defenselessness made her heart thud with alarm. She knew she would not be able to resist him, any more than she had been able to withstand Christian's entreaties to take liberties. Yet she knew if Gerard ever kissed her again she would be lost, lost to the all-consuming need that seethed inside her like a raging sea.

Tina suddenly realized that James was addressing her. "I . . . I beg your pardon?" she stammered, flushing as though they could all know what had occupied her mind.

"I said I would very much enjoy seeing your sketches. Felicity has been telling me what a talented artist you are."

She could feel the viscount's scrutiny. "I am afraid Felicity exaggerates," she said uncomfortably. "My talent is nothing beyond commonplace."

For once Libby failed in her role as ally. "Now that is untrue, Valentina." She turned to James. "Why, you have simply to give her paper and pencil and you will see for yourselves."

To Tina's dismay, the requisite materials were soon procured, but before she was obliged to put them into use, Felicity sallied into the room arrayed in a sprigged muslin gown better suited for a warm spring day than a cold winter one.

"Good morning, everyone!" she said, smiling vivaciously. "Am I truly the last to rise?" She blinked at James. "But what is this? Do not tell me you *do* have the gout after all!"

"The gout?" James looked nonplused. "What on earth makes you say that?"

154

Felicity made a fluttering gesture. "Oh, that is what Tina said. Only of course she meant it for Lord Laverstoke, not you." Tina fought a desire to squirm as her cousin turned to address the viscount, who had risen politely. "Tina said you were bound to be goutish, in consequence of the dissipated life you have led. But I said—"

"Felicity," Tina interposed in some embarrassment. "His lordship is not interested in our stupid talk. Here, have a muffin. I am persuaded you must be hungry.

"Famished," agreed her cousin without a moment's hesitation. She flounced over to sit next to James. "These look delicious. May I have my chocolate in here, Cousin Laverstoke?"

While Felicity's sustenance was being attended to, Lord Laverstoke leaned closer to Tina. "Not a very flattering conclusion," he remarked, very softly.

A quick look at his face told her nothing. " 'Twas nothing but a jest between us," she said in chagrin.

The dark brows arched, and though he did not pursue the matter, Tina had the uneasy feeling that it was not the last she would hear of it. Instead, he said, in a lazy tone, "What are you going to sketch for us?"

"Oh, is that what you are doing?" asked Felicity, dusting crumbs from her fingers. "Why don't you send for your sketchbook? It's upstairs in your room. I know it is because I saw it."

"You saw it?" echoed Tina, a little sharply. Had Felicity gone prying into her things? The last thing she wanted was for Felicity to see her drawings of Christian.

But her fears were put to rest when Felicity answered, "Yes, don't you remember? I watched you tuck it into the wardrobe." She bestowed a smile on James. "You simply must see her sketchbook."

"No." The single syllable was too quick. Tina swallowed and drew a quick breath. "I mean, why bother when I have paper right here?" She forced a smile. "I shall draw Cousin James."

"Shall I strike an attitude?" inquired James. "How about

this?" He gave her a view of his profile, his hand clasped to his brow as though he were buried in thought.

Felicity chattered and ate while Tina deftly delineated James's form into a few graceful lines. Then she concentrated on the face, capturing the silhouette with its firm mouth and high, noble brow.

"There," she said, as she shaded in the hair. "It's very rough, but I think I've captured the likeness." As she turned it around so they could all see, Felicity squealed and bounced.

Unaccustomed to being the center of attention, Tina could feel herself blushing. In a way it was gratifying, yet it was not an arena she wished to occupy for very long. If any of them demanded to see her sketchbook, she would have to come up with some other excuse. The book was as personal as a diary, and for no one's eyes but her own.

"It's very good."

The quiet praise came from Laverstoke. She looked at him quickly, unable to detect anything but sincerity in his voice.

"Thank you," she replied, caught off guard by her own stab of pleasure. Why should she care if he liked it?

"Have you ever thought of portrait painting?"

"No. I wasn't taught. We had no money for such things." Fearing she sounded self-pitying, she quickly added, "I've always found what I do to be sufficient. I enjoy it, and do it for myself, not for others." It was as delicate a hint as she could make that her sketchbook was for no one's eyes but her own.

He nodded. "Yes, of course."

"Oh, Tina," exclaimed Felicity. "I almost forgot to tell you. I had the most splendid notion this morning. Mama sent my white ball gown, as you know, but it seems a little plain. What if we embroidered little hearts all around the hem and bodice? Wouldn't that be beautiful?"

Tina's heart sank. She knew perfectly well that *we* meant *her,* as Felicity was hopeless with a needle. Before she could think of a reply, Felicity was seeking James's concurrence.

156

"It sounds capital," replied James with the heartiness of a man who knows nothing about feminine fripperies. "You'll be the belle of the ball."

"Little red hearts around the bodice," Felicity continued, "and larger ones around the hem. Or perhaps they should be pink?" Her brow wrinkled for an instant, then the frown melted away. "Tina will know. She is so clever about these things. She embroiders beautifully. Mama always says so."

Tina's face must have reflected her loathing for the project, for Lord Laverstoke stated, "There is no need for your cousin to do the work. There is an excellent needle-woman in Norton. My mother frequently employed her for such things."

"Oh, but Tina will not mind doing it. And I do not have to pay *her*," explained Felicity artlessly. "You do not mind, do you, Tina?"

"Whether your cousin objects is not the issue," retorted the viscount with authority. "While she is a guest in my home, she will not be doing servant's work."

Felicity eyed him in astonishment, her small mouth forming a silent "O." Then she shrugged. "Very well, Cousin Laverstoke. If you wish to pay someone else to do the work, it is all one to me. Of course, Mama will not be pleased."

The words were left to hover in the air like a shadow.

Tina glanced at the viscount, her blue eyes pleading with him not to interfere. "Felicity and I will have to discuss this between ourselves," she said quietly. "It is not beyond my capabilities to embroider a few hearts. And embroidery is not servant's work."

"Valentines," Felicity corrected, her happiness restored. "For my Valentine's Day ball gown."

Gerard had not anticipated that having Valentina residing under his roof would make his life a living hell. He had thought to use the time to become better acquainted with

157

her, and had even expected to enjoy himself while doing so. He had found, however, that simply knowing she was near created a temptation that was nearly irresistible. He had finally admitted to himself that he wanted her, and though his interest in her was more than physical, it was her physical presence that was driving him insane. Above all, he wanted to hold her, to kiss her, to peel the clothes from her body and cover her with himself. He wanted to burrow into her softness, to taste her sweet femininity, to hear her moan his name. He'd even dreamt of it, for God's sake, awakening in the dead of night covered with sweat and filled with the frustration of knowing exactly where her room was and how simple it would be to go there. Instead, he'd forced himself to lie in the dark and think of anything but that lush body and that lovely pink mouth. Even during the daytime, he'd had to exert an iron control over himself, maintaining a polite aloofness that was very much at odds with his real inclinations.

It was chiefly to escape this strain that he had gone out to shoot hares with his brother. Out there, he could forget her for a time, cool the heat in his loins, and focus on other things. But not for long, for it was fast becoming an obsession to him that he solve the mystery of her dislike. Allegra and Christian were to arrive tomorrow, and with those two around, he rated his chances of private conversation with Tina small to nonexistent. More to the point, he could scarcely hope to overcome whatever prejudice she cherished against him if he did not know what that prejudice was. It had occurred to him that Miss Steeple might know, but he was strangely reluctant to pursue that course. Whatever the problem was, he wanted to hear it from Valentina herself.

Valentina.

Her very name was rich and velvet-soft, conjuring images of love and passion. That such a magnificent woman should be obliged to play drudge to Felicity Winton filled Gerard with a fury he could scarcely contain. That business of embroidering hearts on Felicity's ball gown made

158

him simmer with rage. The silly little twit ought to do her own sewing, he thought wrathfully.

Tonight would be their last evening together before his sister and brother-in-law arrived. It might be his last chance.

Very well, then. Tonight he would make his move.

Having no inkling of what Gerard was planning, Tina pleaded a headache and retired to her room immediately after dinner. The mere notion of spending another evening feigning indifference to his presence was more than she could bear at the moment, particularly when her nerves were frayed thin from the knowledge of what—or who—the morrow would bring. But her room did not seem so appealing when she reached it. It seemed to close in on her and make it difficult to breath.

She glanced down at Gretchen, who had followed her upstairs. "Let's go somewhere else, shall we?"

Gretchen sat down and scratched, then chased a flea with her teeth.

Tina dug her sketchbook from the wardrobe, knowing it was the best way to deal with her fidgets. Tucking it under her arm, she stood pensively, wondering where she could go to work undisturbed. Gretchen yawned and looked expectant.

"Let's try the Long Gallery," she told the dog. "I think sketching one of those Marchant ancestors might be fun."

Gretchen scrambled to her feet.

The Long Gallery was silent and dark, but this was easily remedied by lighting the candles in the wall sconces. When the room was ablaze, Tina settled a chair in front of the Marchant ancestor who resembled Gerard and sat down. She gazed up at the portrait, silently studying the hard mouth and jaded, world-weary eyes.

There *was* a resemblance. Of course, the hair was different; the man in the portrait had dark, flowing tresses, reminding her of paintings she had seen of Charles II. But the dark, heavy brows were the same, as were the shape of the nose and mouth. Like Gerard, he looked elegant and arrogant.

Turning to a fresh sheet of paper, Tina bent over her work. Time passed—how much time she could not have said, but she had nearly completed a very detailed drawing when she heard the familiar footsteps.

He walked toward her almost leisurely, but there was that in his gaze that made the pencil slide from her fingers. When he was close, he stooped down and picked it up. "I sent a maid to your room to be sure you needed nothing. She told me you were gone."

Tina moistened her lips. "I . . . couldn't sleep."

"And so you decided to hide here, where I couldn't find you." His voice was calm, yet it lacked its usual impassivity.

"But you did find me," she pointed out.

He gave her a flat look. "I meant to ask you to play chess with me tonight. I wanted to spend some time with you, but you, as I recollect, had the headache." His eyes narrowed. "So you came to draw old Simon instead. An apt choice. He was the most depraved of my ancestors, one of Charles Stuart's most debauched courtiers. Unlike me, he probably did have the gout."

"I thought he looked like you," she whispered.

Something flashed in his eyes, an emotion that might have been anger or frustration or sorrow. Then, before she could protest, he tookn her sketchbook and tossed it and her pencil onto the floor.

"Enough of this," he said, in a quiet, deadly voice. He reached for her wrists and pulled her slowly, inexorably, to her feet. "I want you to tell me, right now, what I have done to earn your contempt. And don't say nothing. I want the truth."

Tina stood frozen in his grasp. *Tell him,* shrilled the voice in her head. *Tell him now, quickly, before you lose courage.* She closed her eyes, searching for the anger that would make it possible to explain. Scenes flickered in her

160

mind: Christian, smiling down at her; Christian, whispering of his love; Christian, telling her how happy they would be when they married and had children of their own.

Children.

It was the key word. She had always yearned for children, and now Christian had a son and she did not. Perhaps she never would. All the might-have-beens rushed together, welling upward, cascading out and over the dam she had created to hold in the pain.

She opened her eyes. "I think I shall tell you," she said coldly. She leaned over and scooped up her sketchbook, flipping it open to some of its earliest pages. Selecting one, she turned it around for Gerard to see.

"Do you recognize this man?"

He stared at the picture. "It's my brother-in-law," he said in confusion. "How—?"

"It is a portrait of the man I loved. The man I was once promised to marry," she told him harshly. Her own words fed her emotion, renewing a bitterness that had nearly faded.

His brows snapped together. "Rewe was betrothed to *you?*"

"Do you pretend you did not know?" she said scathingly. "Yes, Christian was mine once. We were betrothed. Everyone knew it. It had not yet reached the London papers, and the marriage settlements had not been drawn up, but in my eyes, and in the eyes of my family, my friends, and my neighbors, it was final."

Gerard was very still.

"And then he inherited a title and went off," she went on, "but he still loved me. It was not until he met your sister that I lost him." Conveniently forgetting her belief in Allegra's guilt, she said, "I make no doubt she fell in love with him, for who would not? I do not hold her to blame. No, it is *you* I hold responsible. You were your sister's guardian. But you, the great diplomat, the hero of England"—her voice was shaking with fury—"you could not

161

concern yourself with such mundane responsibilities. I daresay you were too busy chasing opera dancers to bother!"

Gerard was very pale. "Tina, I . . . truly did not know that it was you."

"Oh," she marveled, "and if you had, no doubt you would have done differently!"

"No, I cannot say that I would." He spoke heavily. "In fact, I did know that there was a girl in his life . . . a fiancée in the country. But there were circumstances—" He cleared his throat. "I am not at liberty to discuss my reasons for permitting the marriage."

"Of course not." Tina tried to pull away. "And I obviously wasted my time in telling you this." Unaccountable tears pricked at her eyes, but only dimly did she realize that they were not for Christian. "Perhaps now you will understand why it is so distasteful for me to be under your roof. I am only here at Felicity's behest, and the moment this *outlandish* Valentine's Day ball is over, I intend to go somewhere where I shall not be forced to see *you* day and night!"

He would not release her. "Tina, calm yourself. For God's sake, you are shaking." He pulled her a little closer, staring down at her with tormented eyes. "My dear girl, I would give anything to make you happy, but I will not tell you I am sorry for that. Rewe would have made you a damnable husband. You cannot know what you escaped."

"And yet you encouraged him to wed your sister? What a hypocrite you are, Gerard. I pity the woman who becomes *your* wife."

"In time, I hope to change your mind about that," he said quietly. "For now, I think it best that you go to your room and rest—"

"I shall do what I please," she retorted, starting to struggle. "Go and dictate to your servants, but not to me."

"My God, what a termagant you are. If you will just listen to me—no, you're in no condition to be reasonable, are you?" And then, without waiting for an answer, he

162

pulled her against his chest and kissed her with a ruthless purpose that deprived her of sensible thought.

It was as though the touch of his lips tore a hole in her heart, draining it of the rancor she had fought so hard to invoke. Just as she'd feared, she was lost within seconds, drowning in his assault upon her devastated senses. It was wildly unfair and exactly what she needed, the part of the healing process of which she had been deprived.

Human contact . . . warmth . . . love.

Tina's brain disconnected from her body as she twined her arms around his neck, pressing closer, arching against him with an abandon that seemed as natural as breathing. Excitement shot through her as his arms tightened, his mouth raining kisses across her face while her own hands, as of their own accord, slid from his neck to his shoulders to his chest.

"Oh, Tina," he murmured, his mouth trailing down to the base of her throat, "I've wanted to do this for days. You have no idea what you do to me." His breath was warm and urgent, his hands roving over her body with such fierce hunger that a moan dragged from her lips.

It was at this precise moment that Gretchen barked.

Tina's eyes snapped open as Gerard swung around, but there was no one there save the dog. Gretchen's tail thumped in mute expectation of a frolic.

"She thinks we're playing," he muttered.

Yet the interruption was enough. As Gerard's arms tightened once more, Tina's common sense came rushing back, sensation arrested in mid-flight, reality replacing delirium.

"Let go!"

Frantically, she pushed at his chest only to find herself released without protest. She staggered backward and swallowed convulsively. "You should not have done that," she whispered. "It was wrong. Very wrong."

"It did not feel wrong to me," he countered. He held out a hand. "Come back to me, sweetheart."

"No." She shook her head, steeling herself to resist.

"What you feel is no concern of mine. You may be used to participating in sordid episodes like this, but I am not. Nor do I wish to be." Slowly, she backed away from him, her eyes stark with anguish. "Good night."

His hand dropped to his side. "Good night," he echoed, with infinite weariness.

It was not until Tina reached the sanctuary of her room that she realized she had left her sketchbook behind. Yet as she sagged against its sheltering door, she knew she did not care. Its secret had been revealed. Gerard finally knew the truth.

How strange that she should feel no triumph.

Eleven

In the end, Tina was to witness Christian's arrival from an upstairs window.

She had just come up from downstairs, where James was instructing Felicity at billiards and Gerard was entertaining Libby with descriptions of Vienna. She had listened for a while, but Gerard was such a compelling speaker that she'd found herself sliding under his spell. He had painted a portrait that was too real; she could so easily imagine the romantic Viennese allée known as the Prater promenade with its golden chestnut trees and merry-go-rounds, wandering minstrels and air of gaiety. Lulled by his voice, for a few seconds she'd daydreamed of going there herself, and as if that were not insane enough, the daydream had included having him at her side.

Unable to bear it, she had mumbled an excuse and fled the room, but her bedchamber offered no comfort. Her head ached, her eyes felt heavy, but somehow she could not sit; instead she wandered over to the window embrasure to look outside. And then fate played its sly trick—for the moment she did so, a small entourage came into view, lumbering along the snow-packed gravel on its way up to the house.

The two carriages were piled high with baggage. The first was an opulent chariot pulled by a team of four, colored a dark green with flamboyant crests on its doors. The second was a bright yellow post-chaise, also drawn by a team of four. Coachmen, footmen, and postilions abounded; Tina watched, wide-eyed, as it all halted before the great front doors of Laverstoke Park.

Her hands clenched hard on the sill as the steps to the chariot were let down. Holding her breath, she leaned forward, straining to catch a glimpse of the man she had not seen in five long years.

Oh God, there he was. *Christian.*

He stood unmoving in the sunlight, his feet planted wide apart, his dark head held at an angle which cast his features into relief against the bright, white snow. Then he turned to look toward the chariot, where a small, gloved hand was extending to the waiting footman.

Tina's tension mounted as she viewed the woman who emerged. Even from this distance she could see that Allegra, Lady Rewe, was everything she had ever wanted to be and was not. Christian's wife was, to put it plainly, the quintessence of femininity, a tall, ethereal golden goddess, a masterpiece of womanhood. Then, before Tina had time to grow jealous, her attention was drawn to the postchaise, where an elderly servant was holding out her arms to a small, golden-haired boy.

Watching the child, she suddenly realized it wasn't jealousy she felt. It was emptiness. Very slowly, she turned away from the window, her hands fisted at her sides. How could emptiness hurt so much? Was she going to be able to face them, after all?

Pride.

It was the only weapon she had. She had never been beautiful or witty or clever, but deadly pride—she had more than her fair share of that. Very well, then, she would use it. No matter what transpired, she would conduct herself as though Christian were nothing more than an old acquaintance. She would cling to dignity and pride. Pray God it was enough.

She deeply regretted telling Gerard about Christian; just knowing that he knew the truth was going to make things that much more difficult. And how she wished she had not permitted him to kiss her again! It had been a devastating mistake, one that had kept her awake for the better part of the night. However, the deed was done, and could not be undone. And to her shame, she now knew for certain that where men were concerned she had no self-restraint at all.

As for Gerard, he obviously did not see her as a lady, for why else would he kiss her as he had? It had not been a chivalrous kiss; it had been a burning, ravenous assault upon her senses. And she'd not wanted him to stop—that was what slayed her. In her heart, she'd wanted him to sweep her into his arms like a conquering knight, to carry her off to some shadowed corner of his home to make love to her until she died of pleasure. She'd wanted him to override her protests, to still her doubts, to annihilate her scruples.

And deep inside she still wanted that.

Suddenly, a painful new fear erupted. If she were so susceptible to a man she disliked, how much more susceptible would she be to the man she had once loved? *Still* loved, she corrected. She still loved Christian, didn't she?

Tina considered this with a frown. To her surprise, a clear answer to the question did not present itself. Perhaps, she pondered, if God were merciful she would find that her love had faded, but that was something she could not know until she faced Christian again.

And face him she must. Now.

Yet it took her another twenty minutes to screw up her courage sufficiently to go downstairs. In the end, it was the fear that Gerard would think her a coward that spurred her to action. Not, she assured herself, that she cared a fig what he thought of her, but pride demanded that she present him—and the rest of world—with a courageous front. And so, head held high, she made her way along the corridor, past bustling housemaids busily preparing rooms for the house party.

Her steps slowed as she neared the drawing room.

"Nana!" squealed a childish voice. "I want Nana! Where's Nana?"

"Hush, darling." Allegra's voice was exactly as Tina had imagined it—cool and smooth and well-bred. "You'll go up to Nana in a minute. Right now I want you to be here so your uncles can see you. Don't crush Mama's gown. No, dear, don't touch that either. Come and sit next to Mama on the couch."

Tina's heart fluttered in anticipation of hearing Christian's voice, but instead it was Gerard who spoke. "The child has been sitting for hours, Allegra. He needs to stretch his legs."

"Perhaps he's hungry," she heard James say. "I would be."

"So would I." This was Felicity. "Are you hungry, Dickon? Would you like a biscuit?"

The voices murmured on, and Tina nodded to the footman to open the door.

Heads turned.

Her breath held, Tina's gaze swept their faces, passing and returning to Gerard. Christian, she discovered, was not even in the room.

"Come in, Tina," Gerard said quietly. "Come and allow me to present you to my sister. Allegra, this is Miss Jardine. Tina, Lady Rewe."

Extending her hand, Allegra acknowledged the introduction with the majesty of a queen. Yet her tone was not unfriendly. "Gerard tells us you are our cousin, Miss Jardine. Miss Winton has been good enough to explain the connection, which I find confusing. Nevertheless, I am pleased to make your acquaintance." She slanted a look at her brothers, adding, "No doubt your presence here will enliven things. Ah, here is my husband."

Tina froze as Allegra beckoned to someone behind her back. "Christian, come and meet Miss Jardine. She is another of our cousins."

Tina turned slowly. Behind her, Christian stood framed in the doorway, tall, solid, real—and wearing a guarded look. Of course, she thought. Letters had been exchanged. He would have known she was here.

While her heart pounded, Christian took two steps into the room and made a small, formal bow. "A pleasure to meet you, Miss Jardine." His eyes focused on a point midway between her eyes.

He behaved as though she were a stranger.

Stunned, Tina could do nothing but respond to the salutation with the same degree of formality.

How could he? How dared he?

Filled with irrational anger, she shuddered as he walked past her to swing his son into the air. As the child squealed he said casually, "Have you met Dickon yet?"

Tina hesitated. The remark appeared to be addressed to her, but his gaze scraped past her as though she were invisible. It also seemed he did not want an answer, for already he was striding toward the door. "I'll take Dickon up to Nana now." He threw the remark over his shoulder, this time to his wife. "She'll be getting anxious."

And he was gone.

Vaguely, Tina was aware that Gerard had been very still during the exchange. Now he spoke, a thread of gentleness in his voice. "Come sit down, Tina. I'll pour you some sherry."

Feeling deflated, she did as he suggested, accepting the sherry with a small, brave smile. Oddly, her brain seemed to have lapsed into something akin to paralysis, so that the ensuing conversation floated round her like fog, wispy and insubstantial, a mix of pleasantries which held neither meaning nor interest.

"Miss Jardine?"

Tina was jerked from her lethargy by Allegra's voice. "I beg your pardon, ma'am?"

"I asked what you thought of Laverstoke Park." Allegra shot her an assessing look. "Have my brothers given you the tour?"

Somehow Tina replied, her lips forming a string of words that must have been a sentence. Fortunately, she was not required to say anything more, so she relapsed into silence. Hazily, she knew Felicity was talking, chirping away like a sparrow about the Valentine's Day ball. Allegra seemed to share her enthusiasm, though she hid it behind a veil of cool sophistication. At one point, she saw Gerard frown, which had the curious effect of forcing her to pay attention.

"—and of course we shall draw lots. That is the way it is done," finished Allegra with the smug smile of a hostess anticipating a successful celebration.

"Draw lots?" The query came from James.

The perfect blond ringlets bounced with her nod. "Yes. I shall write the names of all the house guests onto slips of paper, and at the start of the house party we shall have a lottery. The gentlemen will draw from the ladies' names, and vice versa. The name you draw will be the person to whom you give a valentine. Typically, the giver composes some sort of verse, witty or complimentary, or whatever seems appropriate."

"Sounds arduous," James grumbled.

"It will be most diverting," said his sister firmly. "At any rate, brother dear, you do not sign the valentine. They must be given anonymously."

Tina glanced at Gerard and found his pensive gaze on her face. For a moment their eyes locked, then she flushed and looked away, her pulse racing madly. How embarrassing it would be to find herself obliged to give Gerard a valentine. And, oh God, even worse, what would she do if she drew Christian's name? Even anonymously, how could she bear it?

"'Tis a pity you had to include that horrid Buckden woman," Allegra was saying, "but of course we must have Millie. Is she still the frightened little mouse she used to be? James, you always had a kindness for mice. I will appoint you Millie's caretaker, for lord knows her mother will do nothing to see to her happiness. It will answer the purpose nicely."

James smiled wryly. "A duty I will gladly discharge—if Lady Buckden allows me within a furlong of Millie, that is."

Allegra's brows arched. "Oh? Does the foolish woman still have her sights set on Laverstoke? 'Tis nonsensical when he has his choice of almost any girl in the realm." She turned to Gerard. "Miss Gladstone or Miss Fenchurch would be more suitable. Why, even Miss Rudgwick—" She broke off to glance suspiciously at Felicity. "Ah well. I daresay you've a mind to remain a bachelor."

"For the present," Gerard agreed, a warning edge to his voice. "Though I daresay I shall eventually come about. You have set us such an example of married bliss, Allie."

Tina wondered at Allegra's flush. "Yes, I have," she said defensively. "Rewe is a wonderful father. Did I tell you Dickon is to have his own pony? Rewe insists upon it, though I fear he is too young."

"You must enjoy being a mother," Tina said in a careful, toneless voice. It was the first voluntary statement she had made, and Allegra seemed surprised.

"Enjoy, Miss Jardine? Well, I suppose I do. He is a sweet child, though sometimes"—she shrugged—"well, of course he can be tedious."

Rather shocked by this unmotherly sentiment, Tina pressed her lips together. How unfair, she thought, how odiously unfair that this woman should be the one to bear Christian's child. She obviously cared nothing for her son.

"I wish Rewe would come down," Allegra cried pettishly. "What in the world can be keeping him? He has merely to give Dickon to Nana, for pity's sake."

"Perhaps," Gerard suggested, an ironic note in his voice, "you might care to go and see for yourself."

Allegra glared, then rose to her feet. "I believe I shall do that," she said stiffly.

On the pretext of going over some estate matters, Gerard retired to his library for the interval between teatime and dinner. In truth, he and James had gone over everything early that morning, but he could trust his brother not to mention that fact.

171

The day, he reflected, was proving to be more of an ordeal than he had expected. He had never cared for his brother-in-law, and his dislike was rapidly increasing. Under the circumstances, he knew that Rewe had chosen the best course, but he still damned him for the bloody coward he was. Gerard would be willing to swear that Tina had not understood, that she had expected some sign of recognition, some hint of warmth from the man she had once loved. That such a sign would have been a hellish violation of propriety, of what was right . . . that was wholly irrelevant. Gerard was still disgusted. On the other hand, he reflected, if the bastard *had* dared to smile at her—his hands clenched at the thought—he'd have been hard put not to plant him a facer.

It pained him to see Tina suffer. Even though he had not known of her broken betrothal until it was too late, he felt guilty for introducing Rewe into the household. That guilt, however, was tempered by the knowledge that it was probably all for the best. Tina had obviously been carrying a torch for the fellow, and if he was to woo her himself, he wanted that torch extinguished once and for all.

Ah, God, was he ready to admit it? Was he ready to admit that he wanted her for his wife? Surely he had not known her long enough, he thought uneasily. He was being abnormally impulsive, something a trained diplomat ought never to be. He ought to wait a few months, or even a year, before deciding upon such a drastic course. Marriage was more than a discreet liaison.

Marriage was permanent.

His lips curved as he recalled a friend who had courted a young woman for eight years before he'd finally made her an offer. God, eight years. He couldn't imagine waiting that long for Tina. Even eight months would be too long. Or eight weeks. Of course his friend had kept a succession of mistresses during the interim, which must have made it a great deal easier.

Gerard frowned. If it were Tina he wanted—which it was—he did not think he would care to go to bed with

172

Beatrice. Surely not. His lips thinned with distaste. To own the truth, he was rather surprised by the discovery. He had always assumed that when he wed, he too would keep a mistress. It was simply what gentlemen did, what he had long accepted as the norm. But it was not what Viscount Laverstoke would do. When he married, he was going to make damned sure it was his wife who warmed his bed at night.

Valentina.

He tapped the desk with his fingers. Yes, he did feel badly that she was forced to meet her first love under such intolerable circumstances. But perhaps it was the best way for her to learn what a blackguard the man was. Her eyes must be opened, and of their own accord.

With an abrupt movement, Gerard moved back and pulled open the wide center drawer of his desk. Tina's sketchbook lay safely within. He had already examined its contents.

It was, of course, an invasion of her privacy, but he had done it anyway, with only a twinge of guilt. He had done it because he desired, desperately, to discover some clue, some hint of how he should proceed in his courtship. And he was not sorry, because he had found the sketch she had done of him and because she dated all her drawings, very lightly, in the bottom right corner. And the date corresponded to the day that they had kissed in the snow. The day he had felt her passion.

He found that encouraging. Not conclusive, but encouraging.

Again, he was acting on instinct. It was the same instinct that had told him that Castlereagh was right in his dealings with Russia—when everyone from the Whig Opposition to their own Tory Cabinet attacked the beleaguered foreign secretary's policies as too bold. He had known in his bones that England must stand firm in its refusal to allow the Russian Tsar to consume Poland in its entirety. Just as he knew that Valentina's sketch of him was significant.

She was not indifferent to him. Well, he had sensed that

ever since that second kiss, but this additional evidence was welcome. It convinced him that he stood a chance, even if she was still wearing the willow for Rewe.

Once more Gerard scowled. He had to admit that his brother-in-law was a handsome, romantic-looking fellow. Rewe had a devil-may-care attitude that women adored—and invariably swallowed hook, line, and sinker. So somehow he must do something to convince her that he, too, was a romantic fellow. He cast his mind about, wondering what he could do that might prove effective and yet remain within the boundaries of propriety. Then, suddenly, he knew.

He would give her a valentine.

Of course, the odds were against his drawing her name in Allegra's lottery, but he would give her one anyway. He would compose something that would not only melt her hostility, but would teach her that he was not a heartless rake, incapable of feeling or caring.

Washed with a wave of optimism, Gerard unlocked a small drawer on the left-hand side of his desk and rifled around inside. Within lay the sum total of his life's creative efforts, a bundle of papers tied together with a yellow ribbon. Long ago, he had scribbled poetry in his spare time, though what he had written had never satisfied him sufficiently to allow anyone else to read it. Browsing through, he grimaced as a ribald jingle about his Oxford days caught his eye. The muse had certainly deserted him that day, he thought.

However, there were many others of a more seemly nature: madrigals, sonnets, even the first three stanzas of an epic. He had forgotten all about his epic. As a whole, it wasn't very good, but here and there he discovered a line that pleased him. Perhaps if he had worked harder, revised more . . . With a sigh, he stuffed the papers back into the drawer. He had always liked the fluidity and ambiguity of poetry, the feeling that one might almost express what lay within one's soul. Yet he had always known that his own poems lacked the spark that would make them great.

Even so, he would write Valentina a sonnet. He was no Shakespeare, but he had determination on his side. And after all, she liked sonnets.

He frowned suddenly. At least, he believed she liked sonnets. After all, she still had his book in her possession. Perhaps, however, he had better do some additional research on the subject.

In answer to the light tap, Tina opened her door to find a young chambermaid standing in the corridor. "Yes?"

The girl curtsied. "His lordship requests your attendance in the library, miss."

"He does?" Tina cleared her throat, hoping she did not look like she'd been crying. "Why?" she said gruffly.

"I'm sure I couldn't say, miss." The girl bobbed another respectful curtsy, her lips folded primly.

"Very well, Alice. Thank you for telling me."

As the chambermaid departed, Tina stood very still, her shoulders slumped. What could Gerard want of her? If he wished to play chess again, she must certainly decline. Even to be in the same room with him was difficult after what had transpired between them last night. Still, she supposed she ought to go down.

With a deep, shuddering breath, she marshaled her courage. She would abide by her decision to face this with fortitude, to keep her feelings hidden from the others. This would be good preparation; if she could behave normally with Gerard, then perhaps she could do so with Christian.

Turning to the mirror, she composed her features into an emotionless mask. "Very well, Gerard," she said aloud. "I shall come down to you." She picked up her shawl and left the room.

To her relief, Gerard was alone in the library. He was seated behind his great mahogany desk, his posture casual, his golden head bent over a pile of what looked like legal documents. As she paused in the doorway, he looked up.

"Ah, there you are," he said, rather gravely. "Come in.

How are you feeling?" He was holding a letter-opener, tapping its steel tip against the elegant frogging of his waistcoat.

Tina took a few wary steps into the room. "I am perfectly well, thank you."

Tossing the letter-opener aside, he stood and came around his desk. "I thought you were looking out of sorts earlier." He walked past her and closed the door. "There. Now we may speak privately."

"Is this wise?" she said uneasily. "What will your sister think?"

"What she thinks is of no consequence. Tina, we have to talk."

"Do we?" She kept her voice carefully cool.

He took her arm and led her to a couch. "Tell me how you liked the book."

Surprised, she barely noticed when he sat beside her. "You mean the sonnets?"

"Yes. Which was your favorite?" There was real interest in his voice.

"Oh, I don't know." She lifted a hand, too tired to think clearly. "I cannot say I have a favorite. Do you?"

He cocked a considering eyebrow. "I'm not sure. I admire them all, but there is a bit too much of the 'devouring time' theme in them to please me. The Renaissance mind seems rather obsessed with the idea." His mouth curved, and she was struck anew by his charm. *"Devouring Time, blunt thou the lion's paws, and make the earth devour her own sweet brood.* Rather dreary, eh? And then there's this one: *My grief lies onward, and my joy behind.* You see what I mean," he added apologetically.

Despite her efforts to remain aloof, Tina's lips twitched. "So you do not care for Shakespeare's poetry?"

"On the contrary, the imagery fascinates me. His expression of universal emotion is without equal." He moved a little closer. *"Shall I compare thee to a summer's day?"* he said, very softly. *"Thou art more lovely . . ."* His voice drifted off. "That's rather nice, isn't it?"

Tina's breath caught in her throat as, for a stunned moment, she thought he was applying the words to her. Then reality intruded, and the pleasant fantasy faded. "You've memorized them?" she asked.

"Not deliberately. I've read them and they simply . . . stay in my mind." He shrugged. "It's one of my assets, Castlereagh would tell you."

"Good grief," she said in amazement. "No wonder you play chess so well. How can I ever hope to outfox a mind like yours?"

"Nonsense, of course you can defeat me. I'm not infallible. I've lost before. But when I play, I always play to win." All at once, he rose and walked to his desk; when he came back he was holding her sketchbook. "I thought you'd want this back."

Tina hesitated, then took it from his hand. "Thank you," she said awkwardly.

He did not sit down, but stood looking down at her, a tight set to his jaw. "Tina, I've been wanting to apologize for my behavior last night. It was not the conduct of a gentleman, but I . . . meant it for the best. I meant to comfort you but instead"—he paused, clearing his throat—"instead I acted badly."

Tina flushed scarlet at the reminder.

He looked equally uncomfortable. "I also want you to know that I understand how difficult this is for you. And if there's anything I can do, I hope you'll tell me."

"There's nothing," she mumbled, gazing down at her lap.

There was a short silence. "You do like poetry, don't you?" he asked suddenly. Anxiously.

Tina's gaze flew up. It seemed such an excessively odd thing for him to say that for a moment she wondered if he were mocking her. But there was no trace of mockery in his face.

"Yes, I do," she replied, studying him. "I'm very fond of it. Particularly sonnets. Although, like you, I prefer them less dreary."

"Good," he said simply.

And as he smiled down at her, something shifted in her heart.

Twelve

Odd as it seemed, it was her interview with Gerard that enabled Tina to survive her first evening in Christian's company. His apology had stirred her, awakened her to the fact that he truly did regret the awkwardness of her position. Moreover, the simple pleasure of the hour they had spent discussing poetry lingered in her mind like a spectacular sunset. It had warmed her, filled her with a glow that even Allegra's presence could not dispel.

At dinner, he further displayed his contrition by seating her at his right hand, far from Christian, which made it a good deal easier for her to relax. And because she was relaxed, she was better able to contrast the behavior of the two lords.

Where Gerard was politely impassive, Christian was clearly in the sulks. He had little to say for himself, and took no pains to be anything more than civil to his wife. While Felicity and Allegra babbled of balls, he stared at his food, at his fork, and into his wineglass — anywhere but in her own direction, Tina noted painfully.

As for Gerard, he dominated the room, playing the part of host with an ease that reflected his sophistication. Yet she sensed he was not as self-composed as he appeared. Why? Was it because of her?

Suddenly, she yearned to understand him. Since this afternoon, her feelings toward him had undergone an undefined change. Deep down, she longed to come to terms with this change, to explore it as one would explore a daring new idea. At the same time she was afraid, rejecting it as weakness, a base outgrowth of her own erotic cravings.

"How sad," Allegra remarked midway through the second course, "that we should be an uneven number. Four ladies and three gentlemen. Shame on you, Gerard."

"We'll have a houseful to feed soon enough," James remarked.

"Yes, 'twill be splendid indeed. I so adore company. This Valentine's Day notion was a stroke of genius."

While Allegra went on to enumerate the various personages she planned to invite, Tina allowed her thoughts to drift. She pushed her food about her plate, wondering whether Gerard had really meant what he'd said about wanting to kiss her for days.

"Don't you like it?" he asked.

The quiet question made her start. "Like what?" she said stupidly.

"The sauce."

Looking down, she stared at her broccoli as though it were of sudden, great interest. "Yes, of course. It's very good."

"Some people don't care for Continental cuisine." She could feel him probing her with those astute gray eyes.

"Laverstoke's cook is French," Allegra put in. "I wish *we* had a French cook," she threw at her husband. "Our vegetables are never served with a sauce. Our dinners are as varied as this beastly weather. I wish we had gone to Italy for the winter."

"There's nothing wrong with our cook," said Christian irritably. "There's nothing wrong with good English cooking either."

"The French use a great deal of butter," said Miss Steeple tactfully, "which makes it difficult to keep one's figure."

"There, Allie, you see?" James waved his fork at his sister. "What you want is a little of Miss Steeple's sense."

Allegra pursed her lips.

The remainder of the meal was no less awkward, so that when the time came for the ladies to leave the gentlemen to their port, Tina was thankful to escape.

In the drawing room, Allegra took charge. "Tomorrow," she announced, "we must write out the cards for the ball. Since my brother does not employ a secretary, I shall require assistance from at least one of you."

Tina waited, expecting the ax to fall upon either her shoulders or Libby's, but surprisingly it was Felicity who volunteered. For a moment, the two spoiled beauties studied each other, then Allegra nodded.

"Very well, then, Miss Winton. We shall have to act quickly so as to give people adequate time to respond. I have already sent out the invitations for the house party itself, which Laverstoke wishes to keep small. Other than the Buckdens, I have included the Earl and Countess of Ruscombe, Lord and Lady Wantage, and the Bradfields. They all spend their winters here in the Cotswolds and will have nothing else to do."

"Are there to be no young people?" asked Felicity forlornly.

"Indeed there will be." Allegra gestured vaguely. "The Ruscombe's have two sons and a daughter of marriageable age, and the Bradfields have two sons. And Lady Wantage has two daughters by her first husband. Both girls were introduced to the *ton* last Season, but neither of them took. Jane, I believe, is the prettier, but she has nothing to say for herself. Rather like James's Millie. I have also invited Mr. Chetwoode and Lord Flaundon. They are both bachelors," she added. "Mr. Chetwoode is fashionable and charming. And Lord Flaundon is"—her smile grew dreamy—"divinely handsome."

Then she sighed. "As for the ball itself, I expect we

shall have above a hundred and fifty people. It won't be what one would call a squeeze, but for this time of year it will be grand."

While Allegra went on to describe some of the more fashionable 'squeezes' she had attended, Tina noticed Libby watching her in quiet concern.

"You look tired," murmured the elderly woman. "Do you have another headache, my love?"

"A small one," Tina admitted. In truth, she was utterly exhausted; she'd had, at best, no more than four hours' sleep the night before.

"Then why do you not retire for the night? I am sure none of us will object."

Tina hesitated. What would Gerard think if he found her gone? Or if she stayed, would she be able to go on pretending she did not know Christian? As it was, she could barely put a sensible sentence together.

"Perhaps that would be best," she agreed, rising.

Allegra broke off from her description of her newest ball gown. "You are leaving us, Miss Jardine?" At that moment, her luminous gray eyes were every bit as piercing as Gerard's.

Tina resisted an urge to fidget. "I'm very tired," she replied. "I did not sleep well last night."

"I am sorry to hear it. I hope to have an opportunity to talk with you tomorrow. I should like for us to become better acquainted."

As polite as it was, there was something in Allegra's tone that made Tina uneasy. "I would like that," she responded, quaking inwardly. Dear lord, had Christian told his wife about her? If so, what would Allegra say?

She could feel Allegra's gaze following her as she moved toward the door. "Pleasant dreams, Miss Jardine," uttered that soft, well-bred voice.

Upstairs, Tina collapsed on her bed, her brain swirling with bits and pieces of the past twenty-four hours' events. Then, gradually, it all faded to nothingness — a nothingness that lasted perhaps as long as half an hour.

Then came the knock on her door.

"His lordship requests your attendance in the Long Gallery, mum," said the young servant girl who stood outside.

Blinking the sleep from her eyes, Tina gripped the edge of the door. "He requests my attendance . . . now?"

"At once, mum."

The girl curtsied and withdrew, while Tina stared after her in perplexity. What possessed Gerard to make such an extraordinary request? Surely such a meeting was most unwise.

Fortunately, she had not yet disrobed, although her hair had been freed from its confining coil. Should she take the time to redo it?

No.

She wanted Gerard to see her with her hair down again. It was clean, it was beautiful, and he liked it. Her pulse raced as she imagined what he might say, what he might do. Her throat went dry. In her present state of mind, she knew she would be unable to resist him if he wished to touch her, and as scandalous and foolhardy as that was, she did not care.

She moved quietly and took no candle. Knowing that Gerard would wish her to be discreet, she passed over the carpets like a whisper, her feet making less sound than her own thudding heart. What could he want? Was she insane? If anyone had told her a week ago that she would be doing this, she would not have believed them. She was a well-bred, respectable woman, not a lightskirt who agreed to clandestine meetings with arrogant, overbearing viscounts.

It was black as pitch in the Long Gallery—the sconces were unlit and there was no moon. Regretting the lack of illumination, she stepped forward, gazing about uneasily. "My lord?" she said softly.

With heart-stopping abruptness, a tall shadow separated from the rest of the darkness. "You got my message," it said.

Tina drew back in horror, the blood rushing from her face. "Christian!" she gasped. "Wh-what are you doing here?"

"I had to talk to you." He was walking toward her as he spoke. "I thought this a safe place. No one ever comes to this god-forsaken room."

"*You* sent the message?" she stammered.

She could almost see his shrug. "Of course. You didn't think it was Laverstoke, did you? I bribed the maid to say 'his lordship' in case anyone overheard." His voice changed, chiding her gently. "I assumed you would know it was me."

"Well, I did not." Somewhere inside her head shrieked a voice telling her to flee, but her knees were shaking too badly to do anything of the sort. "I . . . I did think it odd of him," she added, in a last-ditch effort to hide the truth.

But Christian had noticed nothing. "God, Tina, it's so good to see you again." Somehow, his hands found her shoulders.

"For pity's sake, Christian, you must be mad to do this. What do you want? What will the others think?"

"They'll think I've gone to the privy," he answered with a touch of humor. "Though of course I didn't tell them so."

She was not amused. "You must go back, this is madness!" Then, as of its own accord, her tongue formed the painful words. "Oh, Christian, why? Why did you pretend not to know me?"

He gave her a little shake. "I *had* to! Don't you see? Allegra doesn't know about us. And she mustn't either, because—oh, never mind why. But I had to see you, Tina. I had to tell you I still love you."

"Don't." Vaguely, she knew that she was icy cold, and that every part of her body was trembling almost uncontrollably. "Don't say that, Christian."

"I must. There's so much more I want to say, but we can't talk now. I'll invite you to go driving tomorrow, if I can. Then we'll talk."

"No, we won't," she protested with rising anger. Strength surged through her, giving her the impetus to push him away. "You're married now, Christian. You have a wife."

He stood unmoving, but she could feel his beckoning warmth through the darkness. "I'm well aware of that, but marrying Allegra was a big mistake. I don't love her."

A tiny sob rose in her throat. "What of your son? I assume you love him? As his father, you owe it to him to conduct yourself with honor. And meeting me here like this—it is not honorable."

"I don't care," he countered. "Don't you understand? Fate has offered us a second chance. We would be fools not to take it."

As she searched for his meaning, he laughed softly. "You were always such a prim little thing on the surface. I always liked that. But I know what's underneath. You can't fool me, Tina. I know you still love me or you'd have married by now."

Before she could answer, he was turning away. "I must go. Good night, darling. Dream of me tonight." And then he was gone, melting into the darkness as though he had never been there at all.

Very slowly, Tina made her way back to her room. She couldn't absorb what had just happened, didn't quite understand what he had been trying to say. Whatever it had been, the crux of the matter was that he thought she still loved him. And he still loved her. Was there ever a worse muddle?

Sinking onto her bed, Tina covered her face. What a foolish, spineless creature she was. Why hadn't she simply told him that he was wrong, that she did not care for him anymore? *Because she was not sure.* Because she was a fickle, flighty, addle-brained creature who did not know her own mind.

Dream of me tonight. What a cruel thing to have said, she thought bitterly. She had been dreaming of him for years, but of course he would not realize that. He was a man. Men did not feel things the same way women did. Men were fundamentally different, the opposite of women. They viewed life from another angle—a male, masterful, dominant angle. Except in courtship, they did not need to strive to please—and even there, she thought cynically, they did not toil too greatly.

Almost light-headed with fatigue, she rose and proceeded to undress for the night. As she climbed into bed, she remembered with what enthusiasm she had rushed to the Long Gallery, simply because she had believed it would be Gerard waiting there. What madness had seized her? To have gone to him with her hair down, ready to permit him to embrace her as he had before . . . it was unthinkable. Shocking. Scandalous. She shivered in mortification.

Yes, her worst fears were confirmed; she most definitely had a wanton streak. Mercifully, it had lain dormant since Christian, but Gerard Marchant had brought it alive. He was handsome and virile, his body hard with a robust, male strength that called to her femininity. Even now, she ached for him. As tired as she was, she wanted to wrap her arms around him, to meld herself to him as sealing wax to paper. She wanted to explore him with her hands while his lips trailed fire over her flesh. She wanted to feel the heat of his manhood, to experience the most primal and wonderful of all acts, the physical joining of a man and a woman. The act of love.

It was folly even to think of it.

With a tortured groan, she buried her face in her pillow. She was headed down the road to disaster with such thoughts. Well-bred ladies did not even think about such things, much less yearn for them. And she was a spinster, which meant it was her destiny to spend her life alone. Alone, untouched, and unloved.

Gerard did not blame Tina for finding an excuse to absent herself from the drawing room that evening, but without her the hours seemed to drag on interminably. As Felicity made another inept discard, Gerard struggled to conceal his annoyance at her lack of aptitude for the game of whist.

Felicity was a hopeless card player. For perhaps the twentieth time that hour, he wished it were Tina in the seat opposite him. Tina, he reflected, would have noticed if she held a quart-major in her hand. Tina would have recalled what card he had led with. Tina would never have forgotten which suit was trump.

Felicity talked so much she forgot everything.

"Are we boring you, Gerry?" inquired Allegra, during one of Felicity's rare silences. Her teasing tone was lightly laced with curiosity. "You look like you'd rather be anywhere but here."

As he made a noncommittal answer, Gerard's eyes shifted to his brother-in-law. Rewe was hugging his cards against his chest, his handsome, swashbuckler face closed and taciturn. Wondering whether the bastard was thinking about Tina, Gerard concealed a scowl. Normally, he was adept at reading facial expressions, but not tonight.

"A pity Miss Jardine did not stay," commented his sister to no one in particular. Her eyes slid slyly over to Gerard. "She seems a pleasant young woman. A trifle colorless, perhaps."

Gerard almost snapped that Tina was not colorless, that she had more vitality in her little finger than Allegra had in her entire body. Instead he brusquely commanded her to cease her prattle and play. God forbid that any of them should guess that he had fallen in love. He was the

187

self-contained member of the family, the one who never let his passions override his common sense. It was how he had avoided marriage for so long; it was how he dealt with everything in his life.

Until now.

For the first time in memory, Gerard wanted to let go of his reserve. He wanted to fling out his arms and sing to the clouds, to dance and shout and tell the world of this wonderful woman he had found.

But of course he would not do it. Instead, he would put it all into his sonnet. Somehow he intended to convey everything he felt in three quatrains and a couplet. Within a rigid fourteen-line framework, he would present his romantic sentiments in logical, orderly progression. The idea pleased him enormously.

Several hours later, however, he stared down at a blank piece of paper and wondered whether he could do it. He was tired. Since it was well after midnight, he did not feel particularly creative. Briefly, he considered borrowing one of Shakespeare's lines. Surely the old fellow wouldn't mind.

Shall I compare thee to a summer's day?

Or perhaps he should liken her to something else, something more original. A buttercup? A rose? Imagery, Gerard, imagery. Create music with words, sing your song with metaphors.

She was more exotic than a buttercup, he decided. He supposed he should compare her to something prim-looking, yet wild and beautiful. Perhaps an orchid? Honeysuckle? A primrose? At least that one had the word 'prim' in it.

Gerard rubbed at his eyes and sighed wearily. This wasn't going to be easy. And he was certainly no Shakespeare.

"Miss Winton and I will deal with the invitations," announced Allegra at breakfast the following morning. "We must also plan a schedule of events to fill the hours for our guests. Naturally, we will have cards and dancing and musical entertainment, but I think some games might be diverting as well. As for the food"—her eyes went to Gerard—"naturally everything must be of the finest. The Marchants never stint."

Before she whisked Felicity off, however, Allegra made a point to solicit Tina's opinions. Did Miss Jardine have anyone she wished to invite? Did Miss Jardine have any thoughts on how they might decorate the ballroom? Did Miss Jardine have any ideas she wished to share?

Tina disclaimed, at the same time wondering why Allegra should show such unprecedented interest. Was it merely kindness? Or had she somehow discovered what her husband had done last night?

She was still worrying about it later when she commenced the despised task of embroidering tiny red hearts on Felicity's ball gown. Fortunately, she had convinced her cousin that hearts encircling the bodice *and* the waistline *and* the hem were simply too much. The white gauze and satin ball gown was already heavily flounced and trimmed with lace, pearls and rouleaux of zephyrine. She had told Felicity that small red hearts did nothing to improve it, but Felicity was unconvinced. They had therefore compromised on a discreet sprinkling of hearts across the bodice beneath the square-cut neckline.

A fire crackled in the grate of the small, first-floor sitting room where she had decided to work. Cousin Libby had fallen asleep in a nearby chair and was snoring peacefully. Gretchen sprawled at Tina's feet, her canine toes twitching as she dreamed whatever dogs dreamed.

When the first heart was complete, Tina leaned back and wondered what Gerard was doing. She knew that Allegra and Felicity were closeted in the Red Saloon, a room Christian's wife had taken over for herself. Christian, she knew, had gone riding with James, but Gerard had disappeared after breakfast with no word of his objectives. Not, of course, that the master of the house need explain himself to anyone, least of all her.

Yawning with boredom, Tina at last set the ball gown aside. There was no need to complete all the embroidery-work at once; the ball was days away. And Mrs. Winton was not here to complain if she chose to do something else for a while.

She had no specific plan in mind. She simply wanted to stretch her legs, to wander about the house for a bit. She had absolutely no intention of searching for Gerard—whatever he chose to do was no concern of hers. However, when Tina found herself outside the door to Gerard's library, she realized she had been fooling herself, that it was where she had intended to come all along. When a footman stepped forward, she shook her head, indicating that she did not require him to announce her. Instead, she lifted her hand and knocked.

"Come in." The cool, authoritative voice struck a chord in her heart, and she paused nervously. What was she doing here? What would she say? Then, telling herself not to behave like a simpering fool, she pushed open the door.

Like yesterday, Gerard was working at his desk. "What is it?" He did not look up, and his voice was curt.

"I'm sorry," she faltered. "You're busy. I'll go away."

His head came up sharply. "Tina," he said in an altered tone. Immediately he gathered his papers and shoved them into a drawer. "Come in." He sounded uncommonly glad to see her, and also, strangely, a little nervous.

"I don't wish to disturb your concentration," she protested. "You're obviously doing something important."

He stood, smiling oddly. "Yes, but it can wait. Come and sit down. What can I do for you?"

"Actually, I . . . the reason I'm here is that"—as he approached, she let her eyes rove over the shelves

190

crammed with hundreds of weighty-looking tomes—"I was wondering if I might look for something to read."

"But of course." The dark brows lifted. "My library is at your disposal. I hope you're not bored. What have you been doing?"

Tina was unused to gentlemen looking at her quite so intently, nor was she accustomed to such flattering interest in her doings. Gerard's charm was potent. It seeped under her skin like an aphrodisiac, bringing back the aches and yearnings she had been working all day to suppress.

"I have been sewing," she said in a rush. "Felicity is determined to have hearts on her gown."

He was standing so close she could see the tiny muscles in his jaw tighten. "I told Felicity that woman in Norton could do that. I see no reason for you to slave over her dress."

"I am not slaving," she said quietly. "Embroidery is something I am well equipped to do."

"But you dislike it," he insisted. "Your artist's soul feels constrained by such rigidity."

"I never said that."

Before she could protest, he captured her hands. "You do not need to," he replied. "Your face gives you away. Your face tells me a great many things you may not realize."

"It does?" she said warily.

"It does." His lips curved in amusement. "For instance, I know why you came to the library, and it was not to borrow a book."

Heat surged to Tina's cheeks. "I don't know what you mean," she stammered.

"Don't you?" His smile broadened. "You came to challenge me to another game of chess. And I accept your challenge."

Weak with relief, she said severely, "You, Lord Laverstoke, are a manipulator. Is this how you served your country? By planting ideas in peoples' heads?"

He burst out laughing. "You've guessed it. The trick is in making a person think my ideas are his own. Or *her* own," he added, more softly. "How about it, Valentina? Dare you challenge me? Or are you one of those women who really believes that the male mind is superior?"

"I am not!" she said indignantly. "Why, I used to beat Papa quite often, and he was a first-rate player." She knew that he was baiting her, but at that moment she did not care. She could only think that it was the first time she had heard him laugh, and that it was the most delicious, seductive sound she had ever heard.

She watched him set up the chess pieces, marveling at the peace and serenity flooding her spirit. As attracted as she was to him, the satisfaction she found in this man's company was far more than physical. When she was with him, she felt strong enough to deal with life's vicissitudes. She did not feel like a woman who was destined to remain a spinster. She did not feel alone.

"Ebony or ivory?"

"Oh, I think ivory this time," she answered, tingling with the knowledge of her power and femininity. "Perhaps I will have a change of luck."

"People make their own luck, Tina. Nothing happens by chance."

"Our meeting was by chance," she said without thinking. Then she flushed and lowered her eyes, her heart thudding with embarrassment.

"True," he acknowledged. "Unless one believes that it was preordained. Do you think that might be possible?"

"I think, my lord, that we had best leave such discussions for another occasion. If I am to defeat you, I shall need all my wits about me."

This time his laugh was soft, a brief, comfortable sound that soothed her embarrassment as effectively as a kiss.

"Very well. Play your best, my girl, for I won't fall without a struggle."

And struggle he did. For the next three hours they fought, man against woman, mind against mind. She was making no mistakes, he observed with approval. This time she did not underestimate him, nor did she do anything reckless. Gerard could almost see the wheels turning in her mind as she weighed every option and predicted his intentions with an accuracy that would have made Castlereagh stare.

As he waited for her to move, it occurred to him that she was the most relaxing woman he had ever known. Instead of assailing his ears, she challenged his mind. She excited his body and stimulated his intellect, which was precisely what he had been looking for all these years. Watching her face, he realized that with her he could be himself. He could imagine confiding in her, just as he could imagine her nurturing his children—bearing them, suckling them, laughing with them.

He wanted her in his future.

He recalled that at first he had found her looks a trifle quiet. Now he found her—every lovely inch of her—pleasing beyond measure. Though she was not petite, her features had a definite dainty quality. Her eyes were wide-spaced and blue, her brow clear and pale, her cheeks delicately blushed with rosedust. *Blushed with rosedust.* Now there was a nice phrase. Perhaps he could work it into his sonnet.

He had written enough words to fill ten sonnets by now, yet he had not achieved the exact combination of words that expressed what lay within his churning soul. He would work on it some more tonight, he decided, after everyone was asleep.

In search of inspiration, he stared at Tina's lips, allowing the memory of their taste to wash over him in clear, cleansing waves.

"My lord?" Her reproving voice interrupted his thoughts.

He had been woolgathering so deeply he had missed the movement of her hand. Refocusing his attention, he frowned. "Wait a minute. What the devil happened?"

Tina's eyes gleamed with mischief. "I believe you will find you are in check." Her demure air made him want to laugh with delight.

"That was very neat," he said approvingly. "You know you have me caught?"

She nodded, looking pleased with herself.

He moved his king, then watched her slide her queen triumphantly across the board. "Checkmate, my lord."

He leaned back, thinking how beautiful she was when she was smiling. "Will you think me arrogant if I say that you're the first woman ever to beat me?"

"Terribly arrogant," she agreed. "I've thought so from the first."

"Have you, now?" He pondered this. "And yet it appears that I'm forgiven."

Under his fascinated gaze, her cheeks slowly shaded a delicate pink. *Rosedust,* he thought in bemusement.

Without warning, the door to his study swung open. "Oh, there you are," said his brother-in-law, lounging casually against the jamb. "I've been wondering where everyone was. I see you are monopolizing Miss Jardine."

Gerard glanced at Tina just quickly enough to observe her change in color.

"Trust you," Rewe continued, "to snatch the loveliest lady and keep her to yourself. The post arrived, by the way. There's a very fragrant letter for you from Lady Chalfield."

"My letters are none of your concern," uttered Gerard in sudden fury.

Rewe merely smiled. "Sorry, old fellow. I don't mean to pry. I only came by to see if Miss Jardine would care to take the air. The roads are clear enough to use the gig."

"Miss Jardine is occupied," snapped Gerard.

"I am perfectly capable of answering for myself." Tina's voice, unlike his, was quiet and full of dignity.

"Well, answer then," he said tightly. *Tell the bastard to go to hell*.

To his astonishment, she stood and dropped him a formal curtsy. "Thank you for the chess game, my lord. I think"—she spoke carefully, he noticed—"I would like to take the air with Lord Rewe now." She glanced over at the man in the doorway. "If he will give me a few minutes to make myself ready."

Rewe smiled the foxy smile that Gerard loathed. "Of course, Miss Jardine. Take all the time you need. I'll await you in the hall. Be sure and dress warmly."

"I shall," she said calmly. She walked halfway to the door, then looked back at Gerard, as though trying to convey some message. "Thank you again."

Gerard merely nodded. For once, he could think of nothing to say.

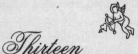

Thirteen

"I knew you'd agree," Christian said. He flicked the reins, and they started off down the drive.

"I almost didn't," she informed him. "And I'm not at all sure this is wise . . . Lord Rewe." She used his title to put a distance between them, her stomach tying into knots at the idea of what Gerard must be thinking.

There was a shift in Christian's expression. "Don't call me that. For God's sake, we don't have to stand on points with each other in private."

"You are Allegra Marchant's husband," she retorted. " 'Til death, I believe."

That silenced him for a moment. "You hate me," he said finally. "You hate me for marrying her."

The accusation hurt.

"No, of course I don't." Her protest was automatic. Hate? Christian? She glanced at him, her mind rejecting such an alien emotion. How could she hate this beautiful man with his sulky, little boy's smile? No matter what he had done, he was still the man she had loved so dearly, the man she had wanted to wed. But did she still love him? What did she feel?

"Don't hate me, Tina. It wasn't my fault I had to marry her. I couldn't help it."

He was charming, earnest, repentant. Himself. Christian had not changed a bit.

Unable to bear the pain of looking at him, Tina gazed

196

blindly at a spot on the horizon. "Your letter arrived on my birthday." Pride demanded she keep the emotion from her voice. "Almost five years ago. It was not a nice gift."

"Jesus," he muttered. "I didn't know. There was so much happening that I . . . I must have forgotten."

"Obviously." The cold blurred her eyes.

"There were other things than you on my mind," he snapped. "There was the estate to claim, and all that money. I had to take control. There were people to meet. I met Allegra at a nearby house party. She was eighteen and rigged to the nines."

The admiration in his voice blew away whatever tactful statement she'd been going to make. "So you simply forgot about me," she said flatly.

"I didn't *forget*," he insisted. "You were never out of my mind for an instant. It was just that—oh, damn." Several seconds went by. "Allegra was different from you. Forward. Uppity. But beneath her uppityness. she wanted me."

"So did I," she murmured, a lump in her throat.

He sent her a sidelong look. "Yes, but what Allegra wants, she takes. I didn't realize that until it was too late." Again, that tinge of admiration. "But I didn't bring you out here to tell you that," he added in a far different tone.

"Then why *did* you bring me?" she flashed.

He halted the gig and turned to look at her. "Oh, Tina," he said softly, "I really botched things up for us, didn't I? Yet all is not lost. We're together now, and that's something I never thought would happen." His eyes were beseeching. "Can't we patch things up? Can't we cry a truce and be . . . friends?"

Tina hesitated. The thought of having Christian in her life again was both painful and glorious. Living without him had been hell. Could she risk it?

"Remember what good times we used to have?" he

urged. "Do you remember the apple orchard, Tina? Do you remember how we used to go there and hold hands and talk? Do you remember the first time I kissed you?" He went on, pulling out memory after memory like lace and ribbons from a drawer.

Tina stared down at her lap. She remembered. She remembered everything, perhaps in greater detail than he.

"—we can have all that again," he ended. "I can't say it will be easy, but—"

Of course it won't be easy, her reason scoffed.

How? questioned her thudding heart.

"How?" She examined the fur edging on her gloves. "How can we possibly have all that, Christian?" she said evenly. "Are you suggesting you will divorce Allegra?"

"Divorce?" He was clearly startled. "Good God, no!" He slipped an arm around her shoulders and gave her a gentle squeeze. "My darling, you were always so naive. Of course I can't divorce Allegra. You've no idea of the expense, not to mention the social stigma." He shuddered visibly. "Divorce won't wash, and there's no grounds for annulment. I signed no prenuptial agreement, you'll recall."

She recalled all too clearly.

"Now, listen to me, Tina. I'm going to explain this to you. The thing for you to do is to make a *mariage de convenance.*"

"What?" Stunned, she looked at him.

"A marriage of convenience," he explained, as though she were slightly stupid. "You need a husband. We can't be together if you go on living with Felicity Winton's family. At any rate, you were never meant to live your life as someone's else slave. You're no passionless drudge like Miss Steeple."

"Miss Steeple was never a passionless drudge!" she shot, latching onto the less infamous statement. "And you've no right to say so."

"Forgive me," he said with uncharacteristic humbleness. "Of course I've no right. I'd forgotten how close you were to the woman."

Ignoring this, Tina gave full attention to his suggestion. "A marriage of convenience." She repeated the words, testing their sound. "Are you serious?" she asked in amazement.

Christian's dark, exquisite face bent so close she thought he meant to kiss her. "Yes. Ever since I learned that you were here, at Laverstoke Park, I've been thinking about what we should do. We can take advantage of this, Tina." She could feel his excitement, his sincerity. "I've come up with a plan. And the first step of the plan is for you to marry James."

"James!" For the second time in a minute, Tina was nearly struck dumb. "Why James?"

"Who else is there?" he retorted. "Not Laverstoke. He's not interested in marriage, and if he was, he wouldn't choose you."

"I don't think James would marry me either," she said stiffly. "I believe he cares for Lady Millicent."

Christian dismissed this with a snort. "He'll never win her and he knows it. His prospects are too dim to dazzle her mother. The old cow wants Laverstoke for a son-in-law."

"Lord Laverstoke would never wed Millie."

"You think not? I'll lay odds he does." Christian's tone was more matter-of-fact than cynical. "She's an heiress, Tina. Her dowry is huge."

"So?" she countered. "Laverstoke does not need to marry wealth."

"Every Viscount Laverstoke marries wealth. His father married an heiress, and so did his grandfather before him. It's a tradition that goes back for generations. Centuries, even. Haven't you wondered how it is that Laverstoke Park is so magnificent? It's like a damned ducal estate, for God's sake! The Regent himself has been known to sigh over the place."

Tina sucked in a breath. "So you think I should wed James," she said slowly. "Assuming he is agreeable, how would that . . . serve us?"

"James lives at Laverstoke Park," Christian said patiently. "He is his brother's steward. And with that leg of his, he's never likely to be anything else. His soldiering is at an end. He has no estate of his own."

"So?"

"So you will live here, too. And whenever Allegra and I visit, you and I can be together."

"Together," she repeated, as his meaning sunk in. "And what of James? Do you think he will countenance this?"

He had the grace to flush. "He will if he has any sense. He ought to be damned grateful to have you for a wife. Dash it, Tina, don't look at me like that. I know it's not perfect. I don't want you married to another man. I love you!" As if to prove this, he slid his arm around her waist and kissed the side of her mouth.

She jerked away. "Don't!"

"Don't?" he repeated, a quizzing look in his eye. "But why?"

"How can you ask me why?" she exclaimed, her voice shaking. "Besides the small fact that anyone might come along and see, you are *married,* Christian. *Married!*"

He made a noise that was both frustrated and amused. "Haven't you been listening to a word I've said? What in heaven's name do you think the purpose of all this is? I want you as a man wants a woman. When you're married to James, we can have that. Discreetly, of course."

When she only looked at him, he shifted uncomfortably. "Dash it, Tina, most married women have lovers! It's not at all uncommon! Why, my own mother carried on with a man for years—after she had me, of course. And my father never cared, for God's sake. Why should he, when he had a mistress of his own? And with James, there won't be the problem of an heir, for there'll be nothing to inherit—"

"Please take me back," she requested in a low, curt voice. "I'm very cold."

He cast her a dubious glance, but, thankfully, did not argue, or indeed speak at all during the return journey. Likewise, Tina simply sat, struggling to absorb what had just transpired. Shards of emotion catapulted within her, splintering her heart, numbing her mind, making it impossible to speak.

When the gig drew up to the door, Christian reached over and squeezed her hand. "It's the only way," he said again. "You think about what I've said, love, and you'll see it makes sense. My sweet, sweet Valentine's Day girl. I've missed you so much."

For the tenth time that hour, Gerard reread his sonnet with a critical eye. He was particularly pleased with the last line. *Thou art the heavenly garden of my soul.* It flowed. He allowed himself the pleasure of imagining Tina's expression when she read it, then released a frustrated sigh. The rest of it was not right yet. He would have to work some more.

While he was pondering, James wandered into the room. "Hullo. What are you doing?" He limped over to the desk and peered over Gerard's shoulder.

Gerard repressed a childish urge to shield his poem with his hands. "Writing a sonnet," he answered, his voice challenging.

"Writing a what?"

"A sonnet."

James continued to stare.

"S-O-N-N-E-T," said Gerard irritably.

"I know how to spell it," James said mildly. He reached down and picked up Gerard's most recent effort. *"Shall I compare thee to a summer's day?* By jove, I like that. You wrote it?"

"Actually, that line is Shakespeare's. I wrote the rest of it."

"Oh," said James. "Isn't that cheating?"

Gerard surveyed his brother with growing annoyance. "No. It's called borrowing. I'm sure Shakespeare would have been highly flattered."

"I don't know, Gerry. I think you ought to give the old fellow credit." He frowned. "Your handwriting is atrocious."

Gerard snatched the sonnet away.

James grinned and planted himself in a nearby armchair. "I assume it's for Valentina?" he asked casually.

"Yes." Hearing his own brusqueness, Gerard adjusted his tone. "It's for a valentine."

James gazed at him fixedly. "You think you will draw her name in the lottery?"

"No. I, er, will give it to her privately."

"Hmmm, not a bad idea. Perhaps I should write one for Millie."

"A sonnet?" Gerard lifted a brow.

"Of course not," scoffed his brother. "I couldn't write a sonnet if my life depended on it. I was thinking of something simple. You know: 'Roses are red, violets are blue, you are sweet and I love you.' That sort of thing." Another thought struck him. "Unless Shakespeare has one I could borrow?"

"I doubt it. Here, see for yourself." With a satanic gleam, Gerard tossed him the book of sonnets.

Catching it neatly, James browsed through the pages for a while. "Hang it," he said at last, "I can't understand most of this, and the little I do understand is wildly unsuitable. Listen to this." He cleared his throat. *"My mistress' eyes are nothing like the sun; Coral is far more red than her lips' red; If snow be white, why then her breasts are dun; If hairs be wires, black wires grow on her head."* He glanced up indignantly. "Hang it, Gerry, that's dashed insulting!"

Gerard regarded his brother over his steepled fingers. "Write one yourself," he advised. "Something that comes

202

from your heart."

"The only words that come from my heart are 'I love you'," said his brother simply. Then he heaved a sigh. "Well, mayhap I will, though how I'm to give it to her without her mother knowing . . ." He shook his head gloomily.

"That's the least of your worries," Gerard assured him. "I've already planned for that."

"Have you, now?" James straightened. "How?"

"You can slip it under her door during the night."

James's brows shot up. "Isn't that risky? What if one of the maids picks it up?"

"Well, she won't open it, will she? All you need do is put her name on it. Believe me, Millie will think you a terribly dashing fellow."

"Very well, I won't argue with you." James stretched his arms and yawned. "Where is Valentina?"

Gerard could feel himself tense at the question. "Rewe took her for a ride in the gig." There was strain in his voice.

"He's a cool bastard, isn't he?" James leaned back, his eyes pinned to Gerard's. "What are you going to do about it?"

"What can I do? I can't forbid her to talk to him."

James hesitated. "No, but you can prevent your servants from taking his bribes."

"What?"

"As your steward, I feel it's my duty to tell you. Mrs. Bissett informs me that one of her girls was caught with a half-crown in her possession. When she could not account for it, Bissett accused her of stealing. The girl broke down and confessed that Rewe had given it to her."

"For doing what?" Gerard asked harshly.

James shook his head. "No, not that. Rewe has more discretion than to tumble the housemaids." Briefly, he provided a summary of Lord Rewe's tactic for meeting Tina alone.

Gerard absorbed the tale in silence, his insides cold with fury. "So the girl told Tina to meet Rewe in the Long Gallery," he said tightly. "Did she go?"

"I'm afraid I've no idea."

Jealousy was a new experience for Gerard. He had never cared about any one woman enough for it to signify whether or not she was constant, or preferred another man to himself. It had never mattered that he was not the only man in Beatrice's life. She made herself available to him when he wished it; when he did not, he knew she satisfied her appetite with other men, none of them her husband. Until now he had found the arrangement unexceptional.

"When Rewe gets back, tell him to come to the library," he said roughly.

"I'll do that," said James.

Gerard used the subsequent half hour to consume two fingers of whiskey, and was seriously considering pouring himself another when his brother-in-law strolled into the room.

"You wanted to talk to me?" Rewe said in the jaunty, faintly insolent tone he reserved for Gerard.

From his vantage behind the desk, Gerard favored his sister's husband with a cold, hard stare. The ability to crucify a person with a mere look was an art which had been perfected by every Viscount Laverstoke for generations. Relations claimed that it came with the title; first sons were simply born with it.

However, Gerard had seldom found it necessary to employ The Stare. It was not diplomatic. It was not even nice. But Gerard was feeling neither diplomatic nor nice. Only once before had he leveled that rapier look upon his brother-in-law, and from the way Rewe stood, shifting his feet like the weak-kneed milksop that he was, it was clear that he also remembered the occasion.

"Well?" Rewe said boldly. "What have I done?"

"I think you know."

"Well, I don't." Rewe hunched a shoulder.

"Then allow me to explain." Gerard's fingers tapped the edge of the desk. "Quite simply, I do not condone bribery in my house."

"Bribery?" The word was midway between a squeak and a growl. "What the devil are you talking about?"

"Last night you bribed one of my housemaids with a half-crown." Gerard leaned forward, his eyes like chinks of ice. "You forced her to deliver a message to Miss Jardine."

To his annoyance, Rewe threw him a cocky grin and sat down, uninvited. "Is that what troubles you? Good God, man, I simply wanted to further my acquaintance with an attractive woman. Why the deuce should you care?"

"Miss Jardine," responded Gerard, enunciating carefully, "is a virtuous young woman of birth and breeding. She is off-limits to you. Do you understand?"

"No, I don't," Rewe shot back, exhibiting more defiance than Gerard expected. "If Miss Jardine wishes for my company, what the deuce does it matter to you? She's a comely armful, but I'll remember my manners."

Determined to learn whether Tina had actually gone to the Long Gallery, Gerard searched for a way to do so without betraying his ignorance. "Have you remembered them yet?" he inquired. "Asking a lady to rendezvous with you secretly is hardly the way to show respect."

Rewe bared his teeth in a semblance of a smile. "Oh, she didn't mind," he retorted. "She was quite entranced by my innovative methods." Making himself comfortable, he honed right in on the chink in Gerard's armor. "I know what it is. You're jealous of my success. You wish it were you she came to meet!"

Gerard flung this aside with contempt. "Don't flatter yourself that I see you as a rival, you bastard. It is Allegra who concerns me. You married her—"

"At your behest!"

"—and by God you are going to remember your vows. I'll not have my sister humiliated, do you hear?"

"I wouldn't do that! Damn it, Laverstoke, I'm fond of Allegra!"

"Then show it. Stop dangling after other women and pay her some attention. And stay away from Tina."

Rewe's brows rose. "Oh, so it's *Tina*, is it?" He rose to his feet, a taunting glitter in his dark eyes. "You randy dog, you want her for yourself, don't you? I'll wager you've been sniffing around her skirts since the day she arrived."

All this time, Gerard had forgotten that beneath his desk lay a dog. Gretchen was not, perhaps, the most intelligent animal in the world, but she knew the word "dog" when she heard it. Rewe's gaze shifted and changed as the beast emerged, her stance taut with unblinking canine menace. All at once Gerard remembered that his brother-in-law was afraid of dogs.

"Nice doggie."

Gretchen's lip lifted at the hypocrisy. A low growl rumbled in her throat.

"Why's it doing that?" Christian stepped back nervously.

Gerard smiled. "She doesn't like you."

"Well, do something! Call the creature off!"

"Sit, Gretchen," said Gerard quietly.

Gretchen sat.

Gerard looked at his brother-in-law, searching to see what it was Tina saw in him. He supposed there was a manly beauty in the broad, high cheekbones and sculpted nose. He supposed, too, that there was a certain masculine presence in Rewe's height and physique. However, Gerard found the fellow's eyes over-crafty. And he did not care for his lips, particularly when he imagined where they might have been. His own lips folded in revulsion.

206

"Get out of here," he uttered, his voice very low. "Go ahead, Gretchen won't hurt you. The threat is from me, you fool."

As Rewe backed toward the door, he recovered a portion of his *savoir-faire*. "If you want your precious sister happy, Laverstoke, you'd best save your threats. I'll talk to Miss Jardine if I choose. Thus far, she seems delighted with my company."

When he was gone, Gerard's eyes slid shut. What had possessed him to be so unsubtle? Years of self-discipline and practice had taught him how to handle a hostile personality, yet with Rewe he had been reduced to common threats and insults. Then his face darkened.

The bastard talked about Tina as if she were a dog.

Gretchen nudged his leg as she crawled back under the desk and resumed her previous position. Gerard reached down and scratched her head. "Good girl," he murmured. "Excellent, discriminating animal."

Gretchen slurped at his hand and snorted blissfully.

By the following day it seemed clear that Allegra, for reasons of her own, was very curious about Tina — far more so than she was about Felicity. Tina pondered this nervously on her way to the Red Saloon. Why had Allegra sent for her? Was she aware that Christian had taken her for a drive? If so, what would she say?

But Allegra's first words were almost ordinary. "There you are, Miss Jardine. James tells me you wish to borrow one of my ball gowns." She came closer, studying Tina with almost meticulous absorption. "Turn around, please. Yes, that's good. Hmmm. Of course, you do not have my coloring, but"—her fair head tilted consideringly—"we are much the same height. My figure is a little fuller, perhaps. Because I've had a child."

Tina flushed. "I don't know exactly what your brother said, Lady Rewe, but I am certainly not expecting you to lend me anything—"

"Do you have a ball gown?" Allegra cut in.

"No, but—"

"Then what do you intend to wear to the ball?"

Tina bit her lip. "Well, I . . . do not know. But I would feel uncomfortable borrowing one of yours."

"Oh, fustian. I shall enjoy dressing you up." Allegra patted her curls. "My red silk ought to become you. I adore the color but it doesn't flatter me at all. Come to my room later and you may try it on. No, don't thank me." She waved airily. "It would be too boring."

"But I must thank you," Tina said helplessly. "You are too kind, I am sure."

Allegra's mouth quirked. "You think so? Poor Miss Jardine. You are doomed to disappointment if you think me any sort of paragon. I am only kind when it suits me. I choose to be kind to you because"—she paused, as though choosing her words with care—"because you interest me profoundly."

"But . . . why?" Tina braced herself for the answer.

Moving to the sofa, Allegra settled herself with grace. "Oh, I don't think I shall tell you that just yet. Come sit with me. Have you been to the portrait gallery?"

Filled with foreboding, Tina did as Allegra suggested. "Yes, as a matter of fact I have."

"Ah." Allegra's lips curved. "Then you've seen our ancestors. A gruesome lot, are they not?"

"I don't think so. Many of them are quite striking."

"The men, perhaps. The women are pathetic, except for one or two. Doubtless they were all miserable. Every one of them was wed for her wealth."

"Not an uncommon practice, even today," Tina said without thinking.

"Very true." Allegra's smile flashed then faded. "You've no money, I collect? No, of course you do not, else why would you play drudge for Felicity Winton? Tell me, have you had much experience with men?"

"I . . . I beg your pardon?" Every muscle in Tina's

body tensed at what sounded like a subtle accusation.

Allegra merely waved a hand. "Oh, I do not mean *that* sort of experience. I know you are unwed. I mean, have you known many men? Are you shy with them? Can you tease? Can you"—she gestured—"keep up with their conversation? Read their moods?"

"I'm afraid I do not take your meaning, ma'am."

Allegra sighed. "It is of no consequence, Miss Jardine. I was merely . . . thinking. You know, it was not until after I was married that I realized exactly how permanent marriage is. Before that, the wedded state seemed only a rainbow of golden dreams." Her brow puckered. "The reality is so different."

Abruptly, she switched the topic to fashion, a subject that dominated the rest of their visit. As for the reason for Allegra's interest in her, Tina was more mystified than ever.

Dinner that evening was another stilted affair, as was the stretch of hours afterward. To avoid Christian, Tina agreed to play piquet with James, at the same time straining to hear Gerard and Christian's heated political debate on the other side of the room. It seemed to her that no matter what stand Gerard took on a subject, Christian would take the opposite. And while Christian argued without purpose, Gerard seemed bent on goading him into making a fool of himself. It distressed Tina almost as much as Christian's suggestion that she set her cap for poor, unsuspecting James.

Before she retired that night, Tina sat down and made a quick sketch of Allegra. The woman was not at all what she expected, she mused. Allegra, Lady Rewe, was a beautiful woman, but she was also a very unhappy one. Was it because she did not have her husband's love? If so, Tina could only pity her.

The following morning she was summoned to Allegra's bedroom to try on the ball gown. While her maid helped Tina into the dress, Allegra stood still and watched, sipping at her chocolate.

"Dickon is out for his walk with Nana," she told Tina. "Sometimes I take him out myself. Does it feel like spring yet? How I loathe winter. It makes me feel so trapped." Setting down her cup, she wandered over to the window. "As a child, I used to love winter. I used to skate on the pond over there"—she pointed to a spot in the distance—"with my brothers. It was the only thing I could do better than them."

Tina said nothing.

"Some of the houseguests will be arriving today. Lady Buckden and Millie will be first, of course. Lord Buckden won't come—he's a recluse." Allegra glanced over her shoulder, but instead of making some comment on the dress, she said fiercely, "I don't want Laverstoke to marry Millie!"

While the maid pinned in the waistline, Tina wondered if this accounted for Allegra's interest in her. "Surely that is up to him?"

"Faugh, he doesn't want her. But I don't trust that Buckden woman. Did you know she was a Cit's daughter? She trapped poor Buckden into marriage, no one knows how." Allegra turned back to the window. "But she's haughtier than Buckden, whose family goes back nearly as far as the Norman Conquest. As his wife is so fond of pointing out," she added with heavy sarcasm.

Tina thought of the dark little mouse of a girl she had met so briefly. "Poor Lady Millie," she said softly.

"Poor Millie indeed." Allegra spun around. "She's an heiress, you know. That's why I'm afraid."

"Afraid?"

"Every Viscount Laverstoke for centuries has married an heiress, Miss Jardine."

Tina feigned an indifference she did not feel. "Why are you telling me this, ma'am?"

Allegra sent her a strange look. "I thought you'd be interested. Aren't you?"

"Well . . . I suppose so. I think it a pity that James is not allowed to court Millie. He so obviously wishes to."

"Yes, it *is* a pity. To wed the wrong person is a terrible thing, Miss Jardine. I should know." She paused. "Miss Winton spends too much time flirting with James. I wish she would not."

"Felicity is merely a high-spirited girl," Tina said. "She also has a young man she misses extremely. Unfortunately his duties are keeping him . . . away at the moment. An invitation to the ball might bring him here."

"Indeed? Then we shall send him one. Hopefully he will come at once and fetch her away. I find her very much *de trop*. That dress suits you. I knew it would."

"If she went, I would have to go with her," Tina reminded.

"No! No, you must stay." Allegra drew a deep breath. "You must stay. He likes you, Miss Jardine. And . . . I like you, too. I think I would like to have you for a sister."

"I am employed by Felicity's parents—"

"That must not be allowed to continue. I shall see what can be done about it, but let us not discuss it anymore. Come, turn around. Yes, the color is marvelous with your black hair and pale skin. Agnes, see that these alterations are made, and then we will try it again. I think the hem needs to be taken up a bit, too. You'd better pin it up now."

When Tina left the room twenty minutes later, it was with the belief that she understood Christian's wife a great deal better than she had when she entered. If her suspicions were correct, Allegra had selected her to be Gerard's bride. Moreover, it seemed Allegra intended to do everything she could to make sure she got her way! Her motives were less clear, but Tina had received the impression that there was a stronger bond between Allegra and her brothers than she had at first realized. In short, Allegra wanted her brothers—both of them—to be

211

happy, and that, curiously enough, was enough to banish the last of Tina's dislike.

Searching for Felicity and Libby, she headed for the first floor, where she instead encountered Gerard at the foot of the grand staircase.

"What perfect timing," he said, with a smile that stole the strength from her limbs. "I wanted to ask you to go riding with me."

Since Tina still stood on the last step, she found herself gazing directly into the viscount's penetrating gray eyes. For a moment, she was utterly mesmerized, lost in that direct masculine look that her body understood far better than her mind. "I . . . I'm afraid I did not bring my riding habit, my lord." There was no need to mention that it was nonexistent.

"My lord?" he repeated, his tone quizzing. "I thought we'd gotten past such formality. I wish you would call me Gerard."

"I can hardly do so when your sister—"

"I'll speak to Allegra. She's always been a stickler for formality." His voice was low, his look intimate. "I've had enough of it to last me a lifetime."

Very conscious of a nearby footman, Tina smiled uncertainly. "Very well, then, if it pleases you. But I have no habit."

"You shall borrow one of Allegra's." Very slowly, he ran one finger along the curve of her jaw, then flicked the tip of her nose. "I'm sure she's brought several along. No, don't argue with me. The fresh air will put some color into your cheeks. Or don't you ride?"

Her flesh tingled where he'd touched her.

"I was used to," she admitted, "before Papa had to sell his horses. It's been a long time."

"Then I shan't mount you on anything spirited," he said. "I'll put you on Lady, my mother's old hack."

"Oh, no!" she said involuntarily. When his brows shot up, she stammered, "I did not mean . . . I only meant

212

that I've not forgotten how to ride."

"We must take no chances," he said smoothly.

"My lord—"

"Gerard," he corrected.

"Gerard," she warned, "if you mount me on a slug, I will never forgive you! I'll wager I can ride as well as anyone in this house. Including you."

His eyes lit with amusement. "What would you care to wager?"

A kiss. The words hung in the air like an unspoken promise.

Tina's eyes flew to the hovering footman. "As to that," she said with a saucy smile, "I shall wager nothing. I would not like to take advantage of you twice in two days."

He reached up and placed his finger under her chin, lifting it just a trifle. "My dear Valentina," he said, in a very soft voice, "you may take advantage of me any time the fancy strikes you."

Fourteen

At the crest of the tallest hill they paused, gazing over a sweep of landscape that was only extraordinary because they viewed it together. Side by side, they absorbed the sun-sparkled snow and playful clouds; side by side, they listened to the rustlings and whispers on the shifting breeze. Then Laverstoke's black stallion pawed the ground, demonstrating an impatience which quickly transmitted to Sheba, Tina's feisty mount.

Patting the mare's neck, Tina glanced over at Gerard and found that he was no longer studying the terrain. Instead, he was watching her, his expression direct and intent and focused on her face. His eyes glittered silver in the sunlight, slicing and keen, a reminder of his intelligence. She was so conscious of him that when he smiled, it was as though he had stroked her with his hands.

When they started down the hill, she purposely fell a little behind so that she could feast her eyes on his physique. He sat his saddle with ease, his back straight, his riding breeches stretched across his long, muscled legs. Of course, she well knew that a lady of breeding and refinement ought not to notice such things as a gentleman's legs. However, she rationalized, her artist's eye was trained to observe, so she could do so with a clear conscience.

So far they had spoken naught but the merest commonplaces, yet in the light of her new awareness, each look, each gesture, each ordinary remark seemed intimate beyond measure. No ghosts haunted her at this moment; Christian's image was as absent as if it had never been. Yet Tina was not without qualms. Dare she hope for love from this man? Dare she fall in love again? Especially when family tradition demanded that he marry wealth?

Perhaps she was mad to dream of it. Her heart plummeted at the possibility that the awareness might all be on her side. She could very well be imagining everything. What she needed to do was think. Love was something that should be approached cautiously, not with the wild, reckless abandon her disposition demanded. If she were wise, she would go back and review lessons learned.

Of course, it all came back to that streak in her nature, that wild, passionate streak that yearned for the physical love of a man. It was her flaw, her weakness. Yet she must subdue it, for above all she wished Gerard to think well of her. She was a lady. She had to remember that.

"Why are you frowning?" he asked suddenly.

"Oh—" Tina forced a smile. "It's nothing. I am merely concerned about"—quickly she searched for some reasonable answer—"Felicity."

"Felicity?" He looked slightly taken aback. "Why?"

"Oh, well, she misses her young man, you know—" She chattered on, explained the gist of her cousin's problems with Eugene St. Hillary.

"I know St. Hillary," he remarked.

"You do? How?"

He shrugged. "I know a great many people, at both the Home and Foreign Office. St. Hillary seems a fine young man. Felicity could do worse."

"Her mother does not think so," she told him. "Mrs. Winton expects Felicity to make a splendid marriage."

Gerard's mouth lost its relaxed slant. "What is it about motherhood?" he said derisively. "I've seen perfectly amiable women turn into wolves when it comes time to find husbands for their daughters. An unmarried man is nothing but prey."

Tina shifted in her saddle. "I'm sure most of them only want what's best for their children."

"You think so?" He sounded cynical. "I don't." Then he smiled lazily. "Don't look like that, my dear. I'm not talking about you. I'm sure you would make a splendid mother."

This was dangerous territory, but something inside Tina compelled her to tread forward. "Perhaps," she said lightly, "but I doubt I shall have the opportunity to prove you right."

"Why not? Don't you want children?"

"I would need a husband first," she reminded him tartly. Oddly, she did not think of Christian until after she spoke.

"Yes, of course. I do understand that." For a moment, rich humor rippled his voice, but it died as he went on, abruptly, "Don't think about him, Tina. Not now, not ever."

It took her a moment to decide what to say. "I suppose you mean Christian," she finally mumbled, her gaze riveted on Sheba's left ear.

"Of course I mean Christian," he said impatiently. There was a short pause. Then, harshly, he added, "I know you met him in the Long Gallery the other night. I want to know why."

Tina's involuntary jerk on the reins sent Sheba dancing sideways. "How did you find out?" she said, her voice not quite even.

"I know everything that goes on in my house," he replied. His tone was arrogant, his expression as stern as it had been the night she had met him. "It is my business to know. Under the circumstances, however, I own I am disappointed. I'd thought better of you, my girl."

Her bosom swelled at the injustice. "Oh, you did, did

you? And what right have you to approve or disapprove my actions?"

"No right," he said, scowling, "unless your actions reflect upon the honor of my family. Need I remind you that Lord Rewe is my sister's husband? I am scarcely going to condone any behavior that will cause her distress."

Tina's throat closed on a lump of misery. Their ride was ruined, the magic gone. They were nearly back to the house; even from here, she could see an elegant coach-and-four drawn up before the great front doors. Nothing was the same as it had been a moment before.

"The guests are arriving," she said shakily.

"It's Lady Buckden." For a moment Gerard was indifferent, then his voice blazed out at her once more. "Listen to me, Tina. I will say this once and only once. What's done is done. You are going to have to accept that Rewe is lost to you. And for God's sake be discreet! My sister has invited people to this house party who will scent out the faintest whiff of scandal. They will be only too happy to fault your actions—"

"The way you do?" she cut in hotly. "I'm sure I ought to be flattered by your opinion of me. First you thought Felicity and I arranged a false accident to our carriage just so we could crawl through a mile of freezing snow to your hallowed doorstep—"

"Tina!"

"—and all for the dubious honor of trapping you into marriage! And now you think me capable of the vilest kind of deceit." She paused, her breasts heaving, her eyes sparking blue fire in his direction. "Well, my lord, rest assured that you will have no further cause to complain about my behavior. I am a virtuous woman, I have always been a virtuous woman, and I intend to remain a virtuous woman! And it just so happens that I thought it was *you* waiting for me in the Long Gallery!"

Before he could speak, she used her crop on Sheba's

flanks—not cruelly, but hard enough to send the mare flying toward the house.

Left far behind, Gerard's face wore an arrested expression. "Well, that will certainly teach me to open my mouth," he murmured.

Her temper simmering, Tina entered the house by a side door and went directly to her room to change her clothes. Half an hour later, she descended to the first floor, feeling it obligatory that she present herself in the drawing room even though she was still exceedingly annoyed with Gerard.

As she approached the drawing room, Tina could hear Lady Buckden's strident accents floating down the corridor.

". . . Millicent has been practicing her steps, though of course there is no question of her performing the scandalous waltz. It is not to be considered. I feel certain that you, Lord Laverstoke, must agree. No gently bred female of tender age should behave with such a want of propriety. Naturally Millicent does nothing that her papa and I do not approve."

Tina reached the threshold in time to see Felicity's eyes flash dangerously. "I should love to waltz," she declared with a toss of her auburn curls. "I think it must be the most romantic thing in the world, to be held by a man while one danced! Don't you, Lady Millie?"

"My daughter's name is Millicent, Miss Winton," Lady Buckden said stiffly. "And I am sure Millicent does not agree." The countess's cold eyes swiveled as Tina ventured forward. "Good day, Miss Jardine. How pleasant to see you again." Her lack of warmth contradicted the statement.

Tina took a seat, glancing involuntarily at Gerard, who was standing with his shoulders propped against the mantelshelf, a sardonic look on his face. On a nearby

218

settee sat Allegra and Libby. James occupied an armchair, but Christian was nowhere to be seen.

"Well?" Felicity's gaze challenged Lady Millicent to speak for herself.

Lady Millicent was obviously embarrassed. "I suppose it might be pleasant," she said at last, "that is, if it were seemly . . ." Her voice faded off uncertainly, but Tina saw her cast James a quick, scared look.

"Nonsense," said her mother depressingly. "You know nothing of the matter, my love. Nor, I trust, does Miss Winton."

Allegra hurried into speech. "Should you like to go up to your rooms now? I daresay you will want to rest for a while. Lady Millicent looks weary."

"Yes, I am—" began Millie, who had dark, unhappy circles under her eyes.

"No, of course you are not." Not surprisingly, Lady Buckden addressed the viscount. "I am thankful to say that my daughter's constitution is amazingly robust. Far stronger than mine ever was." She touched a finger to the corner of her eye as though dabbing at a tear. "If I had had Millicent's health, I would have given dearest Buckden many more pledges of my affection. Millicent will not err in that respect," she added.

As Lady Millie went crimson, Gerard said quietly, "Then her husband will be fortunate indeed. Yet I am sure you will both want to rest. We are expecting some of the other guests in just a little while, and I daresay the evening will be very long . . ."

Tina listened in awe as he said all the right words, agreeing with Lady Buckden, complimenting and praising her wisdom and opinions, and in the end, maneuvering her into doing exactly what he wished her to do. By the time the countess left the room, Tina could see she thought the idea was her own.

"Well done," praised Allegra, before rounding on Felicity. "Miss Winton, I would appreciate it if in the future

219

you would refrain from baiting Lady Buckden. You may find it amusing, but—"

"I wasn't baiting her," Felicity protested. "I was merely trying to help Lady Millie stand up for herself. No one else bothers to do so." Her accusing eyes went from James to Gerard to Allegra.

"Your motives are good, but your tactics are impractical," stated the viscount in such dry tones that Tina's temper was provoked.

"Felicity is right," she said, glaring at him. "Someone should help that girl."

Gerard's voice was very bland. "I am sure you are correct," he replied. "What strategy do you recommend, Miss Jardine? How do we make Lady Millie more militant?"

Tina frowned for a moment, bending her mind to the problem. "Perhaps you could help her," she said. "We all saw how skillfully you handled her mother. Perhaps what Lady Millicent needs are . . . lessons."

"Lessons?" He lifted a brow. "You expect me to tutor Lady Millie in the gentle art of"—he glanced at James—"manipulation?"

"Diplomacy," she corrected. "Dealing with people. Winning them to your way of thinking. Making them feel that your ideas are their own. That is what diplomats do, is it not?"

"In part," he acknowledged. "Honey wins more allies than vinegar. But I deal with men, not with matchmaking mamas. Lady Buckden is no Alexander of Russia."

"You're suggesting that men are more reasonable than women?" she said sweetly.

Something unholy glinted in his eyes. "No, I wouldn't say that, but—oh lord." His voice trailed off in an exasperated sigh.

James spoke up. "Her idea's not bad, Gerry. God knows I can't do anything to help Millie. I can't get near her any more. You can speak to her anytime you wish, unchaperoned and unheard."

For a long moment, Gerard did not answer. "Very well, then," he said finally. "I'll do what I can. But Jay?"

His brother looked at him.

"You, too, could benefit from some lessons in handling"—the viscount smiled wolfishly—"your future mama-in-law."

By five o'clock that afternoon, more of the guests had arrived—the Ruscombes, the Bradfields, and the Wantages, as well as those of their offspring whom Allegra had included in the invitation. The eligible bachelors—the fashionable Mr. Chetwoode and the divinely handsome Lord Flaundon—were not due to arrive until the following afternoon, a fact bemoaned by both Lady Wantage and Lady Ruscombe.

However, Lady Wantage comforted herself with the reflection that it would give Jane and Maria time to rest and recover their looks, a remark which prompted Lord Wantage to utter the unfatherly (and rather too audible) sentiment that it would take a long cold day in hell for that to occur.

Ignoring her husband, Lady Wantage immediately sought the opinion of Lady Ruscombe, whose daughter Lizzie, though of lively disposition, rivaled neither Jane nor Maria in beauty. The two ladies were soon huddled together, having formed an alliance whose foremost goal was to prevent the vexatiously lovely Felicity Winton (who *was* she, anyway?) from depriving their Darling Daughters of the chance to snag one of the bachelors. Mrs. Bradfield, who had no daughter to worry about, sat and listened and smiled smugly. Her elder son was betrothed to the daughter of a baronet. She could afford to be complacent.

Neither Lady Wantage nor Lady Ruscombe appeared in the least concerned about Valentina Jardine, who did not put herself forward like Miss Winton. Miss Jardine

221

was (the ladies agreed) well-enough looking, but past the prime of her youth. Not *yet* an ape-leader, of course, but—they shook their heads sadly—already headed toward that melancholy fate. However, since blondes were last year's vogue (no one knew what this year's would be) and since Lizzie and Jane and Maria were all more or less in that category, their fond mamas finally concluded that neither Miss Jardine's midnight tresses nor Felicity Winton's auburn curls posed any serious threat to their hopes. Lord Laverstoke might be a wild card, but the fashionable Mr. Chetwoode and the divine Lord Flaundon would certainly be conversant with the current mode in Beauty.

Much of this, of course, was not discussed within Tina's hearing, but was related to her by Miss Steeple while she was dressing for dinner.

"Because I am quiet, they talk about these things in front of me," explained Libby in her gentle voice. "But I am glad they did, for it helps me to make you see what it is Lord Laverstoke has had to endure."

Tina smiled wryly. "Indeed. General adoration must be very hard to bear." At Libby's troubled look, she added quickly, "Dearest Libby, do not worry. I no longer dislike him. Indeed, he has been"—she paused, forming her comment with care—"most persuasive in changing my opinion of him."

Libby examined her face. "I am glad. If you recall, I did tell you in the beginning what a fine gentleman he was, and how well he always treated his mama, and how courteous and kind he has been to me—"

"I remember, Libby. And I treated it all with a very large grain of salt." Tina sighed. In a low voice, she went on, "I no longer hold him to blame for what happened. I am beginning to see that Christian is . . . very weak and not always . . . wholly honorable." She was on the brink of telling Libby of Christian's proposition when Annie entered the room.

"Shall I do your hair now, miss? I've finished with Miss Felicity."

Tina acquiesced, her mind turning back to the subject of Christian as Libby fell quiet. Christian had tried to speak to her this afternoon, but she had walked away from him. She did not think he had understood. She did not believe he realized that she found his proposal abhorrent, disgraceful, and utterly dishonorable. What staggered her most was that he seemed to find his plan so reasonable. When had he become so lost to common decency? Had he always been this way, and if so, how could she have been so blind?

With a last pat to her handiwork, the maid set down the curling tongs. "Miss?" she asked, waiting for Tina's reaction.

Tina started. "Oh, I'm sorry. Yes, that will be fine, Annie. Thank you."

When the maid was gone, Tina studied her reflection in the mirror. Why, she looked quite nice. Her cheeks were flushed and her eyes sparkled. Her hair looked better than it ever had. Did those women really see her as an ape-leader? Did they truly think no man would look at her? Were they right?

"What is it, Tina? What's wrong?"

With a wistful little sigh, Tina stood up. "Nothing, Libby. Nothing at all." With effort, she squared her shoulders. "I was only thinking." She rose to her feet. "I believe that's the dinner bell. We'd better hurry."

By the following afternoon, Mrs. Bradfield had joined the ranks of those who resented Felicity, for Felicity had had the shocking effrontery to snub her saintly son, Thomas, (while behaving with perfect civility to Lady Ruscombe's son, Richard). Exactly what Thomas had done to incur Felicity's displeasure was unclear, but there were now three indignant mamas huddled together in growling dissatisfaction.

223

To give her credit, Allegra was handling the situation beautifully. While disharmony reigned, she displayed no sign of irritation, nor did she shirk her duty as her brother's hostess. Instead, she herself undertook the formidable task of soothing Lady Ruscombe and Lady Wantage, at the same time dispatching her husband to assuage Mrs. Bradfield's ruffled feathers.

In her youth, Mrs. Bradfield had been a London belle. She had married young, born her commoner husband his heir and never conceived again, in consequence of which she had retained her excellent figure and a very high opinion of her own physical attractiveness. So it was that when Christian singled her out, she at once dislodged herself from the sullying effects of Lady Wantage and Lady Ruscombe (neither of whom had any pretense to Beauty) and discreetly allowed herself to be charmed by the handsome husband of her hostess.

Gerard observed all this with cynical amusement. He had seen it happen a dozen times before, and so did not blame Felicity for being what she was: beautiful, vivacious, and flirtatious, a girl the mamas loved to hate. And since she was compassionate enough not to flirt with James in front of Millie, he allowed her to continue unchecked.

What he found incredible was that Valentina attracted so little notice. She was only a few years older than the other girls, but those years were like an unbreachable gulf in the eyes of the matchmaking mamas. He had actually overheard the whispered word "ape-leader" the previous afternoon, a slur that made his insides churn with rage. They must be blind not to see that Valentina was worth more than all their daughters put together, he mused.

Briefly, he considered the two guests due to arrive at any moment: Mr. Chetwoode and Lord Flaundon. He suspected they had been included more for Allegra's benefit than because they were eligible bachelors who might be inclined to throw their handkerchiefs at Lizzie, Jane, or Maria. From a purely social standpoint, however, he supposed the choices were appropriate. Both gentlemen possessed estates within easy traveling distance of Laverstoke Park; as for their characters, Lord Flaundon possessed a fortune and a rakish air, while Forbes Chetwoode was even wealthier, though a little on the stuffy side.

Lady Buckden, he noticed, had kept herself remote from the fray, but she was there, waiting in the wings, like a fire-breathing dragon. Remembering his promise to James, he had singled Millie out after breakfast for a stroll about the house. He recalled their conversation with a small smile. . . .

"Millie," he had said, after a few minutes of preparatory groundwork, "you are aware, perhaps, that my brother wishes to ask for the honor of your hand."

She shrank away from him. "My lord," she stammered, "I beg you will not . . . Mama would never allow . . . I dare not think of it."

She looked up, unhappiness radiating from her large, expressive blue eyes.

"I know. She wishes you to wed me."

Turning bright red, Millie uttered several inarticulate syllables. "We have known each other for many years," he said gently, "so I know you will not be offended if I say we should not suit. I know it is my brother you prefer."

Millie made more strangled sounds.

"Millie," he said with great patience, "do you wish to marry James?"

"Oh, yes!" That came out clearly enough.

"Then you must decide to fight for what you want. That is the first lesson."

"But . . . my lord . . ."

"You must stop telling yourself that it will never happen." He looked down at her and smiled bracingly.

"Nothing is impossible, after all. I think we can come up with a plan."

"Do you mean . . . James and I . . . should elope?" She gazed up at him in half horrified hope.

He shook his head. "Elopement carries a taint I know you would not like. No, let us first explore our other options."

"But there *are* no other options," she wailed, forgetting to stammer. "Mama wants me to wed a title, not a man. That is what *she* did, and she wants me to be like her."

"I think that would be a very great shame," he replied. "I think you would do better to be yourself. James has asked me to do what I can to teach you how to deal with your mother. I cannot promise you miracles, but if you employ the tactics I teach you, you will certainly have a better chance of success."

"Oh, my lord, *would* you?" Now those blue eyes were shining. "I never know what to say to her! That is what makes me feel so helpless!"

As they entered the Long Gallery, he began the little speech he had prepared. "The first thing you must never do is tell your mother that she's wrong. She *is* wrong, and we both know it, but she will not thank you for telling her so. No matter how angry she makes you, you must control your temper. I fancy you are already rather good at that."

Millie nodded, gazing at him worshipfully.

"Allow her to tell you how she feels," he went on, "and listen to what she says. Show her that you value her opinions and calmly thank her for all that she has done for you. Make her feel that she is important, and that even if there are areas in which you and she do not agree, you see the merit in her opinions."

"That won't be easy." Her voice had a wry note.

"No, but for James's sake, you will do it," he said firmly. "Next you must present to her a list of all the things that you *do* agree upon. Make it as long a list as

226

possible. Stretch the truth if you must, but above all control your temper. The key to handling people is making them feel good about themselves, making them feel important, and being sympathetic to their opinions."

"But how will all this help? How will I convince Mama that James is the only man I could ever—" Her voice cracked.

"Ah, now we must deal with that area where you and she do not agree. The fact that I intend to offer for someone else, very soon, should be of some help. If I am betrothed, then your mother cannot very well expect you to wed me, can she?" He smiled encouragingly.

"No. I suppose not." She sounded unconvinced.

"Let me point out some things about my brother. He is a second son, that is true, but he is by no means penniless. He has, you might recall, the same lineage as myself, so his birth should be no obstacle. Let me point out something else. He is currently my steward. Do you know what that means?"

"N-no."

"It means that he is not lazy. It means that he is a man of pride, who is willing to work, rather than sit around *taking,* as so many in his position might do. Moreover, he was a soldier for seven years. Do you know what that means?"

"That he is brave?" she answered timidly.

"Brave enough to do what he had to do when it was required. Brave enough to endure a ball in the hip and live without bitterness. It also means that he has witnessed the horror of war and endured much of its deprivations. And because of that, he loves life and people all the more. He values peace, and that is a good thing for a man to do."

Millie closed her eyes. "And he is loyal," she whispered. "All these months . . . I wish I could make Mama see."

"And he loves you," Gerard pointed out quietly.

227

Her hands flew to her cheeks. "Oh, I'll never remember it all. I'll never be able to do it!"

"We will go over it all again," he soothed. "You will learn to handle people, Millie. Not only your mother, but everyone you encounter, in London or anywhere else."

"Yes, yes, yes." She trembled. "Tell me again, please."

"Very well. First of all, you never tell anyone that they're wrong."

Fifteen

Allegra directed the drawing of lots for the valentines after dinner that evening. The proceedings seemed to do much to alleviate the cat-and-dog atmosphere that had prevailed earlier, which in turn made it easier for Tina to relax. And then she unfolded her slip of paper and saw whose name was upon it. Her hand closed quickly.

"Under no circumstance must you reveal whose name you have drawn," Allegra was saying in a severe tone. "It must remain a secret. All valentines will be collected the morning of the ball. I will read them aloud at dinner."

"These verses you want us to write, what do you want in 'em?" demanded Lord Wantage, who was clearly the least enthusiastic of the guests.

Allegra sent him a flirtatious smile. "Lord Wantage, as long as you do not embarrass the ladies, you may write anything you like. It doesn't even have to rhyme if you don't wish it to."

Lord Wantage grinned at her forthrightness. "Very well, I'll play your game, m'dear. 'Twill be diverting, I make no doubt."

While Lizzie, Jane, and Maria giggled and cast furtive looks at the bachelors present, Tina glanced over at Gerard. He had been rather quiet this evening. In comparison to the other men, he seemed a cool, shadowy, self-contained figure, a man whose masculinity was so compelling that any woman must be aware of it. In contrast, Christian appeared uncontrolled and tense. While Gerard sat quite still, Christian moved and twitched continuously, crossing and uncrossing his legs, fiddling with his snuffbox, shifting restlessly in his chair.

"And now," said Allegra, clapping her hands, "perhaps some of the young ladies would like to perform for us. The harp has been moved into the drawing room, and of course, there is the pianoforte."

"Millicent will be delighted to play," Lady Buckden proclaimed. "Wouldn't you, dear?"

"Yes, Mama," whispered Lady Millicent dutifully.

As Millie approached the harp, Tina's eyes flew to Gerard's in silent inquiry. He nodded imperceptibly, telling her that he had indeed spoken to Millie. But would it do any good?

As it happened, Lady Millie's performance proved excellent, which Tina found slightly surprising. For some reason she had expected less, perhaps because she had it in her mind that Lady Buckden forced Millie to do things she did not wish. But Millie clearly enjoyed the harp; it was merely performing before others that made her uncomfortable.

Afterward, the other girls took turns. Lady Ruscombe's Lizzie played an indifferent score on the harp, followed by Jane, who sang tunelessly while her sister, Maria, hammered on the pianoforte. While their fond mamas clapped, Lady Buckden remarked, in nasal accents, "I daresay Miss Winton will prefer not to honor us since she finds practicing the pianoforte so dull."

"On the contrary," said Felicity sweetly. "I should be delighted to play. How kind of you to ask."

Suppressing a smile, Tina folded her hands and waited. She knew what to expect.

"It is true that I find practicing dull," explained Felicity, planting herself on the piano bench. "But *playing*—she ran her fingers lightly over the keys—"that is different, you see."

And then the music filled the room—rich, mellifluent music the likes of which neither Lizzie, nor Jane, nor Maria was ever likely to produce. Felicity might lack discipline, but she played flawlessly, with an expressiveness that had everyone—with the possible exception of Lady Buckden—utterly mesmerized.

"I do like that," sighed Felicity at the end of the sonata. "It's by someone called W.A. Mozart. Has anyone heard of him?"

Other than Tina, no one had, but the applause was enthusiastic. With a demure curtsy, Felicity rose and returned to her seat, passing Lady Buckden without a glance. Meanwhile, Lady Buckden's face had turned such a delicate shade of puce that Tina had to look away, just to keep from laughing. And so, naturally, her eyes went to Gerard. Like her, his lips were twitching, but when their gazes locked, something changed. Something subtle. Awareness rippled through her—a queer, flooding excitement that went far beyond anything she had ever experienced.

"Miss Jardine?" inquired Allegra. "Would you care to play for us?"

Tina started. "Oh, well,"—a blush crept into her cheeks—"it has been years since I have had an opportunity to play, Lady Rewe. And unlike my cousin, I do not have an excess of natural talent."

"We are an informal audience," drawled Lord Flaundon. "We shan't be critical."

"Very well, then." Tina took her place at the pianoforte a bit nervously. With a deep breath, she looked down at the keys, thinking back to the days when she'd had the chance to do such things as this. Her mother had sold their instrument a month after Tina's father had died, and as for the months spent in Felicity's home, Tina had never even touched their pianoforte. She hadn't wanted to.

In the end, she chose the song she remembered best,

231

though it carried a sweep of memories almost too painful to handle. It was a romantic Scottish ballad called "Willie o Douglas Dale," one that she had sung for Christian many years before. Perhaps it was dangerous to remind herself of the afternoon Christian had first declared his love for her, but it was the only tune she felt confident enough to play from memory.

Fortunately, Tina's voice did not crack or waver, but came out clear and crystal-true. Fearing mistakes, she watched her fingers at first, but after two or three stanzas she grew brave enough to look her audience in the eye. Scanning the faces, she chose to focus on Felicity, who beamed back at her as fondly as any parent. As for Gerard, his was the only gaze she dared not seek. He'd distract her for certain, make her flounder and miss a note. He'd make her forget to breath.

She looked at Christian though. When she sang the words: *"O will you leave your father's court, An go along wi me? I'll carry you unto fair Scotland, and make you a lady free"* she stared him straight in the eye, curious to know whether he remembered anything at all.

But his face was as blank as if she were a stranger.

And she discovered she didn't care.

It was the end of the song, the moment she'd been waiting for, the moment when she could finally meet the gaze of the only one who mattered. Yet Gerard's eyes, when she turned to him, were a shock of glacial gray that doused her pleasure and froze her heart. Had he somehow guessed the significance of the melody?

While everyone clapped, Tina cast him a quick, pleading look. But it was too late. Already the coldness had been replaced by what must surely be his diplomat's expression—a polite, aloof mask that might mean anything or nothing. Feeling oddly hollow, she wanted to run to him, to tell him that the song meant nothing.

That Christian meant nothing.

But she could only walk back to her seat as Felicity

had done. She had to go on with the evening.

Over the course of the next hour, she had ample opportunity to ponder her new discovery. How strange that she had not realized any sooner that the pain was gone. When had it happened? And how? Had it occurred all at once, perhaps at the moment when Christian had made his infamous proposal? Or had it been happening all along, hour by hour, like grains of sand crawling through an hourglass?

Whatever the case, it didn't matter.

What mattered was that she was wildly, crazily in love with Gerard; equally important, she was out of love with Christian. Completely and irrevocably out of love. Out of pain. Free at last. Free to love again, with the whole of her newly-healed heart.

She glanced over at Christian, viewing his dark male perfection with a dispassion that bordered on distaste. She watched him hunch a shoulder and shift restlessly while Lord Wantage related a fox-hunting story. She saw how he gulped down the whiskey Gerard handed him, then wipe his mouth with his fingers. She saw his expression, sullen and sulky, when his wife whispered some entreaty in his ear.

They were small things, ill-mannered things, and she noticed them now.

Gerard, on the other hand, stood tall and straight, his mouth curved with amusement as Lord Wantage wound up his tale with the words: "And then the sly old hound gave a sniff as if to say—*Fool, hunt it yourself!*"

When the men broke into laughter, Tina heard Gerard's deep, rich chuckle, observed Christian's small, perfunctory smile. Substance and shadow, strength and weakness.

There was really no comparison.

As the conversation droned on around her, Tina sat quietly, her heart swelling with the strength of her love. More than anything, she wanted to tell him, to speak of

233

her love, to give it life and expression. But of course that was out of the question. She must wait, wait for him to court her properly.

If that was what he intended.

For a moment, she was assailed with doubt. Was that his aim? Or was she merely reading too much into what had taken place between them?

It was not until later, as she crawled into bed, that Tina remembered about the lottery. Somehow, against all odds, she had managed to draw Gerard's name. She grimaced, realizing that she was going to have to compose some sort of verse that was fit to be read aloud. What irony. She would not be able to pour her feelings into it, that much was certain.

Of course, it was to be done anonymously, but what if someone guessed? Whatever she wrote, it would have to be very prim and proper. She sighed wistfully. Where Gerard was concerned, she did not feel very prim and proper.

When the last of his guests had gone to bed, Gerard made his weary way to the library. He'd drawn Mrs. Bradfield's name in the lottery, but he was not going to worry about that just yet. His mind was too full of Tina. He closed his eyes and groaned softly. All he wanted to do was to go to her, to gather her soft body close, to kiss her and love her until they were both utterly exhausted, and to fall asleep in her arms.

But of course it was out of the question.

To combat his frustration, he pulled out his sonnet, reviewed it, and felt soothed. Before they could have passion, he had to undo the damage that Rewe had wrought. Tina was vulnerable, suspicious, and defensive right now, but he would woo her with patience, honor her with eloquence—and ultimately, he hoped, convince her that he would never hurt or betray her or violate her trust.

It was the only honorable course.

Of course, there were obstacles in his path, some of them put there by his own foolish tongue. He regretted now the deception he had perpetrated in the beginning— 'twas madness to have pretended to be James—yet in truth he believed Tina's anger over the matter had ebbed. No, it was only her broken betrothal that she held against him, as though he had sought deliberately to ruin her life.

He sighed deeply. Someday he would be able to explain about that, but in the meanwhile he would have to court her trust, teach her to accept him without explanations, without justification or apology. And when the time was ripe, when he felt she would be receptive, he would declare his love and ask her to marry him.

His heart lifted at the thought. Yes, he was in love with her; he knew it as surely as he knew the sun would rise tomorrow. To own the truth, he was also a little dazed, for he had never actually expected to find himself in the throes of what was commonly called "a lasting passion."

He rubbed at the stubble on his chin and yawned. Yes, at the age of three-and-thirty, he had finally fallen in love. Why now, with this particular woman? And how had it happened so quickly? The answer was as elusive as smoke, as tangled as a half-forgotten dream. He merely knew that he *was* in love, and that in some indefinable way, he was altered by that fact. The man who had watched two half-frozen young ladies warming their hands before his fire had been a different man, a man who had not understood that love could be, *should* be, more than the joining of two bodies.

Suddenly, his mouth hardened as he recalled the romantic ballad she had sung that evening. Her voice had been so sweet and pure, so expressive that he had been deeply moved. And just at the moment that he had indulged himself with the fancy that she might be thinking of *him* as she sang . . . she had looked straight at his brother-in-law. And he had known with gutwrenching certainty that the song meant something to the two of them, that it was Rewe who occupied her thoughts at that moment.

Not him.

His jaw tight, Gerard leaned back and closed his eyes, fatigue drifting over him like a dense fog. Dignified, controlled gentlemen did not become jealous, he reminded himself. Good diplomats assessed a situation, then looked for ways to turn it to their advantage. Unfortunately, the stern admonishment had no noticeable authority over his emotions, which were a far cry from their usual levelheaded condition.

It was going to be difficult.

Difficult to court her, difficult to overcome her pining for Rewe, difficult to prevent himself from plunging his fist into his smirking brother-in-law's face. While the house party lasted, he was obviously going to have to be stoic, but when it was over, when the guests had gone, when Rewe was gone, then, *then* . . .

Shifting slightly, he gazed upward at the frieze, restlessness washing over him in a palpable wave. God, he wanted her so badly. His sonnet would help, *must* help to prove to her that he was worthy of her love. It came from his heart, after all. And when the proper time came, he would express with his lips and hands anything that his pen had inadvertently overlooked. After all, there were some things one simply couldn't express verbally.

Needing time alone, Tina began taking Gretchen for early morning walks, usually at an hour when no one but the servants was about. After the first day, she stopped using a leash, though this usually meant that the dog took off in pursuit of a hare five minutes after they left. However, since sooner or later Gretchen always returned (usually later), Tina saw this as less of an inconvenience than having her arm wrenched from its socket or her nose clogged with snow. As long as they were not connected by a lead, she and Gretchen got along famously.

As the days passed, Tina's worries increased. She had not yet composed a Valentine's Day verse for Gerard, though vaguely she hoped inspiration would strike while she watched the sunrise or listened to the sound of Gretchen's barks. However, all she could compose were the words *I love you*—naked sentiments she could scarcely write upon a valentine that was to be read aloud before the other guests.

She did not tell Gerard about her walks, partly because she had no opportunity—they were never alone for a moment—and partly because she suspected he would slip out and join her if he knew. And as much as the possibility made her shiver with excitement, she was aware of the gossip which would arise if any of the guests got wind of it. Gerard himself had advised her to be discreet, and that, she must remember, included her dealings with him.

And of course another object of these solitary tramps was to clear her head of the impossible dreams that crept in during the night. The sensible part of her was trying, desperately, to come to terms with the possibility that her love was destined to go nowhere. After all, marriage might not be as close to Gerard's thoughts as it was to hers. She might be his fancy of the moment, but the fact remained that she was a penniless spinster of slightly inferior birth. And while Gerard clearly had no *need* to espouse an heiress, it was obviously expected of him. In the eyes of the world, any other choice would be considered a mismatch, a *mesalliance*. Tina was not so naive she did not understand that.

But while she struggled to retain her spirits, the truth

was she was worried. For the past several days she had watched Gerard single Millie out time and again, and though she knew he did not wish to wed the girl, she was well aware that his guests viewed these quiet talks as significant. This concerned her a great deal. She had observed Millie's increasing confidence—she no longer allowed her mother to answer every question for her—but if push came to shove, she did not know whether Millie could withstand pressure from her mother. To the other guests, she feared it looked as though Gerard were making Millie the object of his attentions; certainly her mother believed that to be so. Only yesterday, Tina had overheard Lady Wantage wager Lady Ruscombe that Laverstoke would declare himself at the Valentine's Day ball.

Another of her problems was Christian, who had begun giving her long, smoldering glances when no one else was looking. Fearing someone would see, Tina always looked away, yet he did not seem to be getting the hint. Therefore, Christian was another reason for slipping silently out of the house, for she would not put it past him to follow.

However, it was not Christian but his wife who intercepted her in the corridor two mornings before the ball.

"So this is what you do while the rest of us are abed."

Looking breathlessly lovely in a pink satin dressing gown, Allegra stood, hands on hips, her gaze leveled at Tina. "I rose to watch the sunrise yesterday and saw you and that wretched beast from my window." She hesitated, her eyes dropping to Gretchen for a moment. "I was wondering if I might join you. Or would that be . . . intruding?"

"Why, of course not, Lady Rewe," replied Tina, concealing her dismay.

Allegra looked pleased. "Give me ten minutes to dress, then."

True to her word, Allegra returned within the promised

interval. "Ordinarily, I do not care to rise before eleven," she remarked, hastily pulling on her gloves, "but I need to escape these harpies. This is the only moment of the day when I am not on duty as hostess. The closer we come to the ball, the more I have to do, even though we have increased the size of our domestic staff for the occasion."

"I hope you will tell me if there is anything I can do to help," Tina said.

"You *are* helping, Miss Jardine, in more ways than you can know. Isn't Lady Buckden the most horrid woman? James is utterly mad. And Lady Wantage is so dreary—"

As they tramped over the snow-encrusted ground, Allegra unburdened her soul of its exasperation with some of the guests, particularly Christian's conquest, Mrs. Bradfield, whom she felt "put on airs." As for the gentlemen, she found no wrong in Mr. Chetwoode or Lord Flaundon, but as for Lady Wantage's fancy (expressed one evening while the gentlemen lingered over their port) that Lord Flaundon appeared charmed by her daughter Jane: "What fustian! The man has no more interest in Jane than he has in Maria or Lizzie," she scoffed, underscoring the remark with a slash of her arm. "However, at least they are keeping their talons out of Laverstoke for once. His so-called attentions toward Millie are taking care of that."

"Yes." Tina's reply was subdued.

"The women all bore me to tears," Allegra went on. "And their husbands are dull as well. Lord Wantage talks of nothing but fox hunting, while Lord Ruscombe and Mr. Bradfield—all they do is ignore their wives and lose money to each other at cards! They have no conversation, no spark, no *anything*. It makes me so out of reason cross."

Suspecting that the real root of the trouble was Christian, Tina felt a twinge of pity for Allegra. "At least you have your son with you," she offered. "That must bring

239

you some comfort."

Allegra brightened a little. "True, but I am out of patience with his nurse. She spends more time moaning about her aches and ailments and rheumatism than she does attending to Dickon. And she has not been taking him outside often enough. Children need fresh air."

"Then why you don't you do it?"

Allegra looked startled by the suggestion. "Yes, I should, shouldn't I? Perhaps I shall some afternoon when the sun is bright and warm. I would like to show him the pond where I used to skate. Childhood seems so long ago, doesn't it?" She sighed. "I daresay you must envy me. Here I am, married to such a handsome man, mother to such a beautiful child. I suppose you think me a poor creature to complain."

"I think you have a great deal to be thankful for," Tina said tactfully.

"Yes, I suppose I do. I *am* thankful for Dickon, however it may appear. It is just that lately Christian has been so—" She broke off, frowning. "You are easy to talk to, Miss Jardine. You appear so interested that my tongue rattles more loosely than it should. Yet I have a feeling that you would not betray a confidence."

"No, I would not," said Tina frankly, "but I beg you will not confide anything you will regret. After all, we scarcely know one another—"

"But we are *cousins,*" cut in Allegra, her tone faintly mocking.

"Yes, but I did not come here to exploit the relationship," Tina retorted quickly.

"So vehement! Did I suggest you had?" Allegra's eyes crinkled with amusement. "I am perfectly aware that *your* intention was to visit Miss Steeple, but Miss Winton's mama had other ideas, did she not?" Displeasure colored her voice, lending it a sour note. "She must be in raptures over this ball business. 'Tis practically as good as a come-out ball, and at no expense to her."

When Tina said nothing, Allegra laughed. "However, Laverstoke can afford it, so why worry? The ball is going to be a huge success. Did I tell you that the final count is near two hundred? Of course, no one in their right mind would turn down an invitation to Laverstoke Park. I only pray it does not snow! And if the musicians do not arrive, I do not know what we shall do . . ."

Allegra rattled on, voicing concern over the myriad small things that could go wrong. When at last they turned back toward the house, she said, "I would like to do this again tomorrow. Of course, it will be even more hectic what with it being the day before the ball. There will be a million things for me to do, but"—her head tilted consideringly—"perhaps in the afternoon I could slip away for a short while." She smiled suddenly. "I could bring Dickon. You would like that, wouldn't you?"

"Of course," Tina responded automatically.

Allegra looked at her intently. "Good," she replied. "Then it is settled. You see? I knew you would be able to help me."

Tina only wished she had someone to help *her*. Late that night, she sat at the small writing table in her room, laboring to compose a verse to go on Gerard's valentine.

"Curse Allegra and her silly ideas," she muttered.

She rubbed her eyes, knowing she was going to have to write something. Everyone had agreed to do their part and so must she. wishing she were not so tired, she dipped her quill in the ink and frowned down at the pink-tinted paper that Allegra had provided. Very well, then. She would stop thinking and start writing. Perhaps that was the key.

She spent the next hour composing, scratching out, recomposing, and scowling until at last she sat back and read what she had written:

A Valentine for Laverstoke
Whose gracious hospitality
Has filled our visit with such joy
And great conviviality.

We're flattered he could spare the time
Far from Vienna's esteemed hall,
Where diplomats applaud his words,
To host for us this lovely ball.

His pleasant mien, his sage gray eyes,
His golden hair untouched by time,
A sharp young wit with age's wiles
To me, he's England's Valentine.

Well, it rhymed in all the right places, but, oh God, could she ever bear to let anyone read it? Surely it was a perfectly dreadful poem! And yet, she reflected, it was deliciously impersonal—no one would ever guess that its author was head over heels in love with England's Valentine!

Filled with new respect for Lord Byron and his kind, Tina glanced down at her brooch-watch. Good grief, it was past midnight! Stifling a yawn, she hastened into her night clothes, then went back to read her poem one more time. It would simply have to do, she decided, for anything cleverer was beyond her capabilities.

If only she could keep from blushing when they read it aloud.

Sixteen

As Allegra had predicted, the following day was a busy one. While Gerard and James kept the other guests occupied with various diversions, Tina found herself swept up in the complicated business of preparing for the ball. It seemed there were a dozen small tasks that were too consequential to be performed by servants, but as Allegra said: "Someone must do them, and you are the only person I can abide to have assist me. You do not object, I hope?"

Tina denied this, feeling that anything was better than being obliged to listen to the matchmaking mamas.

"We shall begin the ball with a pair of country dance—'Brighton Camp' "—Allegra tapped her chin thoughtfully—"and 'My Lady Cullen.' Then I think a minuet would be nice, and then a waltz. Yes, definitely a waltz—I love waltzes, don't you? They make me feel young and beautiful. Then we must have another country dance—'Amarillis,' I think. And then another waltz, and then a cotillion just before supper—oh, and we must decide where to place the tables. Come, Miss Jardine, you can assist me with that . . ."

And so it went until the middle of the afternoon, when they were both exhausted. Pushing back her golden curls, Allegra suggested they take her son for a walk. "I noticed I slept better last night," she added, "so perhaps the fresh air will help me again."

To assure that they were not seen, they left the house

by a side door. "For it would be too vexatious for words if one of those women decided to join us." Allegra's lovely features scrunched into a horrid face at the thought. "Dickon, my love, stay with us!"

Tina watched the golden-haired child scamper ahead. "He is a beautiful child," she felt compelled to say. "So healthy and strong." Despite the knowledge that she no longer loved Christian, she still felt a twinge of melancholy when she looked at the little boy.

"Yes, he is." Allegra's eyes filled with a maternal pride that had been absent on other occasions. "Not every woman can bear their husband so fine an heir. The midwife said I'd the hips for childbearing. You do, too, I think."

"I doubt I shall ever bear a child," Tina answered wryly. "I shall be three-and-twenty tomorrow, Lady Rewe."

"On the shelf, in other words? Well, I own I thought so myself at first. But"—her voice took on an odd note—"you seem the sort of woman who *would* marry. Did you never have an offer?"

Tina hesitated, debating the wisdom of a frank answer. When she spoke, her voice was low. "Yes, I did have one once. Long ago." A brief pause. "I even accepted."

"What happened? Did he die?"

"No. He married someone else."

Allegra grimaced. "How odious. Did you hate him very much for it?"

"No," Tina replied. "I didn't hate him at all. For a very long time I continued to love him."

"How odd. *I* would have hated him. You must be very different from me." Allegra gave her a sidelong look. "So I suppose you think you will never love again—Dickon, do come back! Stay near to Mama, love." Several seconds passed before she went on, casually, "To own the truth, I had a notion that you were rather fond of my brother."

244

"Oh?" Tina said guardedly.

Amusement lurked in Allegra's voice. "My husband and I actually had a disagreement about it the other night. Rewe said you were partial to James, but I insisted it was Gerry you held in affection. Am I right?"

Tina hesitated. She was starting to realize what she was going to have to do. Things had been different when Allegra had been an adversary, but now that she liked Allegra, now that the woman had come a fair way toward becoming her friend, the rules had changed.

Very quietly, she said, "Lady Rewe, there is something I should tell you, something I think you should know."

"What is it? Dickon, don't do that, love. Keep your mittens on."

"It concerns your husband."

"Christian? What of him?" Allegra's eyes were on her child.

Tina drew a breath. "I am better acquainted with Lord Rewe than it may seem. You see, he is from Kent and so am I . . . and we were neighbors . . ." She paused, searching for the correct word, the correct phrase that would make this simple to explain.

"Do go on." Allegra's voice had grown sharp.

"This is very difficult for me to tell you—"

Allegra reached out, her small hand clamping onto Tina's arm. "Shall I guess? I am not entirely stupid, you know. My husband was once your fiancé, is that what you're trying to say? It would certainly explain why he's been behaving so strangely."

"We never meant to deceive you," Tina said unhappily. "At least, *I* did not."

"Indeed." The single word held a wealth of irony and bitterness.

Then there was silence and they walked on, following Dickon, who turned and called out in his high, childish voice, "Mama, where is the pond? You p'omised to show me the pond!"

"That way, darling, behind the beech trees." Allegra pointed absently off to the left, and glanced at Tina. "You were very brave to tell me," she said dryly. "Braver than my husband."

"I suppose he did not wish to hurt you," Tina replied. "Nor do I wish to. But I thought you ought to know, and I hate all this pretending."

Allegra's face was rigid. "Half my life is spent pretending," she said roughly. "Pretending I do not love my husband, pretending I do not care when he smiles and flirts with other women. I am not very good at it either." She cleared her throat. "Why was the betrothal broken?"

"Because of you," Tina said gently. Without bitterness.

Again, there was silence. Allegra seemed to be thinking, her lips pressed together in a tight line. Then, in her harshest voice yet, she said, "Did he seduce you?"

Tina's breath drew in sharply. "Did he—No. No, he did not."

"You are fortunate. He seduced *me*. That's why I married him." As though she felt the urge to clarify, she added, "I was breeding, Miss Jardine. *That* is why you lost him, not because he fell in love with me."

Tina just kept walking, stunned to silence.

"I knew it almost immediately. Only two weeks went by when I began to suspect. I felt so dreadful, you see." Allegra gave a small, humorless laugh. "You see what can happen at a house party? If it weren't for Gerry, I'd have been ruined. Christian certainly had no intention of offering for me, but my dear brother brought him to the point fast enough. I begged him to help me, you see. I was terrified of facing the consequences on my own."

"I . . . see."

Oh, yes, Tina did indeed see. Day by day, her scope was widening, encompassing so much more than the narrow little tunnel she had used to look through. Not only had she wronged Gerard, she had wronged Allegra. She had also given Christian credit where none was deserved.

She had been completely mistaken about everyone, and she felt like the greatest fool in existence.

"As it happened, I miscarried the child two months after we were wed," Allegra went on. "Dickon did not come along 'til almost two years later." She paused briefly. "You were telling me the truth, I hope. As his wife, I need to know."

There was appeal in Allegra's voice, a faint hint of something that struck an answering chord in Tina's own heart. Should she tell Allegra what had truly happened? Surely it was kinder not to let her know. And strictly speaking, no seduction had occurred.

"No, Lady Rewe," she said firmly. "Nothing happened. That is the truth, as God is my witness."

At once she knew it was the right response; Allegra's face blatantly reflected her relief.

"He told me he loved me," she confessed. "I didn't believe it, but I wanted to. He doesn't, of course, but for better or for worse we are married, and it has not been so very bad, after all. And as you said before, I have Dickon—"

"Where is he?" Tina cut in suddenly. She pointed, her eyes narrowed against the glare of sun on snow. "He was right there a moment ago."

Allegra froze, staring white-faced in the direction of the pond. "Oh, God, the ice! I did not think—"

The rest of her sentence was lost as Tina hitched up her skirts and ran. Behind her, she heard Allegra screech, but whatever she said was blown away on the wind.

Until now the pond had been hidden by the trees, but as Tina raced down the hill she saw it, a shimmering patch of brilliance against the sea of white. Dickon had taken only a few steps out.

"Dickon!" she called. "Stay there! Don't move!"

Her heart sank as the child looked up, smiling as though it were a game. "Catch me," he said, quite clearly. Then, happy as a puppy, he turned and ran toward the middle of the deadly glaze.

Panting from the exertion, Tina came to a halt at the pond's edge, watching Dickon stop and poke the ice with a stick. Praying that the ice was thick enough to bear weight, she tested it with her foot. It flexed and shuddered alarmingly.

"Dickon," she said carefully. "Come here, dear. At once. Your mama needs you."

"Why?" He grinned at her, taking a step backward.

By now Allegra had arrived, gasping for air, shrilling her son's name.

Dickon only giggled.

"How deep is it?" Tina rapped out.

"Not deep, but deeper than his height. Oh God!"

"Hold out your arms to him! Call to him. Promise him candy, or anything else you think he'd like."

Allegra obeyed, cooing endearments and assurances to which the child remained visibly unswayed. When he took another step backward, they both realized that the ploy was useless.

"We need a game." Reaching down, Tina picked up a stick and tossed it a few feet onto the ice. "Can you get the stick, Dickon?" she urged. "Come over and get the stick."

Interest gleamed in the cherubic blue eyes. "Why?" he demanded.

"Because I want to see if you can do it. Perhaps you cannot," Tina said softly.

"Yes, I can." Thus challenged, Dickon toddled a few steps toward the women. Then he stopped. "No," he said stubbornly. "Don't want to."

"Why not?" Allegra cried. "Darling, fetch the stick. Pretend you are Gretchen, darling. It's a game."

"Where's G'etchun?" Dickon asked with interest.

"Gretchen is in the house. Darling, please!"

Once more, Tina put a foot on the ice. "I'm going to have to go to him," she warned Allegra. Then, to

Dickon, she said provocatively, "I can get the stick before Dickon does."

"No!" Roused at last, the little boy plunged toward the stick. There was a fearsome crackle, like the pop of burning firewood, then a slow, splintering sound that seemed to last an eternity. As Dickon disappeared, Tina threw herself forward.

Her heart shuddered and nearly stopped as the icy water took her, a great, merciless hand squeezing the air from her lungs. Surely she was either dying or in the grip of some ghastly nightmare, surely nothing could be as cold or as wretchedly, horribly painful as this. For a moment she felt an inexorable futility, then her feet touched the bottom and reason returned. She could stand here. As she pushed herself up, Allegra's screams filled her ears, impelling her to break off ice with her hands in an effort to move closer to that small, gaping hole where Dickon had gone down. She had managed to take a few quick steps before the ice had given way, which meant that she must be quite close to Dickon.

But how close?

He had to be only a few feet away. Her half-paralyzed arms stretched out, searching, clawing at nothing. "Am I near him?" she shouted.

"Go farther, farther!" Allegra shrieked.

Taking a breath, Tina dove under, ignoring the way her stomach cramped at the cold, biting water. She searched blindly, eyes squeezed shut against the bitter chill, then miraculously, she touched something solid. . . .

Afterward, she could never quite remember how she did it, but somehow she held on to Dickon and hauled him back through the hole. Somehow her deadened arms supported him as she fought her way to Allegra. She would only remember that she had passed the choking, spluttering child to his sobbing mother just as her own strength gave out.

Then she was on her knees in the snow, gasping commands Allegra could barely understand. "Put . . . him down. . . on his stomach." Her lips were almost too cold to speak intelligibly, her body too frozen even to shiver.

Operating on pure instinct, Tina bent and pressed hard on the little back in an effort to force out the water that was causing him to choke. At once liquid spurted from his mouth; the coughing ceased, replaced by loud, lusty sobs that proclaimed his lungs to be in excellent condition.

"Hush, darling, hush," Allegra crooned. "You're safe with Mama now. I'm going to take you back to the house, back to Nana." Heedless of anything but her son, she clutched Dickon to her bosom and started back up the hill.

Tina had never been so cold. The sharp February wind pierced as though she were wearing nothing; her eyes and mind blurred so she scarcely knew where she was. But behind the numbness there was a warmth that had not died, a person whose name she could cling to, a face she could remember.

Halfway back to the house, she heard Allegra call her name. "Miss Jardine—*Tina!* Can you manage? Dear God, I thought you were right behind me!"

Teeth chattering, Tina hobbled toward Allegra, who came back and seized her by an arm she could not feel. "Come on," she urged, dragging her forward, "you can make it."

Another hundred yards and they were within view of the house, where a lone footman stood sweeping the slush from the steps. His head jerked when he saw them, then he sprinted forward to take the little boy.

"I've got him, fool," said Allegra sharply. "Help Miss Jardine."

Perhaps it was Allegra's tone which cut through Tina's haze, or perhaps it was the footman's expression when he turned to her. Whatever the case, she had a sudden, very vivid picture of how she must look, bedraggled as a half-drowned cat, her clothes clinging to her shaking body, her wet hair plastered to her head and neck.

"I c-cannot go in the f-front door like this," she stuttered as he took her arm. She bit her lip to keep the tears from welling. "Another way, p-please."

"Yes, miss," he said dutifully. Taking her arm, he led her away, leaving Allegra to continue up the main steps of the house.

It seemed to take forever, but in reality it must have been less than a minute before she was inside, in a quiet corridor near the north end of the house. The way was familiar—she had used this route frequently on her early morning ventures. Pausing near a flight of stairs, she leaned one shoulder against the wall.

"I can find my way," she told the footman, rather haltingly. "Thank you for your assistance."

"Are you sure, miss?" He sounded doubtful.

"Quite sure," she mumbled. "I won't drip too much. My dress is nearly frozen stiff."

"Not to worry, miss. We'll mop up."

By some miracle, she made it to her room without being seen by either guests or servants. She was shivering uncontrollably, but managed to ring for a maid and stagger over to the fire. Thank God it was still burning; now if only the girl arrived quickly.

Her next thought was to remove her sodden boots, but it took several frustrating minutes to accomplish because her fingers were so stiff they were practically useless. Wishing the maidservant would hurry, she wondered whether the girl had heard the bell. It was quite possible she had not—between the ball and the uproar that would have been created by Allegra's dramatic entrance, the whole house was probably topsy-turvy. Struggling with the hooks of her pelisse, Tina sighed. It did not signify. She could undress and warm herself.

A loud scream and a reverberating crash alerted

Gerard to the fact that something had occurred. In the act of lining up a shot at the billiard table, he froze, listening. The shrieks continued. Cursing softly, he threw down his stick and strode swiftly toward the source of the sound, which seemed to be coming from the Front Hall.

He arrived there precisely in time to see Mrs. Bissett slap the housemaid whose strident cries were rending the air. Silently applauding the action, his eyes swept the scene, taking in the broken glass, the weeping housemaid, his sister, pale and trembling—and the sobbing, sodden child.

"My God," he ejaculated. "Allie, what happened?"

And then it was pandemonium—the housemaid started wailing again, Allegra babbled incoherently, and what seemed like the entire retinue of his guests and staff popped out of the woodwork to gawk or ask questions. With some difficulty, he was at last able to ascertain the essentials: that Dickon had fallen through the ice but had survived unscathed, thanks to Tina, who had rescued him.

"Where is she?" he demanded in a low, tight voice. "Is she all right?"

To his exasperation, Allegra looked uncertain. "I think so. She did not want anyone to see her so one of the footman took her around to a side door. Where is my husband?" she added in a shaking voice.

At that moment, Christian pushed his way through the press of people, his face stark with concern. "Bissett just told me," he said grimly. "Come on, let's get the boy to the nursery." He took the whimpering child from his wife and, to Gerard's surprised approval, hugged his son close.

While a dozen voices chimed with instructions, husband and wife hurried upstairs, followed by Mrs. Bissett and several maidservants. In her own quiet fashion, Miss Steeple would have followed, but Gerard detained her with a hand. "You're going to her?" he asked.

The elderly woman looked worried. "Someone should. I think it ought to be me." Then, so softly that only he could hear, she added, "Or you, my lord."

Gerard turned and uttered a few soothing words to his guests, sending them back to their billiards, their cards, and their gossip. "Keep them occupied," he told James and Felicity. Then he turned back to Libby. "I'll go," he said. "I know it's not proper but"—he made a small, frustrated gesture—"you understand, don't you?"

"Aye, my lord." Libby's gray head nodded knowingly. "I understand. But if she needs me, I expect you'll let me know."

"Of course," he promised.

Tina threw the last of her clothing onto the floor. Her teeth still chattered like castanets every time she left the fire, so she simply pulled on her dressing gown—not a satin affair, but serviceable flannel—and looped the sash. Then, swaddled in a blanket, she huddled on the floor as close as she could get to the fire.

She wished she had the strength to comb out her hair, but at least she'd been able to towel it a bit. She lacked the energy to ring for the maid again, too; the cord was on the other side of the room, by the bed, and it simply wasn't worth the effort. She would ring when it was time to dress for dinner, but in the meanwhile she would rest and recover from this absurd weakness. She had done what she had to do, she thought drowsily. There was no need for her to worry about anything, no need for her to think, no need to look beyond the flickering flames.

The knock on the door came just when her eyes were sliding shut. How tiresome, she reflected, that the maidservant should come now. Blinking blearily, she bade the girl to enter. Without turning, she said, "At last. I thought you did not hear the bell."

"Tina."

"Gerard!" she gasped, twisting around.

He was beside her in two steps, kneeling down to pull her roughly into his arms. "Tina," he murmured, crushing her against him. "Tina, Tina, what will they tell me next? You chose the wrong time of year to go swimming, my dear."

"I know." No longer sleepy, her heart pumped furiously as she pressed her face into his shoulder. It felt solid, warm, and so gloriously right that she started to tremble with the sheer wonder of it.

His lips grazed the dampened mass of her hair. "God, it must have been awful for you. Confound it, you're shaking."

She looked up and saw that he was frowning. "I'm well enough," she quavered, pulling out of his arms. "How is Dickon?"

"Dickon is fine," he said, almost grimly. "Dickon has two parents and a score of other people to care for him." Regardless of the blanket, he stripped off his coat and draped it around her shoulders. "Why the devil isn't anyone caring for you?"

Her eyes fell to the top button of his waistcoat. "I rang," she explained in a small voice, "but no one came. I . . . I daresay they are all occupied with other things."

"Other things bedamned. You need a hot drink and a hot bath. I shall arrange for them directly." He started to rise.

Without knowing why, she clutched at his arm. "Please don't. I don't want anyone except . . . except you, if you don't mind staying . . . for a bit." Her face crumpled with emotion. "I feel much better with you here."

His face altered, grew oddly still. "I don't mind at all," he said, after a queer silence. "Of course, my methods of warming a lady are rather makeshift, but"—he pulled a flask from his pocket—"I did think to bring this along, just in case."

"What is it?" she asked warily.

He pulled out the stopper and held it to her lips. "Just drink," he ordered. "Slowly."

It was brandy, and it slid down her throat like fire, spreading down, warming and relaxing her like nothing else could have done. She coughed a little. "I hope no one saw you come in here," she said.

"No one saw. They're all downstairs." Gerard recapped the flask and returned it to his pocket, then put an arm around her shoulders and pulled her close. Tina allowed her head to nestle against his shoulder, feeling as though she would dissolve from pure contentment. For several minutes, they stared into the flames, then: "Would you like me to comb your hair?"

He murmured the question against her ear, his voice soothing and hypnotic as wine. She lifted her head to look at him, only to be caught by the fascinating way the fire silvered and glittered his eyes. While he sat, waiting for her response, she studied the dark fringe of his lashes, the planes and contours of his face, the tiny, exciting smile lines at the corners of his mouth. "If . . . you like," she answered breathlessly.

He retrieved her comb from the dressing table, and began, with infinite care, to untangle the snarl of wet, matted curls. Her eyes drifted shut, a small smile curling her lips. His hands were so gentle she scarcely knew he was there, and yet she was aware of him—of his fingers grazing the nape of her neck, of his breath rustling the tiny tendrils near her ear.

"There," he said, after a little while. "I think I've made you presentable. Turn around and look at me."

She did as he commanded, shifting until they sat face to face. Slowly, he reached out to touch her cheek, then both hands extended to frame her face.

"Now I'm going to warm you another way," he said, very softly.

And he lowered his mouth to hers.

255

Vaguely, she knew that she was unsurprised, that a part of her had been expecting this as the natural outcome of the scene. And, as she had known she would, she accepted him, reveling in the touch of his mouth, in his taste, and in the delicious sensations he aroused.

It was a long, exploratory, sensuous kiss; at the end of it he tossed aside the coat and blanket, enfolding her entirely in the warm, splendid security of his embrace. Eyes closed, she tilted her head back and offered her lips once more, craving his touch too much to be shy.

This time he was neither gentle nor patient. His tongue entered her mouth, entwined with hers, then probed her with deep thrusts that sent pagan tremors through every nerve in her body. When he lowered her to her back on the blanket, she moaned and reached for him blindly, tugging until his body shielded her from the coolness of the room. Then he was kissing her again, deeply, his hands gliding over her in a demanding quest that triggered her deepest urges.

When at last they paused to breathe she felt his smile against her cheek, a slow, crooked smile that melted her heart with its charm. "Tina," he whispered. "What are you doing to me? I can't resist you. You're so beautiful, so perfect."

Beautiful words, she thought hazily. He even sounded as though he meant them. Perhaps he did love her. Perhaps her dreams for the future were not impossible. But the present was all that mattered right now. Dreams were formless, this was real. And she had to seize what was real before it evaporated, before she turned old and there was no more time, no more dreams.

Impelled by these thoughts, she clutched at him wordlessly, her lips moist and parted, her hands slipping under his waistcoat to caress him through the thin lawn shirt. But as her urgency increased, she felt him hold back, felt him kiss her more slowly, his lips just brushing the pulse at the base of her throat. Puzzled, she looked up and saw him gazing down at her with the oddest expression.

And then something changed. He made a low, impatient sound in his throat, a kind of growl, and yanked at the tie to her dressing gown.

As he spread wide the flannel, he shook his head, his eyes roaming over the length of her with a hungry, unfocused look. "Perfect," he said hoarsely. "You're too perfect and beautiful to be real. Are you a sprite, Valentina? I swear there's witchcraft in your lips. Will you disappear if I touch you?"

As if to test the theory, his hand skimmed lightly over her flesh, spreading a heat reminiscent of the fire from the brandy. Then his mouth went to her breast and the last vestiges of her self-consciousness vanished. Tina's breath sucked in and her back arched, her arms flailing blindly for whatever part of him she could reach. And then it stopped, abruptly, and he murmured the words she did not want to hear.

"If we're going to stop, it has to be now."

She opened her eyes. He was sitting back, straddling her, his chest rising and falling in an unsteady rhythm. His cravat was untied, and somewhere along the line the top three buttons of his shirt had come undone. She looked at him and swallowed. He was staring at her with such yearning that, without thinking, she reached for him once more.

"Not yet," she whispered.

He seemed to lack the will to argue, for he came down to her at once, his mouth burning her while his hands roved across her sensitive flesh and down, down between her thighs to a place of magic and secrets. Emboldened, her hands went out, knowing instinctively that he would wish her to reciprocate. When she stroked the straining fabric at the front of his trousers, she saw the muscles in his throat constrict.

She half thought he would stop her or argue, but he

only groaned her name and lay down, giving her freer access. For a moment she hesitated, knowing the buttons would be difficult to undo. His eyes were half closed, his face taut with strain, but when she reached for them he caught at her wrist.

"Are you sure this is what you want? I want very much to make love to you, but do you understand what this means?"

"What does it mean?" she whispered. The question sounded stupid, but it was all she could think of to say.

Now those gray eyes were fully open, piercing her with their gleam. "It means that you will be mine," he said softly, "for now and forever, mine and mine alone. Are you willing for that to be so?"

Suddenly confused, she turned her head away from him, toward the fire. There, in the flames, she saw Christian's face. And for a moment doubted.

Words were nothing.

Promises could be empty.

"You're not sure," he stated, reading her hesitation. "God, Tina, you're shivering again. What a brute I am to do this to you."

He covered her quickly, retying the sash of her robe as tenderly as though she were a gift. Then he picked up his coat and stood, looking down at her.

"What you need right now is a hot bath," he said, with quiet authority. "After that you will get into bed and stay there until Miss Steeple says you can get up."

He strode to the door, stopped, and looked back at her from the shadows. "Thank you, Tina. Thank you for rescuing my nephew." Then he wrenched open the door and walked out.

Seventeen

The sonnet was as complete as it would ever be, Gerard thought wearily. He had written and revised and pondered and composed until he no longer knew whether the lines he wrote made any sense at all. He could do no more. He was going to give it to her tonight.

He pondered this, then smiled to himself. The sonnet would reassure her that his intentions were honorable— something this afternoon's episode might lead her to doubt—and give her time to grow used to the idea of becoming his viscountess. It would show her that he was a sensitive, understanding man, a man who was willing to go to a great deal of exertion to assure her happiness. Yes.

As for his proposal of marriage, that was for the morrow. He did not know much about romance, but he rather fancied that Valentine's Day was the perfect time to offer his heart and soul to the lady he loved. Women appreciated that sort of thing, did they not? Therefore, he would give her the sonnet tonight, while tomorrow, *on* Valentine's Day, *on* her birthday, he would formally offer for her hand.

Exactly how and when he would give her the sonnet was still at issue. He had not set eyes on her since the afternoon, when they had come so close to forgetting everything but their desire for each other. Yet the encounter was perilously near the surface of his mind, a dragging undertow of excitement that had been haunting him for hours.

In retrospect he realized that he should have sent Miss Steeple, that he should never have gone to her himself, that it had been wildly indiscreet. But the urge had been too powerful, and besides, no one had tried to stop him. No one had dared. And now he must suffer for it, suffer the memory of her soft, yielding body, of the taste of her silken lips, of her sweet, searing responsiveness to his touch. . . .

His breath hissed out in mute frustration. The embers of the fire still burned—simply thinking about her had brought his body alive with need, something his very tight inexpressibles were doing nothing to conceal. With a soft groan, he closed his eyes and ground his teeth and willed himself to relax.

Perhaps it was as well that she had not come down for dinner, he reflected. After all, this was something that could as easily have happened splat in the middle of his drawing room. It was a horrifying thought, made even more horrifying by the knowledge that another minute, perhaps two, and he would have to return to his guests. He could not hide in his library for long. He would have to go out there and behave normally, talk and play whist or billiards or dice or some other damned game he did not care about, and pretend that he was not thinking about Valentina.

Which he was. He thought about her all the time now. Consciously or unconsciously, she was there every moment, superimposed over everything else, influencing his every action.

Lifting his head, he stared up at the ceiling and made a concentrated effort to think along more elevated, gentlemanly planes. He made himself recite his sonnet, then tried to imagine her reaction to it. Then he envisioned himself going down on one knee to make his declaration, which he had more or less composed in his head. Last but not least, he pictured her blushing acceptance — the most important part of all.

He hoped she would not wish for a long betrothal. He was perfectly willing to do it any way she pleased, but his heartfelt preference was that they wed as soon as possible. Now that he had at last acknowledged the lack in his life, now that he had recognized that he would never be completely happy until he had made her his own, he wanted to get on with it. He wanted a bride, and he wanted her soon — in his life, in his arms, in his bed. . . .

. . . and he was back to that subject again.

Damn.

Self-control, Gerard. Patience, resolution, tenacity, self-control — these were the virtues that had never yet failed him. In the past years he had, when necessary, resisted beautiful women quite successfully. It was merely a question of mind over body.

"Here you are," said a voice, interrupting his thoughts.

James stepped into the library and closed the door, his handsome countenance betraying his curiosity at Gerard's behavior. "What the devil are you doing in here? Everyone has been asking for you. Chetwoode, Flaundon, and the others are ripe for some faro, though some of the ladies are protesting. Ruscombe's son is playing piquet with Felicity." He grinned. "Letting her win, too. She's got that one on a hook."

"And Rewe?"

"Oh, he's paying court to Mrs. Bradfield again, but if you ask me, his heart isn't in it. He and Allegra had a row, did you know? I don't know what it was about, but the amazing thing is that they seem to have patched it up. Little Dickon's narrow escape has had its effect on everyone."

Gerard looked at him. "Have you gone up to see him?"

"Dickon? Yes, but he's sleeping. I understand you were there, too."

"For a while. After I . . . saw Valentina."

"How was she?" The question seemed nonchalant; James perched on the edge of the desk, his weak leg swinging idly.

"Cold." Gerard avoided his brother's eye.

"I assume you took care of that."

He glanced up to see the smile tugging at his brother's mouth. "As you say," he agreed, with an answering gleam. "Whose name did you draw in the lottery?"

James's smile vanished. "Lady Buckden's," he grumbled. "What luck, eh? Believe me, it wasn't easy to come up with a verse for her, but I managed it. And I wrote one for Millie."

Gerard cocked a brow.

"I did what you suggested," James said defensively. "I wrote from my heart. It was short, sweet, and very direct. Look, are you sure Tina is all right? She hasn't come down."

Gerard frowned. He knew that Miss Steeple had fussed over Tina and insisted she remain in her room for the rest of the day. When he'd expressed concern, Miss Steeple had quietly assured him that Tina merely needed to rest—and to think. Gerard could only believe that her thinking had to do with him—or with Rewe. The latter possibility disturbed him, but the former filled him with elation. He could have sworn it was love he had seen in her face this afternoon. Yet, suddenly, he was assailed with doubt. What if she simply desired him? What if it was Rewe she loved? Just the thought made him want to pick something up and smash it.

"I think so," he said with a sigh. He rose to his feet, satisfied that he could now face his guests without blushing. "Meet me here later, when they've all gone to bed. Then we can decide what to do about these valentines of ours."

* * *

Fortunately, the prospect of the ball the following night induced the guests to seek their beds early, so that it was only a little past midnight when the last of them retired.

"Thank God," James sighed, throwing himself into a chair. "I half feared we would be obliged to sit up 'til three again, and I'm too devilish tired for that."

Gerard settled into the chair behind his mahogany desk. "I saw you talking to Millie," he remarked.

James's face filled with light. "Yes, and there was nothing her mother could do about it, short of running away from the whist table. Millie says your little lectures have been helping her a great deal. She is very grateful. And so am I."

"She's catching on," Gerard acknowledged. "Did you bring the valentine?"

James drew a folded sheet of pink-tinted paper from his pocket and tossed it onto the desk. "Here, put a seal on it, will you? Y'know, I've been thinking about this notion of yours, to slip these things under the girls' doors." He sighed. "I don't know, Gerry. When I'm as tired as I am now, my leg aches like the devil and . . . I make too much noise when I walk." He sounded frustrated. "You'll have to do it for me."

While Gerard put his wafer on James's epistle, he considered the situation. He knew which room was Millie's, just as he knew which was Tina's. He was capable of moving quietly—it was something he was rather good at, in fact. But the mere idea of standing outside Tina's room in the dark, remembering what had almost taken place there, knowing that she was on the other side of the door . . . his mouth went dry. It was not wise. He had already found that where she was concerned he had almost no willpower. If he wanted to sleep at all that night, he knew he had better stay as far away from her as possible.

"No," he said finally. "I don't think that will answer

263

the purpose." He leaned over and reached for the bell-pull. "I've another idea."

His butler must have been hovering nearby, for he arrived within seconds, his long face set in a lugubrious expression.

Gerard looked him over. "Bissett," he said, "you're a competent man. James and I have a mission for you."

"A mission, my lord?" Bissett permitted himself to blink.

"A mission," he repeated. "We need you to deliver some correspondence."

"Some correspondence, my lord?" Bissett, too, must have been tired, for this time he betrayed his bewilderment.

Gerard reached into his drawer, where his sonnet lay carefully wrapped and sealed with his wafer. "I require this"—he waved it, then tossed it onto the desk—"to be slipped under Miss Jardine's door sometime between now and tomorrow morning. It must be done with stealth and the utmost discretion."

"Yes, my lord." Bissett had recovered his impassivity.

"Do you know which room she occupies?"

Without actually displaying affront, Bissett indicated that it was his business to be acquainted with such details.

"Good." Gerard gestured. "Jay has one also."

"Mine is for Lady Millicent," explained James hastily. "Put it under her door for me, will you, Bissett? And tiptoe quietly."

"Very good, sir," agreed Bissett without a bat of his eye.

Gerard suppressed a smile at the vision of his dignified butler tiptoeing down the corridor like a thief in the night. "Do you have any questions?"

Bissett did not.

When he was gone, James cast Gerard a doubtful look. "The old fellow looks tired. You don't think he'll botch it up, do you?"

Gerard stared off into space, then sighed wearily. "Don't worry," he said. "Bissett will manage. He always does."

Bissett had performed many assignments during the course of his career as a nobleman's servant, some of them not entirely within the range of his exacting sense of decorum. Nonetheless, in his office as premiere servant to The Rt. Hon. the Viscount Laverstoke, he had never been called upon to undertake any task inconsistent with his age, station, or dignity.

Until now.

However, he was not one to neglect his duty. He would do as he was told because it was his duty, even though he felt foolish. This so-called mission obviously had something to do with Valentine's Day, he reflected stoically. Mrs. Bissett would say that there was romance in the air, but Bissett did not hold with such doings. Bissett could scarcely remember his own courtship, which had been conducted with propriety, with none of this havey-cavey sneaking around in the middle of the night.

Reaching the upper corridor where the two young ladies slept, Bissett began to tiptoe. He felt very foolish. What if one of the ladies looked out and screamed? What would he say? Tossing this around in his head, he stooped down and with a quick prod, poked Mr. James's missive under Lady Millicent Quigley's door. There, thank God. Only one to go and he could head for his bed.

Still tiptoeing, he proceeded along the passageway, holding his candle aloft. The blue bedroom, that was where Miss Jardine was. A nice young lady she was, too, with proper, genteel manners. So his lordship had taken a fancy to her, had he? *What was that?* Bissett froze. Had it been a door? He looked around, but saw nothing. Despite the chill, perspiration beaded on his brow.

He tiptoed closer to Miss Jardine's door. Again, a

sound. Heart hammering crazily, he rammed the viscount's sonnet under the door and scurried off, seeking the shelter of the staircase at the other end of the corridor. Five minutes later, he was safe in his snug apartments near the kitchen, relating the tale to Mrs. Bissett.

"I knew it," sighed the viscount's plump housekeeper. "I knew it ever since the night they arrived. He changed his plans to leave, didn't he? That's when I knew, only at first I thought 'twas Miss Felicity that had caught his eye." She went on talking as she fussed over him, passing him his nightly cup of hot milk, removing his shoes, rubbing his stiff shoulders. "And 'tis only right and proper," she added. "I reckon a fine gentleman like his lordship deserves to find a lady he can love."

"I suppose so," said Bissett glumly. "Only I felt like such a fool."

"Never mind," soothed his loving wife. "You won't feel like that when we've got a new mistress. You'll be glad you did what you did." She stunned him by adding, almost coyly, "You gave me a valentine once, when we were courting. You were quite a romantic fellow, Mr. Bissett."

Bissett could not recall. "I was?" he said cautiously.

"You were," she affirmed. "I still have it, too." She bent and kissed the back of his neck. "Would you like to see it?" she whispered.

Reaching out, Bissett forgot decorum and kissed her back. "I'd like that, Margery. Later."

Lady Buckden had been lying awake, fantasizing about the wedding she would give for Millicent. She would spare no expense; her daughter would be married with as much pomp and pageantry as possible. People must say it was the match of the Season—the same people who looked down their noses at *her* because her grandfather had been a wool-merchant.

Her hands clenched at the memory. A *Cit* they called her behind her back, never mind the fact that her mother had been as blue-blooded as any of them. The fact that her husband was an earl made no difference when that earl had always been considered an eccentric, even before the riding accident that had injured his spine and turned him into a recluse. And without him to lean on, Lady Buckden was unable to command the respect she wished or to assume the place in society she dearly desired.

Lady Buckden's mouth hardened to an obdurate line. Well, she would have the last laugh when her own sweet Millicent carried off the most sought-after bachelor in the realm. As Viscountess Laverstoke, Millicent would have the entrée her mother had been denied. *She* might never have set foot in Almack's, but Millicent would. *She* might have been snubbed by some of London's leading hostesses, but Millicent never would be. As wife to one of the foremost peers in the country, no one would dare. They would see, all those arrogant, supercilious women. They would see that it was *her* daughter, not theirs, who brought the viscount to his knees.

Her bosom swelled as she pictured herself standing in St. George's, Hanover Square, watching her husband (if he could but do it) give his daughter away before the eyes of the envious *ton*. It would be the greatest triumph of her life, the moment she had waited for all these years. She only wished Millicent would cease her languishing over James Marchant.

As she brooded over this, her sharp ears pricked up. Her eyes opened. She'd heard something—something that sounded suspiciously like the shuffle of feet in the corridor. Lifting her head from her pillow, Lady Buckden listened intently. Surely Millicent would not dare leave her room? Millicent had been rather self-willed lately, but surely she would not be so undutiful, so indiscreet? Surely she would not do anything to jeopardize the progress she was making with Lord Laverstoke?

Throwing the covers off, Lady Buckden slipped silently across the carpet and laid her ear against the polished wood door. Faint sounds. Someone was out there, near Millicent's room. She could hear him breathing. Her scalp prickled eerily, but she waited, biding her time, holding her breath, determined to do nothing unless it had to do with Millicent.

Then, nothing.

The whisper of sound moved on past her own door, floating along the corridor and away toward the end. Several seconds passed. Finally roused to irresistible curiosity, Lady Buckden eased open the door the veriest smidgen, and peered out.

And through the darkness, she glimpsed the shadowed outline of a man.

A tall, thin man.

Who?

She watched him bend down to fumble near the floor, but as she widened her door, he surged up and plunged into the blackness, not troubling to hide the sound of his footsteps. Lady Buckden stared after him, unsure whether to be alarmed or simply outraged by such unorthodox goings-on.

Eyes narrowed, Lady Buckden debated her options. She could either go back to bed, investigate on her own, or raise a hue and cry. The latter course was distasteful simply because it would inspire scandal. And to own the truth, as long as it had nothing to do with her plans for Millicent, she did not care what it meant. But she had to be certain.

Fetching the single candle still burning by her bed, Lady Buckden stepped over to Millicent's door and tried turning the knob. It was locked.

She wavered.

Then, raising her dressing gown so she would not trip, Lady Buckden moved down the corridor to where she had seen the prowler crouch. She paused, counting doors. Yes, it had definitely been Miss Jardine's room; she was sure of it.

Glancing around to be sure she was unseen, Lady Buckden bent down to peer under the crack. She was rewarded with the pale fragment of paper stuck out the merest fingernail's length. Lips compressed to the point of pain, she again held her breath, alert to any sound louder than the beat of her own heart.

Silence.

Expelling air, Lady Buckden scraped at the paper, working it bit by bit until she could grasp its tip. Pulling it out, she picked up her candle and scurried back to the safety of her bedchamber, gasping with the effort.

Inside, she sat on the bed and examined her prize with shaking fingers. It was addressed *Valentina,* and secured with a wafer stamped with the viscount's seal. Good God, Laverstoke was sending messages to Miss Jardine— quiet, unassuming, harmless Miss Jardine.

The little jade!

Without compunction, she tore it open, separating the inner from the outer sheet which bore the hussy's name. Casting the one aside, Lady Buckden perused the viscount's sonnet.

By the time she reached the last line, her dreams lay shattered at her feet. This was no innocent communiqué. This was a message of love so ardent it was tantamount to a declaration.

A lone tear rolled down the gaunt line of her cheek. She could hear them laughing, all those fine, high-born ladies, mocking her failure, deriding her ambitions for her daughter. And while they laughed, the door to Almack's slammed shut with a resounding crash.

All was lost. St. Georges, Hanover Square, receded into the mist.

Filled with emotion, she gazed down at the viscount's sonnet. Her first instinct was to crush and burn it, but she had never been an impetuous woman. Was there a

269

better plan?

Suddenly, it crossed her mind that there was nothing in it to indicate who it had been written for, other than a reference to hair and eye color. In fact, the Jardine girl had much the same coloring as Millicent did, which meant—her heart nearly stopped—*the sonnet could as well have been written for Millicent!* Surging to her feet, Lady Buckden returned to Millicent's room and peered under the crack. Sure enough, there was something pushed under there, but this time she could not reach it.

Returning to her bedchamber, she searched the room for something long and thin she could poke under the door, and after a few minutes located a letter-opener in the small top drawer of the bedside table.

Fifteen minutes later she was reading James Marchant's verse, scornfully comparing its paltry simplicity to Lord Laverstoke's elegant composition. So the young fool thought he loved her darling girl, did he?

She regarded James's words, her thin lips curled with contempt. *Roses are red, violets are blue, you are sweet and I love you.* How trite and unimaginative. As for it's impertinent postscript: *"I promise I will find a way to make you mine,"* Lady Buckden snarled at the presumption. Such effrontery passed all bounds!

Seething inwardly, she sat back and considered the situation. Who had delivered these valentines? It had certainly not been the viscount skulking about in the hall, nor had it been his half-crippled fool of a brother. Therefore, she thought craftily, it had to have been a servant.

And servants made mistakes.

Feeling triumphant, she rewrapped the sonnet in the wrapper labeled *Millie* and resealed it with wax dribbled from her candle. As for James's preposterous verse, she was loathe to give it to Miss Jardine, but someone had to receive it or the mix-up would not be credible.

Who then? Lizzie? Jane? Maria?

After several seconds, she came to the reluctant conclusion that it would have to be Felicity Winton. As much as she disliked the girl, Felicity's door was nearest to Miss Jardine's. It would make the servant's blunder that much more plausible.

I will find a way to make you mine . . .

"No, you will not," Lady Buckden spat out softly. "Not as long as I have a say in it."

Felicity Winton could have this worthless scribble of affection, and if she married James Marchant it was of no consequence at all. Nothing signified, as long as her own precious darling received the viscount's love sonnet.

Lady Buckden smiled to herself. Whether he liked it or not, Lord Laverstoke would have to pretend that there had been no mix-up at all. After all, what else could an honorable man do when his sonnet was read aloud in front of all his guests?

Eighteen

Valentine's Day, 1819
Laverstoke Park

The moment Tina awoke, she was flooded with memories of the viscount's embrace. She had already gone over it until she was exhausted, but as the dawn's light filled the sky she relived the scene yet again—every kiss, every word, every splendid, fiery sensation.

What had she done?

She stared at the ceiling, knowing and rejecting. She had done what she had wanted to do from the first—offered herself to him unashamedly, body and soul.

And he had walked away from her.

Had it been chivalry, as he had tried to make her believe? Or had that merely been an excuse, a front to disguise his disgust at her wanton behavior? She groaned softly, mortified to the depths of her soul by the possibility.

Whatever he thought of her, she was hopelessly in love with him. This was not a fancy, nor an infatuation. This was the sort of love that Libby had spoken of—the truest of all loves. What she'd felt for Christian had been a mere shadow in comparison.

She shut her eyes, struggling for the strength she knew she would need to get through this day. She did not know what to do, or how she was to behave toward

Gerard. Suppose he behaved as though nothing had happened? If he pretended, then so must she. She would take her cue from him.

Feeling utterly spent, she rolled to her side and shut her eyes, hoping to be able to go back to sleep. She must eventually have succeeded, for when the soft scratch on her door came, the room was much brighter than it had been before.

"Tina?" Not waiting for an invitation, Felicity slipped into the room and came over to the bed. "Tina, are you awake?"

"Yes." There seemed no point in saying otherwise.

"Good. I have to talk to you." Felicity sat down and waved a page of pink-tinted paper under Tina's nose. "I found this in my room this morning. Someone must have put it under my door during the night."

Stifling a yawn, Tina scanned the paper. "This is from James?" Perplexity formed between her brows. "Felicity, I don't understand."

"I think it means he wants to marry me," her cousin confided.

"But for pity's sake, why *you*?" The response was out of Tina's mouth before she realized how Felicity would interpret it. She groaned inwardly as the face next to hers went hostile.

"Perhaps he has fallen in love with me," her cousin suggested in a chilly tone. "Is it so inconceivable? Simply because Eugene behaves as though I do not exist does not mean that other men are unaware of me. I *am* very beautiful, you know. And James has admired me from the first."

Tina regarded her cousin with distress. Felicity was clearly in one of her wayward moods. She could have no real wish to wed James, but her feelings had obviously been wounded by the fact that they had received no word from Eugene, who had never responded to his invitation to tonight's ball.

Tina mustered patience she did not feel. "True, but it is Millie he cares for," she pointed out, quite gently.

"Is it?" Felicity's face flushed with anger. "Perhaps he has simply come to his senses and realized what an insipid creature she is. All Laverstoke's lessons have not helped her overmuch."

"Don't be cruel, Felicity. Anyone can see she has been trying."

Felicity leaped up, her voice rising hysterically. "I thought you would be excited for me, Tina. I thought you would wish me to be happy."

"Of course I want you to be happy. But why wed James when you are in love with Eugene?"

"Because Eugene will never offer for me!" Felicity's voice shook with emotion. "And because I don't want to spend the rest of my life alone and unloved. I don't want to be like you!" And with this utterance, Felicity ran out, slamming the door with a mighty bang.

"Oh, Felicity." Tina collapsed back onto the pillows with another groan. Happy Valentine's Day, she thought heavily.

Happy birthday to me.

As it happened, she did not encounter Gerard until midafternoon, for in the end she took the coward's way out and ordered a breakfast tray sent to her room. By the time she'd gathered her courage and made her appearance in the drawing room, most of the gentlemen had gone out riding. Tina was left to spend a miserable morning enduring Lizzie, Jane, and Maria's inane giggling, while Felicity flirted desperately with Mr. Chetwoode. Lady Buckden and Lady Millicent did not appear until noon, whereupon Lady Buckden managed to carry a cup of tea too close to Tina and spill it down the front of her best morning gown. Amid gushing apologies and cries of concern, Tina left the room to change her clothes.

Bewildered by an incident that had seemed no accident, Tina headed toward the staircase with a puckered brow. She had just started up the steps when Gerard, accompanied by Lords Ruscombe and Wantage, strolled into the Front Hall.

Not wishing it to appear that she was avoiding him, she paused uncertainly, but he had not yet seen her. For an instant, she studied him longingly, noting how handsome and splendid he looked in riding clothes and top boots. In fact, his riding breeches became him so well that she recalled with heartstopping clarity just how those hard, muscular thighs felt pressed against her own.

As though sensing her gaze, he looked up. "Good morning, Miss Jardine."

So she was Miss Jardine again now.

She lifted her chin as Lords Ruscombe and Wantage bowed and echoed the greeting. Then the two lords proceeded toward the stairs, passing her on their way to the second floor.

As their voices faded, Gerard walked over and rested a foot on the bottom step. "You appear to have had a mishap," he commented.

Tina glanced down at her soiled dress. "Yes, I'm afraid some . . . some tea spilled."

His dark brows pulled together. "I trust you were not burned."

"No." She tried to smile. "But I fear the stain will not come out."

"If it does not, you must allow me to replace your gown." He cleared his throat, scanning her face intently. "I trust you slept well?"

"I . . . yes."

"And what happened yesterday—you are quite recovered from it?"

Recovered? Dear heaven, she would never be recovered. But of course, he was referring to the incident with Dickon.

275

"Quite." In her desperate desire to appear self-possessed, Tina put a bit too much distance into her tone. "Thank you, my lord, but there is no cause for concern. You place too much importance on the incident."

What would he say to that? Oh, Gerard, say something to tell me how you feel. I don't know what to say to you.

But his face masked whatever he was thinking. "I'm glad to hear that. I would not want you to suffer any ill consequences." He paused, his eyes locking with hers. "Happy birthday, Tina."

"Thank you . . . my lord." She was simply too nervous to say his name.

Ever so slightly, his eyes narrowed. "And happy Valentine's Day."

"Thank you," she mumbled again. He appeared to expect something more, so she added awkwardly, "I'm looking forward to the ball."

She had the oddest feeling that she was doing something wrong, that she was displeasing him in some way. But all he said was, "Are you? Why?"

"Well, I have never been to a ball, you know." Under his steady gaze, she went on in a rush, "Your sister is lending me a gown to wear."

He merely looked at her, his gray eyes watchful.

"I . . . I must go and change," she stuttered. "The stain will set, if it has not already done so."

He stepped back. "Then I will detain you no longer."

As she hurried up the stairs, Gerard stared after her in perplexity. Perhaps he should have asked her point-blank about the valentine. Perhaps it would have been the best, if not the most subtle course. But where his sonnet was concerned, he was absurdly self-conscious, and in truth he had expected to read her reaction in her eyes. Even if she did not wish to speak of it aloud, he'd thought she would give him some sign—a smile, a blush, a glowing look.

Something.

Anything, as long as she acknowledged what he had done. But she had given him nothing. What the deuce did that mean?

Still frowning, he strode across the Hall to the nearest footman. "Fetch Bissett," he snapped. "Tell him to come to the library."

"Yes, my lord. Both letters were delivered precisely as your lordship instructed." Beneath his impassivity, Bissett looked indignant.

"Are you certain?" Gerard shot back with a conspicuous lack of diplomacy. "You took care of it yourself?"

Bissett's chest swelled with outrage. "Naturally," he replied, his mien dignified. "No mistake was made, my lord. Miss Jardine occupies the Blue Bedroom. Lady Millicent occupies the Pink Bedroom. I would not mistake those rooms if I were blindfolded and in my grave."

Gerard gave him a hard look, then gestured wearily. "Very well, Bissett. You have my apologies. You may go."

His butler departed in a huff.

Gerard left the library to look for James, and after a short search found him with Allegra in the ballroom. They were occupied with the musicians, who had traveled all the way from London for the occasion.

Ignoring them all, Gerard took James aside. "Something has gone awry," he said curtly.

"What?" James fixed him with a stare.

"Did Millie receive your valentine?"

"I don't know." James's face grew tense. "I do know she is wretchedly pale today. I was afraid it meant her mother had gotten wind of what I had done, but"—his brow furrowed—"Lady Buckden has been all smiles and amiability."

"But wouldn't Millie have found a way to tell you?"

277

Gerard persisted. "I thought the two of you talked with your eyes."

"We usually do, but today she won't even look at me. To be frank, I thought it damned odd, but between her mother and Felicity, I couldn't get near enough to say anything. By the by, Felicity has been behaving very queerly, too. Have you noticed?"

"Not really," said Gerard, his voice absent. His eyes scanned the ballroom, hardly noticing the garlands and wreaths and festoons of red ribbons that his sister and Tina had worked so hard upon. "Let me know if Millie says anything, will you?"

"I'll do that," James said heavily.

For the rest of the afternoon Gerard was kept occupied with his duties as host. Since many of the guests were traveling a considerable distance to attend the ball, some were to arrive that afternoon and spend the night. As the carriages streamed in, he was busy greeting and conversing, introducing those who did not know one another, and listening to gushing praise of his past glories in the service of the government. Yet all the while he was plotting how to have another word with Tina.

But it was not to be. Either she was avoiding him or fate was simply being perverse, for each time there was an opportunity to approach her, either someone would interrupt or she would already be involved in some other activity or conversation. And as the day progressed, his impatience grew.

As the dinner hour approached, he at last conceded that he would have to wait until the ball to talk to her. There, he would not be so thwarted, he thought grimly. He would beg the honor of a dance—preferably a waltz—and then he would probe her with all the silver-tongued agility of which he was capable. Satisfied with this plan, he allowed himself to be swept into a game of billiards with an elderly marquess and a baron who stuttered.

Tina sat quietly while Annie dressed her hair for dinner, barely attending to the maid's chatter or the painful tugs on her scalp. The style, she noted detachedly, was more elaborate than usual, an arrangement of braids and curls and red ribbon that Annie deemed suitable for a such a grand occasion as a ball. Was it truly as flattering as the maid claimed? Tina was in no fit state to judge the answer.

All day she had been trying to fight her melancholy, but right now her shield was down and it seeped in — all the doubt and worry and dread. Was there truly a possibility that her future might include Gerard, or was that merely the foolish illusions of a maiden spinster? If only she knew what he felt, what he thought! Did he condemn her? Did he regret what they had done? She had lived with uncertainty since her mother's death, but never had it troubled her as much as it did now, and never had the prospect of a life alone seemed so bleak.

Dismissing the maid, Tina sat a few minutes longer, gulping air, gathering courage for the evening ahead. Somehow she had made it through the afternoon, but the ball still loomed in front of her like a labor of Hercules. Nervousness quickened her pulses, but it was not the crowds or the splendor that caused it. No, it was the knowledge that Gerard would be there, looking marvelous and elegant and dear — dear beyond her wildest dreams.

To add to her unease, Felicity had not spoken to her all day — which meant that she was still nursing her grievances — while Christian's behavior was making her positively apprehensive. During these past few days, they had spoken only of polite trivialities, yet his smoldering glances had not ceased. Tonight, she promised herself, if

279

he requested her hand for a dance she would accept only to give herself the opportunity to tell him once and for all that what he'd suggested was impossible, unthinkable, and obscene. It would doubtless be unpleasant, but it would settle one of her problems.

Satisfied with the decision, Tina made a final inspection of her appearance, fingering the ruby necklace that Allegra had insisted she borrow. Now that it had been altered, the red silk gown suited her better than she had expected. True, the neckline seemed extremely low, but Allegra had insisted that to raise it would be akin to labeling herself a prudish old spinster. And that was something that Tina was not about to do.

With a surge of new determination, she lifted her chin. This was her birthday and no one—not Felicity, nor Christian, nor even Gerard—no one was going to spoil it for her. She was going to be strong.

At dinner she was seated between Lord Wantage and Lord Flaundon, both of whom behaved so flirtatiously that she was obliged to wonder if her neckline was responsible. Gerard occupied his usual seat at the head of the table, with two of the highest-ranking guests on either hand.

At the beginning of the meal he had stood and made a pretty speech about the three guests of honor who "shared" a birthday coinciding with Valentine's Day. And while everyone drank to their health, Gerard had looked straight at her with a gleam in his eye that made her heart rise up and do pirouettes. She dared not think what it might mean—not here, not now—yet wild new hope blossomed inside her. *Perhaps she was more than a passing fancy to him, after all.*

"And now we are going to read the valentines," Allegra announced at the end of the meal. Her lovely eyes shimmered with pleasure at being the center of attention.

"Our guests who have been here all week know what I am talking about, but for those of you who were not, allow me to explain. It was a little game, you see. Each of us drew a name—" Allegra went on, sweetly detailing the "fun" they had all had composing their verses. "Above each verse, the author was to have indicated who the verse is for, and was not to have signed his or her name. I shall read each one aloud."

This was the part of the dinner that Tina had been dreading. Her hands clenched in her lap as she sat, taut and waiting, listening to Allegra read. She knew that if she had not been so nervous she would have enjoyed it, for some of the poems were really quite good. Of course, others were less so, while a few completely ignored iambic meter and mixed their rhyme schemes horribly. One caught her attention with its simplicity—a limerick for Lady Buckden which actually brought a sour smile to that lady's face.

The verse written for Tina was a clever little triolet which made a play on her name. Lord Wantage gave her a nudge when it was over. "Pretty good, eh?" he whispered conspiratorially. "Worked on it 'til I damned near went blind."

Tina smiled, trying to imagine fusty Lord Wantage making such an effort. Then her smile faded as the words of her own composition rang out for all to hear: *"A Valentine for Laverstoke . . ."*

Every muscle in Tina's body went rigid with the effort of keeping her face absolutely impassive. As Allegra read on, she dared not look around at the faces for fear she would catch Gerard's eye.

"To me, he's England's Valentine!" Allegra finished with a dramatic flourish. She regarded her brother with a smile. "Well! That was most flattering, was it not?"

While everyone clapped and murmured appreciatively, Tina's shoulders sagged with relief. Thank heaven it was over. No one had laughed, no one had pointed a finger or said it was silly or ill-composed. Everyone had liked it. And now that fear was removed, she could risk a quick peep at Gerard.

That was a mistake. To her discomfiture, he was looking straight at her, the glint in his eye even more pronounced than before. And as Allegra's voice washed over their heads, he raised his glass and offered her a silent toast.

He knew.

The knowledge flooded through her like potent wine, scorching her cheeks with color. He knew she had written it and appeared to be *amused*. Mortified to the quick, Tina stared down at her lap. Was she only a source of amusement to him, then? In his eyes, perhaps she was only a silly little spinster who was stupid enough to fall in love with him. England's Valentine indeed! How ridiculous he must think her.

She scarcely heard the few remaining poems, or the buzz of conversation that followed. In fact, she heard nothing at all until Lady Buckden hoisted herself to her feet to say, waggishly, "My dear Lady Rewe, I do have one little thing to add, if you will permit me. My darling Millicent has received the most delightful valentine, and I should like to read it aloud. It was sent to her in the most romantical way possible"—she rolled her eyes significantly—"under her door in the dead of night!"

As everyone grew quiet, Tina glanced at Felicity, then further down the table at James, who was frowning. Millicent's face, she noticed, had gone chalk white. What in the world was going on?

Lady Buckden cleared her throat.

"Shall I compare thee to a summer's day?
Thus spake the Bard, yet I too must avow
They do my feelings all too much betray
As I behold thy fair and ivory brow
Like pristine clouds, so soft, a sunbeam's kiss,

282

> *Thy modest eyes of pure, bewitching blue,*
> *Thy cheek a blush of rosedust, perfumed bliss,*
> *Thy locks a black swan on a pool of dew.*
> *Dainty enchantress, queen of summer's theme,*
> *I hear thee in each bird's bright morning call,*
> *Thy voice the music in the rippling stream,*
> *Thy wisdom both the owl and me enthrall.*
> > *From light to dark I must thy charms extol,*
> > *Thou art the heavenly garden of my soul."*

Shock rippled through Tina as Lady Buckden smirked and looked down the table at Gerard. He was oddly still, his eyes a shock of chill gray, his expression arrested and frozen as winter ice.

"Of course, we know who the author is, and as Millicent's mama,"—she tittered girlishly—"I can only say I am delighted that my daughter is receiving the attentions of so notable a suitor."

Lady Buckden sat down.

No one could have missed her meaning, Tina realized. Gerard had written Millie an achingly beautiful love sonnet, and Lady Buckden was flinging down a gauntlet, daring him not to follow with a declaration of marriage.

But why? Why had he done it?

A creeping numbness swept through her veins, a numbness as real and paralyzing as that created by the icy pond water the day before. What a fool she had been to think he cared for her. Fool, fool, fool.

Amid the rustle of murmurs, Allegra hurried to her feet. "Well," she said shrilly, "I think it is time we left the gentlemen to their port. Come, ladies."

Gerard could not remember ever being so furious. He didn't know how that scheming, vicious Buckden harridan had gotten her hands on his sonnet, but it was exactly like her to lay him such a ruthless trap. Beneath his controlled exterior, he was spewing expletives that would have made a soldier blush. He had never meant anyone other than Tina to see his work, and now his most intimate feelings had been laid bare to the impersonal eyes of strangers. To have had to sit and listen to Lady Buckden's grating voice pronouncing *his* words—it racked him with an anger akin to agony.

He understood only too well what would happen. During the course of the evening the whispers would spread. Everyone would be expecting him to offer for Millie; everyone would stare, everyone would watch and conjecture and gossip behind their hands. Rage clutched at his throat as he imagined it—the whispers, the titters, the eyes.

Well, he'd be bloody *damned* if he'd surrender to what amounted to public blackmail. Unfortunately, when he did not, poor little Millie would be placed in an awkward, humiliating position—put there, by all that was holy, by the unscrupulous machinations of her own mother. What had he said about Lady Buckden—that she was no Alexander of Russia? No, by God, she was worse!

And Tina.

What the devil must she be thinking? Would she believe he had betrayed her? Or would she realize that a mistake had been made? After the way Rewe had treated her, he was not at all sure that she would. His mouth tightened to a forbidding line.

Seething with impotent fury, Gerard could barely force himself to respond when one of his guests addressed him with a question. And while his lips formed words that must have made sense, his brain was working, tossing around ideas.

The situation needed to be handled delicately. It would take all his diplomatic skill to resolve this successfully, but it could be done. It *had* to be done.

Because his happiness—and James's—depended on it.

284

As it happened, no spat of inclement weather prevented the remaining ball guests from reaching their destination. Tina stood in the receiving line for almost an hour while carriages streamed up to the front door, carrying members of the local gentry from miles around. Somehow she managed to smile as each person was introduced, concealing her agitation behind a mask of grace and dignity.

Judging from the number of people, the ball obviously ranked as a success, though it crossed her mind that Allegra ought to have looked more pleased than she did. In fact, none of them appeared as happy as they pretended. To a discerning observer, James's mouth was tight, Lady Millie looked ready to collapse, and Felicity's smile held a queer, brittle quality. Only Gerard looked as unruffled and self-contained as he ever had, unfathomable even now.

How could he?

Despite what had happened, Tina's mind returned to yesterday, when he had seemed so concerned for her welfare, so warm and passionate and loving. Now she saw him as a stranger—a cool, enigmatic stranger who made love to one woman while he wrote love to another. Which had been real?

Laverstokes always married heiresses.

The words rang suddenly through her mind, a death knell to her hopes and dreams. Perhaps he had merely succumbed to tradition, she thought brokenly. Family tradition could be a powerful incentive, could it not?

The possibility sent hysteria surging through her at the same moment she smiled and shook hands with the wife of a local squire. How could this happen to her *again,* for pity's sake? Every time she nearly gave herself to a man, he turned around and got himself engaged to wed someone else! The pain of it was nigh to unbearable—a searing rip in the very substance of her soul.

She was still grappling with her emotions when the receiving line broke up. And then, before she realized his intention, Gerard came over and took her by the elbow. "I believe this first dance is mine," he said quietly.

Her throat closed with shock. Suddenly furious without knowing why, she said, in her haughtiest, frostiest tone, "I think not, my lord. Surely it must be obvious that it is Lady Millicent you must lead out." She paused, then added distinctly, "Her rank is higher than mine."

His fingers tightened on her elbow, hinting at an inner tension as great as hers. "Not in my affections," he murmured. "Come, Tina, don't be stubborn. You know you want to dance with me."

"Stubborn!" Her mouth fell open with outrage, then she twisted from his grasp. "Go and support Lady Millicent with your smooth words. She looks as though she's about to swoon."

Before he could retort, she spun around and entered the ballroom, only to be waylaid by Lord Wantage, who bowed and twinkled at her benignly. "Evening, Miss Jardine. You look lovely, m'dear. Are all your dances bespoken? If not, I'll take any one you have free."

"You may have the first," she said gratefully. "I'd be delighted to stand up with you, sir."

He blinked in surprise. "The first? Why, that's capital!" He beamed happily and led her onto the floor.

An hour later, Felicity sought her out. "I've talked to James," she said tearfully. "He says there's been a mistake."

"Mistake? What do you mean?"

"I don't think he wants to marry me after all." Her cousin's voice trembled with hurt. "He says my valentine was supposed to have been for Millie."

"Oh?" Tina arched a brow. "Then how did it get to be under your door?"

"He doesn't know. He thinks the butler made a mistake." She sniffed tearfully. "No one will ever want to marry me," she sobbed. "I'll grow old and gray waiting for Eugene. He's not coming, Tina. Oh, why didn't he come?"

Realizing that Felicity was about to create a scene, Tina drew her away and out of the ballroom. Choosing a small, unoccupied saloon a short distance away, Tina bade her cousin to sit.

"Now Felicity," she said carefully, "you are only eighteen. As you so immodestly pointed out to me this morning, you are very beautiful. And though you are not a great heiress, you will have a substantial dowry. The only thing that stands in the way of your happiness is your unruly tongue."

"I . . . know." Felicity's shoulders shook with sobs. "But I would not say cruel things if Eugene would only come. He loves the Home Office more than he does me!"

"Do you think your mother would let you wed him if he did?" Tina asked quietly.

"She would *have* to let me, because if she did not, I would only wait until I came of age and then marry him anyway. And besides"—Felicity tossed her curls mutinously—"Papa likes Eugene. I think I could persuade him to come about if I cried hard enough."

Tina sighed at the Felicity-like statement. "Come, dry your tears and return with me to the ballroom. Even if they aren't all lords, there are a great many handsome young men waiting to dance with you."

"Actually, I wouldn't care if every one of them was a duke," Felicity said with a watery smile. "I just care that they aren't Eugene." But she rose, prepared to do as Tina suggested.

When they turned to leave, Christian was standing in the doorway. "There you are," he said playfully. "I was wondering why you two beautiful ladies were missing from the ballroom."

Noticing her cousin's radiant smile, Tina said quickly,

"Pray go on, Felicity. There is something I must discuss with Lord Rewe."

Christian stared after Felicity. "She's a pretty child," he remarked. "Very pretty." Then his head turned, his gaze sweeping appreciatively over Tina. "That's one of Allegra's gowns, is it not? I recognize it. The necklace, too."

"Yes, she lent them to me."

"Red suits you." He moved forward to grasp her lightly by the hands. "God, what a night. I told Allegra that Valentine's Day poetry business was piffle. Did you ever hear such a collection of rubbish in your life?"

"Actually," she said, "I thought some of them were rather clever."

Christian snorted. "You would," he scoffed. "You were always easy to please." As he leaned toward her, Tina could smell the whiskey on his breath. "I wonder which fool wrote that one about Laverstoke. Lord, I nearly burst out laughing when I heard it. *To me, he's England's Valentine,*" he mimicked. "What bloody rot." When she said nothing, he caught hold of her arms and pulled her close. "Have you given any thought to my proposal?"

"Let go of me, Christian," she said coldly.

"Answer my question, Tina."

Feeling curiously calm, she stared him in the eye. "Look, I should have told you at the time what I thought of your ideas. I don't know why I didn't, but I'm doing so now. What you proposed, Lord Rewe, is both dishonorable and impossible." Instinct told her that wasn't enough of an explanation for him, so she went on, "First of all, even if James offered for me, I could not accept knowing he was in love with Lady Millicent—"

"Fat good it will do him," he interrupted. "She's Laverstoke's now. He'll have to marry her after what her mother did. The old cow's out for blood."

"And secondly," she continued in a desperate voice, "I

would never betray the man who was my husband. Whether I loved him or not."

He frowned down at her, looking a little skeptical. "Are you trying to make me believe you don't want me?"

"Not anymore," she replied. "I have come to realize that I'm glad we did not marry. I don't love you, Christian. Perhaps I never did."

"That's not true!" he protested. "Hang it, Tina, there was fire between us. Don't you remember?"

She closed her eyes, pushing the memory away.

"Don't you remember?" he repeated. Abruptly, he jerked her against his chest. "I do. I remember how eager you were for my kisses. I remember what you look like without all those fine clothes. I remember what it feels like to put my mouth on you, and I remember"—she thought his voice sounded taunting—"how much you liked it."

Before she could object, his mouth was on hers, crushing her lips, exploring with an expertise that five years before would have turned her bones to water. Now, however, his kisses triggered nothing more than a mild revulsion. There was no weakness in the knees, no pin-wheeling senses, no throbbing heat in her belly. Nothing. If she had wanton instincts, they were certainly not in evidence.

She tore her mouth away. "Let me go," she cried. "You are despicable! Even if I wanted you, do you think your wife would simply look the other way? She loves you, Christian! And I most assuredly do not!"

He glared down at her. "Allegra doesn't love me," he retorted, almost angrily. "Where the blazes did you get that idea?" He sounded so incensed by the notion that she instantly knew it was his weak point.

"From Allegra herself," she said, pressing her advantage. "Good God, Christian, don't you know she is in love with you? How can you be so blind? If she walked in here right now you would break her heart."

"Allegra hasn't got a heart," he countered. "Damn it, if she had, I wouldn't—" He broke off from whatever he'd been going to say and scratched his head discomposedly. "Look, Tina, perhaps I was wrong. Perhaps you and I . . . were never meant to be." He did not seem as overset by the notion as he had sounded a moment before.

Tina sighed and stepped away from him. "No, Christian, I don't think we were."

"Look," he said, in a new, rather abrupt tone, "I never thanked you properly for saving Dickon. Allegra told me—told everyone, for that matter—what you did. I thought then that you had risked your life because of your love for me."

She shook her head. "I did it for the child. As you would have done yourself if you had been there."

"Well, it was a brave thing to do," he said soberly. "You could have been drowned."

"Excuse me," put in a breathless voice. "Am I interrupting?" Lady Millicent Quigley stood poised in the doorway, one small hand pressed to her slight bosom.

"No, of course not," Tina said quickly.

"I wondered whether I might have a word with you, Miss Jardine?" Millie paused uncertainly, her eyes flitting from Tina to Christian. "If it is not too inconvenient?"

Showing rare tact, Christian bowed. "I shall go. Thank you again for rescuing my son, Miss Jardine. Allegra and I are eternally indebted to you."

When he was gone, Millie advanced tentatively into the room. "I hope you will not mind, but there is something I must tell you," she said nervously. "I know we do not know each other very well."

Eying her curiously, Tina suggested they sit down. Lady Millicent moistened her lips, then scurried over to one of the chairs, her fawnlike eyes huge.

"I . . . I hope you will not think me forward," she apologized, twisting her fingers together.

"Indeed not," Tina said reassuringly.

"You see, it's about the sonnet that . . . Lord Laverstoke wrote," she whispered. "I'm quite sure there's been a mistake. I'm certain it was meant for you."

When Tina said nothing, the other girl's voice firmed. "You look amazed, but . . . you cannot seriously believe he wrote it for me!"

"But I do believe it." Yet even as she spoke, Tina's hopes resurged. Could the butler have made *two* mistakes? Was that possible?

Lady Millicent leaned forward, fixing her blue eyes on Tina's face. "Think about it, Miss Jardine. Would he say such things to me? Of course not. Why should he when it is you he loves? I've seen the way he looks at you."

"How does he look at me?" Tina asked, very faintly.

"The same way James looks at me." Lady Millicent caught hold of her arm. "You and I both have blue eyes and dark hair, do we not?"

Tina bit her lip. "But I am hardly a 'dainty enchantress'," she protested. "I'm not dainty at all."

"Perhaps to him you are," Millie said softly. "Take heart, Miss Jardine. I know what it is like to despair. But, please, please, come back to the ball. Come and see what is going to happen next."

Nineteen

"You're the shrewd one in the family. Tell me how the devil we play this one!" It was James's first opportunity since dinner to vent his fury, and the harsh pitch of his voice reflected his inner wrath. "Look at her over there, smirking like she just swallowed a damned canary. Dash it all, we can't let her outjockey us like this!"

Gerard spared Lady Buckden a cool glance, then leaned closer to his brother. "Do you have any suggestions?" he inquired.

"Aye, tell 'em it was meant for Tina! Though God knows it puts Millie in an infamous position," James conceded with a black scowl, "but 'tis better than having her marry you!"

"Very true," Gerard agreed wholeheartedly. "Yet I think we can do better than that." He hesitated, keeping his voice low. "A possible alternative has crossed my mind."

"What?" James's head turned, his eyes hopeful.

Several seconds passed while Gerard chose his words. "Rather than claiming the sonnet was *for* someone else," he said finally, "why not say that it was *by* someone else?"

"Go on."

"Let us suppose that *you* wrote it for Millie, and that Lady Buckden simply . . . mistook the signature."

"No one'll believe that," James objected.

"No?" Gerard raised a quizzical eyebrow. "I think they might. The lady is not well liked."

"And what'll you do when she whips out your sonnet, and waves it aloft for all to see? You signed the bloody thing, didn't you?"

Gerard sighed. "That, unfortunately, is the hitch. That, and the fact that it is writ in my hand."

"So?" James eyed him narrowly. "You're suggesting what?"

Gerard scanned the crowd for Tina and frowned. "If we could lay our hands on the original—"

Catching on, James cocked a brow. "Hmmm, not bad. Not bad at all. Ho, here comes Allegra."

Their sister was all smiles as she wove her way through the throng of people, but the moment she reached them her expression sobered. "What happened?" she said without preamble.

Gerard shrugged. "Bissett claims he delivered our verses to the proper ladies. Therefore, Lady Buckden must have had a hand in it. Somehow she switched them."

"The wicked, designing old hag," said his sister bitterly. "There is no limit to her ambition. You won't let her bully you, will you?"

"No." There was steel in Gerard's tone. "Jay and I have a plan."

"Good," she retorted. "Do you need my help?"

"Actually, I do. I was unable to say very much to Millie since the movements of the dance kept us apart." His mouth curved wryly. "And I don't think my leading her out again will serve our purpose—"

"Damned right," James muttered.

Gerard surveyed his sister, touched by the genuine distress in her eyes. "What I need you to do, Allie, is to relay a message to Millie. Tell her she must give you the valentine, or obtain it from her mother if Lady Buckden still has it. After what I've taught her, Millie's well equipped to handle the assignment. Then you must bring it to me."

Allegra nodded curtly. "What do you mean to do?"

"Give Lady Buckden a serving of her own tonic," he said grimly. Once more, he scanned the crowd, and was finally rewarded with a glimpse of Tina. His expression altered as, in the next instant, the musicians struck up a waltz.

Lord be praised, here was his golden chance.

When Tina reentered the ballroom, her emotions were in a chaotic state. She supposed that what Millie suggested was possible—that there *had* been a mix-up of valentines. But having already been hurt very badly once in her life, she was afraid to believe it. Even if it were true, she argued, Lady Buckden's cunning stratagems might well achieve her purpose. Her heart shuddered at the possibility.

Pausing at the edge of the room, she searched the faces for Libby, thinking to find comfort in the elderly lady's presence. But as she glanced around, her gaze caught with Lord Flaundon's, who had apparently opted to sit out this particular set. Immediately, he rose to his feet.

A few seconds later, he stood before her and bowed. "May I have the pleasure of this dance?" he said suavely. "Such a lovely lady ought not to be without a partner."

Grateful to have something to distract her from her worries, Tina curtsied and accepted.

Too late, she spied Gerard.

He was weaving his way through the dancers, his eyes linked to her face, and he stopped dead at precisely the moment she laid her hand on Lord Flaundon's arm. And for the first time that evening the careful mask lifted, exposing the emotion beneath.

Why, he looks almost crushed! she thought in amazement.

As Lord Flaundon swept her away, Tina's chest filled with a great exultation. Without doubt, Gerard had intended to ask her to waltz. Could that possibly mean—? Dare she hope? Could Millie have been right?

During the course of the dance, she caught sight of him once or twice, but strangely, by the end of the set, he had completely disappeared. And as far as she could tell, so had James and Allegra. Christian, she noticed, was surrounded by a flock of ladies, but wore an air of abstraction and kept glancing toward the door.

Knowing it was her duty, Tina searched the room for Felicity, and found her flirting determinedly with Mr. Chetwoode. It was really too bad about Eugene, she thought with a sigh. He was usually such a mannerly young man. However, men were unpredictable creatures. One never knew what to expect from them.

"Do you have it?" Gerard asked.

"Of course." Allegra withdrew the wadded valentine from the bodice of her ball gown and held it out. "You were right about Millie. I don't know what she said to Dear Mama, but whatever it was it did the trick." She turned to James, who was sitting at Gerard's desk. "She's no mouse anymore," she added dryly. "You may be sorry, brother dear."

James smiled and picked up a quill. "Oh, I don't think so. Here, give it to me."

"Copy it carefully." Gerard sat down, tapping his fingers while James wrote. If only he'd reached Tina before Flaundon had, he thought in annoyance. Curse it, why did everything have to be so bloody difficult?

"There," pronounced James at the end of it. He signed his name with a flourish and returned the quill to the standish. "I don't know how the devil you thought of this thing," he said admiringly. "I couldn't write something like this if I lived to be a hundred."

"Don't tell anyone that," Gerard advised. "At least for tonight, you're the budding poet in the family."

James grinned and sanded the ink. "Aye, I'll remember." When the ink was dry, he passed it to Allegra, who folded it tightly and tucked it back inside her dress.

Standing up, Gerard retrieved the original and slipped it into his pocket. "Back to the battlefield," he said ironically.

"Oh, heavens, I almost forgot," Allegra said suddenly. "Millie said to tell you she had a plan of her own."

Gerard stiffened. "What kind of a plan?"

"She didn't say. She only said that she had taken certain steps and you were not to worry."

"Find out what," he instructed, "and let me know."

"I'll do what I can," his sister promised.

When Allegra returned to the ballroom, however, she was at once waylaid by her husband. "Where have you been?" Christian demanded in a proprietorial tone.

"With my brother in the library," she said coldly. "Why does it matter?"

His fingers closed on her arm. "It matters because,"—he paused for an instant—"because I thought you were with someone else, Allie, my love. And I found I did not care for the idea."

She held herself rigidly, not daring to hope. "Jealous?" she taunted.

"Yes, very." His honest answer surprised her—floored her, in fact. Before she could recover, he bent close to her ear. "Dance with me, Allie," he urged. "You never do anymore."

"You never ask anymore," she said breathlessly.

He raised her hand, brushing her fingers with his lips. "I'm asking now. Please, Allie," he said humbly. "I need you."

Allegra swallowed hard. "Do you, Christian? I've never thought so."

He amazed her even more by flushing. "I've always needed you," he confessed. "But until tonight I didn't know—" He shook his head, looking down at her with the oddest expression. "Damn it, I've been such an ass."

This inelegant statement, however true, had a curious effect upon Allegra's pulse rate. For the first time in years her husband was showing interest in her, and she could not afford to neglect this chance. She forgot Millie. Old dreams flooded her heart—dreams for her marriage, for the future, for Dickon, and for the tiny new seed of humanity growing in her womb.

And as the musicians struck up a waltz, Allegra looked up into her husband's eyes and saw reflected in them her own fears, her own insecurities. Was it possible their marriage was not lost? Placing her hand on his broad shoulder, she determined to find out.

Tina was hesitant to accept Lord Flaundon's second invitation to dance. Not only was it indiscreet, but it was the supper dance, which meant that she would be obliged to sup with him afterward, possibly *à deux*, which she did not at all relish. Hoping for rescue, she cast her eyes around the vicinity, but this time, of course, Gerard was nowhere in sight.

Concealing her disappointment, Tina accepted his proffered arm. "You honor me," she said politely.

"On the contrary, the honor is mine." His eyes shifted suddenly. "Or perhaps it isn't," he added pensively. "Pardon, my dear, but England's Valentine looks as though he would take exception to our plans."

Heart leaping, Tina spun around in time to witness Gerard's bow. "My apologies, Flaundon," he said briskly, "but Miss Jardine promised me the supper dance."

Lord Flaundon leveled his quizzing glass rather mockingly at Tina. "Is this true?" he drawled. "My dear lady, you made no mention of this to me."

"No doubt she forgot," inserted Gerard before she could speak. "She has a tendency to do that, poor girl."

Subjected to the stares of both men, Tina gave them each a dagger-look. "Neither one of you is behaving like a gentleman," she admonished. "I find you both extremely ungallant. And it is too late for me to dance with either of you. The sets are already formed."

"What a shame," stated Gerard.

"Indeed," murmured Lord Flaundon.

The two men looked at each other.

Gerard smiled pleasantly. "Flaundon," he said, "there are at least half a dozen ladies without the benefit of a partner. I'm sure any one of them would be delighted to keep you company."

Flaundon's eyes gleamed. "Wallflowers, Laverstoke." Then he smiled wryly, and added, "But better a wallflower than your fist in my face."

He bowed and sauntered off, leaving Tina to say with severity, "That was not very well done of you, you know."

"No? I thought it was exceedingly well done of me." He took her by the arm, steering her along the room's perimeter toward an empty alcove. "We'll sit out this set, shall we? Would you care for some refreshment?"

"No," she began, gathering her wits, "but you know very well that—"

"Good. Then we'll talk," he said easily.

"—you are being—"

"Are you enjoying the ball?" he inquired.

"—overbearing and high-handed—"

"You look ravishing this evening. Did I mention it?"

"I . . . don't believe so," she admitted, thrown out of stride.

"Then it's high time I did. Red suits you," he added with an appreciative glint. "Come, sit down."

"I am not at all certain I wish to sit," she said, stubbornly digging in her heels.

"Then tell me what it is you wish to do," he replied, "and I shall endeavor to oblige."

Unfortunately, the answer to that was far too complicated to embark upon, so she said, rather childishly, "Well, we may as well sit since we are already here."

He smiled. "Sensible girl. There, isn't that better? Now then, there are some things we need to discuss. It's been an extremely trying week for both of us, I think."

"Er, yes," she agreed, willing to give him that one.

"But, in my view, a necessary one."

Tina stared at her hands. "Necessary? I don't see why."

He leaned closer, just a little, just enough to make the breath catch in her throat. "I know you blame me for your broken betrothal," he said gravely, "yet it has been my hope that you might come to forgive me. I also hoped this week might help you to . . . lay your ghost to rest. Do you think it has?"

Flustered, Tina plucked at her skirt. "I . . . I don't know why you should wish to know."

"Don't you?" he prodded. "After yesterday, I would think my reason should be obvious."

She went crimson. "Oh," she whispered, her voice suffocated. Rich strains of music floated around them, but she scarcely noticed. "You cannot think . . . indeed I scarcely knew . . . and I never, ever thought . . ." Her voice faded to miserable silence.

His eyes searched her face. "It was not my intention to embarrass you," he said gently. "What happened was my fault and mine alone. I acted the cad, and you were merely"—now his voice was almost a caress—"the most bonny temptress this side of heaven. But you could scarcely be blamed for that, could you?"

Thunderstruck, Tina stared at him, but before she could even begin to think of a reply, a high shriek pierced the air.

The musicians ground to an uncertain halt.

The dancers stilled.

Everyone was staring at Felicity, who had stopped dead in the middle of the floor, her hands pressed to her cheeks.

Gerard started to his feet. "What the devil is she doing?" he muttered. "Is she ill?"

Tina followed the direction of Felicity's gaze. "No," she said resignedly. "She's not ill."

Felicity's second utterance resolved itself into a single, choked word. *"Eugene!"* Then, unconscious of her surroundings, she rushed forward and threw herself into the arms of a stolid young man with silver locks.

Tina sighed. Felicity's Eugene had arrived.

"I hope you will forgive the intrusion," Eugene St. Hillary explained to Gerard after the commotion had died down. "I did receive an invitation, but due to various factors too complicated to expound upon, I did not actually read it until this morning. Knowing that Miss Winton was here"—he shot Felicity an apologetic look—"I instantly procured a seat on the Mail and—"

"For pity's sake, Eugene," cut in Felicity with impatience, "his lordship does not wish to hear all that! Do forgive him, Cousin Laverstoke. Eugene becomes shockingly prosy when he is tired."

Eugene gave her a pained look. "It is my opinion that his lordship deserves the courtesy of an explanation—"

"No, I don't," Gerard said quickly. "Look here, St. Hillary, why don't you take Miss Winton into supper? I'm sure you must be sharp-set after all your travels—"

"And I'm starving!" Felicity declared.

Eugene favored Gerard with a deferential bow. "You have my eternal gratitude, my lord. Come along, Felicity. I'm sure I don't need to tell you what a spectacle you made . . ." The lecture faded as the two young people drifted off.

Shaking his head, Gerard spun around to look for Tina. Where the devil had she gone *now?* The ballroom was only half full, since most of the guests had proceeded to the adjacent rooms where a cold collation was being served by his army of domestics. Ah, there she was, talking to Miss Steeple. He watched her for a moment, watched her gestures, the tilt of her chin, the graceful way she held her head. Perhaps she was confiding all her secrets. He felt unaccountably piqued by the notion, though he'd overheard enough conversations to know that females told each other things they never told a man. Yet he wanted to be the recipient of those confidences. He wanted to know what lay within her heart.

When he reached them it was even worse than he feared; Tina looked up at him and said, "My lord, will you mind very much if Libby joins us for supper?"

Gerard groaned inwardly. He had planned to use this time to explain about the sonnet, to declare his love, and broach the delicate subject of marriage. Perhaps something of his frustration showed in his face, for Miss Steeple sent him a sympathetic look and said, "My dear Valentina, there truly is no need for that. I shall do very well on my own—"

"Nonsense, Libby. Lord Laverstoke will be delighted, won't you, my lord?"

His irritation melted under those pleading blue eyes. Reminding himself that he was enormously in debt to Miss Steeple for bringing Tina into his life, he favored the elderly lady with a deep bow. "I would be honored if you would join us," he told her firmly. "We would not think of leaving you on your own."

Libby rose and patted his arm in a motherly fashion. "You're a good boy," she stated. "You'll do nicely."

As soon as supper was over, Gerard escorted both ladies back to the ballroom, where the musicians were preparing to recommence.

"I trust you will excuse us," he told Miss Steeple. "Tina has promised me the next dance."

"I did not," Tina objected, to his intense exasperation.

For an instant he entertained notions of shaking her until her teeth rattled, but Libby came to his rescue.

"Oh, but you did, Valentina. You'll have to forgive her, my lord," Libby said indulgently. "The poor child has the most shocking memory. Go quickly now," she urged, before Tina could protest. "Lady Buckden is coming."

Gerard needed no second warning. "What an excellent woman," he murmured, propelling Tina toward the rear of the ballroom as fast as he could. "Good, an empty couch. My luck holds." However, when he tried to steer her toward it, Tina stopped dead.

"You told me," she said mulishly, "that we were going to dance."

Gerard gazed down at her in sudden doubt. Was she truly reluctant to let him speak? Was he simply the greatest dullard alive? Did she still fancy herself in love with Rewe?

Then, slowly, those pink lips curved, and it dawned on him that she was teasing.

"Well, you did claim you had invited me to dance," she said demurely. "So I thought . . . the least you could do is . . . to do it." The invitation in her eyes sent masculine hunger jolting through his entire system.

"Oh, I'll do it," he said softly. "That and more, my little valentine. That and more."

The promise in his voice did queer things to Tina's breathing, and for a moment she regretted the postponement of their talk. But all night she had longed to dance with him, and she had the advantage of knowing that the next dance was a waltz. Her confidence must be rising to a risky level, for she found herself preparing to flirt with him. Was it the wine, or was it the seductive resonance of his voice that made her feel so giddy?

"Oh, so it's to be a waltz," he said a moment later. His soft chuckle sent delicious shivers down her spine. "And you knew it."

She peeped up at him. "How could I, my lord?"

"Oh, so we're back to 'my lord' again," he said lazily. "Is that to atone for calling me 'England's Valentine'?"

Her cheeks stained pink. "You knew!"

"Of course I knew," he said in amusement. "You wore such an innocent look. Come, the music's starting."

And then they were waltzing, and it was every bit as magical as she'd anticipated. At first they simply gazed at each other, then Gerard cleared this throat. "Tina, there's something I've been wanting to say. As I said before, it's been a trying week—"

This time the shriek was not loud, but it carried far enough to wreak instant havoc.

The musicians hesitated.

The dancers spun to a halt.

Everyone goggled at Lady Buckden, who had stopped dead in the middle of the dance floor, her hands pressed to her cheeks.

Gerard twisted around. "This is getting to be absurd," he

muttered. Then his entire stance stiffened, poised to alertness. Tina heard him curse, very softly, under his breath.

Across the room, a tall, dour-faced man stood leaning against the wall just inside the doorway, a silver-headed cane in each hand. Tina had never seen him before, but it was clearly his presence that had made Lady Buckden cry out.

Ignoring the speculative eyes, Gerard drew her along with him as they crossed to the newcomer's side. "Good evening, sir. We're honored you could join us. I'm afraid we did not expect you—"

"I'll wager you did not," the gentleman barked out. His cold blue eyes flicked over Tina. "I won't waste time with pleasantries, Laverstoke. I did not drag my body all the way over here for such frippery nonsense. I want a word with you about my daughter. She and my wife are at odds about your intentions."

"Perhaps we should conduct this conversation in private." Tina's heart sank at the strain and constraint in Gerard's voice.

Lord Buckden's hawklike visage was grim. "In private," he conceded with thin-lipped arrogance. "But with my wife and daughter, if you please. One way or another, we are going to settle this business. I've had my fill of it. Before I leave, I'm going to make damned sure Millicent is betrothed."

It took Tina less than a minute to reach her room. Blinded by tears, she slammed the door, turned, and nearly tripped over Gretchen, who made an indignant yip. Tina sank to her knees, huge sobs rasping from her throat.

"I can't bear it, Gretchen," she whispered, wrapping her arms around the dog's neck. "Lord Buckden is even more heartless than Lady Buckden. Millie will never stand up to them." A shudder ran through her entire frame. "We don't stand a chance. None of us, not Millie, not James, not Gerard. Not me. And I think"—her voice quivered and broke—"this time my heart is truly going to break."

A minute later the knock came, as she had known it would. "Valentina?" uttered Libby through the door.

Tina could not move. She tried to discipline her voice, make it controlled and calm, but it came out choked and thin. "I'm all right, Libby. I . . . can't talk to you now."

"Are you sure, dear? I'm worried about you."

"I'm simply tired, Libby. Please, I . . . I need to be alone." *Alone.* Her throat clogged with misery.

She heard Libby sigh. "Very well, dear. I understand." Libby's footsteps faded away.

And then there was nothing but silence.

After a little while, Tina wiped her tears and lifted her head and sighed. "Come on, Gretchen," she said, poking the dog. "Sit up. Yes, get up. We're leaving, girl. We're going out."

Twenty

They assembled in the library. While Lord Buckden eased himself into a chair, Gerard noted the deep lines his infirmity had etched into his face. His own father, he recalled, had witnessed the reckless soar over the fence that had proven the earl's undoing. Very likely the man was in pain a great deal of the time, which would go a long way toward explaining his choleric temperament.

"Now then," snapped Lord Buckden, plunking down his canes, "I'll hear the tale from you first, Laverstoke."

"Would you care for some sherry, sir? The night is cold and you've—"

"Curse it, do you think me some doddering mollycoddle?" For a moment Lord Buckden looked absolutely furious, but Gerard's steadfast gaze appeared to appease him. "I'll take French brandy, if you have any that's decent," he said shortly.

As Gerard poured the drink, he glanced over at Millie. She sat, white-faced, next to her mother on the couch, her hands folded docilely in her lap. He wondered if she'd remember anything he'd taught her. She looked frightened to death.

Bracing himself for the confrontation, he handed the glass to Lord Buckden. "Now then, sir, exactly what is it you wish to know?"

Lord Buckden tossed off the brandy, then stabbed the air with his finger. "I want to know what's been happening," he roared. "My wife informs me that Millicent is all but betrothed to you, yet tonight—while I'm eating my dinner, if

305

you please!—this vaporish letter from Millicent arrives. Fiend seize it, she's begging me to save her from this marriage and I want to know why!" He glared at Gerard. "Have you compromised my daughter, Laverstoke?"

"Not to my knowledge," Gerard answered coolly. "Did someone suggest I had?"

"Don't try to fob me off with any of your ploys, boy. You might be able to cozen those fools in Vienna, but you'll pay me the courtesy of plain speech."

"I have no intention of cozening you. I doubt I could do so if I wished."

"He wrote her a love sonnet," whimpered Lady Buckden. " 'Twas as good as a declaration."

"He didn't!" Millie gulped, clearly shocked by her own daring. "I'm sorry, Mama, but he didn't."

Lord Buckden's freezing stare shifted from Millie to Gerard. "Well, Laverstoke?" he said. "Are you in love with my daughter?"

"No, sir, I am not," Gerard replied. "I am fond of Lady Millicent, but I am not as fond as that."

"Ha!" Lord Buckden rounded on his wife. "Well, Eleonora? What have you to say to that?"

Lady Buckden's bosom swelled. "But the sonnet!" she insisted. "Millicent, you have it. Show it to your father."

Lady Millie obeyed.

Lord Buckden unfolded the heavily creased sheet of paper, then glanced up sharply. "Eleonora, what is the meaning of this? Can you not read, woman? This is signed 'James.' "

"What?" Lady Buckden started to her feet. "Let me see that!" Rushing forward, she snatched it from his hand. Then she looked at Gerard, angry color staining her cheeks. "This is not the one! Someone is playing tricks!"

"Enough!" bellowed Lord Buckden. "Sit down, Eleonora, and hold your tongue. I think you've leveled enough accusations for one evening. I want to hear Millicent's side of the story. Millicent, what is James Marchant to you?"

Millie darted an apologetic glance at her mother. "James is very dear to me, Papa," she said with only the slightest tremble. "He loves me and . . . and wishes to marry me. And I wish to marry him."

"Millicent!" It was an anguished cry.

Millie laid a comforting hand on her mother's arm. "Mama, I know you love me and care for my happiness," she said softly. "I appreciate that, Mama, truly I do. And do not think I have not considered your advice. I *have* considered it, very carefully and often."

"And what advice is that?" said Buckden sardonically.

"Mama only wants what is best for me," Millie explained to them all. "She wants me to marry well so I shall be provided for all my life."

"Hrumph!" snorted her father. "You're heiress enough to marry a pauper if I will it. Tell the truth, girl."

Millie looked tearfully at her mother. "Mama wants me to have a position of respect in society. She wants that because she loves me so much."

Without warning, Lady Buckden burst into tears. "I want her to have what I never had," she sobbed. "Respect! Respect for her birth and her position in society. I want her to be admired. I want her to have the grand London wedding that I never had. You and I eloped, Buckden! And I have never ceased to regret it."

The earl compressed his lips. "It appears," he said dryly, "that my wife has been trying to force your hand, Laverstoke. Pray accept my apologies. Is your brother in the house? I've not seen him in years. Heard he was wounded fighting old Boney."

"Yes. He took a ball in the hip." Gerard rang for a servant. "Inform my brother that he is needed in the library," he told the menial who appeared.

When James entered the library, his face was set with determination. "Lord Buckden," he said, limping forward to shake the earl's hand. "It is good to see you, sir."

Lord Buckden surveyed him approvingly. "I understand you often call at our house, Marchant. I apologize that I've never left my room to see for myself how matters stood. Millicent tells me you want her."

The earl's straightforward wording caused his daughter to squirm with embarrassment, but James only smiled. "Yes, sir, I want her very much. I love her. Will you give me permission to pay my addresses?"

"Aye, you can have her with my blessing. Your leg pain you much?"

"Some," James admitted. "Depends on the weather and how much I use it." Nevertheless he stood proudly, his posture erect.

Reaching for his canes, Lord Buckden struggled to his feet. "Well, you're better off than I am, so remember it and count your blessings. I'm going home. Eleonora, I want you to come with me."

Lady Buckden moped her eyes. "But I cannot leave Millicent," she protested.

Gerard stepped forward. "Sir, I can offer you a room for tonight, if you like. "Wouldn't that be more convenient for you?"

Lord Buckden grunted. "Aye, I suppose so. Very well then. I'll retire now, and leave these young people alone." He angled a meaningful look at his wife. "Come along, Eleonora."

"Papa?"

"Aye, what is it now?" Lord Buckden surveyed his daughter with resignation.

"May we"—she blushed—"I mean James and I . . . if we decide . . . I mean right now everyone thinks . . . that Lord Laverstoke and I . . . what I mean to say is that . . . that we have put him in the most awkward position!" she finished in a rush.

Her father sighed. "Go ahead, make the announcement if you like. I'm going to bed."

Millie and James exchanged delighted looks.

"What better time to announce our betrothal," James asked quietly, "than at a Valentine's Day ball?"

When indeed? thought Gerard, glancing at the ormolu clock upon the mantelshelf. It was nearly midnight. If he was going to settle things with Valentina, he'd better hurry.

Unconscious of the cold, Tina picked her way through the dark, secure in the knowledge that Gretchen would take her around any large obstacles in their path. Her original intention had been merely to walk until she was calm, but her shaggy companion had ideas of her own. The dog was taking her back to the Dower House, an objective which Tina was content to endorse. Perhaps there, away from Laverstoke Park, she could find some measure of peace.

For the first time in days it was snowing — lazily, as though winter still had all the time in the world to make its mark. As they walked, large, indolent flakes brushed Tina's face and flirted with her lashes and hair. There was no wind at all. It was silent and beautiful and cold and lonely. Achingly lonely.

Somehow she would cope. If Gerard and Millie were to be wed she would deal with it. But not today, not now, not on her birthday.

Not on Valentine's Day.

On Valentine's Day she would not think about the vast, empty vista of her life ahead. She would shut off all thought — all memory of yesterday, all dreams of tomorrow. She would block it all out — every feeling, every emotion. For the rest of this night she intended to be a stronghold, fortified and shielded and armed to the teeth.

Tilting her head, she gazed up and felt the wet tickle of snow on her cheek. Tonight there were no stars to wish upon, no dreams to dream — nothing. There was only snow and pressing blackness, and the tenuous comfort of the animal who trotted beside her. Fortunately, all self-respecting hares had retired for the night; Gretchen was truly her protector.

Not that she needed one. If she had to, she could find her own bloody way through the dark. She could do anything she had to do. She was self-sufficient, capable, and totally in control. She knew precisely where she was and how far she had yet to go and —

Confound it!

Whatever she tripped over was firmer than her resolution not to cry. For a few seconds, hot tears coursed down her cheeks, but she swiped at them angrily and returned to her feet. "Come on, Gretchen. You're supposed to take me around the rocks."

As they started forward, Tina was conscious of pain where her knees had made contact. She had probably just ruined Allegra's ball gown, she thought glumly. She had taken the time to remove the necklace and pull on boots—why hadn't she changed her clothes as well? Trust her to foul even this up. Now her knees were scraped, and she would have to replace the dress, which cost a great deal more than she could afford.

At that instant, the Dower House loomed up before them, huddled small and ominously dark against the black. "Come on," she repeated, more to herself than the dog.

She had to knock for nearly a minute before a servant appeared. "Let me in," she commanded. "It is I, Miss Jardine."

Candle held high, Miss Steeple's housekeeper peered out at Tina. "What's the matter, miss? Has something happened? Is Miss Steeple ill?"

"No, Mrs. Mullins, nothing is wrong. I simply want to come in and . . . reclaim my old room for tonight. I've brought Gretchen along for company."

Her expression grudging, Mrs. Mullins widened the door. "That beast is going to get the floor dirty," she complained.

Tina clung to her last shred of patience. "If you'll procure a rag, Mrs. Mullins," she said evenly, "I will wipe Gretchen's paws."

"Oh, very well." Grumbling under her breath, Mrs. Mullins stalked off, only to return a moment later with her husband. To Tina's relief, Mullins performed the task of cleaning Gretchen, then stumped upstairs to light the fire in her bedchamber.

Twenty minutes later, Tina sat near the hearth, watching the flames, drinking in the warmth. Nearby, Gretchen lay sprawled, the picture of canine contentment.

At least one of them was happy, she reflected.

She sighed. Until this moment, she had not realized just how tired she was, how emotionally and physically drained.

For a moment she found herself wishing she had some of Gerard's brandy to drink — perhaps it would have made her feel drowsy. Instead she felt as though she would never sleep again.

Gerard. Emotion rocked through her at the thought of him. What was he doing at this instant? Was he announcing his betrothal to Millie?

Tina's eyes were closed, but even so she could see him, every inch of him — his face and smile, his beautiful hands, his lean, graceful, athletic frame. She felt an instant's yearning for her sketchbook, but what need was there to draw him when his essence was permanently impinged in her mind?

She supposed the memory of him would fade in time, but right now it was hard to believe. How clearly she could remember his lips, those lips that had only to come near for her to melt like a snowflake in the sun. As for the feel of him . . . ah, the feel of him — *that* was something she would never forget, not if she lived to be a hundred.

For the second time that night, tears stung at Tina's eyelids, but as she dashed them away, something caught her attention. She froze, listening.

How curious. It sounded as though someone was walking around downstairs again, though Mullins and his wife had expressed their intention to return to bed. There, what was that? It sounded like a door being opened. And voices. Surely those were voices?

Tina's heart quickened as light footsteps ascended the same creaking set of stairs she had recently climbed. Suddenly, her entire body was trembling. No, no, it could not be him. It had to be someone else, but who? Who else would come?

Who else was there?

Her heart hammering, Tina sat paralyzed with hope and dread. At the top of the staircase the footsteps paused, then continued along, slowly, until they reached her door.

Gretchen's head came up.

"Who is it?" Tina whispered without moving.

There was no answer. There was only an odd, soft sound,

like the rustle of paper on wood. Half mesmerized, she lowered her gaze to the base of the door, staring at the dog-eared sheet of pink-tinted paper lying where a moment before there had been nothing. As if in a dream, she rose and moved toward it, her hand shaking as she bent to pick it up.

Shall I compare thee to a summer's day?

She read the sonnet through a veil of tears, her throat working as she struggled to contain her emotion. Each word, each phrase was unbearably precious, but with the last, sweet line, an agonized sob escaped her lips.

The door flew violently open. "Tina!" Before she could blink, Gerard's arms were enfolding her, crushing her in an embrace so splendid it brought a fresh wave of tears. Over and over against her hair, he murmured her name like a litany until, eventually, his tone changed, became something between a growl and an urgent plea for understanding. "My love, why are you crying? Why did you run away? What did I do?"

"I . . . I don't know . . . I've never been so . . ." As her tongue tied into knots, Tina sensed his confusion. "I mean I don't know why I'm . . . c-crying." She clutched the sonnet to her heart and gave him a watery smile. "I think because it's so b-beautiful. You must have worked so hard on it."

His flickering smile did not banish the tense look around his mouth. "I wrote it for *you,*" he insisted, as though she still doubted.

"I know." Suddenly shy, she burrowed her face in his cravat. "Millie said you had, but I . . . I wasn't quite sure."

His arms shifted and tightened, pressing the whole of her against his hard length. "I love you." He spoke the words into her hair with repressed ferocity. "I don't know whether you'll ever be able to return my love, but I'm willing to accept that. No, don't say anything. I want to tell you something. You blame me for your broken betrothal, but you don't know all the facts."

"Oh, but—"

"Be quiet"—he gave her a small shake—"and let me speak. Allegra met your Christian at a house party in Oxfordshire.

She and my mother went; I was still in London, finishing some work for Castlereagh. It was just before Christmastide. My sister was young — barely eighteen — and vastly impressionable." His voice was taut. "My mother's health was indifferent, and though she tried, she really wasn't much of a chaperon. So the long and short of it is that my sister was the prettiest, most susceptible female present. Rewe flirted with her and she gratified him by flirting back. Eventually they arranged a tryst, at night after everyone was abed." He heaved a harsh sigh. "My sister claims she never meant to let it go beyond a few kisses. But Rewe had other ideas. He convinced her to . . . let him have his way with her."

Tina said nothing. She could imagine it only too well.

"A month later she told me she was to bear a child. I was furious; she was hysterical. She begged me to help her. She said she was willing to marry him if I could arrange it." He looked down at her with a mingling of apology and dissatisfaction. "So I did. First, of course, I investigated him enough to assure myself that his title and fortune were genuine. I learned he was unwed, but that he had a girl in Kent, a neighbor to whom he was unofficially betrothed. If I ever heard the name I don't remember." His voice grew adamant and tense. "But even if I had, I could not have let it weigh with me when my sister's reputation was at stake."

"I understand," she said softly.

"*Do* you?" Hope flared in his eyes. "I know you think I ruined your life, but—"

"Not anymore," she cut in, her voice filled with tenderness. "I think you saved it."

His expression changed. "Thank God," he said in relief. He drew her close and squeezed her once more. "You don't love him anymore."

"I don't think I ever did. I idolized him, which is not the same thing." Her eyes clouded. "You know those myths where one of the Gods looks down and chooses a mortal woman as his mate? Well, it was like that for me. I convinced myself that it was love I felt, when in truth it was nothing more than being . . . flattered and honored by a man who

. . . who really didn't care for me at all."

He seemed to understand how difficult it was for her to say those words. "Come on," he said, lifting his cheek from her hair. "Let's sit down. It's late and you're tired."

She smiled. "So are you."

"Yes, I am. I've just trekked across a lot of cold ground to find you, my girl"—with a steady pull, he drew her back to her chair—"which leads me back to my other question." He settled her down, then stood over her, fists on his hips. "Why did you run away?"

She peeped up at him in embarrassment. "I thought you were going to marry Millie," she confessed.

"And why the devil would you think that?"

She moistened her lips, misliking the ominous tone of his voice. "Well, what else was I to think? There was her father, looking as though he would run you through if you did not, and everyone thought you'd written the sonnet for her, and"—she looked down at her hands—"and I didn't dare hope you'd hold out against all that . . . only for me."

"*Only* for you? Good God, Tina, I—" He broke off, swearing softly. Then he was down on his knees at her feet. "It's nearly midnight, and I made a vow to myself that I would do this on Valentine's Day." He took her by the wrists, forcing her to look at him. "My precious girl, will you do me the very great honor of becoming my wife?"

She regarded him solemnly. "Are you asking because you think you compromised me?"

"I'm asking you because I'm devilish sure I can't live without you!" he exploded. "Though I did compromise you, there's no gainsaying it. And I'll be most happy to do it again if it'll get me what I want!"

His answer pleased her tremendously. "Oh," she said on a fluttery sigh, "that won't be necessary. I'll marry you."

"When?" he demanded. He retained his hold on her wrists, pulling her toward him so that she must, out of pure necessity, entwine her arms round his neck.

"Whenever you wish," she said promptly.

"Tomorrow?"

"If you like." Her eyes slid shut, her heart doing a crazy little spin as his lips brushed hers.

"It ought to have been today," he mused. "A Valentine for Laverstoke. It would have been appropriate. Perhaps we should wait until next year. Next Valentine's Day."

Her eyes flew open. "Are you serious?"

She could not quite decide if he was teasing. "It would be suitable," he pointed out. "We could puff it off in all the papers. You'd have time to buy your bride-clothes and have a Season. We'd have ample opportunity to plan a nice, long wedding trip to somewhere you'd like. Perhaps Vienna."

"Do you *want* to wait a year?"

His eyes gleamed. "No," he murmured, his eyes sliding down to the very low bodice of her ball gown. "I don't want to wait at all."

Slowly, very slowly, his head lowered until his lips pressed against the sensitive flesh of her bosom. It was only a light kiss, like the touch of a feather, but it made it hard to think or even breathe.

"Let's . . . not . . . wait that long," she mumbled. "It seems silly to me."

"Very silly," he agreed, a whispery kiss later. "We'll wait a month."

"A month?" His lips were distracting her, roving the swell of her breast just above the lace-edged bodice. "It seems a bit . . . long."

"A week?" His tongue dipped into the shadowy cleft between her breasts.

"Are . . . are you seducing me?" she managed.

"Not in front of witnesses." He glanced down at Gretchen, who yawned and stared back. "I'm just flirting a little." His mouth dropped below the neckline to tease her through the thin layer of silk. "I like to flirt."

"Oh," she gasped, clutching him tight, "is that what you call this?"

His golden head lifted, and he grinned. "Yes. Much as I'd enjoy it, I'm not going to make love to you until we're married. We'll do this properly if it kills me. Which it very well may," he added with a ragged sigh. Then he made a horrible grimace. "Speaking of pain, I think my knees have just passed beyond the point of numbness." He sat down with a groan, stretching first one long leg and then the other out before the fire.

Concealing her flash of disappointment, Tina looked down at her hands. "I suppose you think . . . my behavior has been rather . . . wanton where you are concerned."

"Wanton?" His left eyebrow shot up.

"Well," she temporized, "fast. I mean, you keep kissing me, and I haven't objected or . . . or swooned or screamed or . . . anything."

He looked at her incredulously. "You can't honestly think I'd want you to scream when I kissed you?"

"Well, I—"

"Swooning, now. That might not be so bad, as long as you swooned into my arms. Then, out of the purest chivalric necessity, I'd be obliged to carry you to the nearest bed—"

"Gerard!"

"As for objecting, I fear you did do that, my heart, but always after the fact. I admit that encouraged me. That sketch you made also encouraged me."

She blushed. "You saw it?"

"I saw it," he stated. "And I liked it. When we are married, you can fill whole walls with drawings of us and our progeny. Speaking of which, I expect you to provide me with a great many pledges of your affection. I mean to harness all those wanton instincts and put them to good use."

Secretly delighted, Tina felt her blush deepen. "And James?" she asked. "Will he be able to wed Millie?"

"Yes, thank God, her father gave his permission. They'll announce it at the ball, and that will stifle the gossip about—" His head came up suddenly. "Egad, I've got to get you back there. If anyone notices our absence, your reputation will be in tatters." Without further ado, he stood up and reached for her hand.

"Oh, but Gerard," she protested, as he hauled her up, "I cannot. Look at this dress. I fell in the dark, and there's marks on it—"

"Better a stained dress than a stained reputation. We'll sneak in through a side door. You'll go to your room and put your dancing shoes back on, and I'll send Miss Steeple up to you. We'll handle it discreetly. One way or another, we'll keep this from—"

"Gerard," she interrupted.

"What is it?" There was a glint in his eye.

She tilted her chin to look up at him. "Kiss me again."

"Why?" The glint grew brighter.

She moved a few inches closer. "Because I love you. And because that's the only way you're going to get me to go back there tonight."

"Well," he murmured, "if that's the only way."

This time the kiss was long and lingering and thorough, and lasted far longer than either of them expected.

"Any more of that," Gerard promised, when it was over, "and I *will* call you a little wanton."

"Happy Valentine's day," she said demurely.

With great reverence, he lifted her hand to his lips. "Happy Birthday," he replied. "My own sweet Valentine."

Author's Note

Although Valentine's Day did not reach its peak in popularity until the Victorian Era, it was around long before that. According to *The Customs and Ceremonies of Britain* published by Thames and Hudson Ltd., London, the holiday's origins are both obscure and ancient. It apparently has no connection with anyone called St. Valentine, but instead may have arisen from a medieval legend involving birds choosing a certain day each spring to mate.

In earlier times it was the custom to present one's valentine with a gift, however by the mid-18th century it became the practice to write love messages instead — ideally poetic compositions. Eventually these were replaced with commercially printed Valentine's Day cards, which, by the way, came along much earlier than Christmas cards.

Another source, *A Persian at the Court of King George, 1809-1810,* states that February 14 is "the day which the English call Valentine's Day: it is the custom on this day for lovers to send letters and love-poems to their sweethearts, but they do not sign their names. Elegant dandies also send each other caricature drawings as jokes."

I love hearing from readers and encourage you to write to me c/o Zebra Books, 475 Park Avenue South, New York, NY 10016. SASE appreciated.

DISCOVER THE MAGIC OF REGENCY ROMANCES

ROMANTIC MASQUERADE (3221, $3.95)
by Lois Stewart

Sabrina Latimer had come to London incognito on a fortune hunt. Disguised as a Hungarian countess, the young widow had to secure the ten thousand pounds her brother needed to pay a gambling debt. His debtor was the notorious ladies' man, Lord Jareth Tremayne. Her scheme would work if she did not fall prey to the charms of the devilish aristocrat. For Jareth was an expert at gambling and always played to win everything—and *everyone*—he could.

RETURN TO CHEYNE SPA (3247, $2.95)
by Daisy Vivian

Very poor but ever-virtuous Elinor Hardy had to become a dealer in a London gambling house to be able to pay her rent. Her future looked dismal until Lady Augusta invited her to be her guest at the exclusive resort, Cheyne Spa. The one condition: Elinor must woo the unsuitable rogue who was in pursuit of the Duchess's pampered niece.

The unsuitable young man was enraptured with Elinor, but *she* had been struck by the devilishly handsome Tyger Dobyn. Elinor knew that Tyger was hardly the respectable, marrying kind, but unfortunately her heart did not agree!

A CRUEL DECEPTION (3246, $3.95)
by Cathryn Huntington Chadwick

Lady Margaret Willoughby had resisted marriage for years, knowing that no man could replace her departed childhood love. But the time had come to produce an heir to the vast Willoughby holdings. First she would get her business affairs in order with the help of the new steward, the disturbingly attractive and infuriatingly capable Mr. Frank Watson; *then* she would begin the search for a man she could tolerate. If only she could find a mate with a *fraction* of the scandalously handsome Mr. Watson's appeal. . . .

Available wherever paperbacks are sold, or order direct from the Publisher. Send cover price plus 50¢ per copy for mailing and handling to: Zebra Books, Dept. 3642, 475 Park Avenue South, New York, NY 10016. Residents of New York and Tennessee must include sales tax. DO NOT SEND CASH. For a free Zebra/ Pinnacle Catalog with more than 1,500 books listed, please write to the above address.

THE ROMANCE OF LORDS AND LADIES
IN JANIS LADEN'S REGENCIES

BEWITCHING MINX (2532, $3.95)

From her first encounter with the Marquis of Penderleigh when he had mistaken her for a common trollop, Penelope had been incensed with the darkly handsome lord. Miss Penelope Larchmont was undoubtedly the most outspoken young lady Penderleigh had ever known, and the most tempting.

A NOBLE MISTRESS (2169, $3.95)

Moriah Landon had always been a singularly practical young lady. So when her father lost the family estate over a game of picquet, she paid the winner, the notorious Viscount Roane, a visit. And when he suggested the means of payment—that she become Roane's mistress—she agreed without a blink of her eyes.

SAPPHIRE TEMPTATION (3054, $3.95)

Lady Serena was commonly held to be an unusual young girl—outspoken when she should have been reticent, lively when she should have been demure. But there was one tradition she had not been allowed to break: a Wexley must marry a Gower. Richard Gower intended to teach his wife her duties—in every way.

SCOTTISH ROSE (2750, $3.95)

The Duke of Milburne returned to Milburne Hall trusting that the new governess, Miss Rose Beacham, had instilled the fear of God into his harum-scarum brood of siblings. But she romped with the children, refused to be cowed by his stern admonitions, and was so pretty that he had the devil of a time keeping his hands off her.